My Dearest Jo,

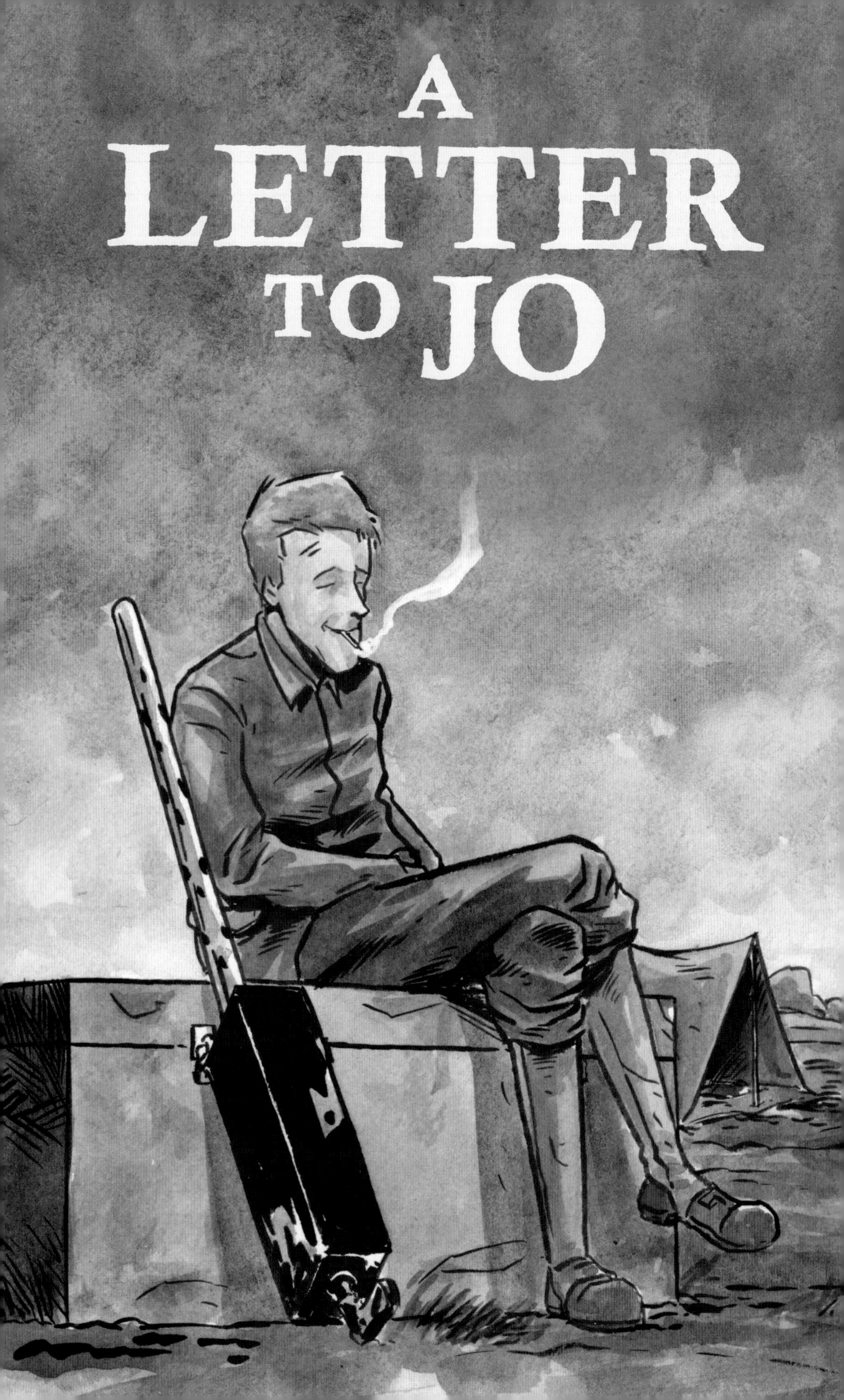
A
LETTER
TO JO

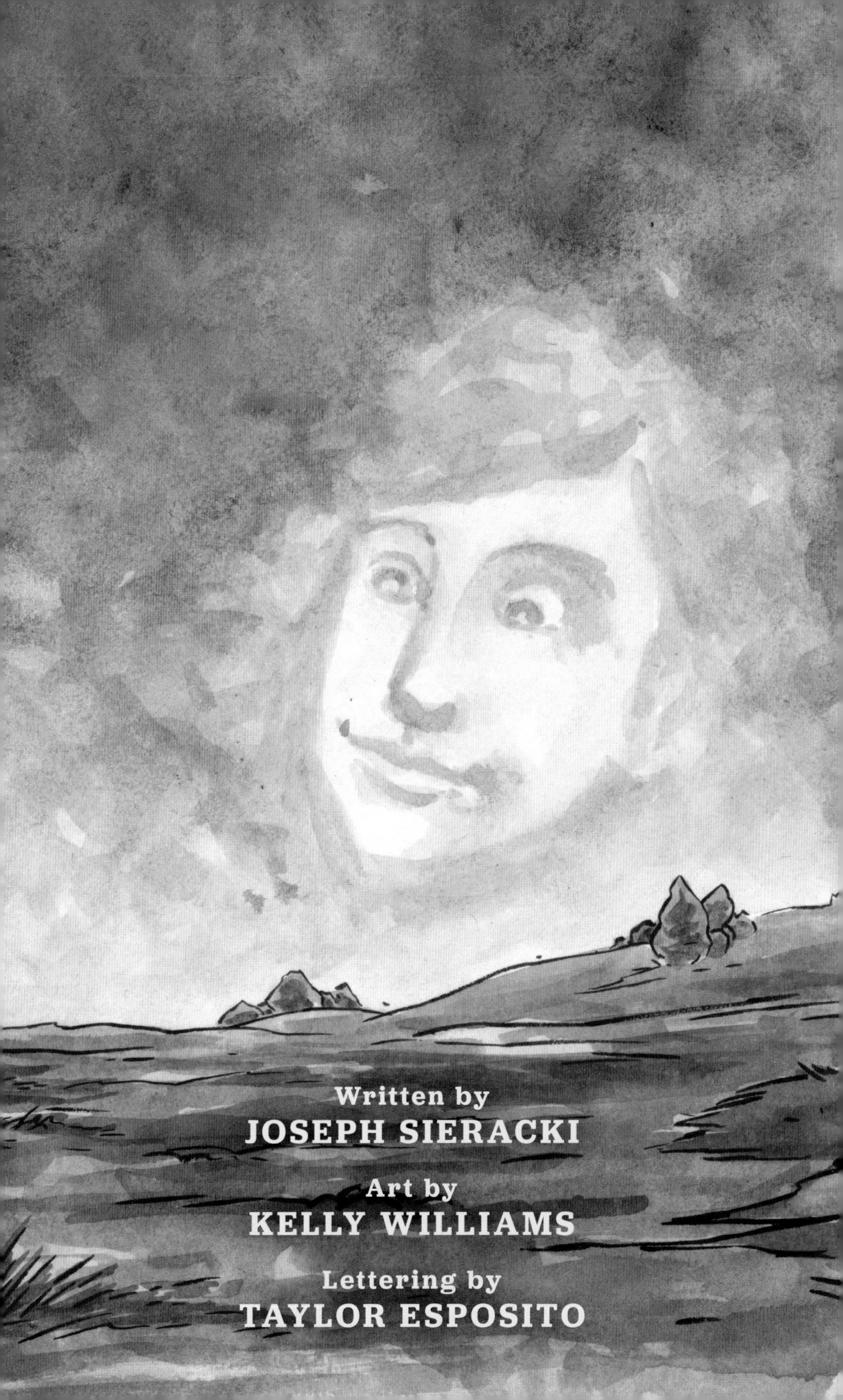

Written by
JOSEPH SIERACKI

Art by
KELLY WILLIAMS

Lettering by
TAYLOR ESPOSITO

In loving memory of Josephine & Leonard Sieracki.
— Joseph

Dedicated to Bernie Wrightson,
who is a large part of why I draw comics.
— Kelly

A Letter to Jo © 2019 Joseph Sieracki & Kelly Williams

Editor-in-Chief: Chris Staros

Edited by Brendan Wright
Designed by Jimmy Presler with Gilberto Lazcano
Production by Conley Presler

Special thanks to Bekah Caden.

ISBN: 978-1-60309-452-8   23 22 21 20 19   1 2 3 4 5

Published by Top Shelf Productions, PO Box 1282, Marietta, GA 30061-1282, USA. Top Shelf
Productions is an imprint of IDW Publishing, a division of Idea and Design Works, LLC.
Offices: 2765 Truxtun Road, San Diego, CA 92106. Top Shelf Productions®, the Top Shelf
logo, Idea and Design Works®, and the IDW logo are registered trademarks of Idea and
Design Works, LLC. All Rights Reserved. With the exception of small excerpts of artwork
used for review purposes, none of the contents of this publication may be reprinted without
the permission of IDW Publishing. IDW Publishing does not read or accept unsolicited
submissions of ideas, stories, or artwork.

Visit our online catalog at www.topshelfcomix.com.

ISBN 978-1-60309-452-8

Printed in China.

Quotation from Slaughterhouse-Five *© 1969, 1997 Kurt Vonnegut, Jr. Reprinted by
permission of Penguin Random House LLC.*

And he said, "You know—we've had to imagine the war here, and we have imagined that it was being fought by aging men like ourselves. We had forgotten that wars were fought by babies. When I saw those freshly shaved faces, it was a shock. 'My God, my God—' I said to myself, 'It's the Children's Crusade.'"

— Kurt Vonnegut, *Slaughterhouse-Five*

PROLOGUE

Ask various members of my family what they remember most about my grandfather Leonard, and they'll each tell you something different. He meant a lot of different things to different people, as did my grandmother Josephine.

My cousin would tell you that he was a devout Republican. I can remember the two having political discussions that I didn't understand as a child and believe that my grandfather's views on politics still echo in my cousin's own beliefs.

My uncle, the eldest of three children, was sort of the black sheep of the family, and liberal to the point of annoying my grandfather. He did drugs occasionally, gambled compulsively, and got divorced at a time when people simply did not do such a thing, especially coming from a strict Catholic upbringing. The fact that he never retrieved my great-grandmother's ring from the woman he divorced is a travesty that haunts my family to this day. "A family heirloom lost because he didn't have the nerve to ask for it back," my grandmother would say.

My aunt was the middle child, and I'm told that my grandfather treated her like a princess, even after she got pregnant at sixteen. If divorce was a hot-button issue, then teenage pregnancy was at least as taboo. Still, he stuck by her side and, along with my grandmother, helped support her and her would-be husband through their trials and tribulations.

Until the day she died, my grandmother would have told you that my grandfather was a saint. But time has a way of distorting reality and, often, after we lose someone, we tend to focus only on the best of them. At least it was that way for my grandmother after my grandfather passed.

My father, however, had a different view. He would tell you that the man was an abusive drunk. For whatever reason, my grandfather was always hardest on his youngest child. Maybe it was because he didn't want to make the same mistakes he made with his previous children. Maybe it was because they had my dad much later in life, clearly by mistake. Whatever the reason, it bred a great deal of resentment in my dad, but probably led him to be the most successful of the three children. My grandparents never had to help my parents out financially or otherwise, as they did their other children, and although he never said so, I think my grandfather was most proud of my dad. Still, sons have a way of remembering the worst of their fathers, and there were many demons that haunted my grandfather.

I have a few distinct memories of my grandfather that stand out in my mind. He died when I was fairly young, so I didn't get to connect with him deeply, but I remember him quietly sitting in front of the television smoking, with the dog by his side. The dog had been my parents', but soon after I was born, they had to give it to my grandparents, as he was not very fond of me. My grandfather was a tenacious smoker, and that dog was always by his side and would, unfortunately, die of throat cancer as a result. My grandmother always blamed him for it.

I remember him making me a pizza one day, stating that all the best chefs in the world are men. Looking back, this is particularly funny, because my grandmother made every single meal for him. For some reason, I picture him wearing an apron and a chef's hat on that day, but I'm almost certain that he wouldn't have been wearing either.

After he was diagnosed with lung cancer and had surgery to remove a tumor in his throat, it was difficult to hear him speak. He wore a microphone and amplifier. My grandmother told me he was nervous that they would frighten me, but when I finally saw him, he made it seem fun.

Above all, I remember the war hero (although he would strongly disagree with that title). I seemed to be the only one in the family who showed any interest in World War II, and that was how we connected. My grandfather was drafted into the war at the age of eighteen, and he earned a number of medals on his tour of duty.

Years later, my grandmother gave me a letter that my grandfather had written her at the end of the war. She said that he would want me to have it. Reading this letter long after he died, I gained a much deeper insight into the man he was and his experience in the war. In fact, until I read this letter for myself I wasn't entirely sure that he had even seen combat, but he saw a great deal of it, more than I had ever imagined. Even more shocking was the duality his words seemed to reveal. On the one hand, the war completely broke him. On the other, he actually appeared to enjoy certain aspects.

I should note that there is no way of verifying the contents of this letter. The only thing I can say for certain is that my grandmother loved my grandfather dearly, despite his many faults. She remained completely devoted to him until the day she died, long after he lost his battle with lung cancer.

CHAPTER ONE

LOVE

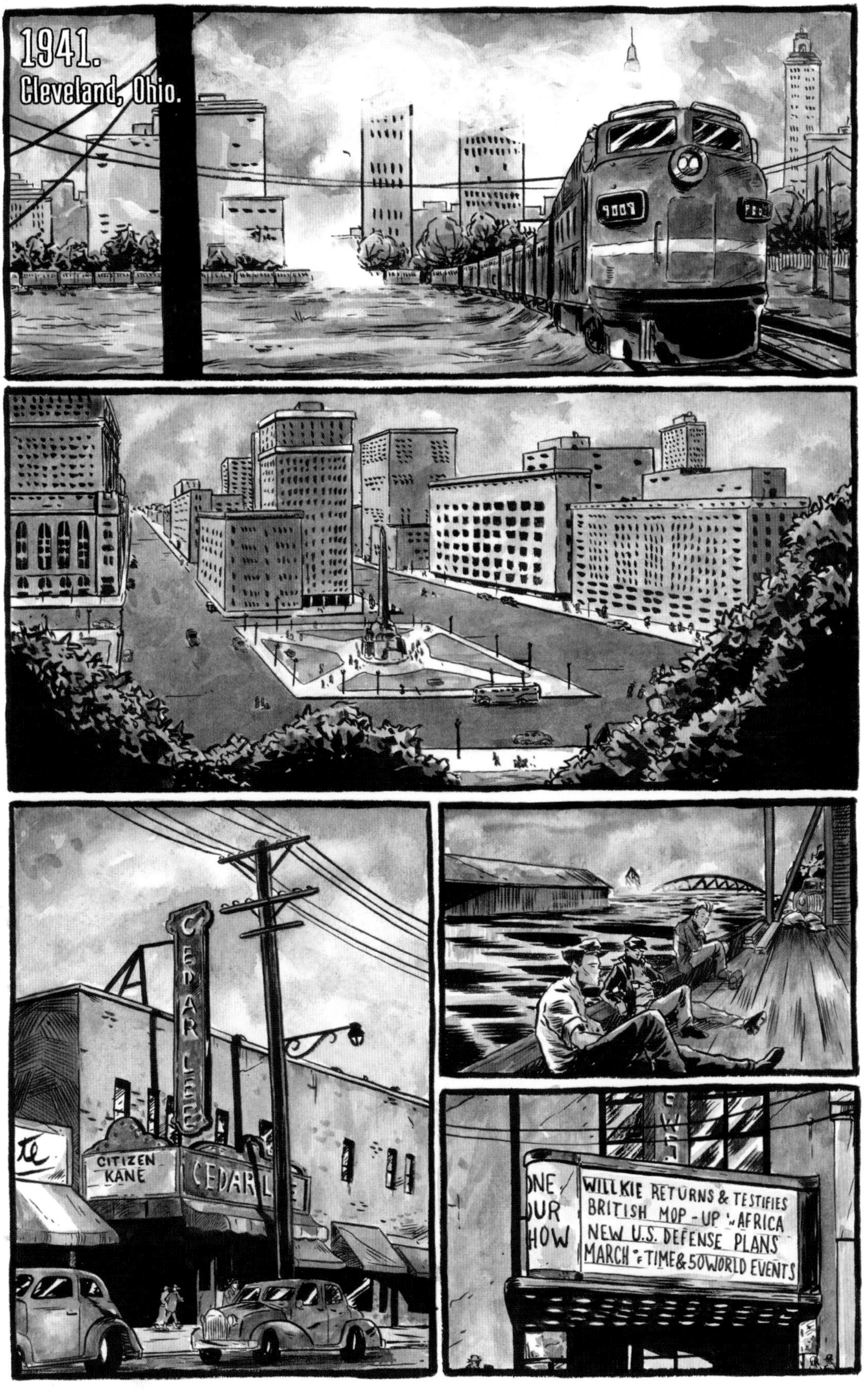

1941.
Cleveland, Ohio.
CEDAR LEE
CITIZEN KANE
WILLKIE RETURNS & TESTIFIES
BRITISH MOP-UP IN AFRICA
NEW U.S. DEFENSE PLANS
MARCH OF TIME & 50 WORLD EVENTS

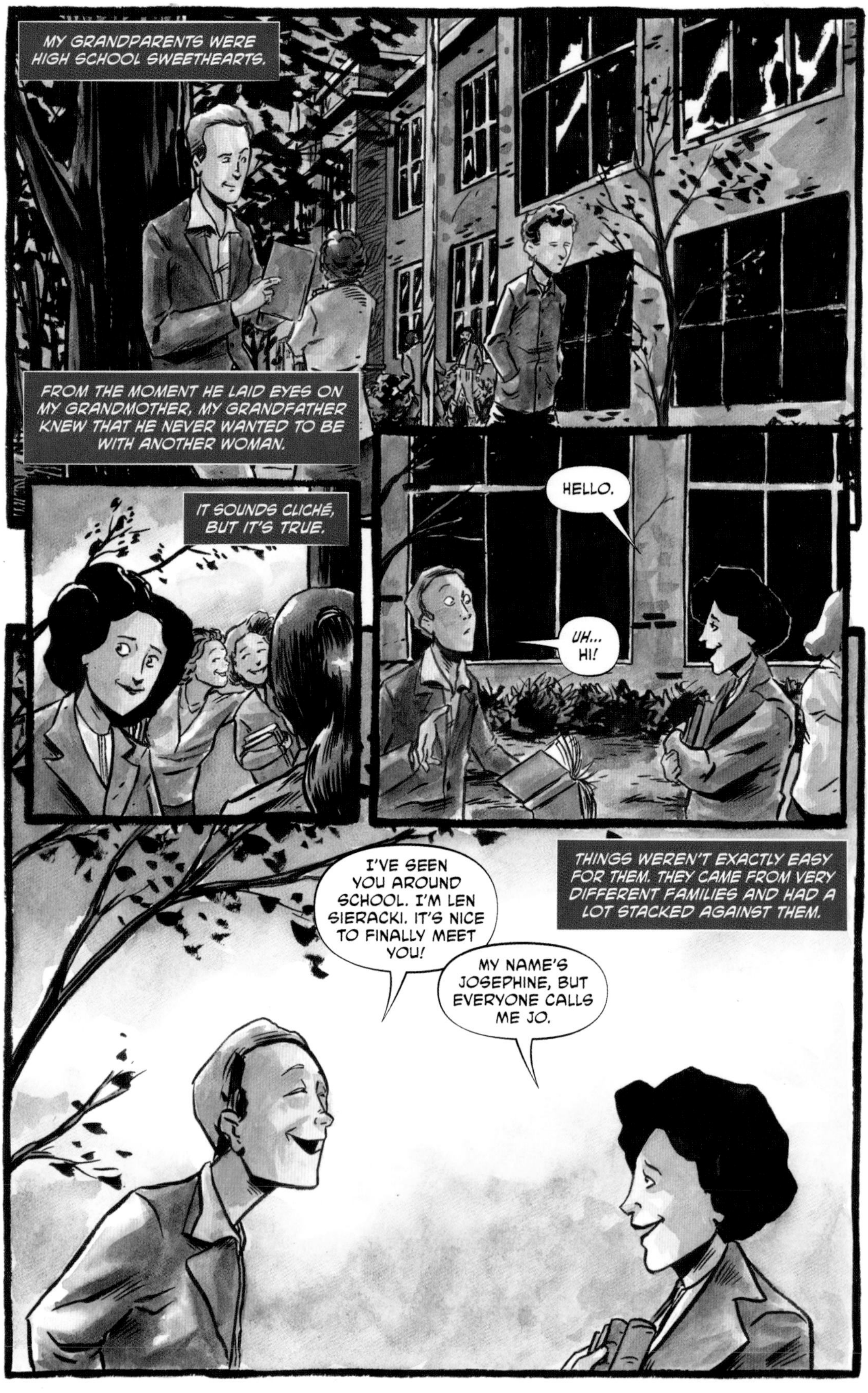
MY GRANDPARENTS WERE HIGH SCHOOL SWEETHEARTS.
FROM THE MOMENT HE LAID EYES ON MY GRANDMOTHER, MY GRANDFATHER KNEW THAT HE NEVER WANTED TO BE WITH ANOTHER WOMAN.
IT SOUNDS CLICHÉ, BUT IT'S TRUE.
HELLO.
UH... HI!
THINGS WEREN'T EXACTLY EASY FOR THEM. THEY CAME FROM VERY DIFFERENT FAMILIES AND HAD A LOT STACKED AGAINST THEM.
I'VE SEEN YOU AROUND SCHOOL. I'M LEN SIERACKI. IT'S NICE TO FINALLY MEET YOU!
MY NAME'S JOSEPHINE, BUT EVERYONE CALLS ME JO.

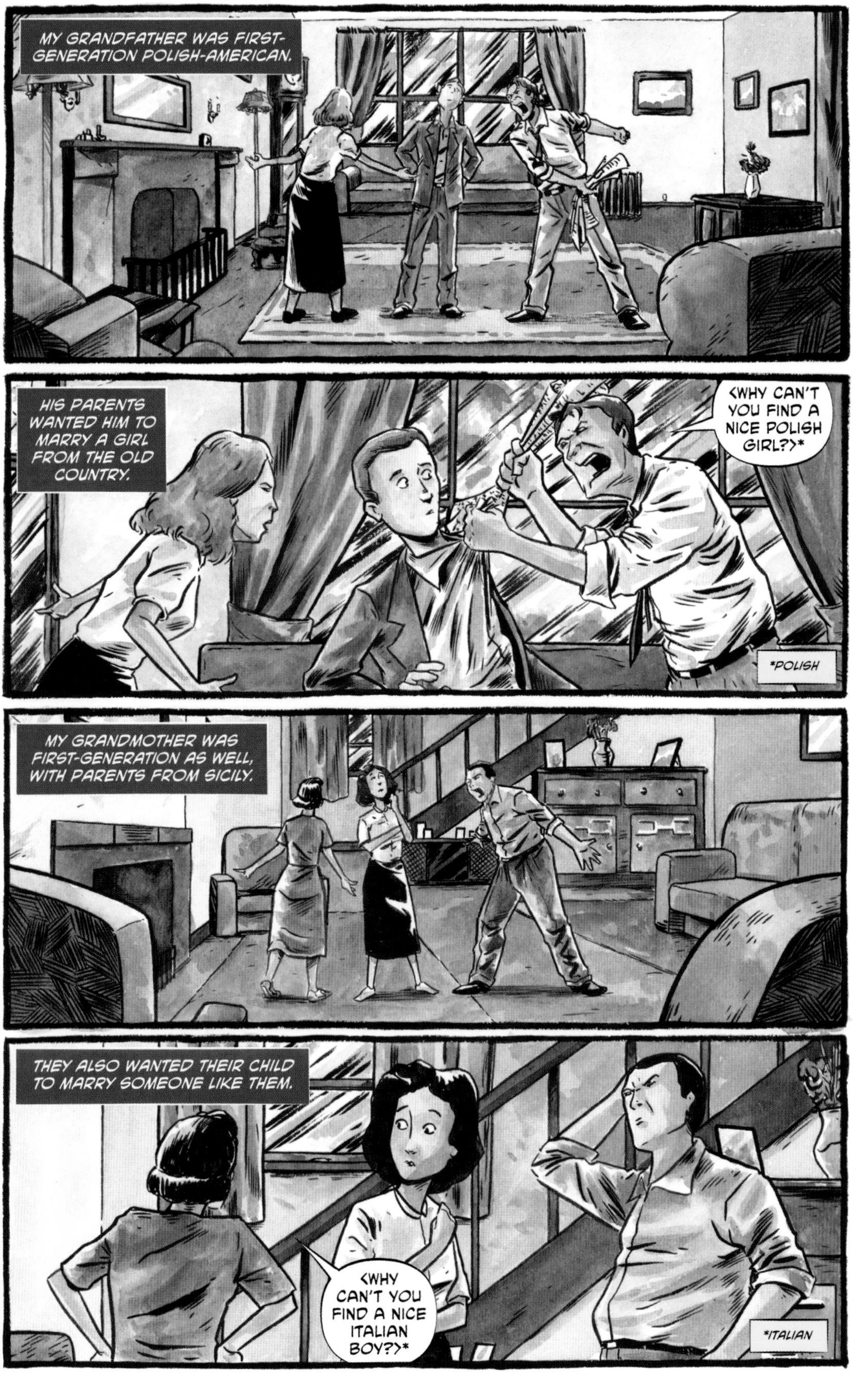
MY GRANDFATHER WAS FIRST-GENERATION POLISH-AMERICAN.
HIS PARENTS WANTED HIM TO MARRY A GIRL FROM THE OLD COUNTRY.
<WHY CAN'T YOU FIND A NICE POLISH GIRL?>*
*POLISH
MY GRANDMOTHER WAS FIRST-GENERATION AS WELL, WITH PARENTS FROM SICILY.
THEY ALSO WANTED THEIR CHILD TO MARRY SOMEONE LIKE THEM.
<WHY CAN'T YOU FIND A NICE ITALIAN BOY?>*
*ITALIAN

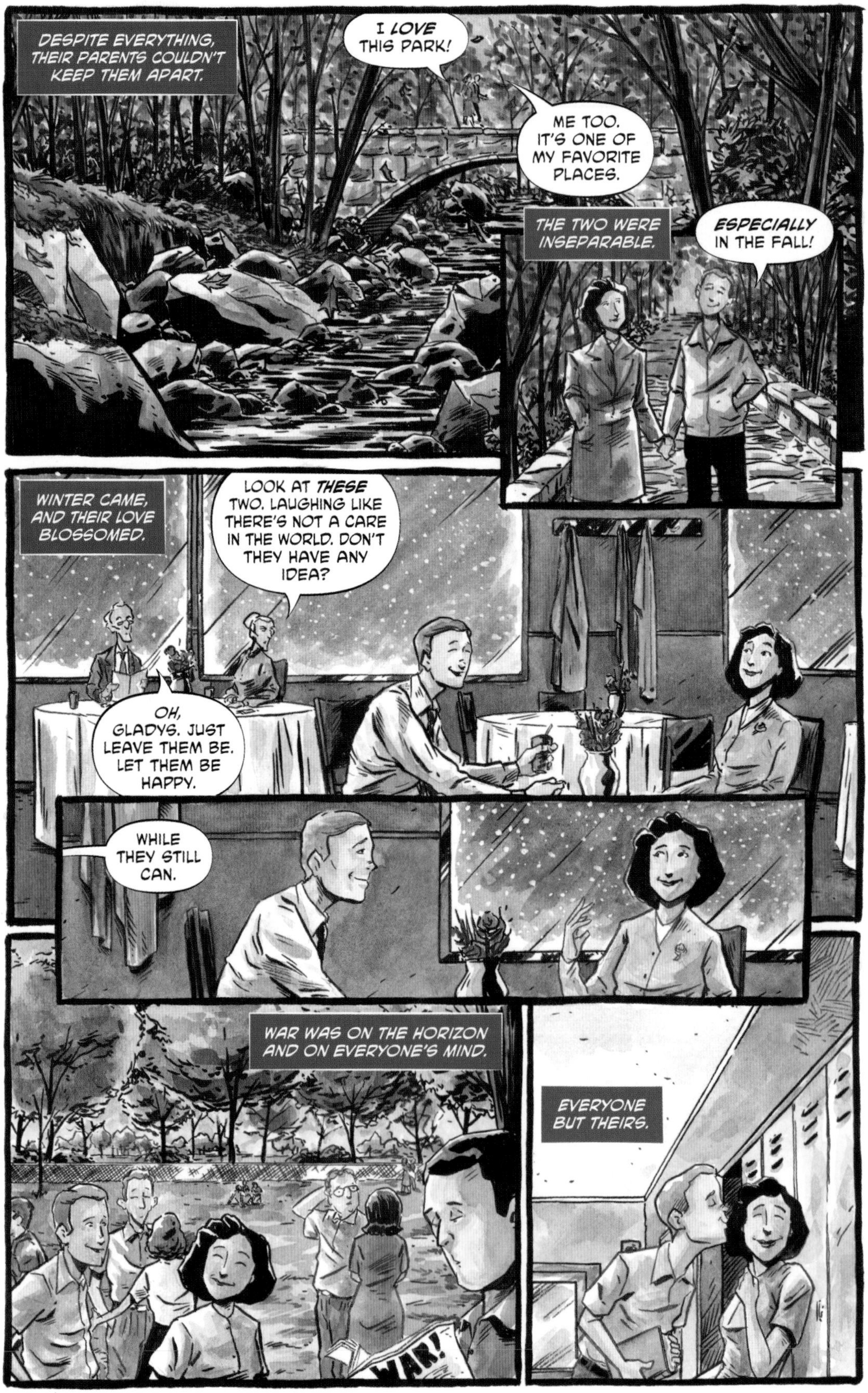
DESPITE EVERYTHING, THEIR PARENTS COULDN'T KEEP THEM APART.
I *LOVE* THIS PARK!
ME TOO. IT'S ONE OF MY FAVORITE PLACES.
THE TWO WERE INSEPARABLE.
ESPECIALLY IN THE FALL!
WINTER CAME, AND THEIR LOVE BLOSSOMED.
LOOK AT *THESE* TWO. LAUGHING LIKE THERE'S NOT A CARE IN THE WORLD. DON'T THEY HAVE ANY IDEA?
OH, GLADYS. JUST LEAVE THEM BE. LET THEM BE HAPPY.
WHILE THEY STILL CAN.
WAR WAS ON THE HORIZON AND ON EVERYONE'S MIND.
WAR!
EVERYONE BUT THEIRS.

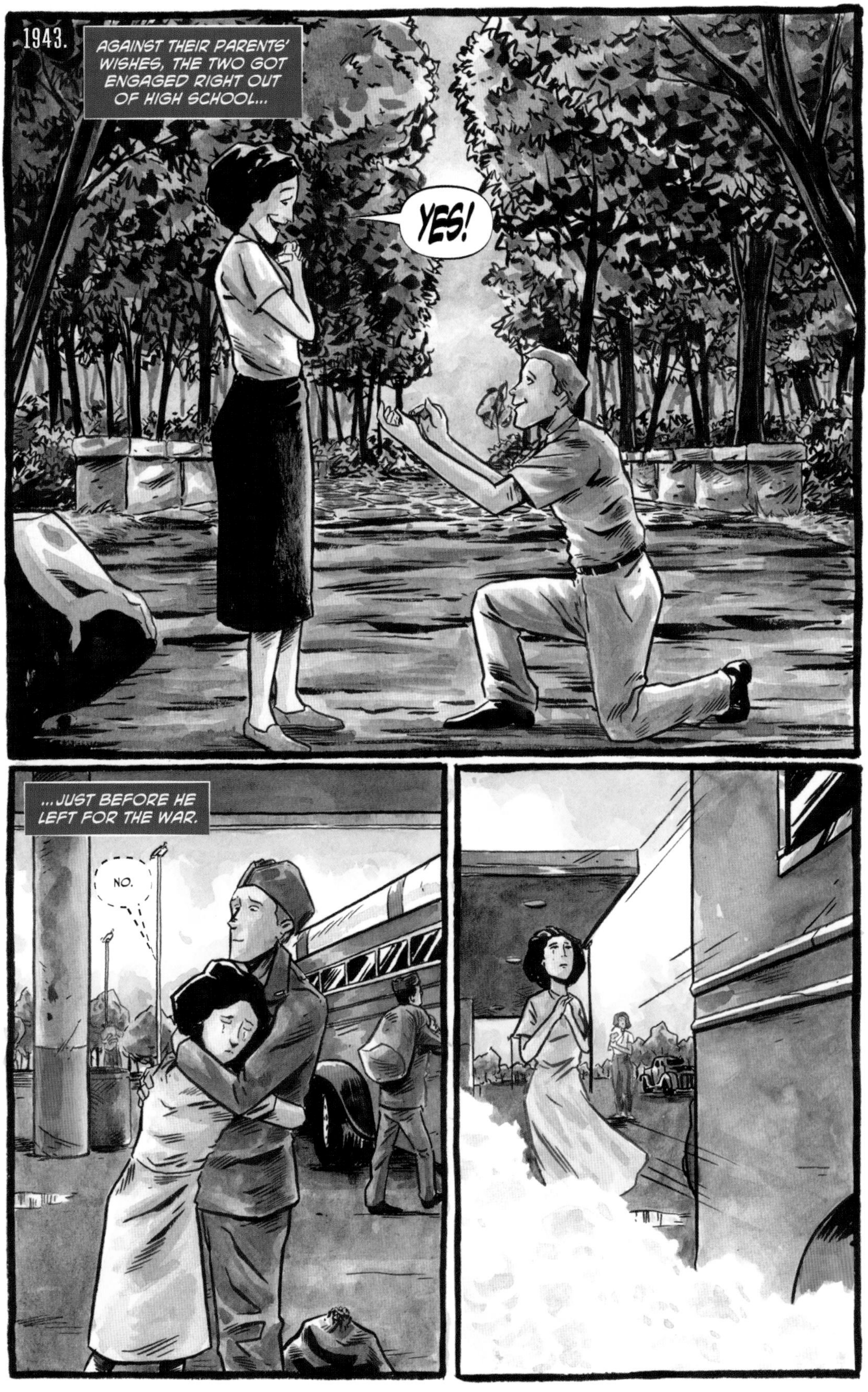
1943.
AGAINST THEIR PARENTS' WISHES, THE TWO GOT ENGAGED RIGHT OUT OF HIGH SCHOOL...
YES!
...JUST BEFORE HE LEFT FOR THE WAR.
NO.

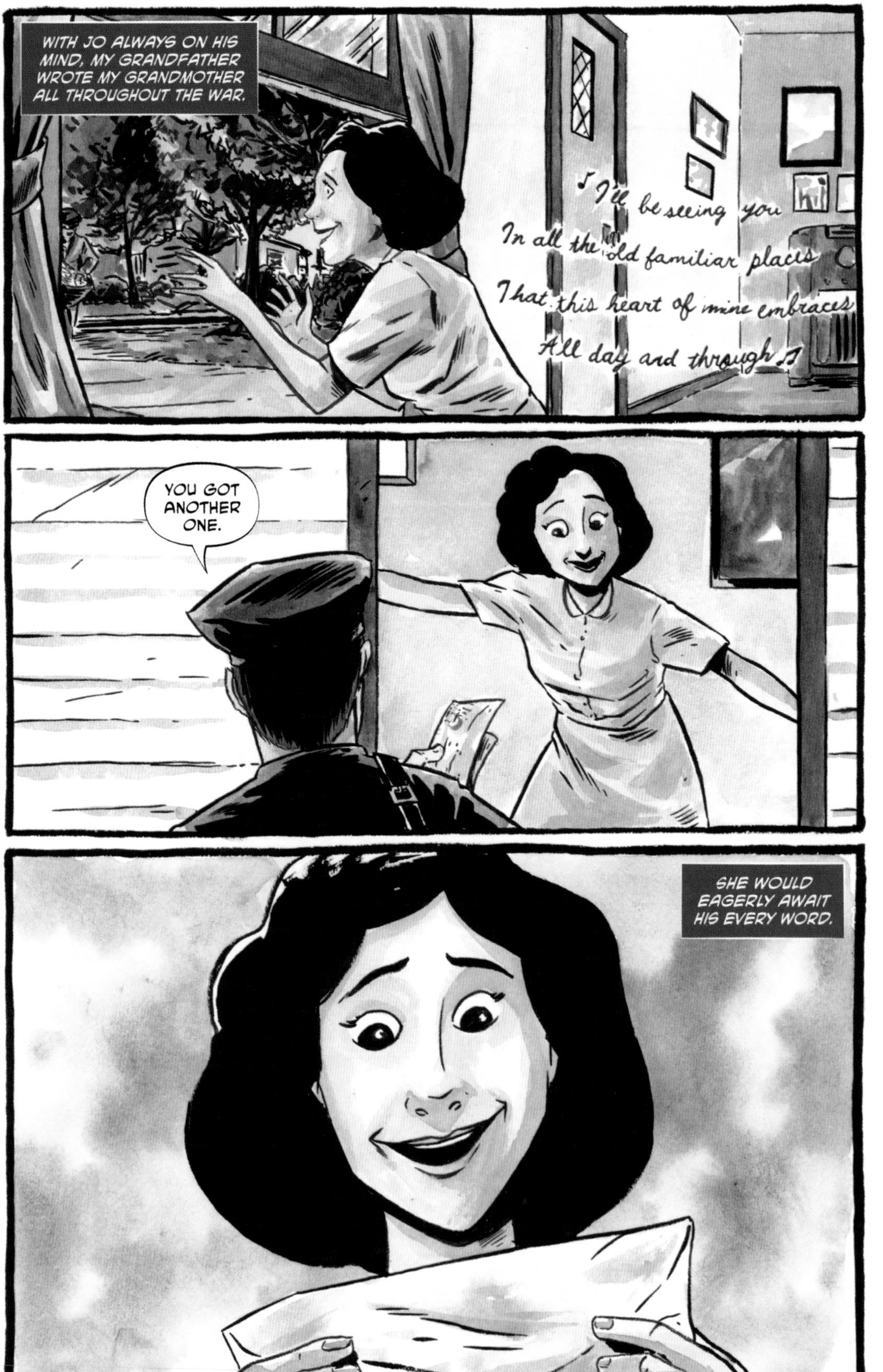
WITH JO ALWAYS ON HIS MIND, MY GRANDFATHER WROTE MY GRANDMOTHER ALL THROUGHOUT THE WAR.
♪ I'll be seeing you
In all the old familiar places
That this heart of mine embraces
All day and through ♫
YOU GOT ANOTHER ONE.
SHE WOULD EAGERLY AWAIT HIS EVERY WORD.

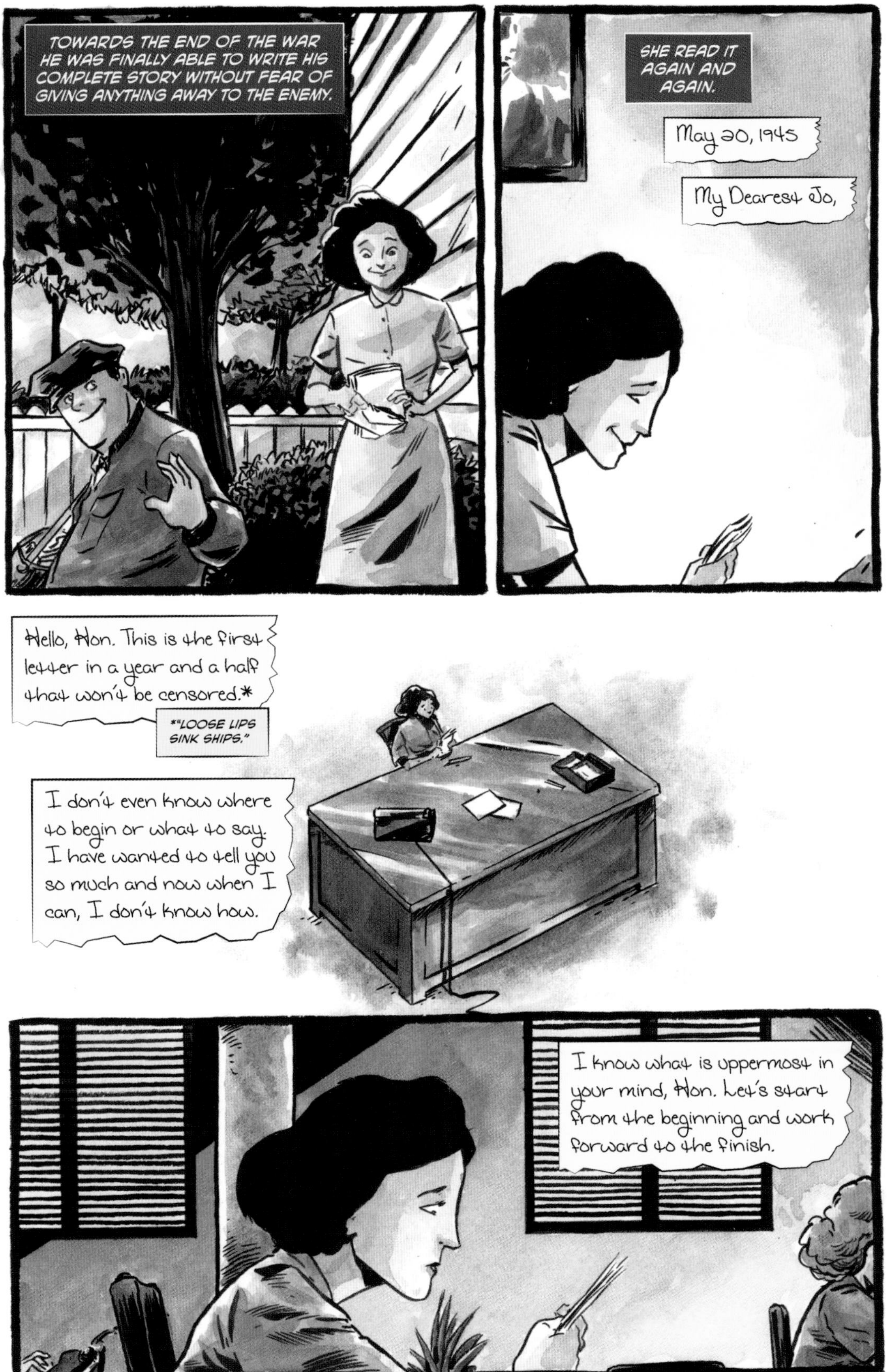
TOWARDS THE END OF THE WAR HE WAS FINALLY ABLE TO WRITE HIS COMPLETE STORY WITHOUT FEAR OF GIVING ANYTHING AWAY TO THE ENEMY.
SHE READ IT AGAIN AND AGAIN.
May 20, 1945
My Dearest Jo,
Hello, Hon. This is the first letter in a year and a half that won't be censored.*
*"LOOSE LIPS SINK SHIPS."
I don't even know where to begin or what to say. I have wanted to tell you so much and now when I can, I don't know how.
I know what is uppermost in your mind, Hon. Let's start from the beginning and work forward to the finish.

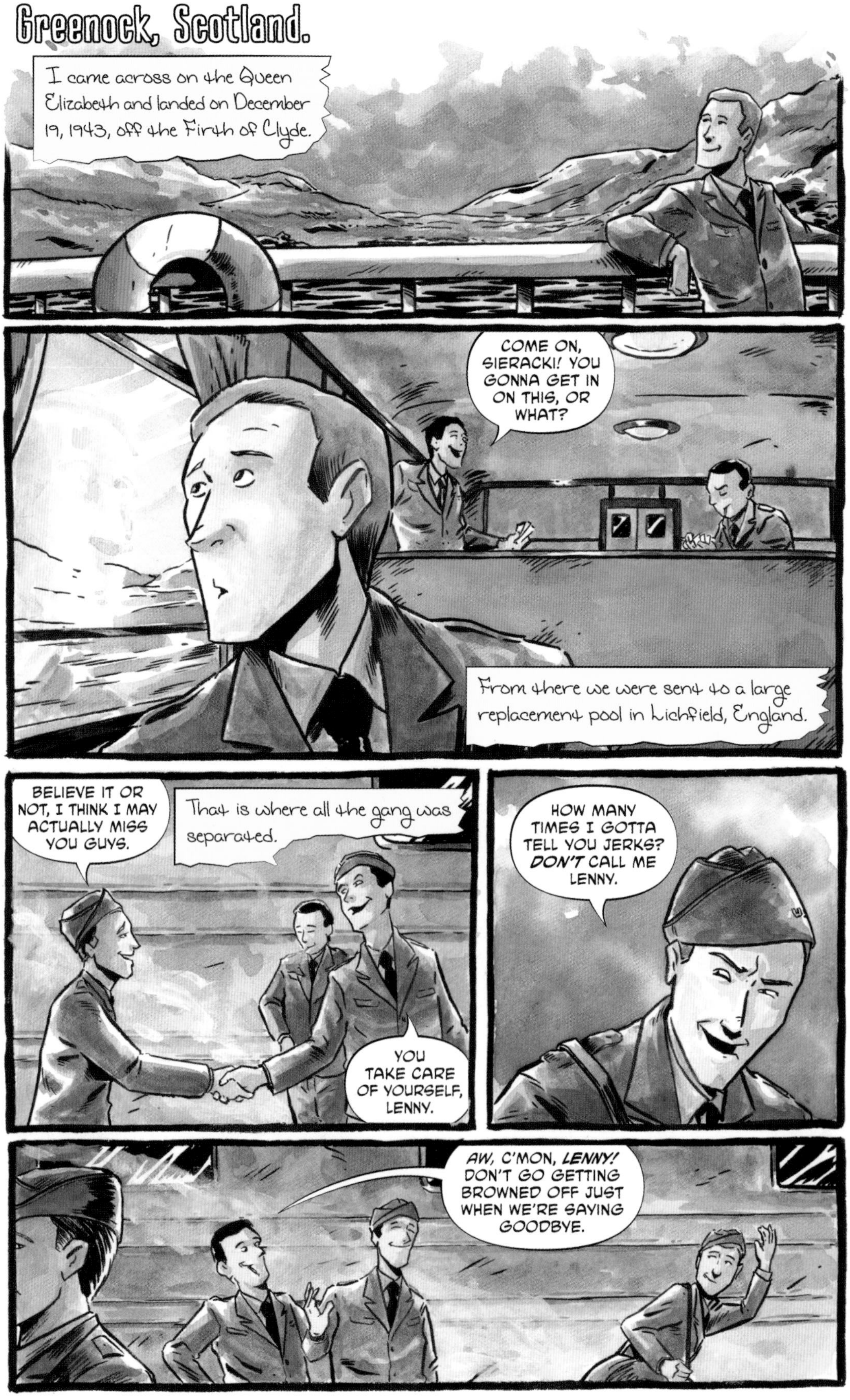

Greenock, Scotland.
I came across on the Queen Elizabeth and landed on December 19, 1943, off the Firth of Clyde.
COME ON, SIERACKI! YOU GONNA GET IN ON THIS, OR WHAT?
From there we were sent to a large replacement pool in Lichfield, England.
BELIEVE IT OR NOT, I THINK I MAY ACTUALLY MISS YOU GUYS.
That is where all the gang was separated.
YOU TAKE CARE OF YOURSELF, LENNY.
HOW MANY TIMES I GOTTA TELL YOU JERKS? DON'T CALL ME LENNY.
AW, C'MON, LENNY! DON'T GO GETTING BROWNED OFF JUST WHEN WE'RE SAYING GOODBYE.

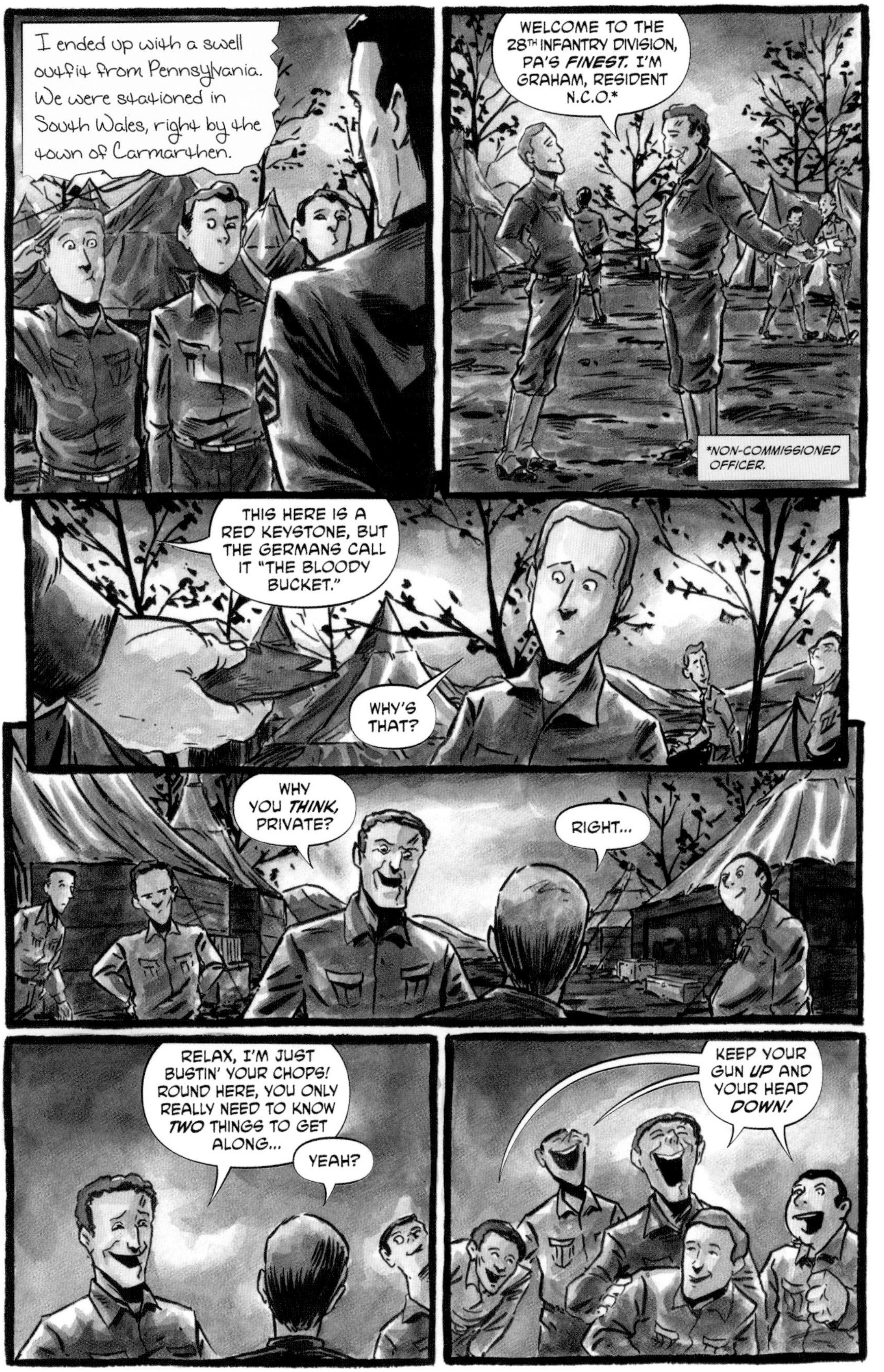
I ended up with a swell outfit from Pennsylvania. We were stationed in South Wales, right by the town of Carmarthen.
WELCOME TO THE 28TH INFANTRY DIVISION, PA'S FINEST. I'M GRAHAM, RESIDENT N.C.O.*
*NON-COMMISSIONED OFFICER.
THIS HERE IS A RED KEYSTONE, BUT THE GERMANS CALL IT "THE BLOODY BUCKET."
WHY'S THAT?
WHY YOU THINK, PRIVATE?
RIGHT...
RELAX, I'M JUST BUSTIN' YOUR CHOPS! ROUND HERE, YOU ONLY REALLY NEED TO KNOW TWO THINGS TO GET ALONG...
YEAH?
KEEP YOUR GUN UP AND YOUR HEAD DOWN!

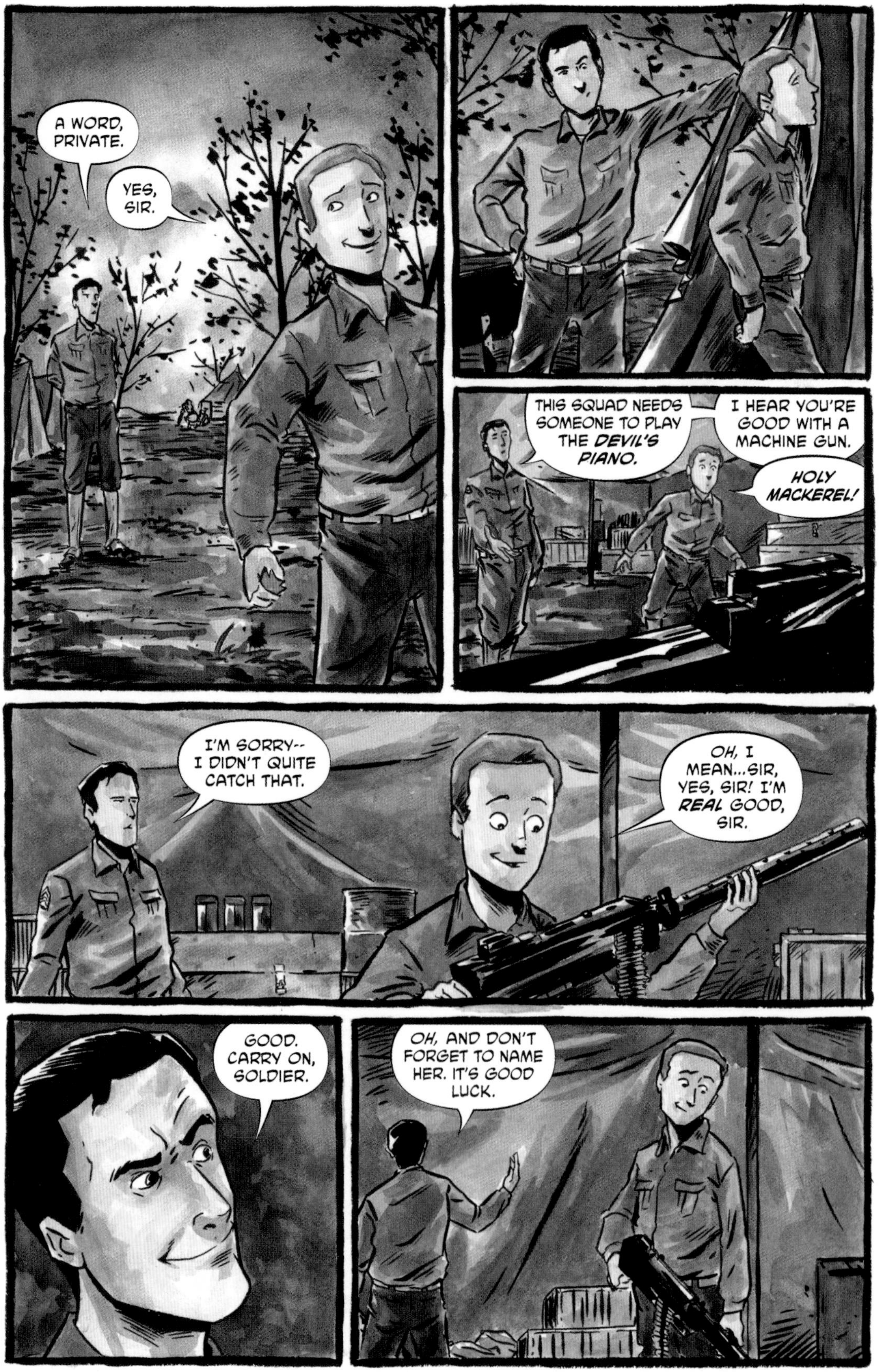
A WORD, PRIVATE.
YES, SIR.
THIS SQUAD NEEDS SOMEONE TO PLAY THE *DEVIL'S PIANO.*
I HEAR YOU'RE GOOD WITH A MACHINE GUN.
HOLY MACKEREL!
I'M SORRY-- I DIDN'T QUITE CATCH THAT.
OH, I MEAN...SIR, YES, SIR! I'M *REAL* GOOD, SIR.
GOOD. CARRY ON, SOLDIER.
OH, AND DON'T FORGET TO NAME HER. IT'S GOOD LUCK.

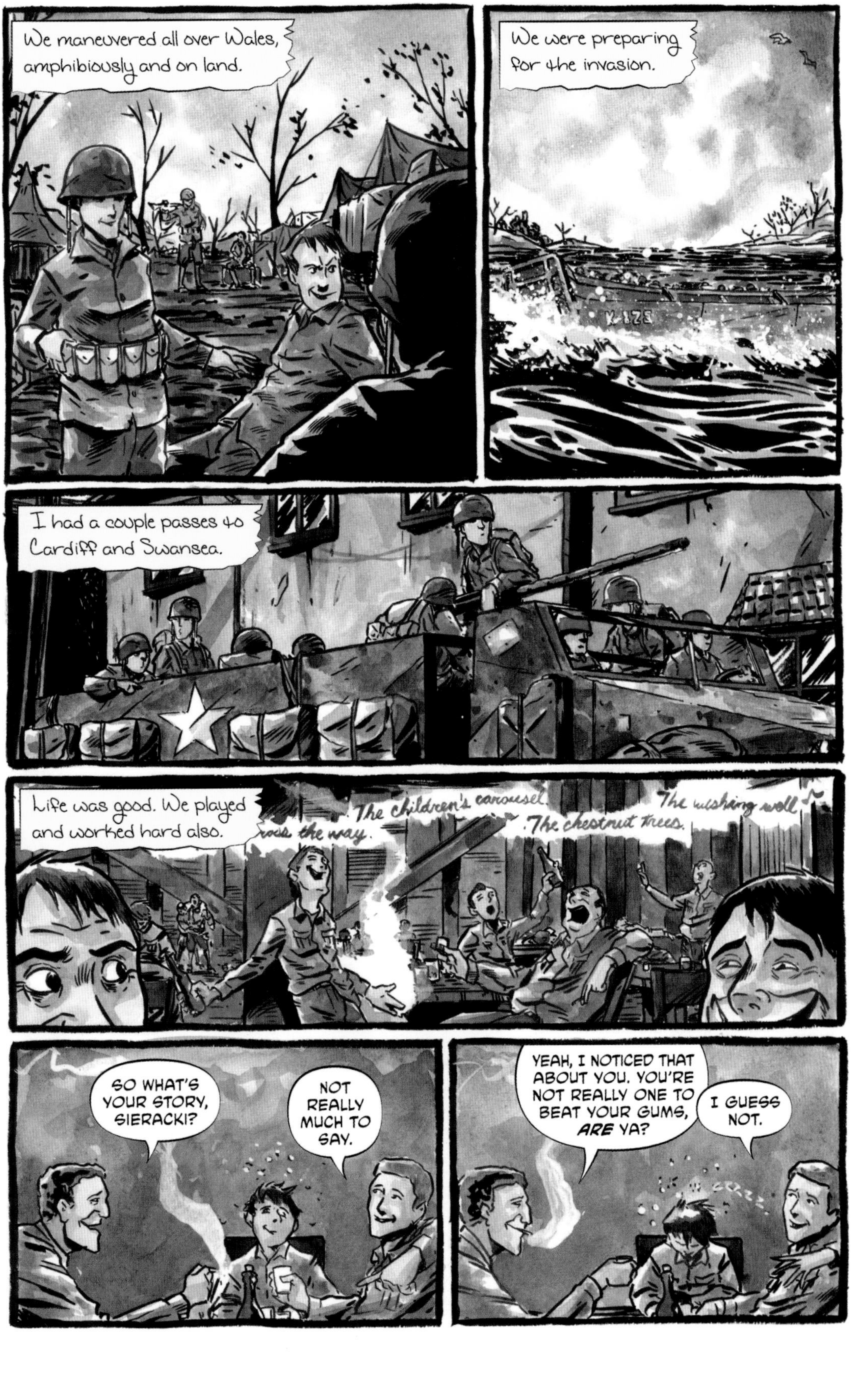
We maneuvered all over Wales, amphibiously and on land.
We were preparing for the invasion.
I had a couple passes to Cardiff and Swansea.
Life was good. We played and worked hard also.
The children's carousel.
The wishing well
The chestnut trees.
the way.
SO WHAT'S YOUR STORY, SIERACKI?
NOT REALLY MUCH TO SAY.
YEAH, I NOTICED THAT ABOUT YOU. YOU'RE NOT REALLY ONE TO BEAT YOUR GUMS, *ARE* YA?
I GUESS NOT.

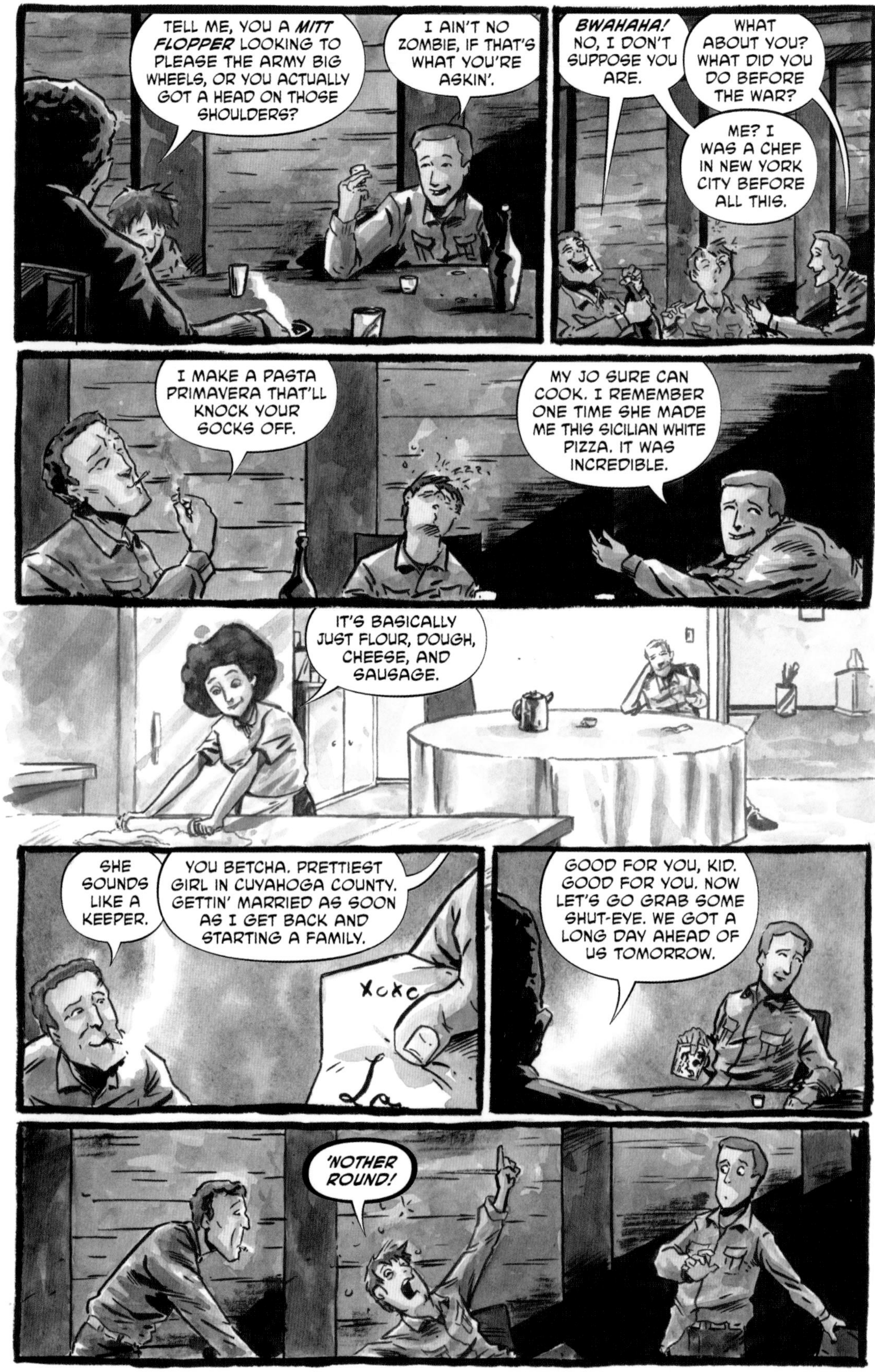
TELL ME, YOU A *MITT FLOPPER* LOOKING TO PLEASE THE ARMY BIG WHEELS, OR YOU ACTUALLY GOT A HEAD ON THOSE SHOULDERS?
I AIN'T NO ZOMBIE, IF THAT'S WHAT YOU'RE ASKIN'.
BWAHAHA! NO, I DON'T SUPPOSE YOU ARE.
WHAT ABOUT YOU? WHAT DID YOU DO BEFORE THE WAR?
ME? I WAS A CHEF IN NEW YORK CITY BEFORE ALL THIS.
I MAKE A PASTA PRIMAVERA THAT'LL KNOCK YOUR SOCKS OFF.
MY JO SURE CAN COOK. I REMEMBER ONE TIME SHE MADE ME THIS SICILIAN WHITE PIZZA. IT WAS INCREDIBLE.
IT'S BASICALLY JUST FLOUR, DOUGH, CHEESE, AND SAUSAGE.
SHE SOUNDS LIKE A KEEPER.
YOU BETCHA. PRETTIEST GIRL IN CUYAHOGA COUNTY. GETTIN' MARRIED AS SOON AS I GET BACK AND STARTING A FAMILY.
XOXO
GOOD FOR YOU, KID. GOOD FOR YOU. NOW LET'S GO GRAB SOME SHUT-EYE. WE GOT A LONG DAY AHEAD OF US TOMORROW.
'NOTHER ROUND!

CHAPTER TWO
FEAR

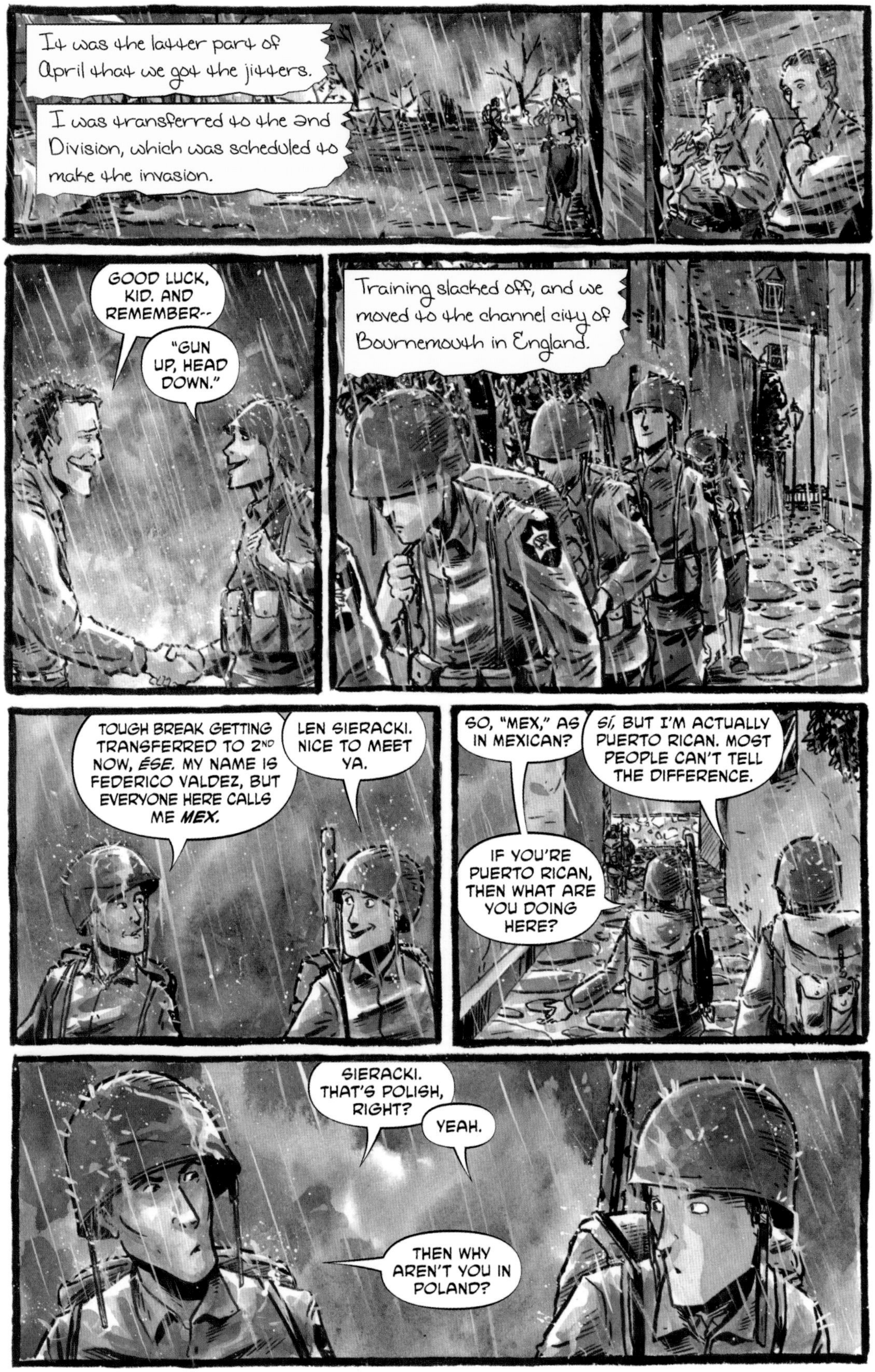

It was the latter part of April that we got the jitters.
I was transferred to the 2nd Division, which was scheduled to make the invasion.
GOOD LUCK, KID. AND REMEMBER--
"GUN UP, HEAD DOWN."
Training slacked off, and we moved to the channel city of Bournemouth in England.
TOUGH BREAK GETTING TRANSFERRED TO 2ND NOW, ÉSE. MY NAME IS FEDERICO VALDEZ, BUT EVERYONE HERE CALLS ME MEX.
LEN SIERACKI. NICE TO MEET YA.
SO, "MEX," AS IN MEXICAN?
SÍ, BUT I'M ACTUALLY PUERTO RICAN. MOST PEOPLE CAN'T TELL THE DIFFERENCE.
IF YOU'RE PUERTO RICAN, THEN WHAT ARE YOU DOING HERE?
SIERACKI. THAT'S POLISH, RIGHT?
YEAH.
THEN WHY AREN'T YOU IN POLAND?

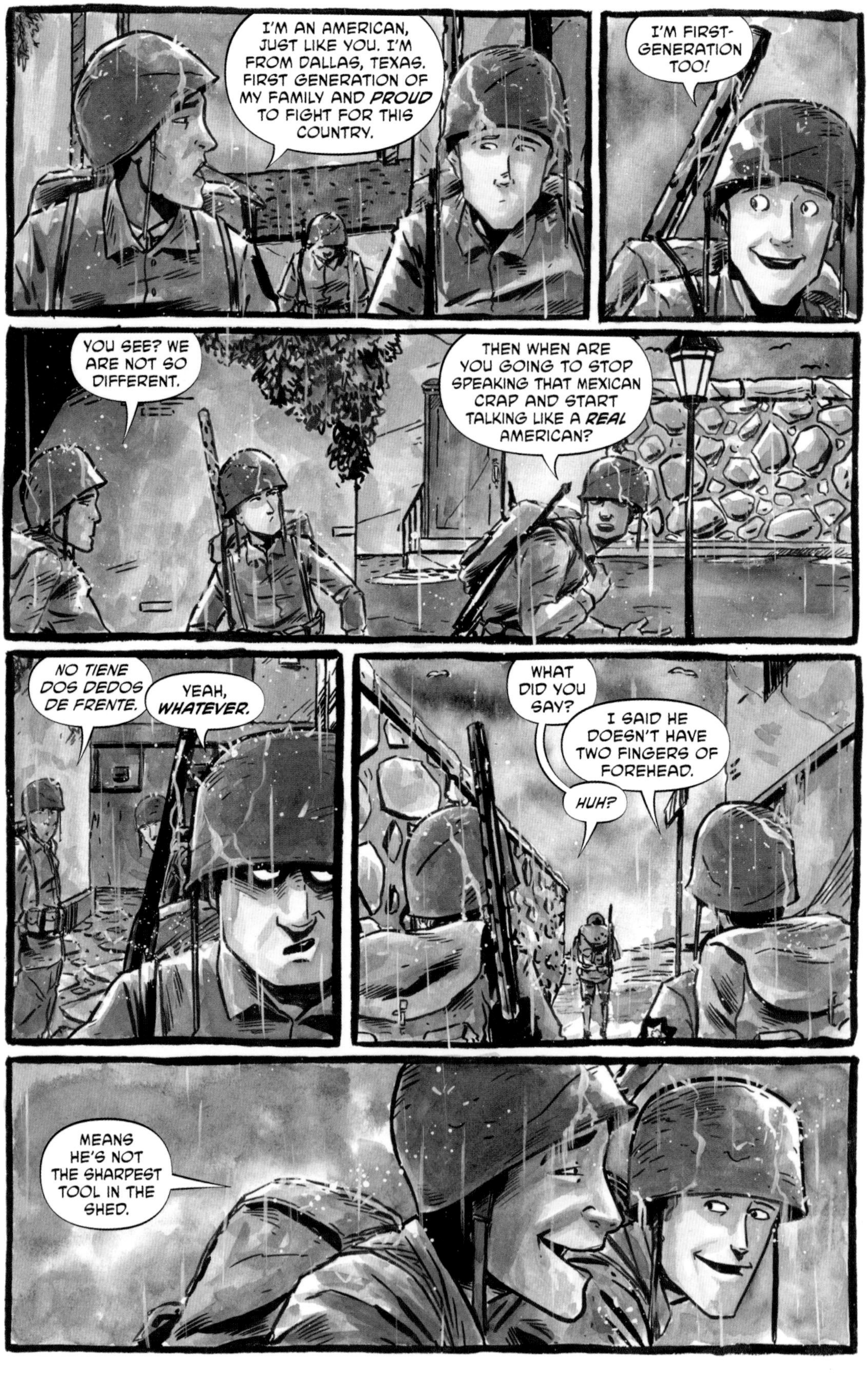

I'M AN AMERICAN, JUST LIKE YOU. I'M FROM DALLAS, TEXAS. FIRST GENERATION OF MY FAMILY AND *PROUD* TO FIGHT FOR THIS COUNTRY.
I'M FIRST-GENERATION TOO!
YOU SEE? WE ARE NOT SO DIFFERENT.
THEN WHEN ARE YOU GOING TO STOP SPEAKING THAT MEXICAN CRAP AND START TALKING LIKE A *REAL* AMERICAN?
NO TIENE DOS DEDOS DE FRENTE.
YEAH, ***WHATEVER.***
WHAT DID YOU SAY?
I SAID HE DOESN'T HAVE TWO FINGERS OF FOREHEAD.
HUH?
MEANS HE'S NOT THE SHARPEST TOOL IN THE SHED.

We played mostly and had little training. I was listed to go in on the third wave, which was a lucky break.

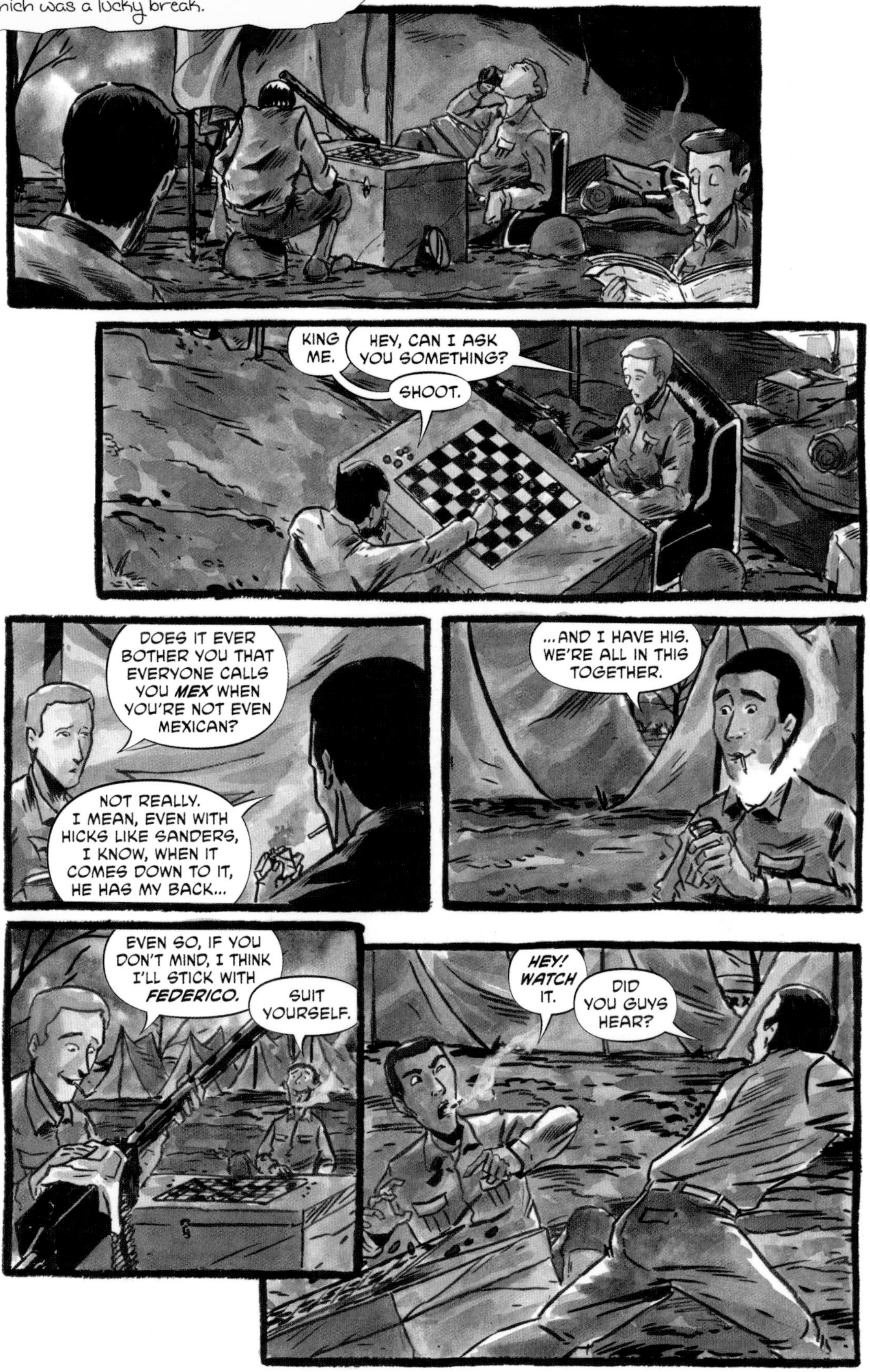

KING ME.
HEY, CAN I ASK YOU SOMETHING?
SHOOT.
DOES IT EVER BOTHER YOU THAT EVERYONE CALLS YOU *MEX* WHEN YOU'RE NOT EVEN MEXICAN?
NOT REALLY. I MEAN, EVEN WITH HICKS LIKE SANDERS, I KNOW, WHEN IT COMES DOWN TO IT, HE HAS MY BACK...
...AND I HAVE HIS. WE'RE ALL IN THIS TOGETHER.
EVEN SO, IF YOU DON'T MIND, I THINK I'LL STICK WITH *FEDERICO.*
SUIT YOURSELF.
HEY! WATCH IT.
DID YOU GUYS HEAR?

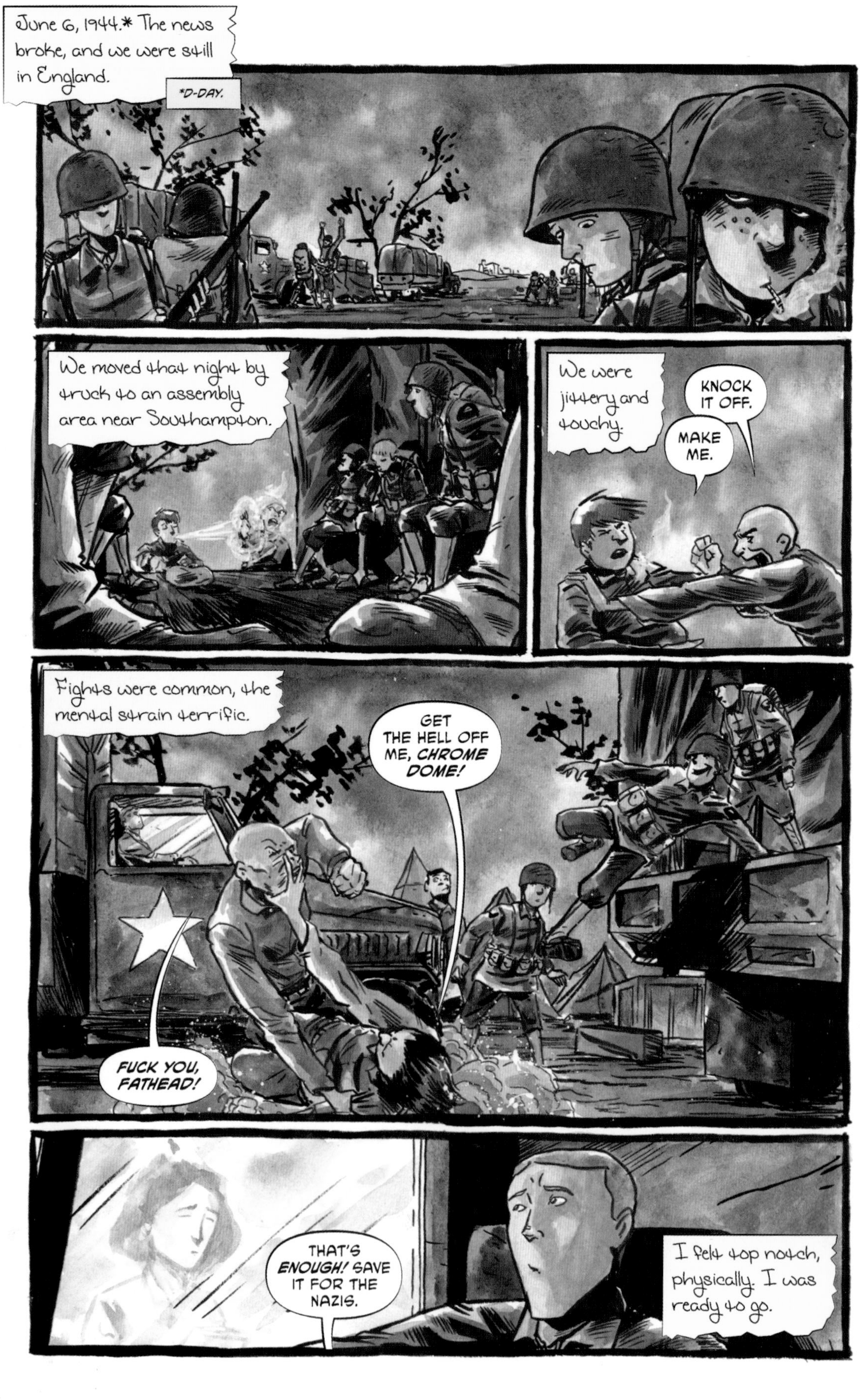
June 6, 1944.* The news broke, and we were still in England.
*D-DAY.
We moved that night by truck to an assembly area near Southampton.
We were jittery and touchy.
KNOCK IT OFF.
MAKE ME.
Fights were common, the mental strain terrific.
GET THE HELL OFF ME, CHROME DOME!
FUCK YOU, FATHEAD!
THAT'S ENOUGH! SAVE IT FOR THE NAZIS.
I felt top notch, physically. I was ready to go.

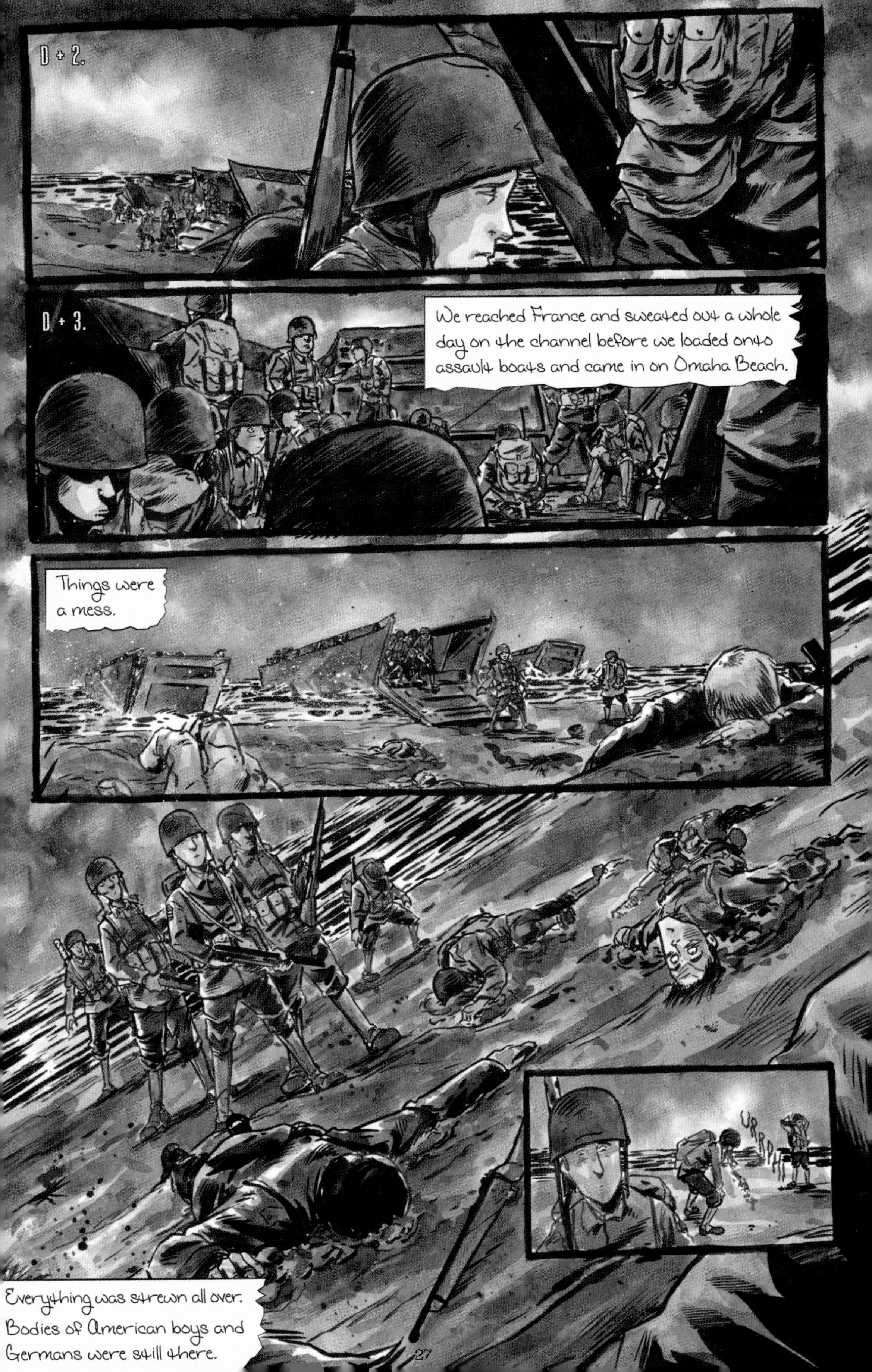
D + 2.
D + 3.
We reached France and sweated out a whole day on the channel before we loaded onto assault boats and came in on Omaha Beach.
Things were a mess.
URRPH!
Everything was strewn all over. Bodies of American boys and Germans were still there.

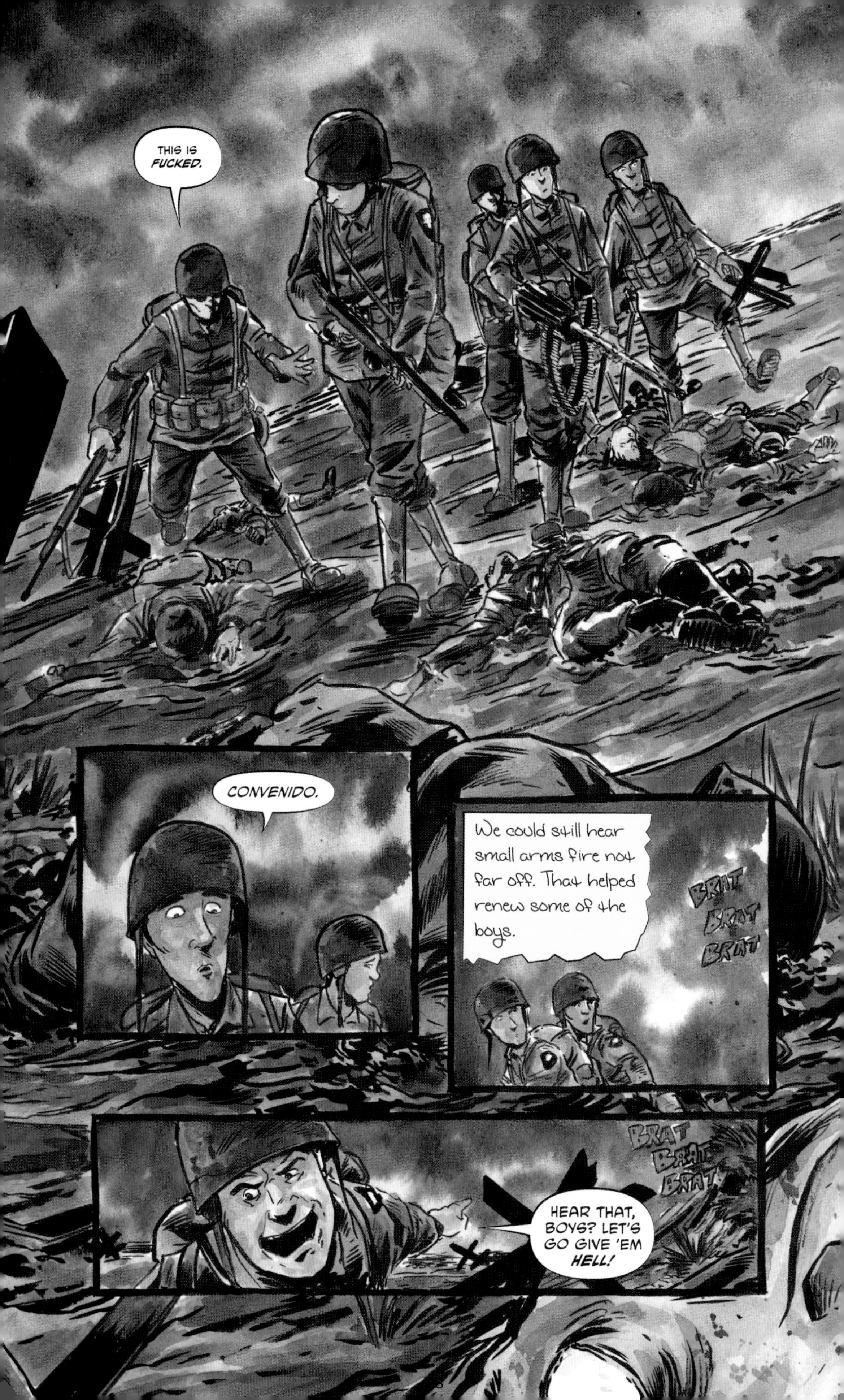
THIS IS FUCKED.
CONVENIDO.
We could still hear small arms fire not far off. That helped renew some of the boys.
BRAT BRAT BRAT
BRAT BRAT BRAT
HEAR THAT, BOYS? LET'S GO GIVE 'EM HELL!

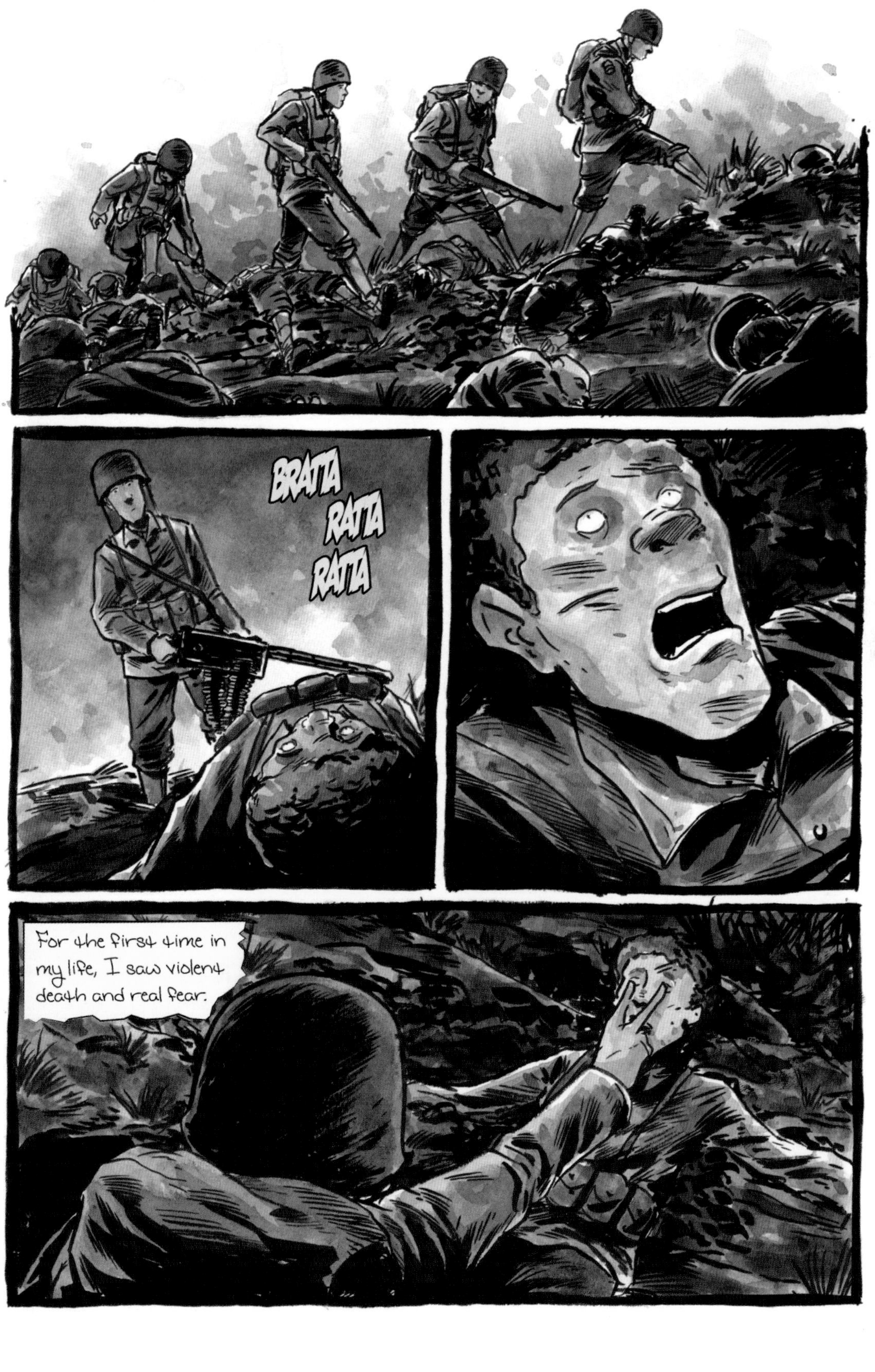
BRATTA
RATTA
RATTA
For the first time in my life, I saw violent death and real fear.

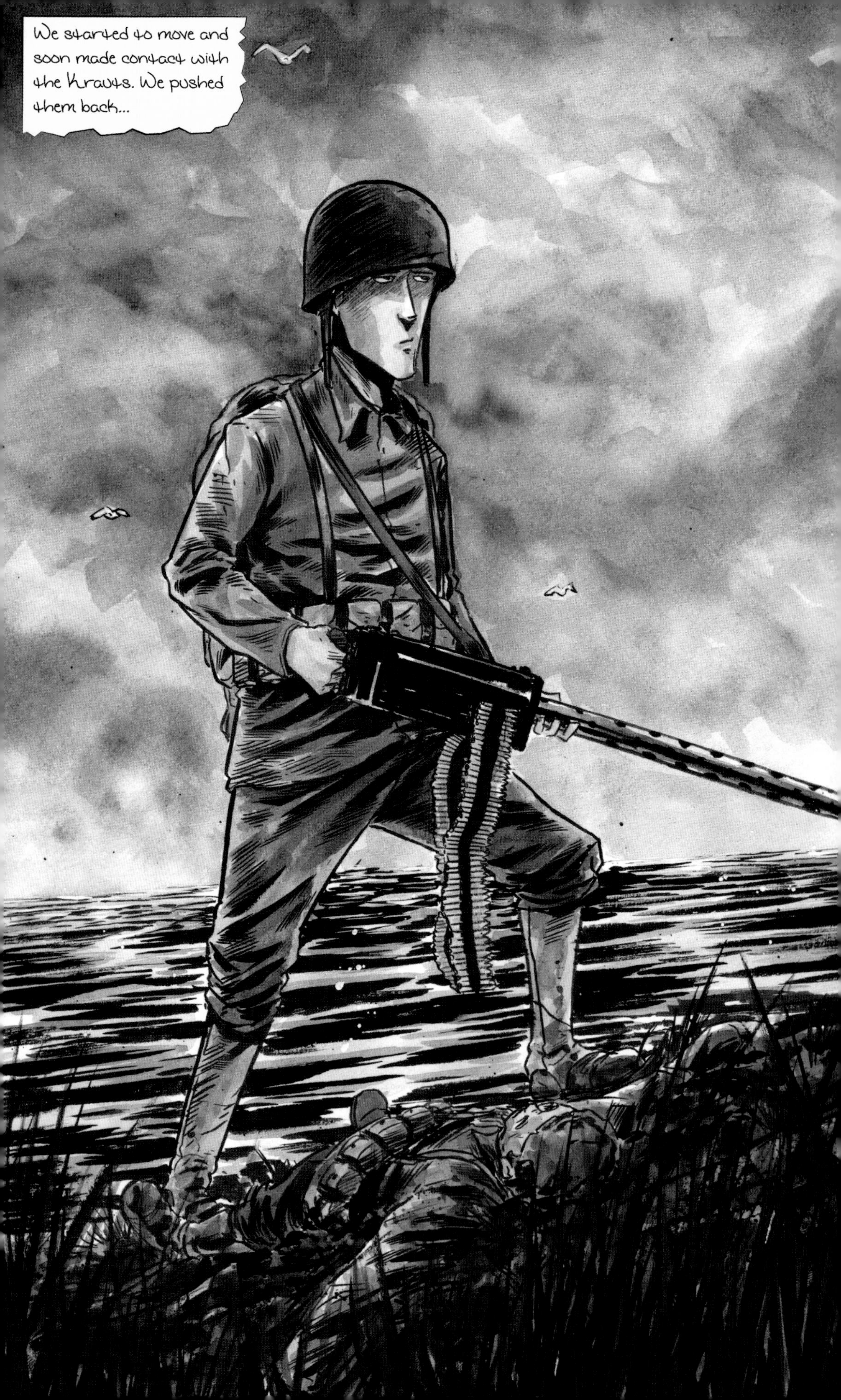
We started to move and soon made contact with the Krauts. We pushed them back...

CHAPTER THREE
WAR

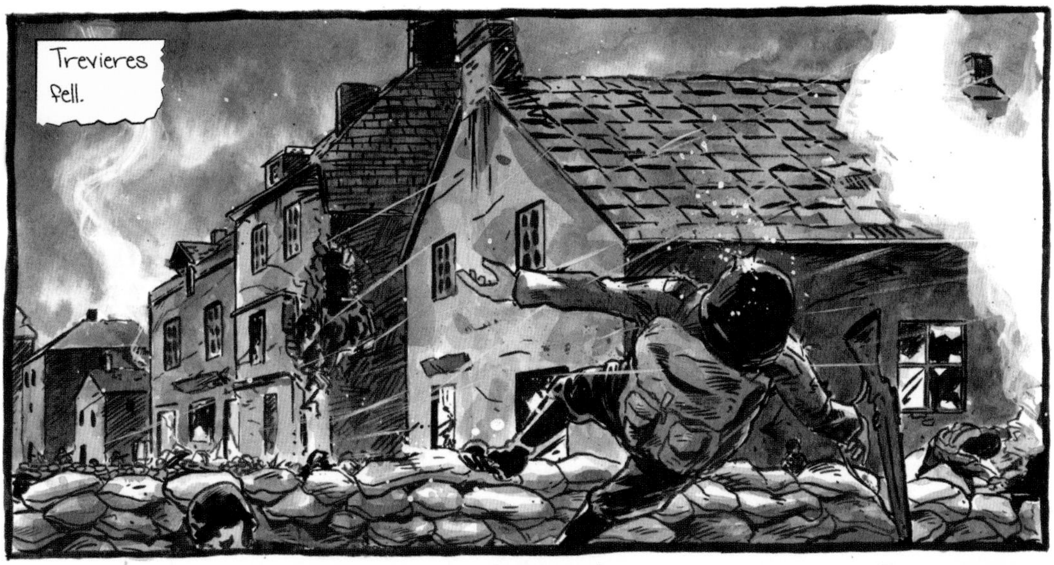
Trevieres fell.

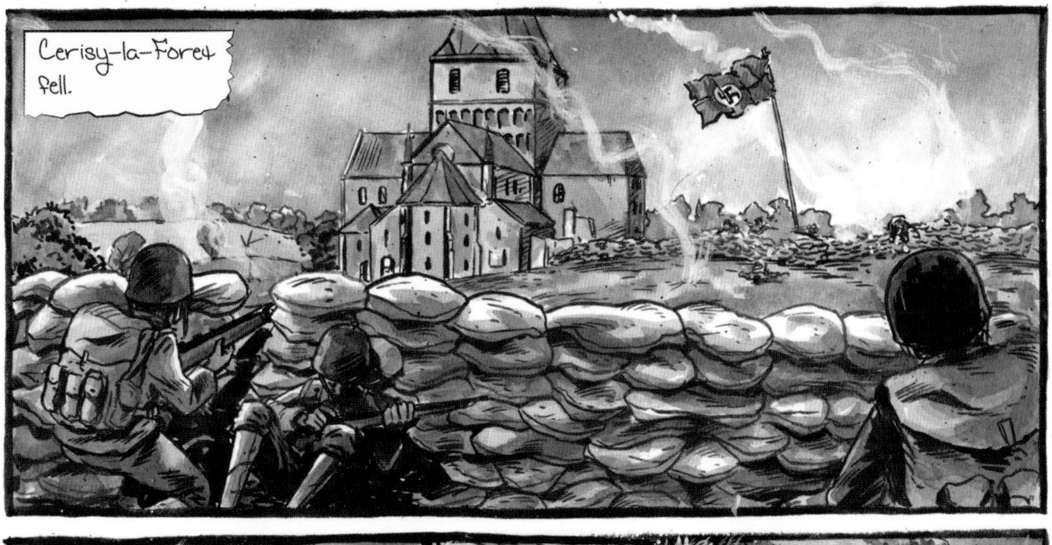
Cerisy-la-Foret fell.

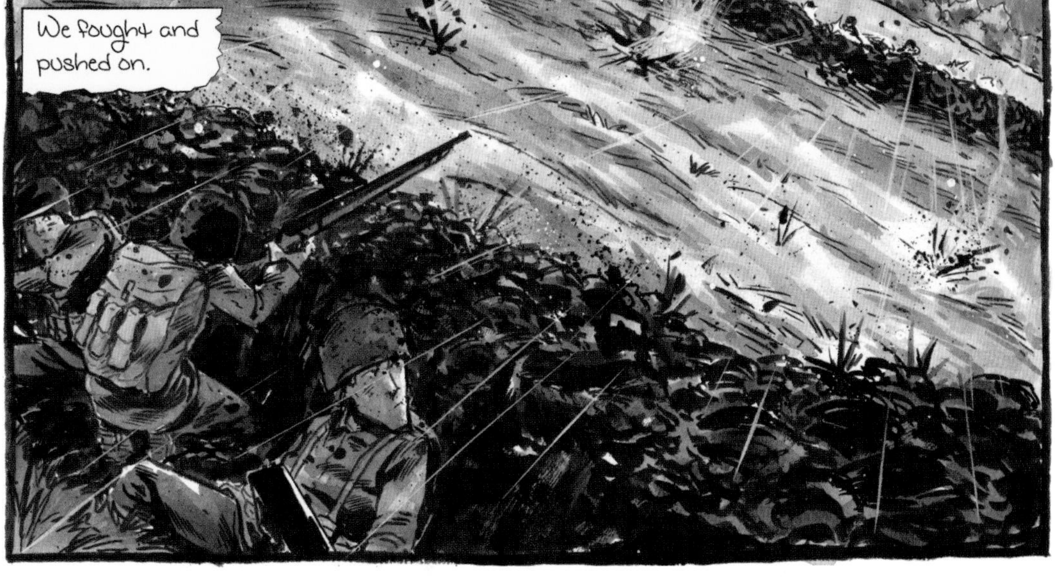
We fought and pushed on.

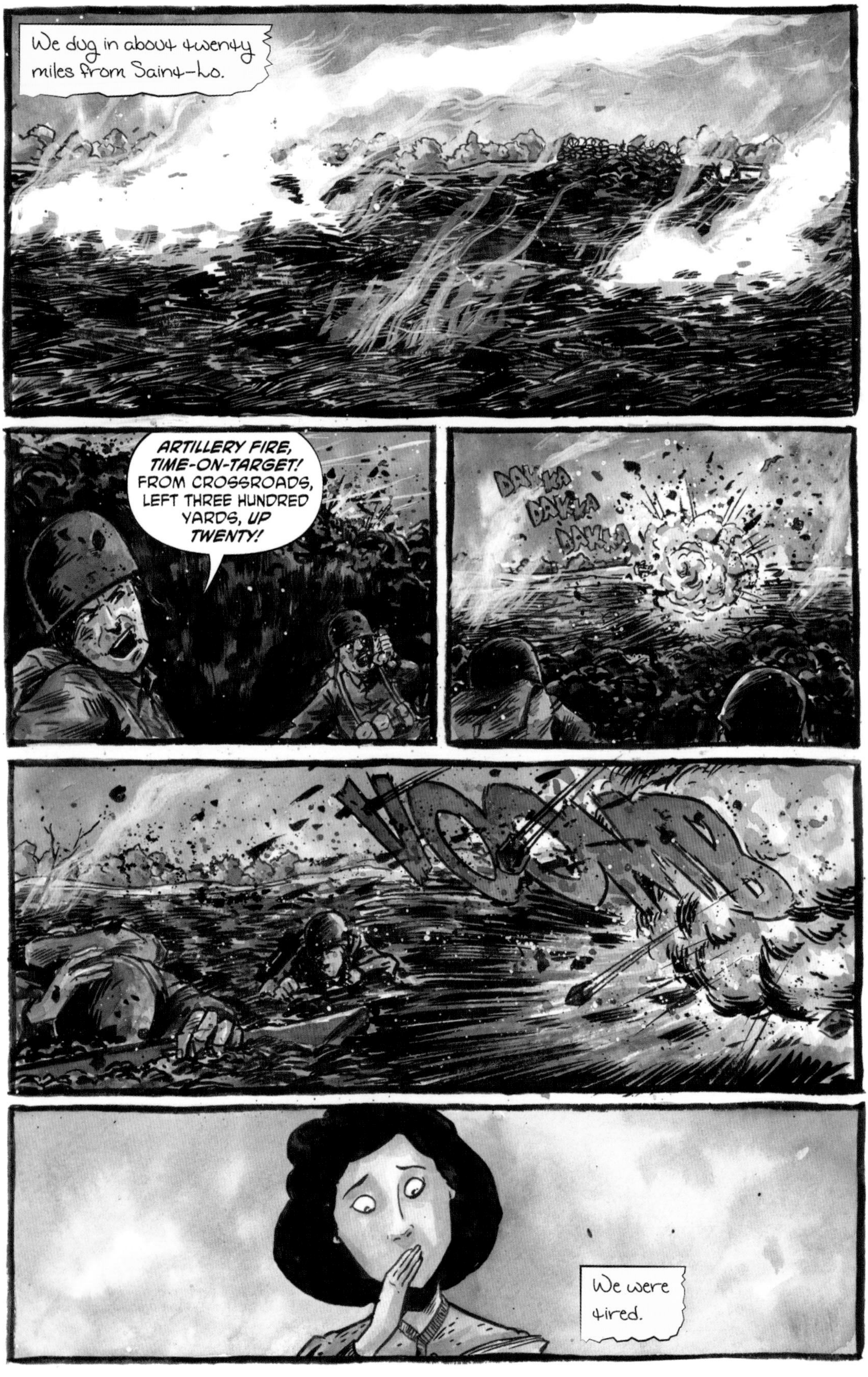
We dug in about twenty miles from Saint-Lo.
ARTILLERY FIRE, TIME-ON-TARGET! FROM CROSSROADS, LEFT THREE HUNDRED YARDS, UP TWENTY!
DAKKA
DAKKA
DAKKA
We were tired.

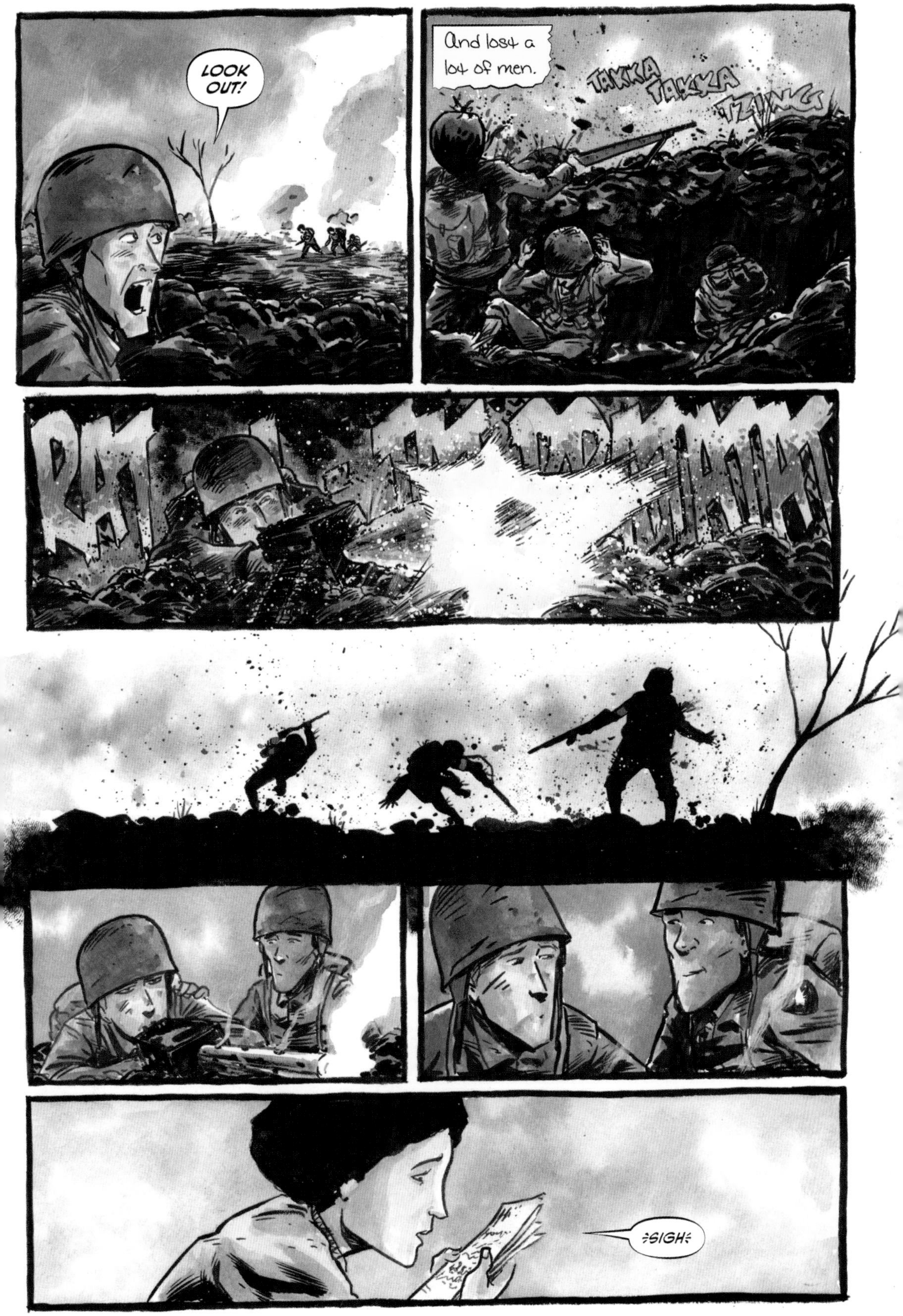
LOOK OUT!
And lost a lot of men.
TAKKA TAKKA
TZINGG
SIGH

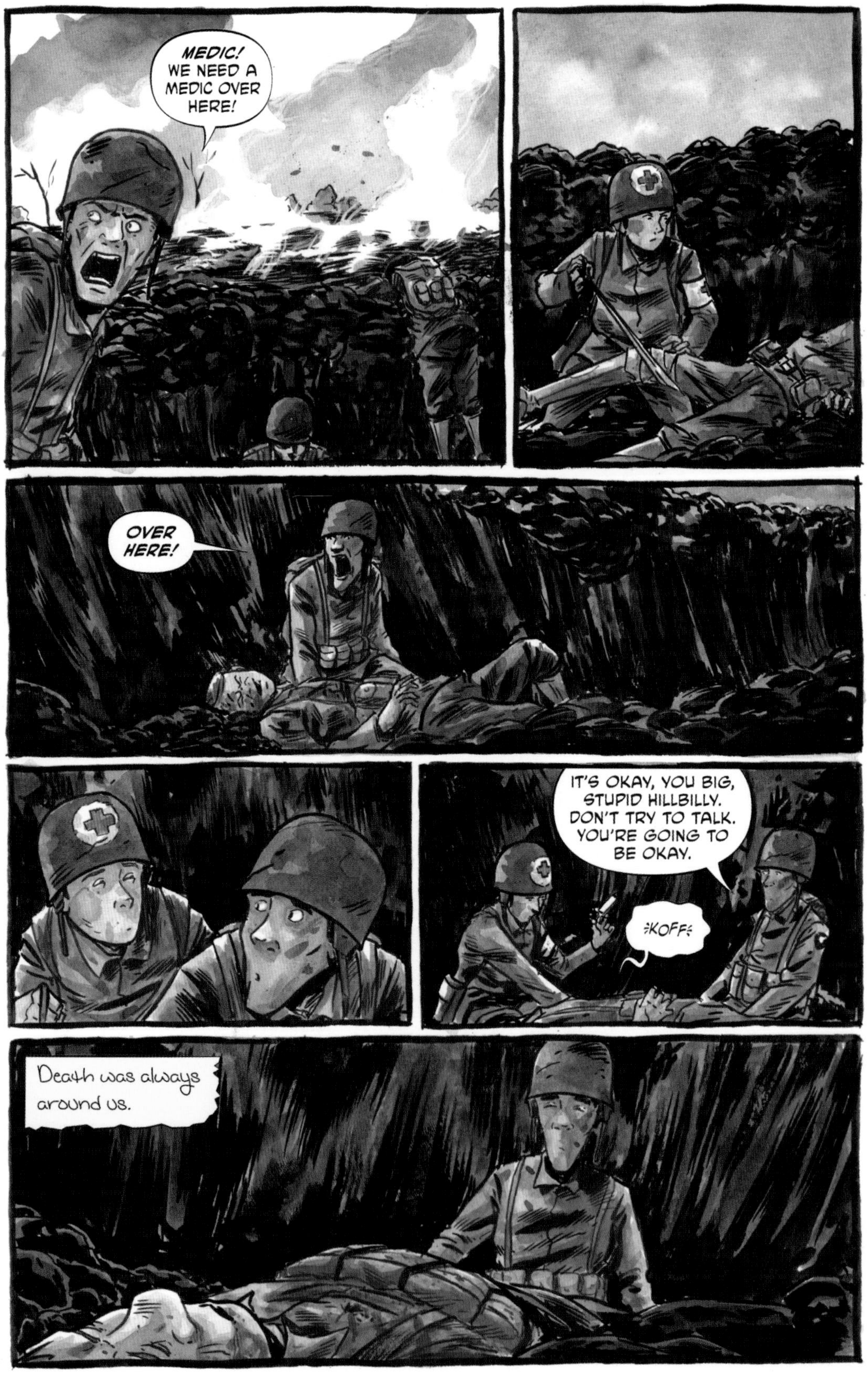
MEDIC! WE NEED A MEDIC OVER HERE!
OVER HERE!
IT'S OKAY, YOU BIG, STUPID HILLBILLY. DON'T TRY TO TALK. YOU'RE GOING TO BE OKAY.
KOFF
Death was always around us.

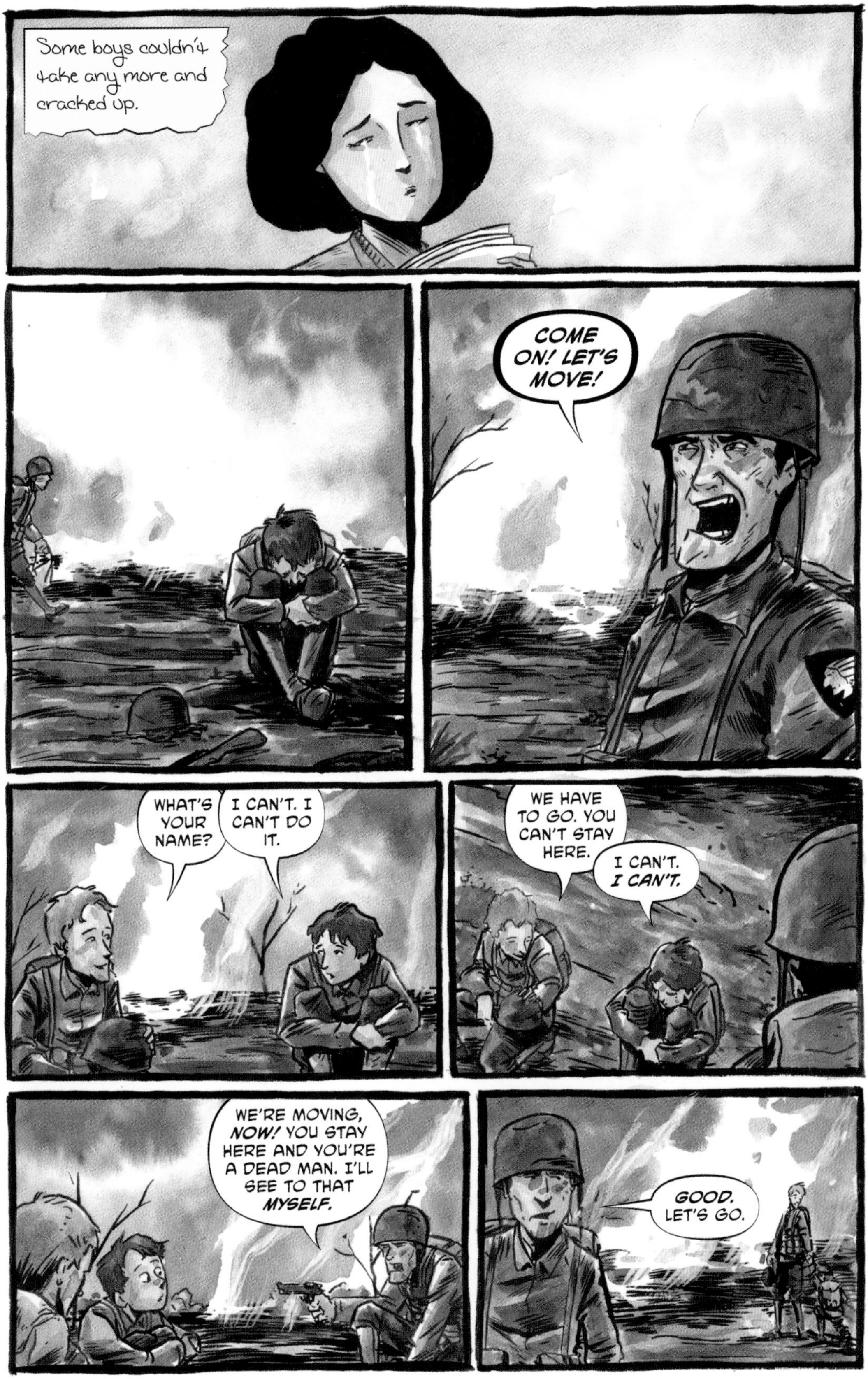
Some boys couldn't take any more and cracked up.
COME ON! LET'S MOVE!
WHAT'S YOUR NAME?
I CAN'T. I CAN'T DO IT.
WE HAVE TO GO. YOU CAN'T STAY HERE.
I CAN'T. *I CAN'T.*
WE'RE MOVING, *NOW!* YOU STAY HERE AND YOU'RE A DEAD MAN. I'LL SEE TO THAT *MYSELF.*
GOOD. LET'S GO.

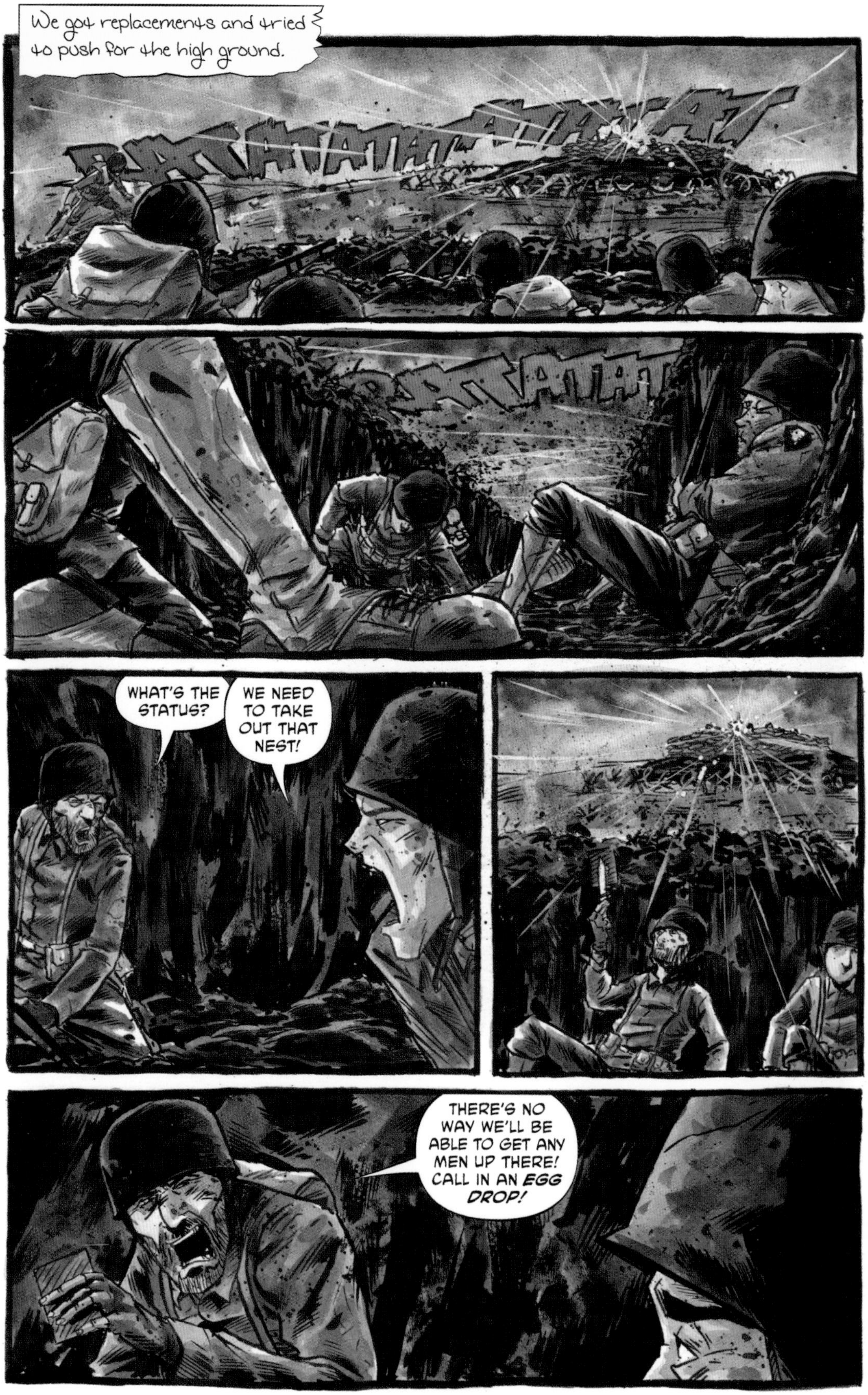
We got replacements and tried to push for the high ground.
BRATATATATATATATAT
BRATATAT
WHAT'S THE STATUS?
WE NEED TO TAKE OUT THAT NEST!
THERE'S NO WAY WE'LL BE ABLE TO GET ANY MEN UP THERE! CALL IN AN *EGG DROP!*

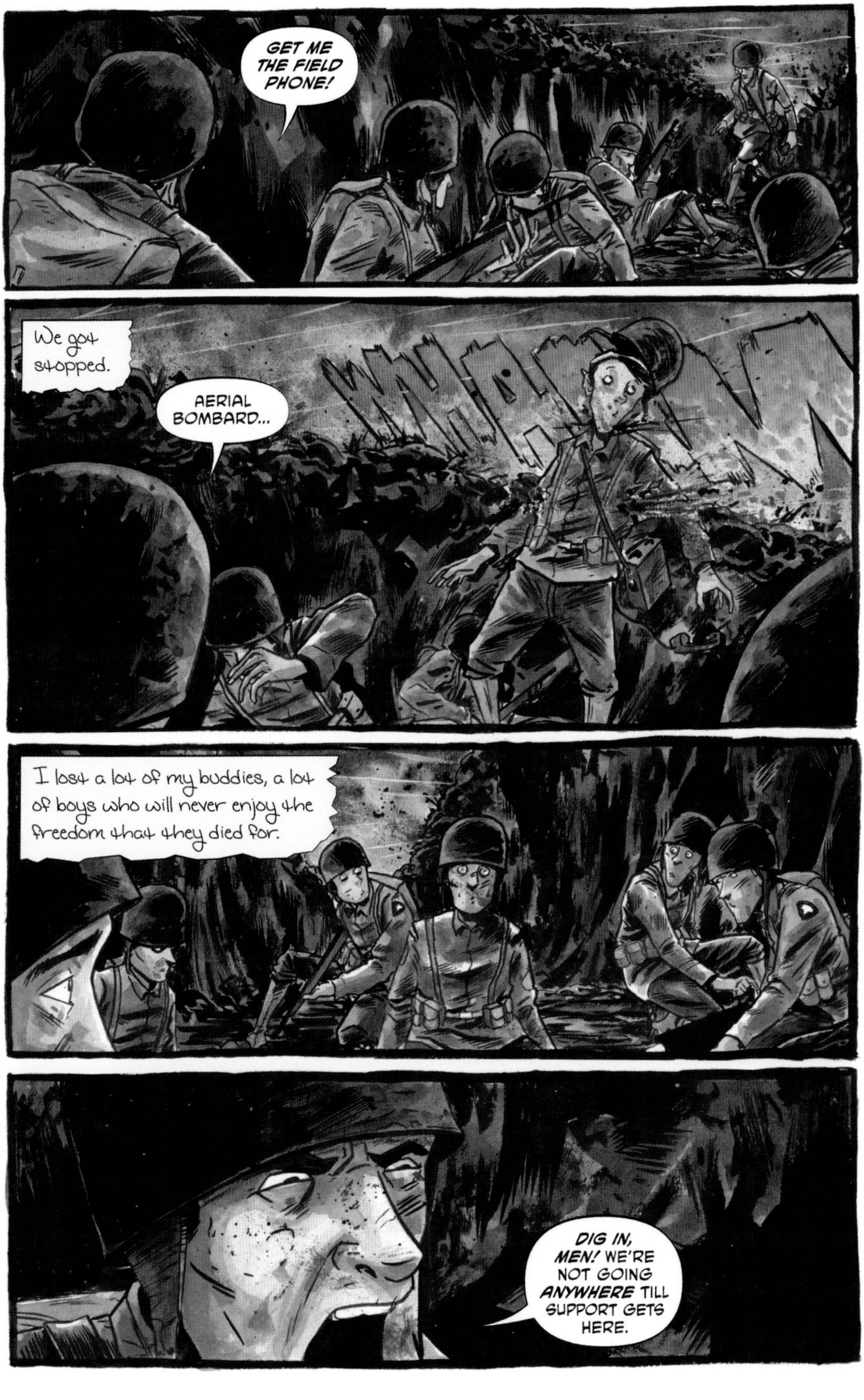
GET ME THE FIELD PHONE!
We got stopped.
AERIAL BOMBARD...
I lost a lot of my buddies, a lot of boys who will never enjoy the freedom that they died for.
DIG IN, MEN! WE'RE NOT GOING ANYWHERE TILL SUPPORT GETS HERE.

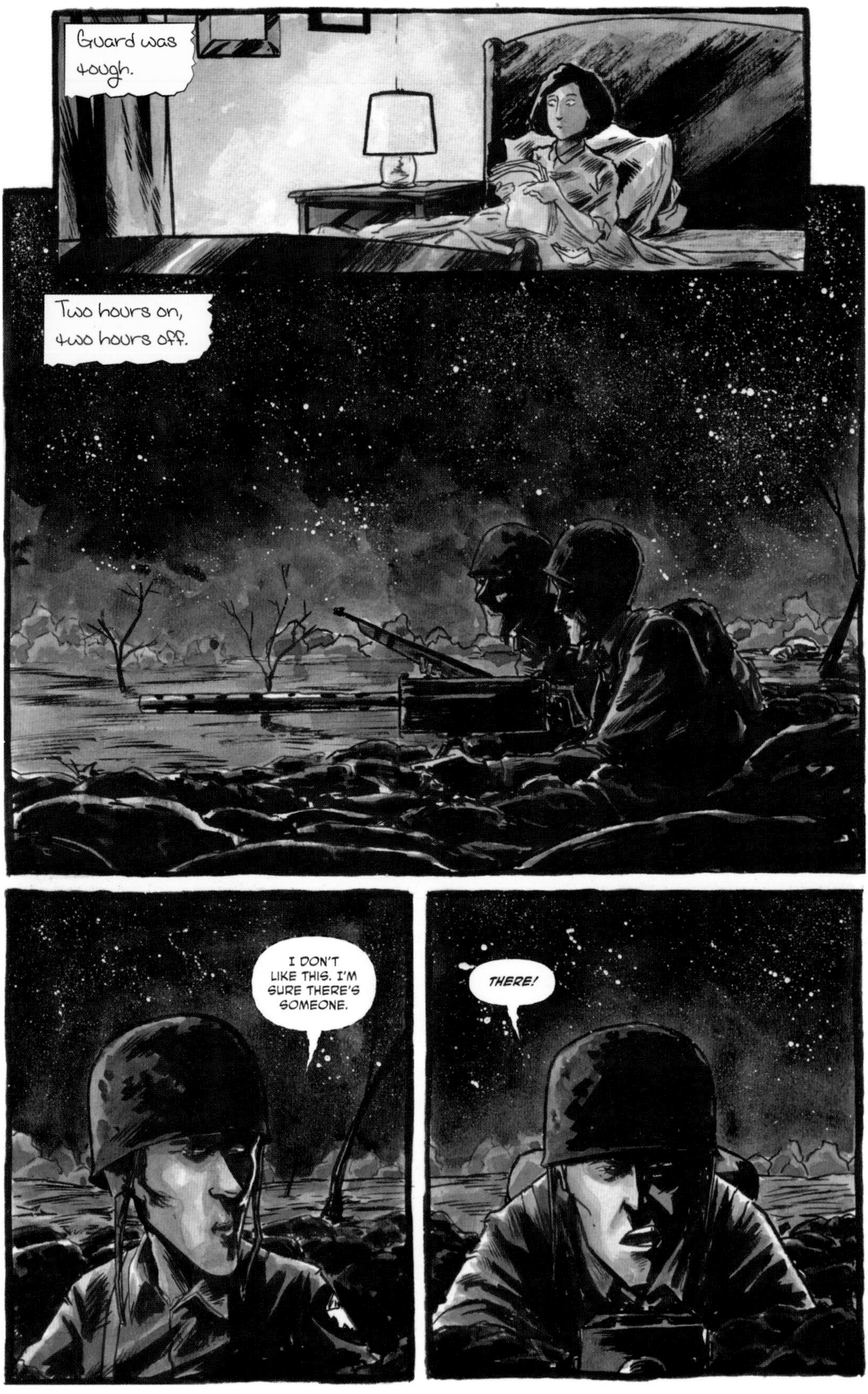
Guard was tough.
Two hours on, two hours off.
I DON'T LIKE THIS. I'M SURE THERE'S SOMEONE.
THERE!

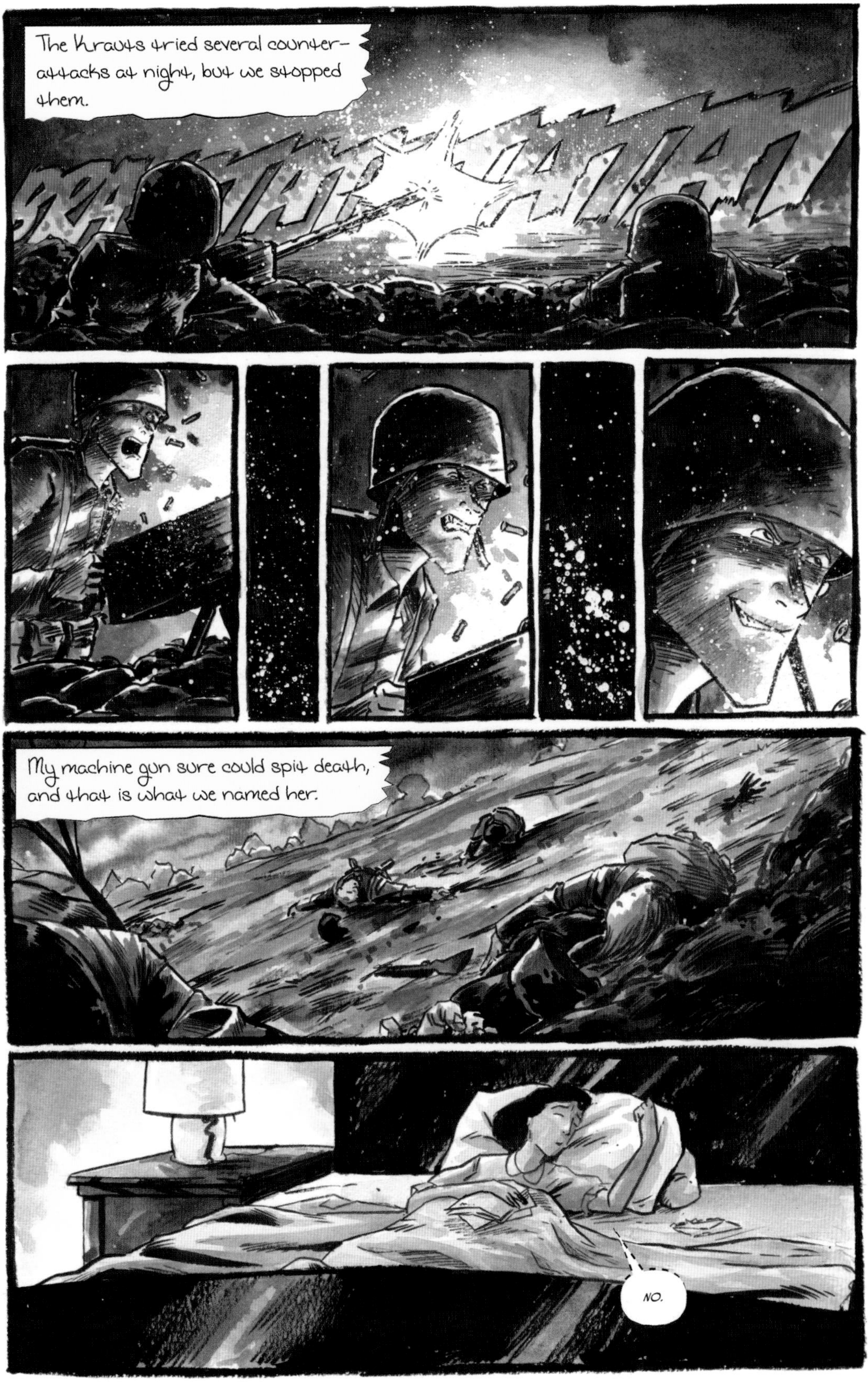

The Krauts tried several counter-attacks at night, but we stopped them.
My machine gun sure could spit death, and that is what we named her.
NO.

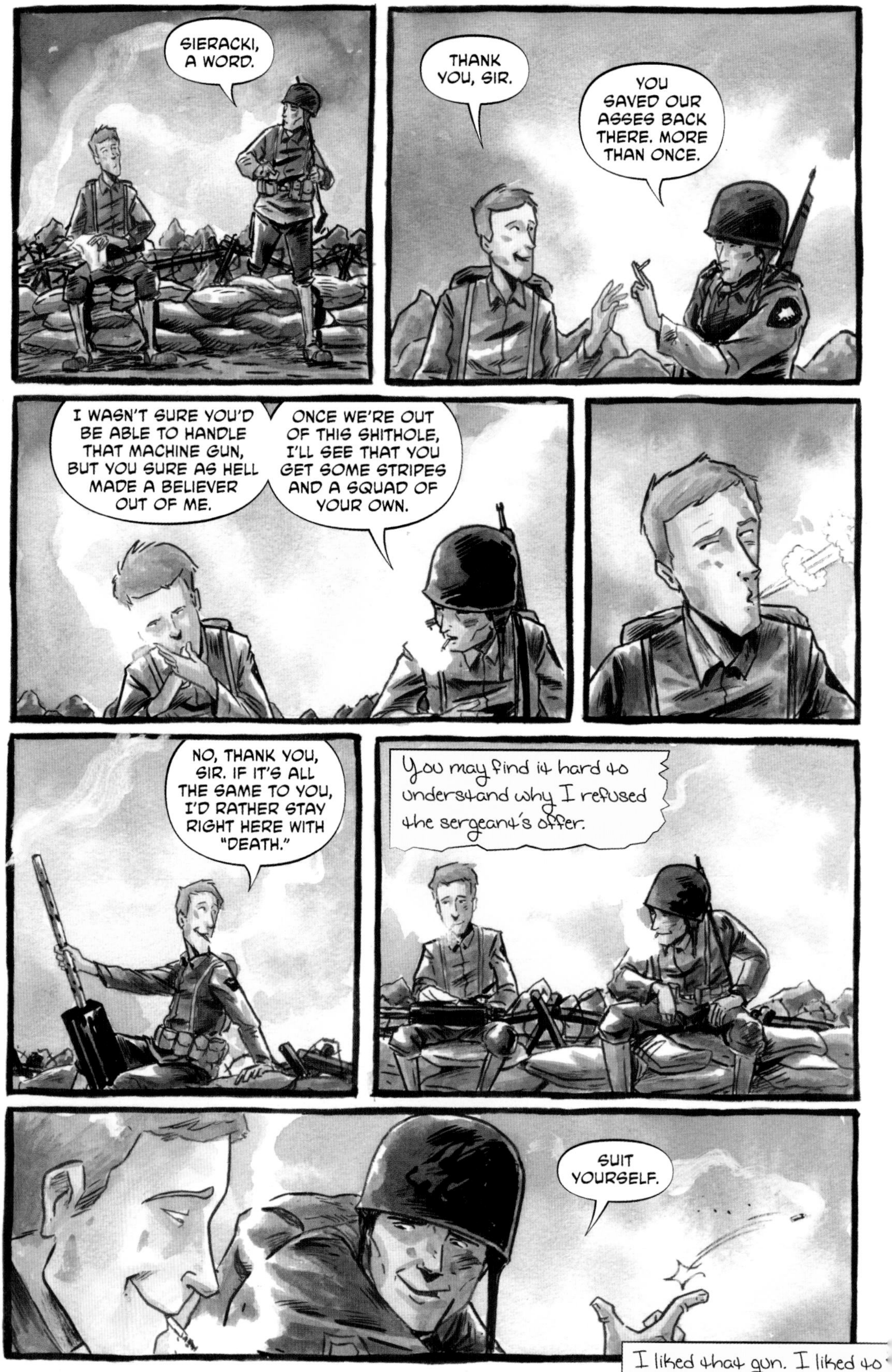
SIERACKI, A WORD.
THANK YOU, SIR.
YOU SAVED OUR ASSES BACK THERE. MORE THAN ONCE.
I WASN'T SURE YOU'D BE ABLE TO HANDLE THAT MACHINE GUN, BUT YOU SURE AS HELL MADE A BELIEVER OUT OF ME.
ONCE WE'RE OUT OF THIS SHITHOLE, I'LL SEE THAT YOU GET SOME STRIPES AND A SQUAD OF YOUR OWN.
NO, THANK YOU, SIR. IF IT'S ALL THE SAME TO YOU, I'D RATHER STAY RIGHT HERE WITH "DEATH."
You may find it hard to understand why I refused the sergeant's offer.
SUIT YOURSELF.
I liked that gun. I liked to fire it too much to leave.

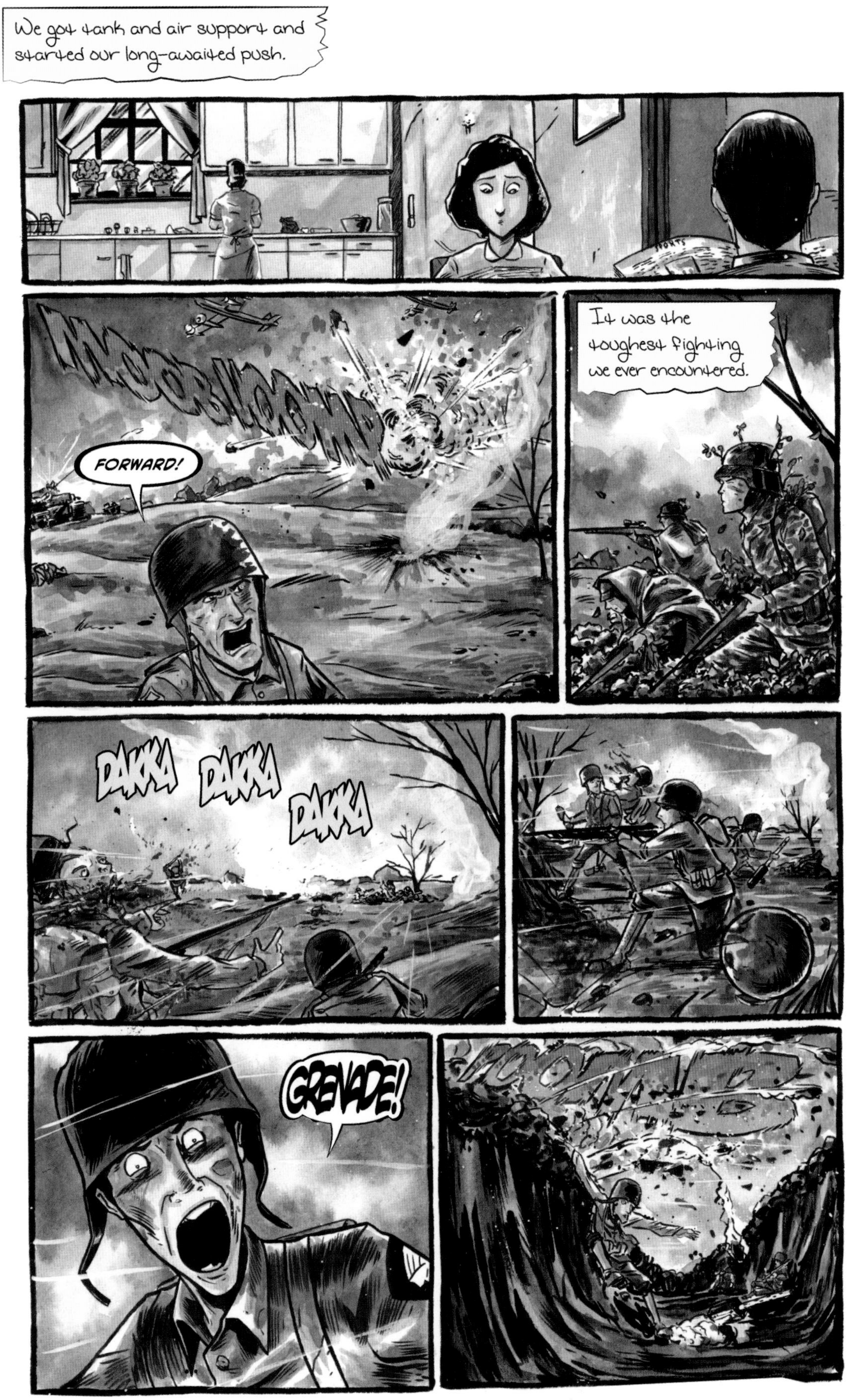
We got tank and air support and started our long-awaited push.
FORWARD!
It was the toughest fighting we ever encountered.
DAKKA
DAKKA
DAKKA
GRENADE!

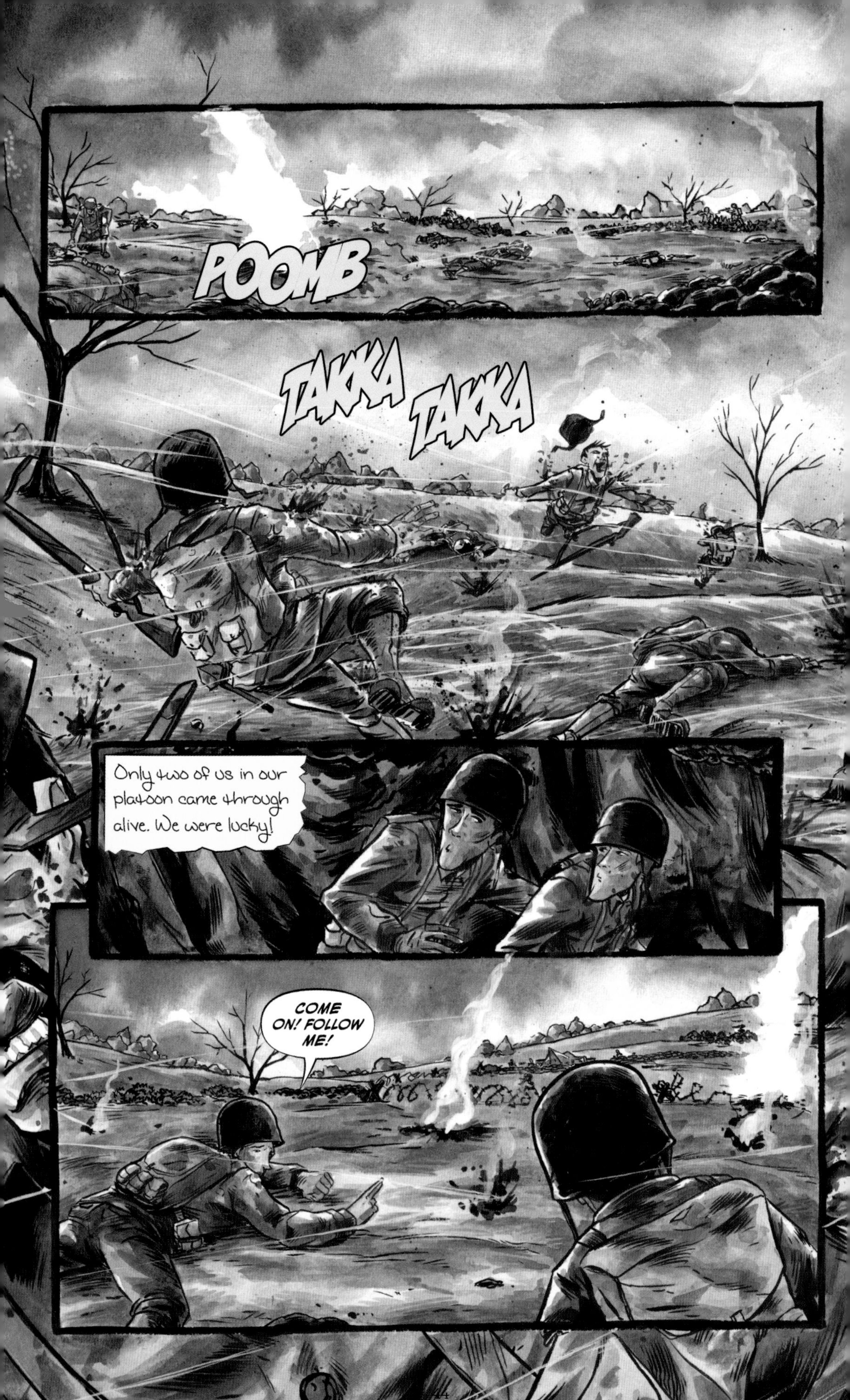

POOMB
TAKKA TAKKA
Only two of us in our platoon came through alive. We were lucky!
COME ON! FOLLOW ME!

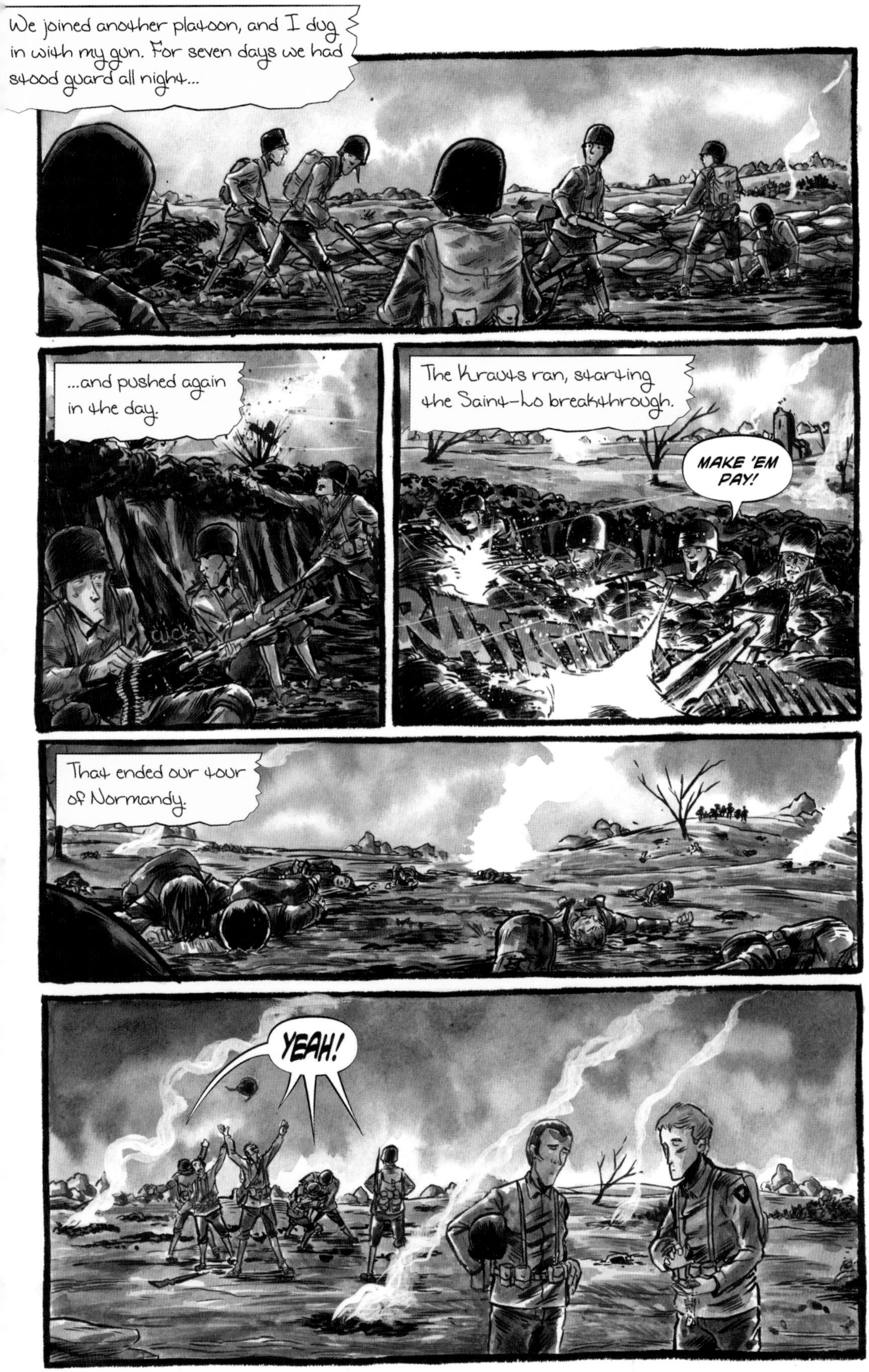
We joined another platoon, and I dug in with my gun. For seven days we had stood guard all night...
...and pushed again in the day.
CLICK
The Krauts ran, starting the Saint-Lo breakthrough.
MAKE 'EM PAY!
That ended our tour of Normandy.
YEAH!

CHAPTER FOUR
HOPE

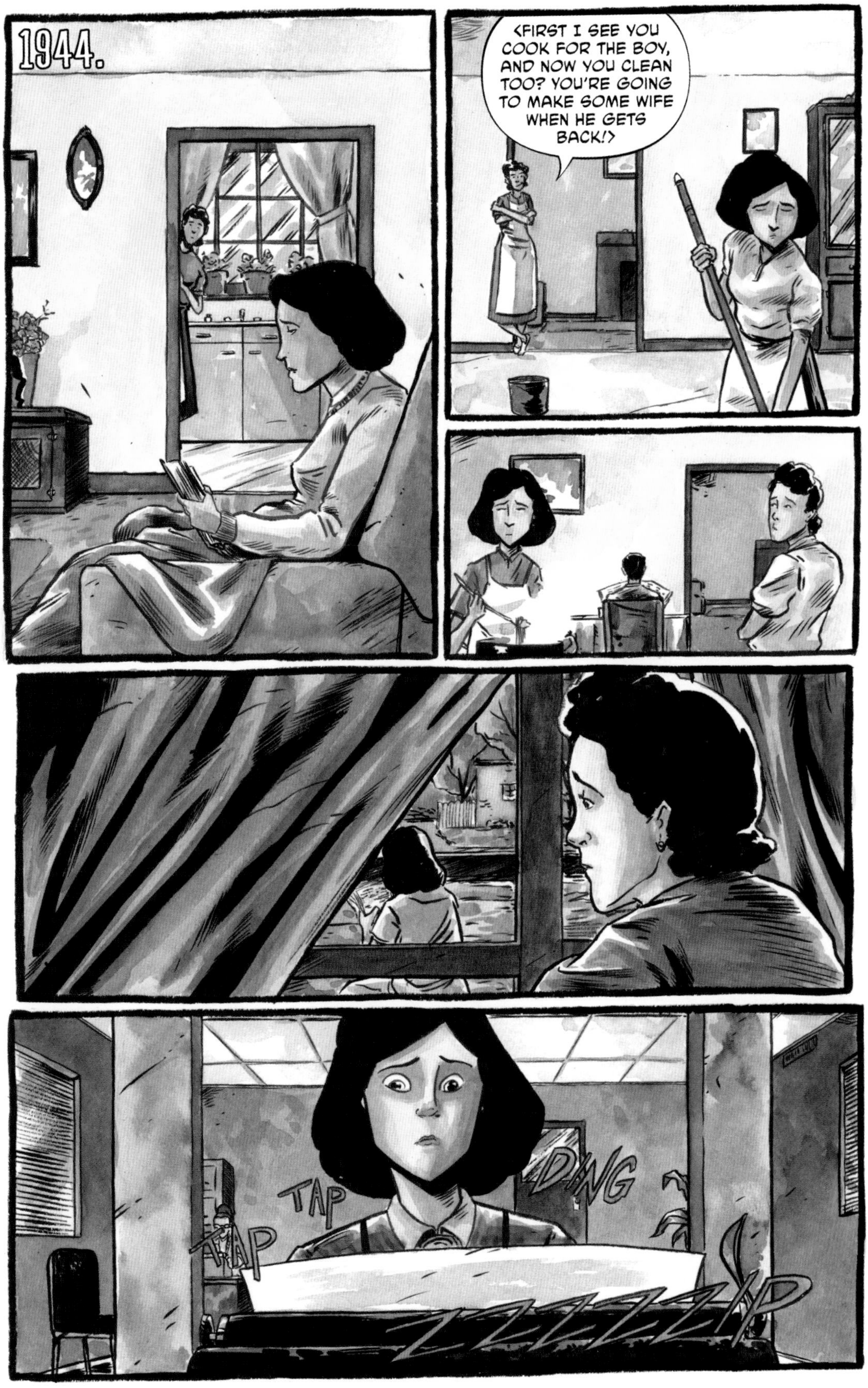
1944.
<FIRST I SEE YOU COOK FOR THE BOY, AND NOW YOU CLEAN TOO? YOU'RE GOING TO MAKE SOME WIFE WHEN HE GETS BACK!>
TAP
TAP
DING
ZZZZZZIP

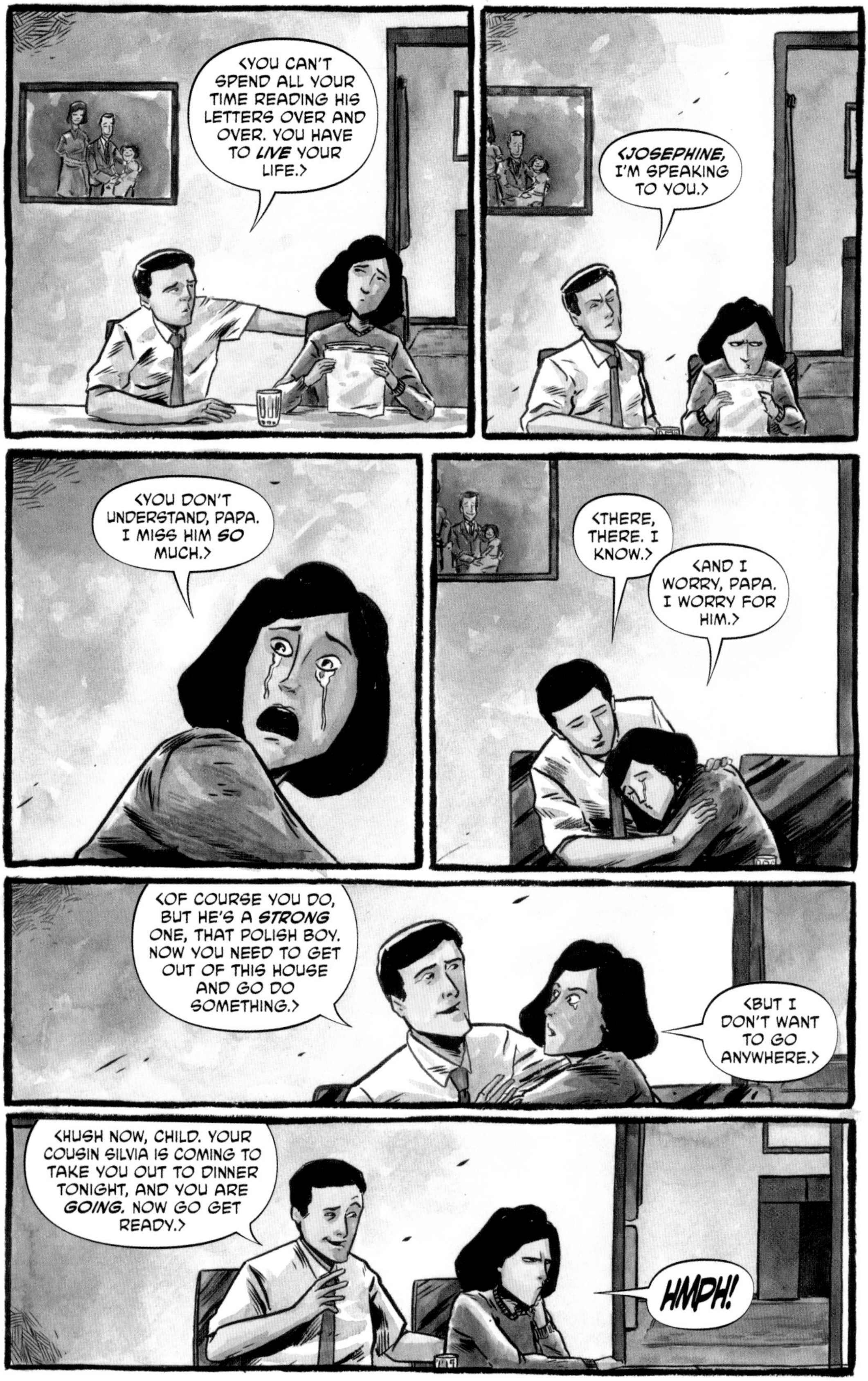
<YOU CAN'T SPEND ALL YOUR TIME READING HIS LETTERS OVER AND OVER. YOU HAVE TO *LIVE* YOUR LIFE.>
<*JOSEPHINE,* I'M SPEAKING TO YOU.>
<YOU DON'T UNDERSTAND, PAPA. I MISS HIM *SO* MUCH.>
<THERE, THERE. I KNOW.>
<AND I WORRY, PAPA. I WORRY FOR HIM.>
<OF COURSE YOU DO, BUT HE'S A *STRONG* ONE, THAT POLISH BOY. NOW YOU NEED TO GET OUT OF THIS HOUSE AND GO DO SOMETHING.>
<BUT I DON'T WANT TO GO ANYWHERE.>
<HUSH NOW, CHILD. YOUR COUSIN SILVIA IS COMING TO TAKE YOU OUT TO DINNER TONIGHT, AND YOU ARE *GOING.* NOW GO GET READY.>
HMPH!

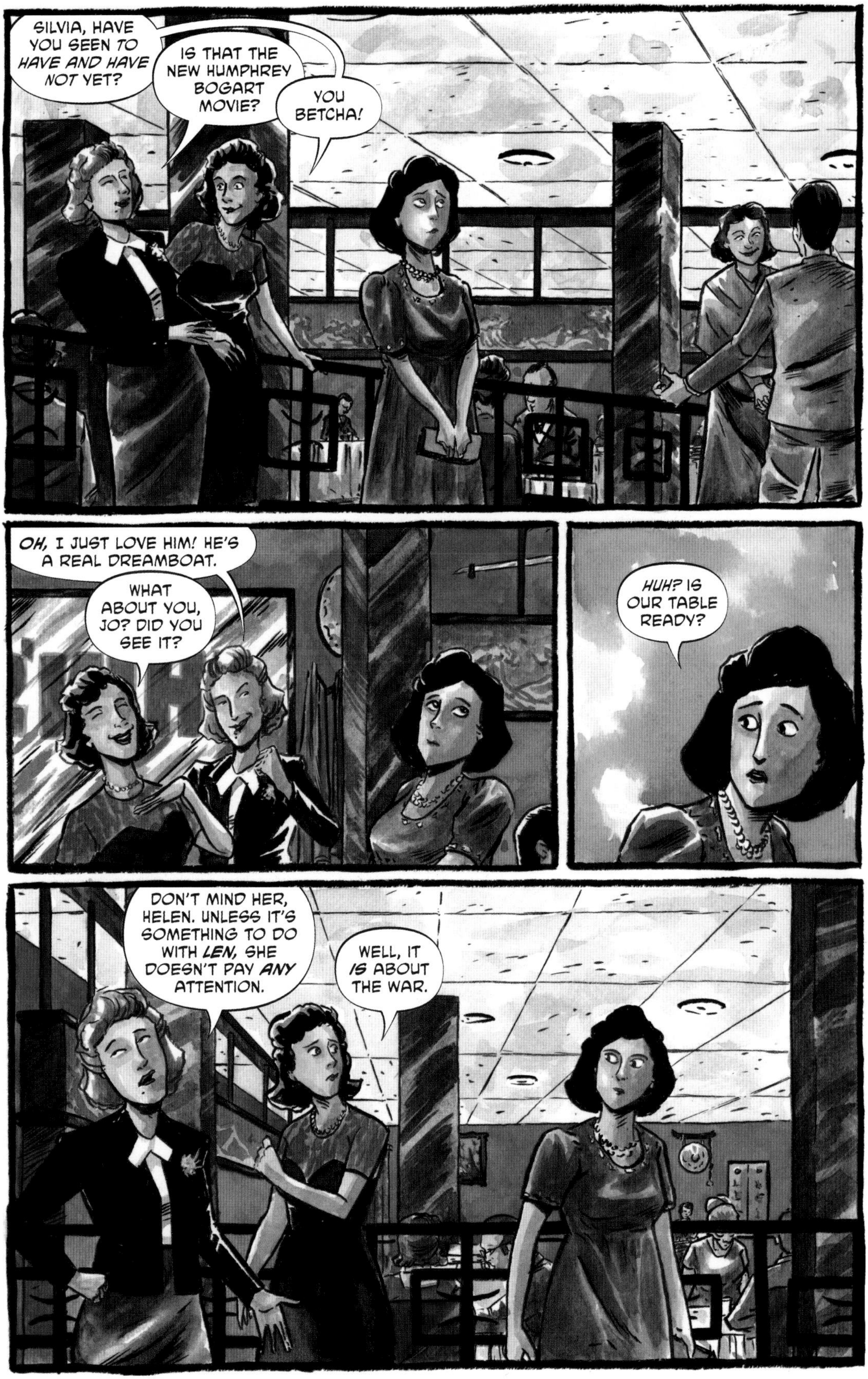
SILVIA, HAVE YOU SEEN TO *HAVE AND HAVE NOT* YET?
IS THAT THE NEW HUMPHREY BOGART MOVIE?
YOU BETCHA!
OH, I JUST LOVE HIM! HE'S A REAL DREAMBOAT.
WHAT ABOUT YOU, JO? DID YOU SEE IT?
HUH? IS OUR TABLE READY?
DON'T MIND HER, HELEN. UNLESS IT'S SOMETHING TO DO WITH *LEN,* SHE DOESN'T PAY *ANY* ATTENTION.
WELL, IT *IS* ABOUT THE WAR.

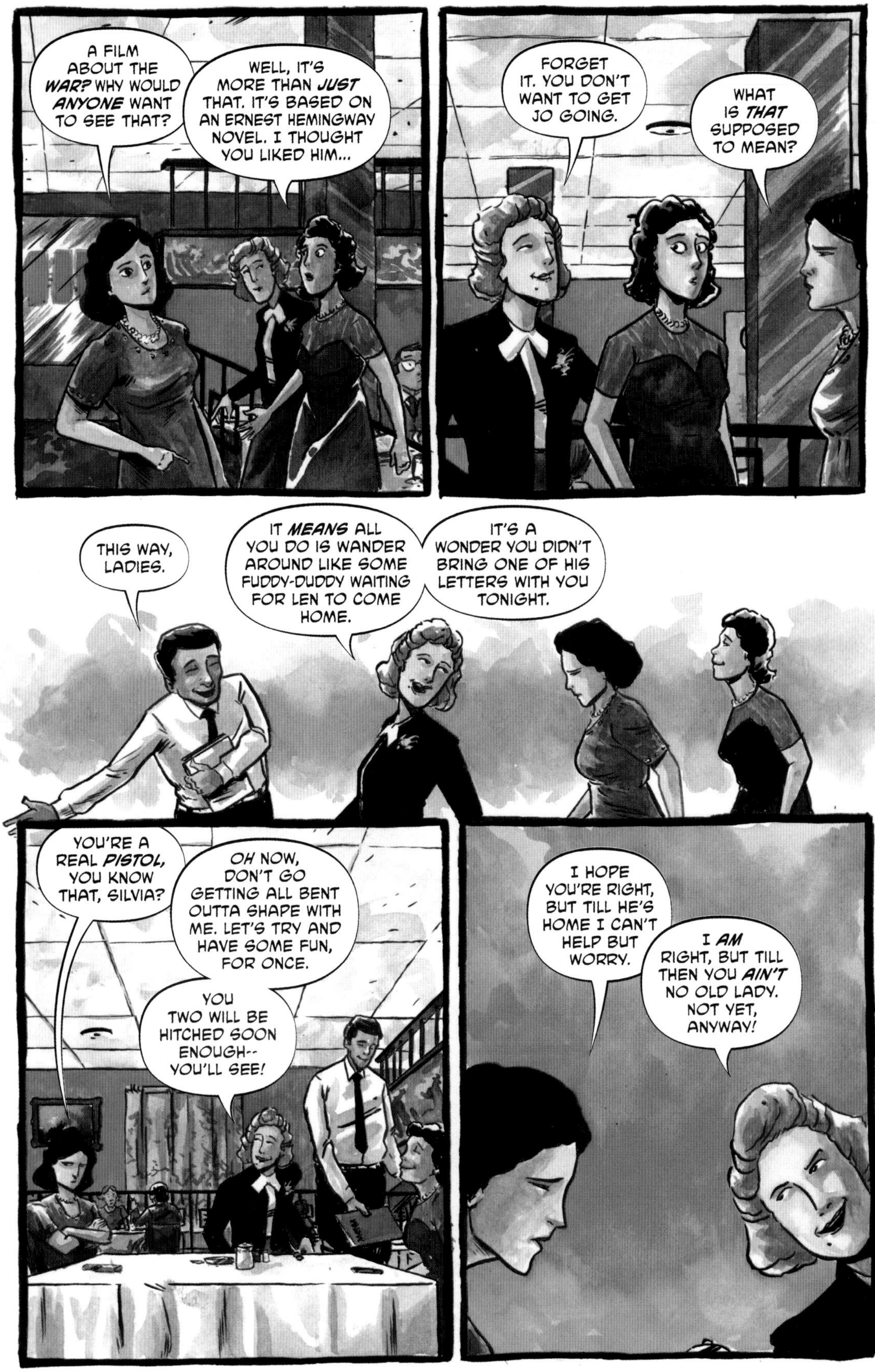
A FILM ABOUT THE *WAR?* WHY WOULD *ANYONE* WANT TO SEE THAT?
WELL, IT'S MORE THAN *JUST* THAT. IT'S BASED ON AN ERNEST HEMINGWAY NOVEL. I THOUGHT YOU LIKED HIM...
FORGET IT. YOU DON'T WANT TO GET JO GOING.
WHAT IS *THAT* SUPPOSED TO MEAN?
THIS WAY, LADIES.
IT *MEANS* ALL YOU DO IS WANDER AROUND LIKE SOME FUDDY-DUDDY WAITING FOR LEN TO COME HOME.
IT'S A WONDER YOU DIDN'T BRING ONE OF HIS LETTERS WITH YOU TONIGHT.
YOU'RE A REAL *PISTOL,* YOU KNOW THAT, SILVIA?
OH NOW, DON'T GO GETTING ALL BENT OUTTA SHAPE WITH ME. LET'S TRY AND HAVE SOME FUN, FOR ONCE.
YOU TWO WILL BE HITCHED SOON ENOUGH-- YOU'LL SEE!
I HOPE YOU'RE RIGHT, BUT TILL HE'S HOME I CAN'T HELP BUT WORRY.
I *AM* RIGHT, BUT TILL THEN YOU *AIN'T* NO OLD LADY. NOT YET, ANYWAY!

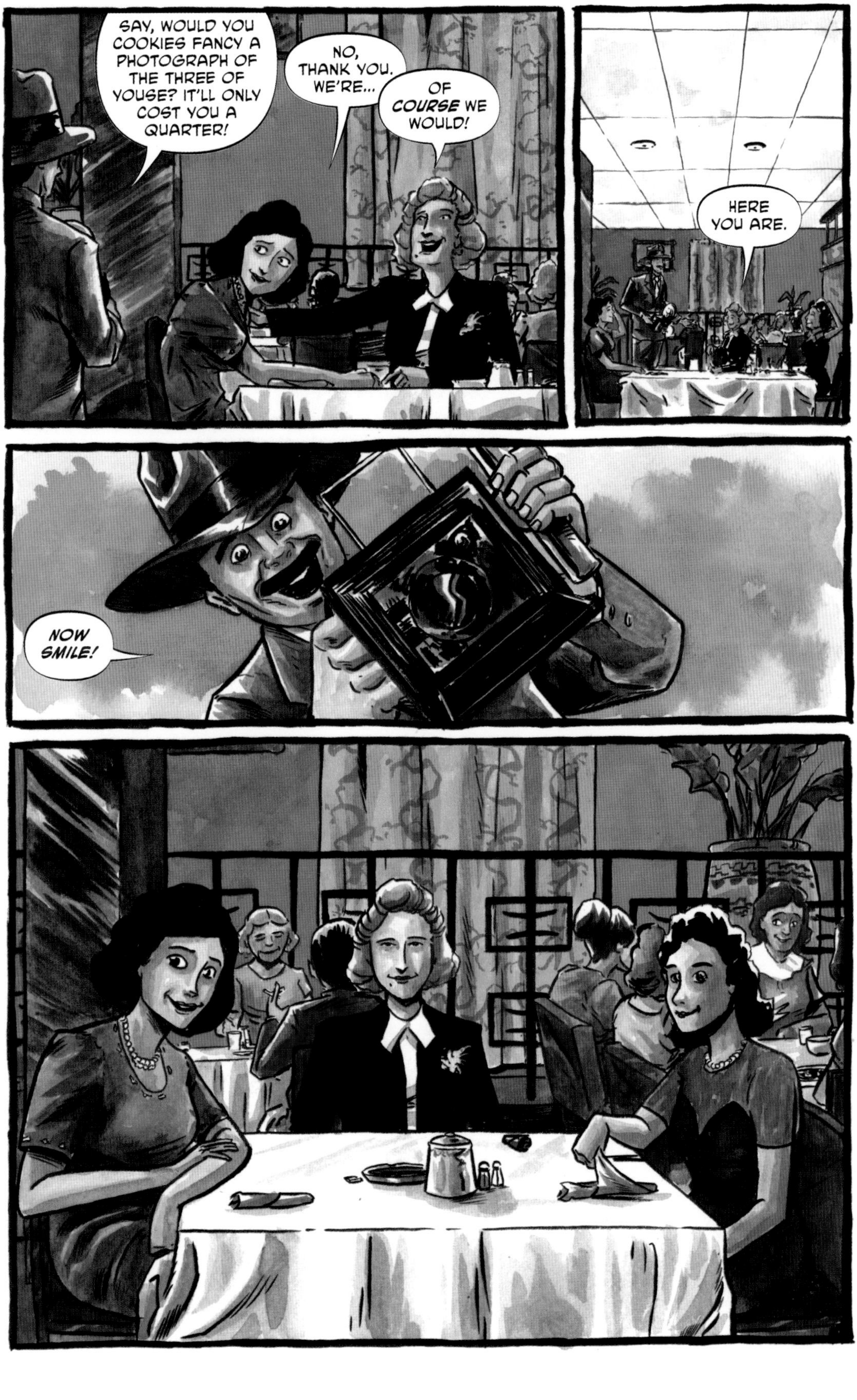
SAY, WOULD YOU COOKIES FANCY A PHOTOGRAPH OF THE THREE OF YOUSE? IT'LL ONLY COST YOU A QUARTER!
NO, THANK YOU. WE'RE...
OF COURSE WE WOULD!
HERE YOU ARE.
NOW SMILE!

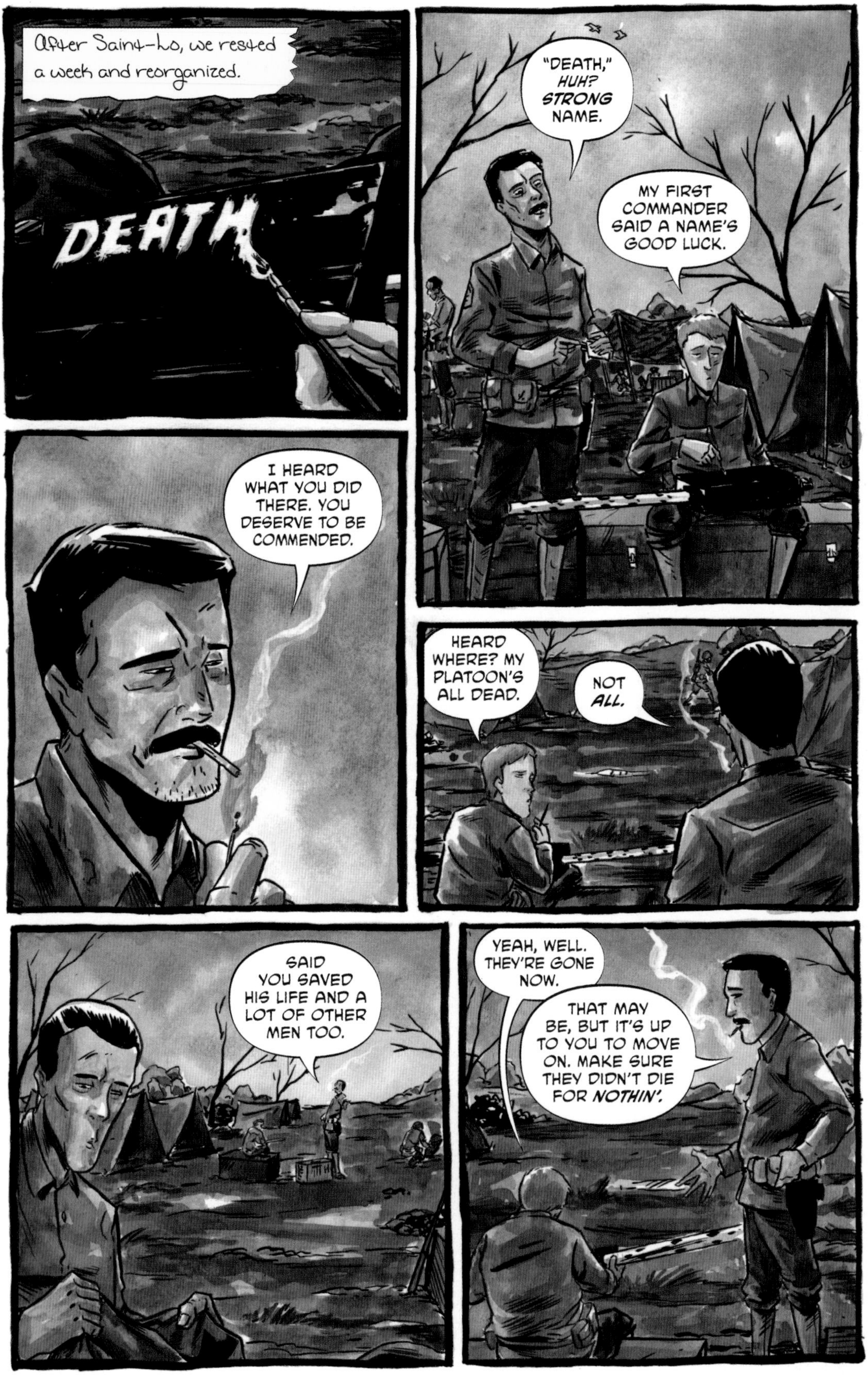
After Saint-Lo, we rested a week and reorganized.
DEATH
"DEATH," HUH? STRONG NAME.
MY FIRST COMMANDER SAID A NAME'S GOOD LUCK.
I HEARD WHAT YOU DID THERE. YOU DESERVE TO BE COMMENDED.
HEARD WHERE? MY PLATOON'S ALL DEAD.
NOT ALL.
SAID YOU SAVED HIS LIFE AND A LOT OF OTHER MEN TOO.
YEAH, WELL. THEY'RE GONE NOW.
THAT MAY BE, BUT IT'S UP TO YOU TO MOVE ON. MAKE SURE THEY DIDN'T DIE FOR NOTHIN'.

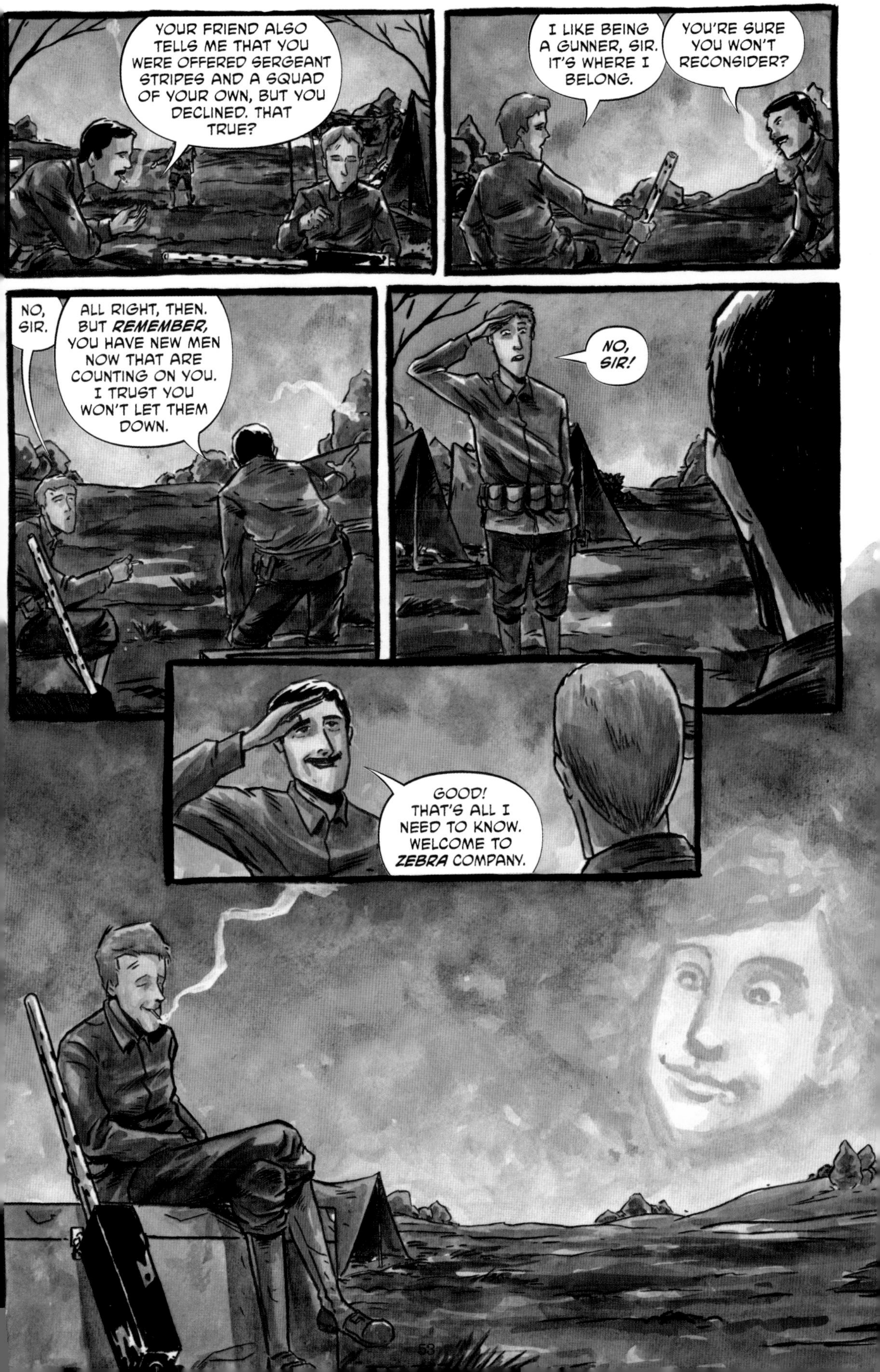
YOUR FRIEND ALSO TELLS ME THAT YOU WERE OFFERED SERGEANT STRIPES AND A SQUAD OF YOUR OWN, BUT YOU DECLINED. THAT TRUE?
I LIKE BEING A GUNNER, SIR. IT'S WHERE I BELONG.
YOU'RE SURE YOU WON'T RECONSIDER?
NO, SIR.
ALL RIGHT, THEN. BUT *REMEMBER,* YOU HAVE NEW MEN NOW THAT ARE COUNTING ON YOU. I TRUST YOU WON'T LET THEM DOWN.
NO, SIR!
GOOD! THAT'S ALL I NEED TO KNOW. WELCOME TO *ZEBRA* COMPANY.

CHAPTER FIVE
LIBERTY

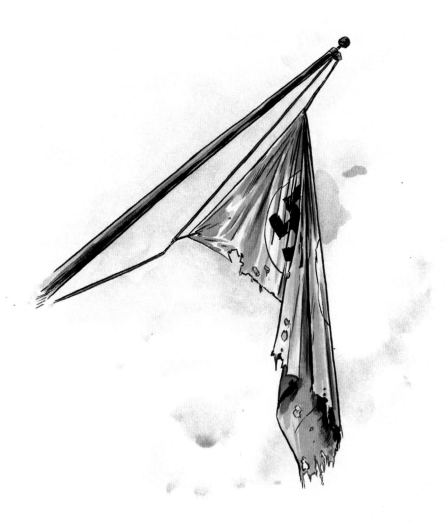

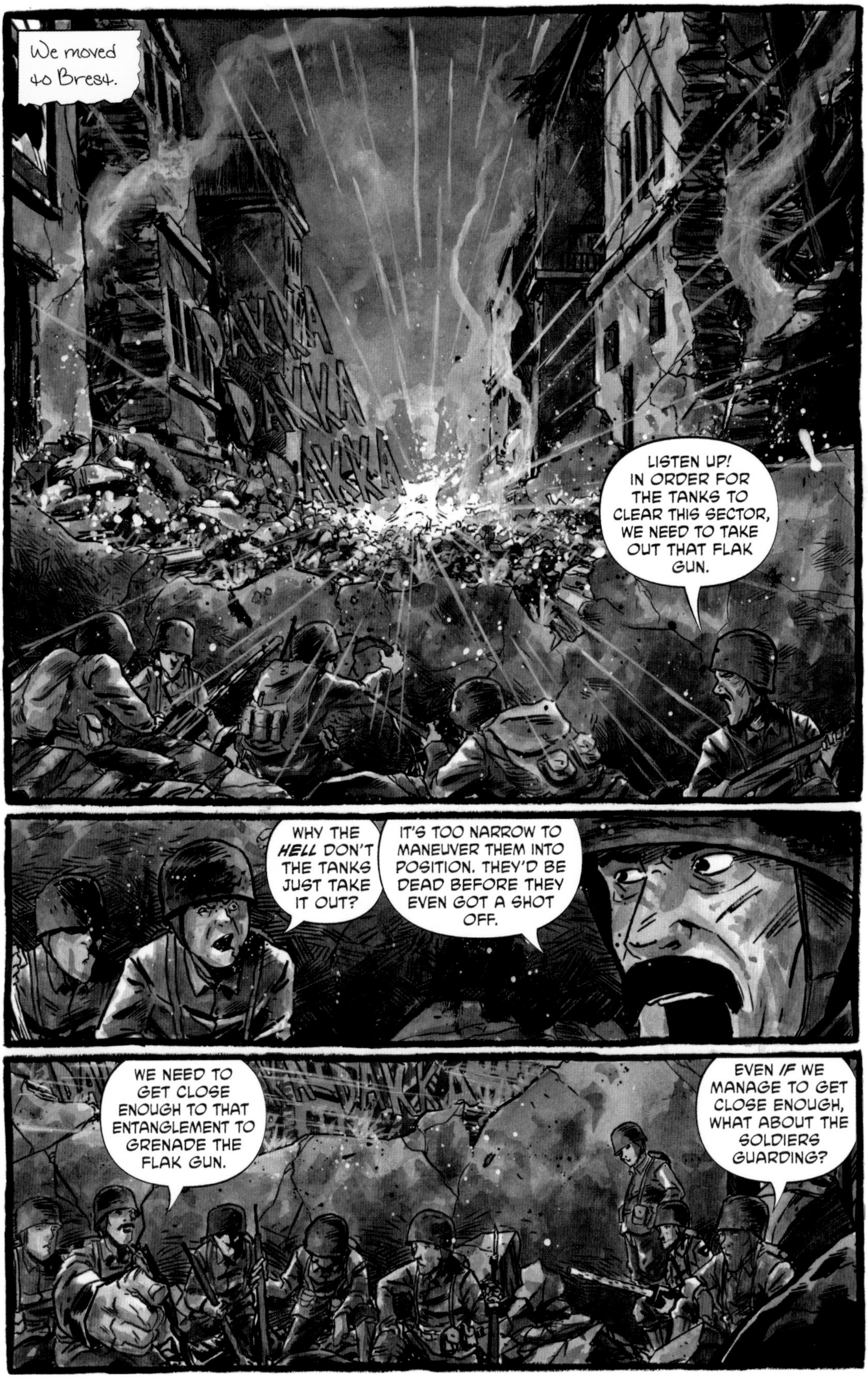
We moved to Brest.
DAKKA DAKKA DAKKA
LISTEN UP! IN ORDER FOR THE TANKS TO CLEAR THIS SECTOR, WE NEED TO TAKE OUT THAT FLAK GUN.
WHY THE *HELL* DON'T THE TANKS JUST TAKE IT OUT?
IT'S TOO NARROW TO MANEUVER THEM INTO POSITION. THEY'D BE DEAD BEFORE THEY EVEN GOT A SHOT OFF.
WE NEED TO GET CLOSE ENOUGH TO THAT ENTANGLEMENT TO GRENADE THE FLAK GUN.
EVEN *IF* WE MANAGE TO GET CLOSE ENOUGH, WHAT ABOUT THE SOLDIERS GUARDING?

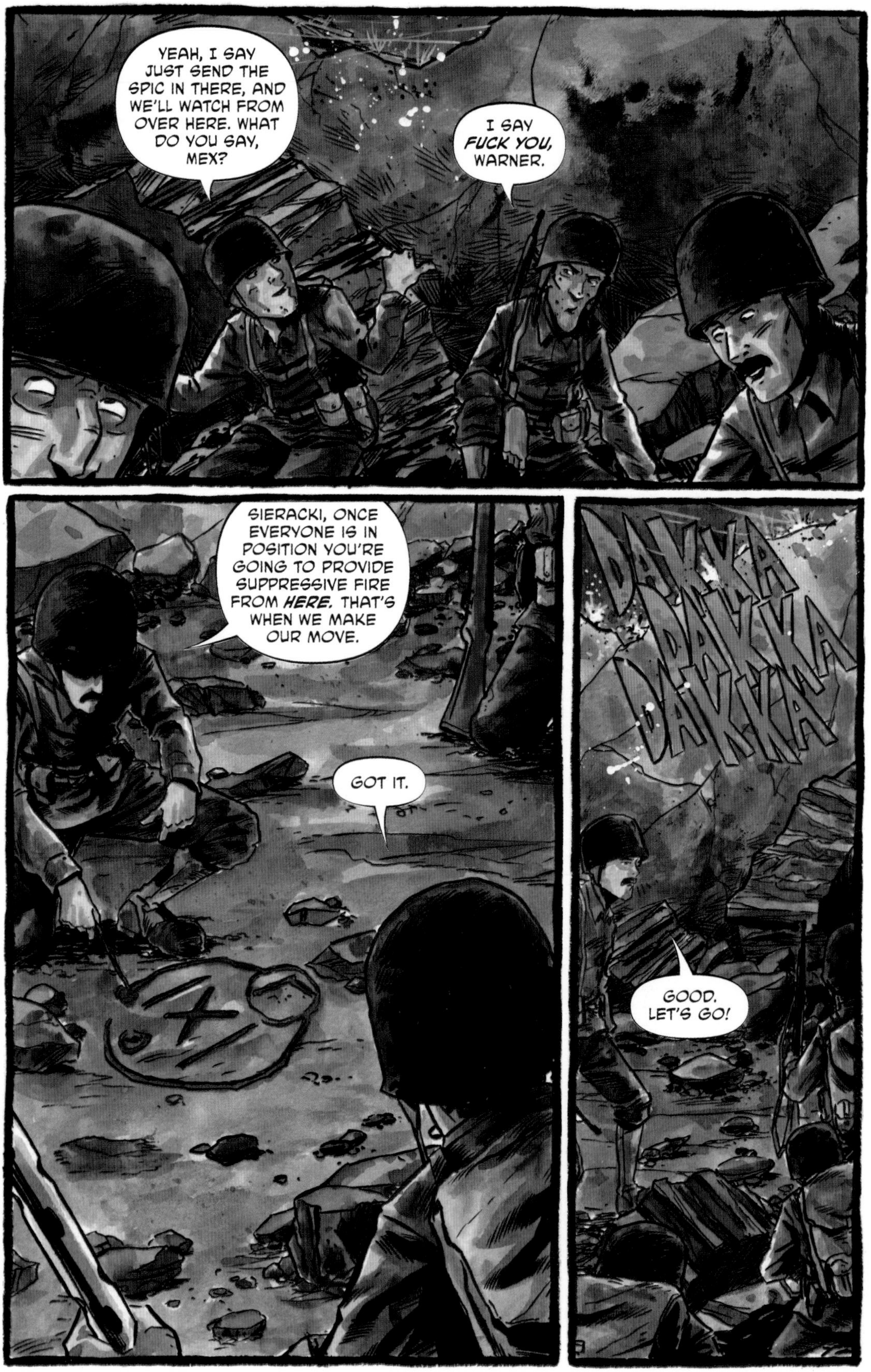
YEAH, I SAY JUST SEND THE SPIC IN THERE, AND WE'LL WATCH FROM OVER HERE. WHAT DO YOU SAY, MEX?
I SAY ***FUCK YOU,*** WARNER.
SIERACKI, ONCE EVERYONE IS IN POSITION YOU'RE GOING TO PROVIDE SUPPRESSIVE FIRE FROM ***HERE.*** THAT'S WHEN WE MAKE OUR MOVE.
GOT IT.
DAKKA DAKKA DAKKA
GOOD. LET'S GO!

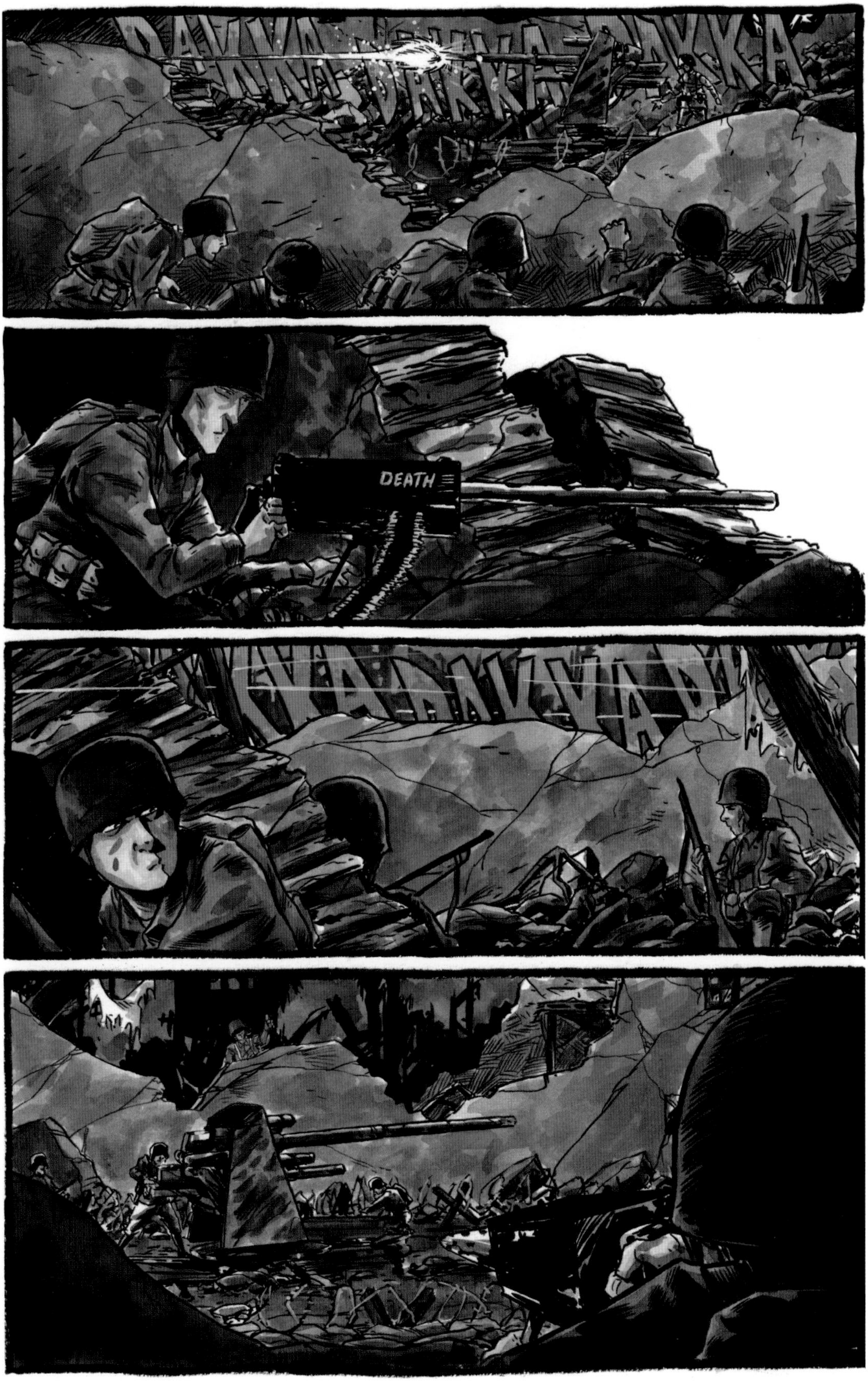
DEATH

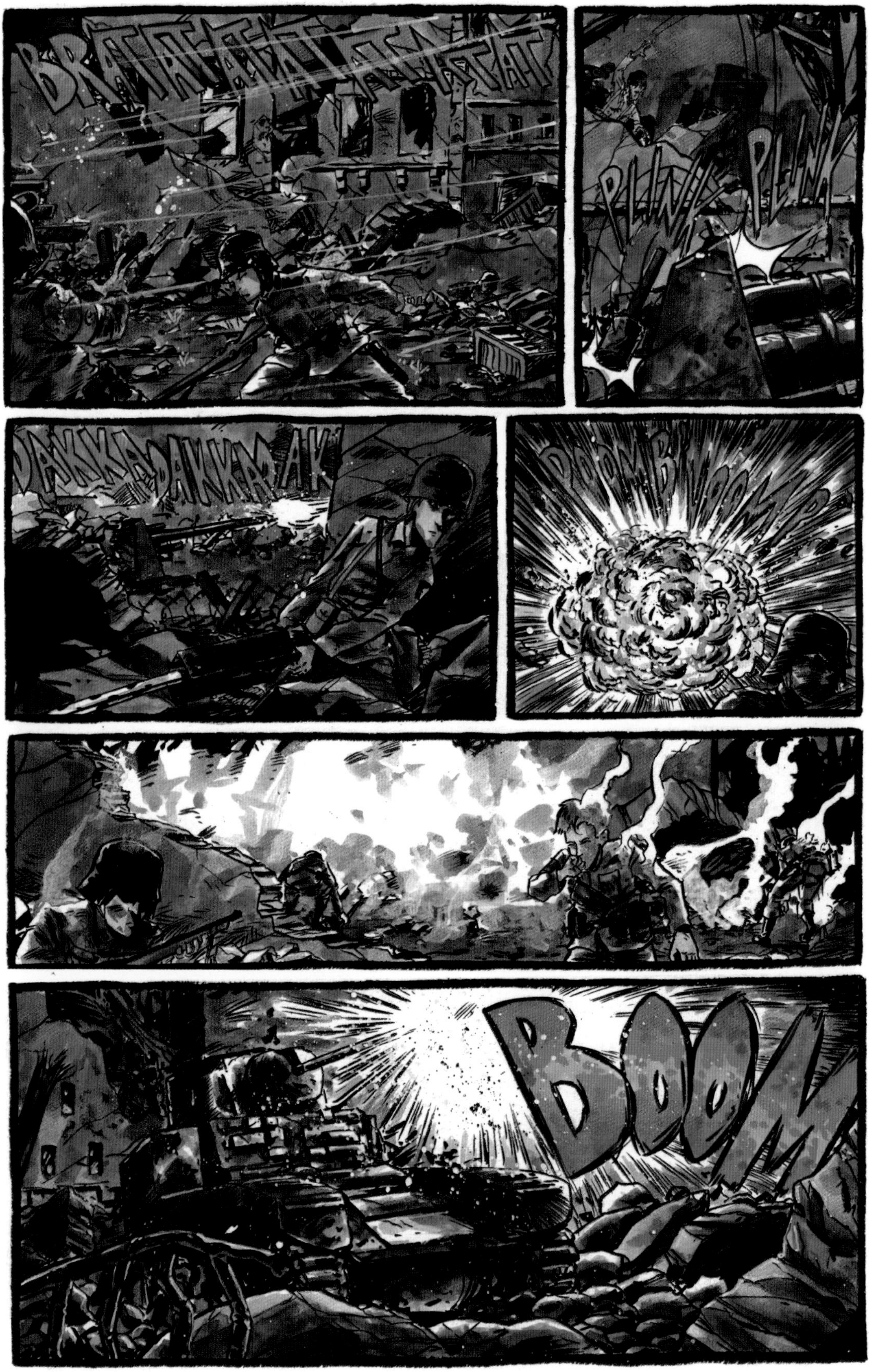
PLINK
PLINK
DAKKADAKKADAK
BOOM

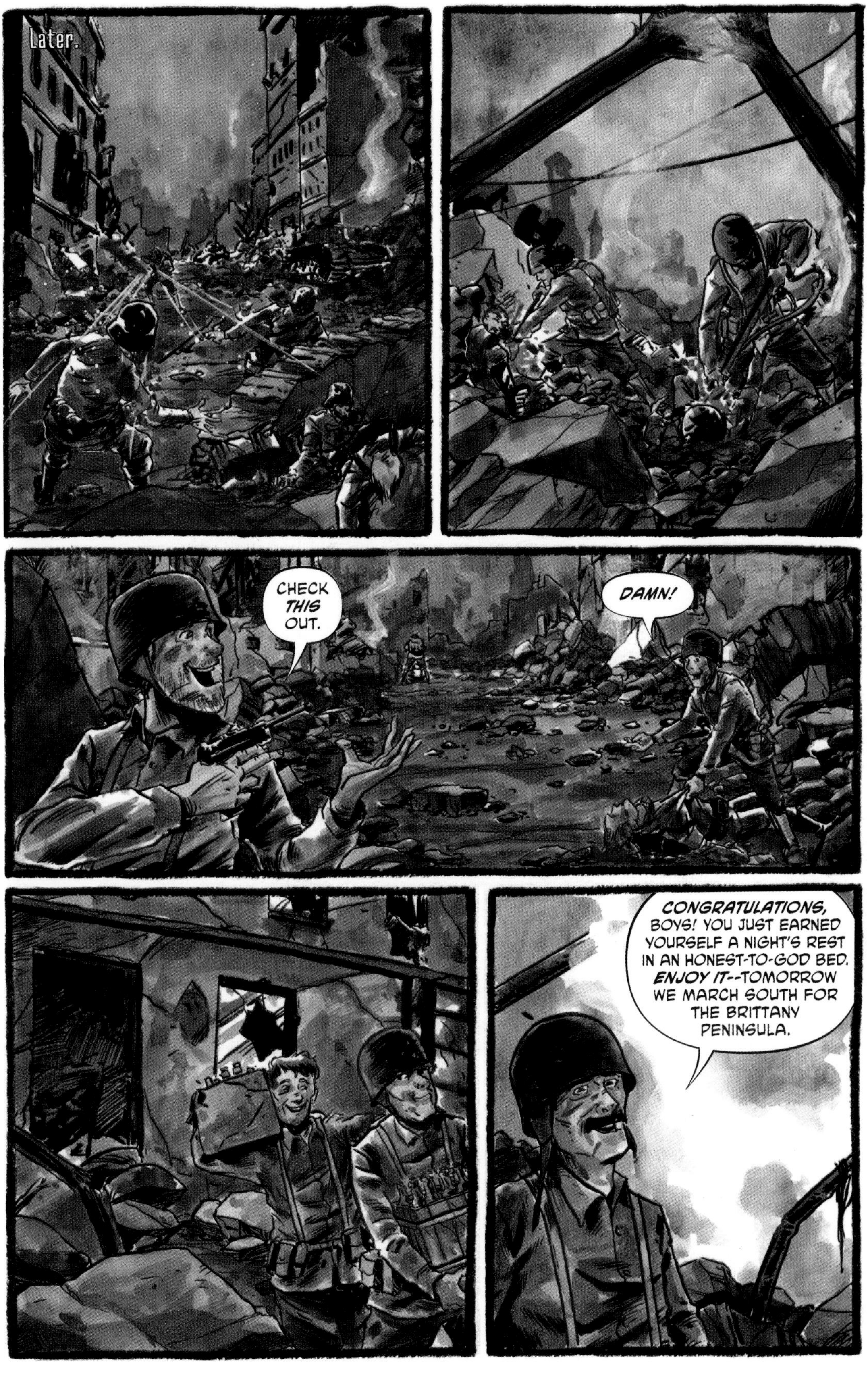
Later.
CHECK THIS OUT.
DAMN!
CONGRATULATIONS, BOYS! YOU JUST EARNED YOURSELF A NIGHT'S REST IN AN HONEST-TO-GOD BED. ENJOY IT--TOMORROW WE MARCH SOUTH FOR THE BRITTANY PENINSULA.

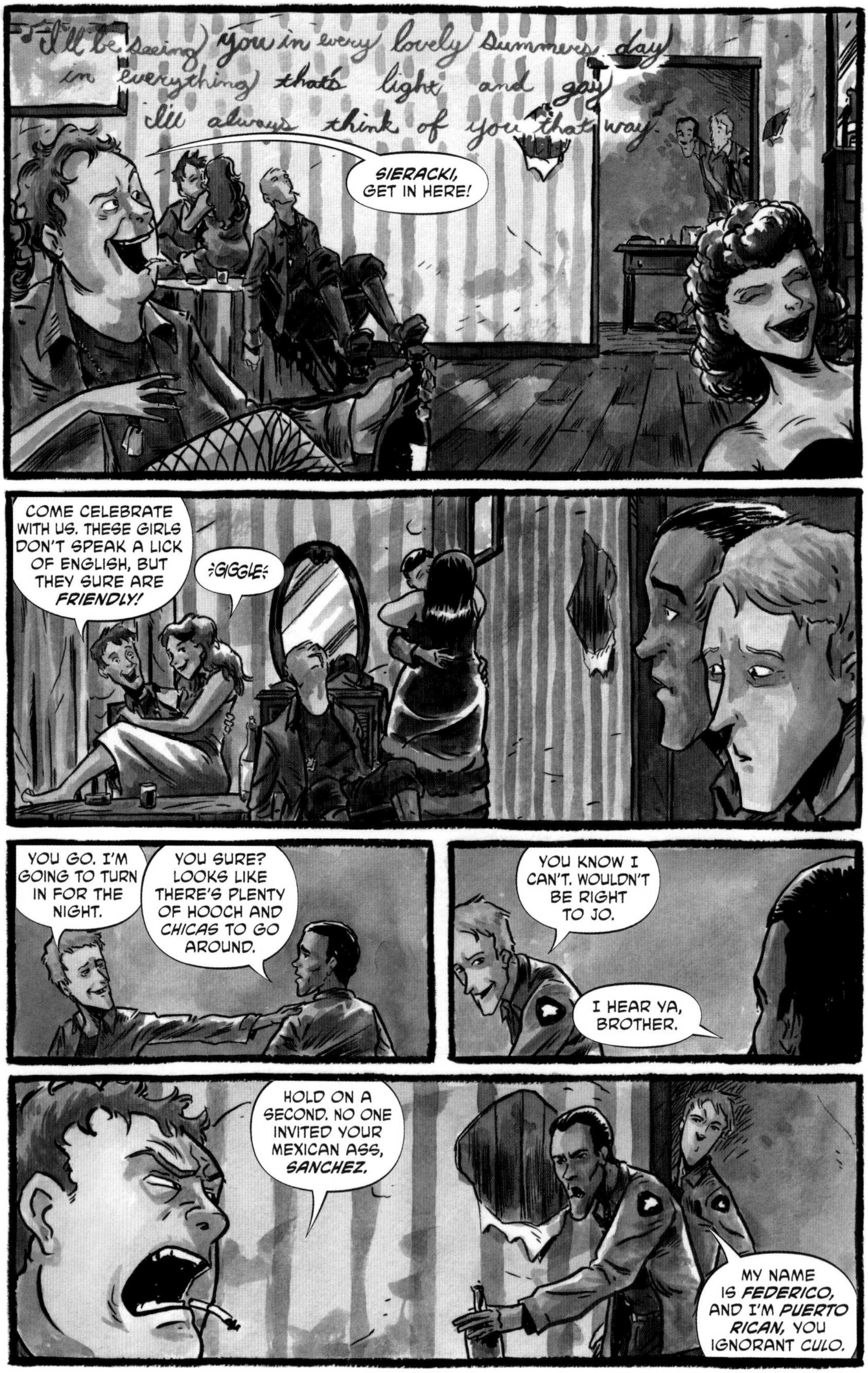
I'll be seeing you in every lovely summer's day
in everything that's light and gay
I'll always think of you that way
SIERACKI, GET IN HERE!
COME CELEBRATE WITH US. THESE GIRLS DON'T SPEAK A LICK OF ENGLISH, BUT THEY SURE ARE FRIENDLY!
GIGGLE
YOU GO. I'M GOING TO TURN IN FOR THE NIGHT.
YOU SURE? LOOKS LIKE THERE'S PLENTY OF HOOCH AND CHICAS TO GO AROUND.
YOU KNOW I CAN'T. WOULDN'T BE RIGHT TO JO.
I HEAR YA, BROTHER.
HOLD ON A SECOND. NO ONE INVITED YOUR MEXICAN ASS, SANCHEZ.
MY NAME IS FEDERICO, AND I'M PUERTO RICAN, YOU IGNORANT CULO.

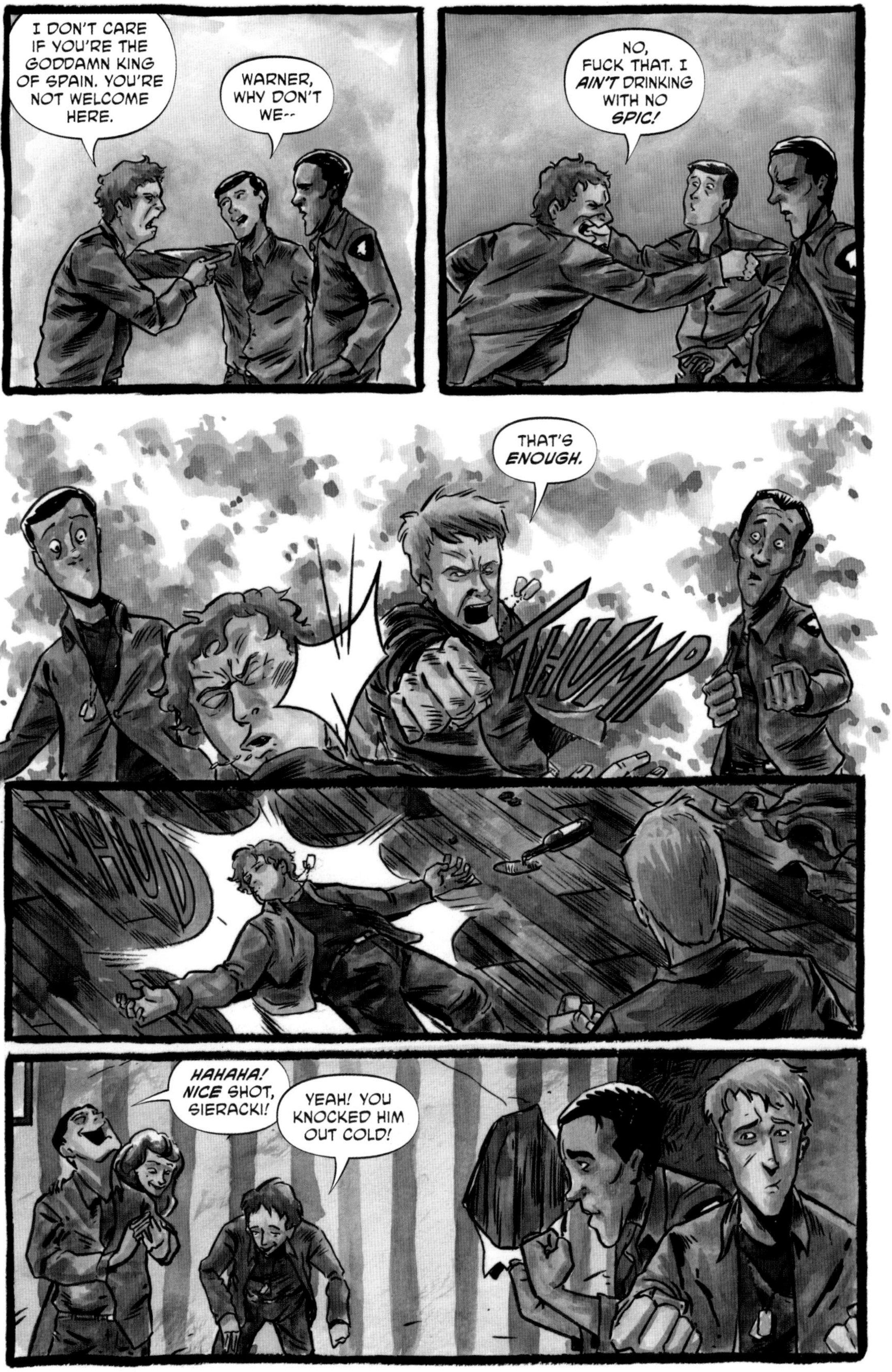

I DON'T CARE IF YOU'RE THE GODDAMN KING OF SPAIN. YOU'RE NOT WELCOME HERE.
WARNER, WHY DON'T WE--
NO, FUCK THAT. I AIN'T DRINKING WITH NO SPIC!
THAT'S ENOUGH.
THUMP
THUD
HAHAHA! NICE SHOT, SIERACKI!
YEAH! YOU KNOCKED HIM OUT COLD!

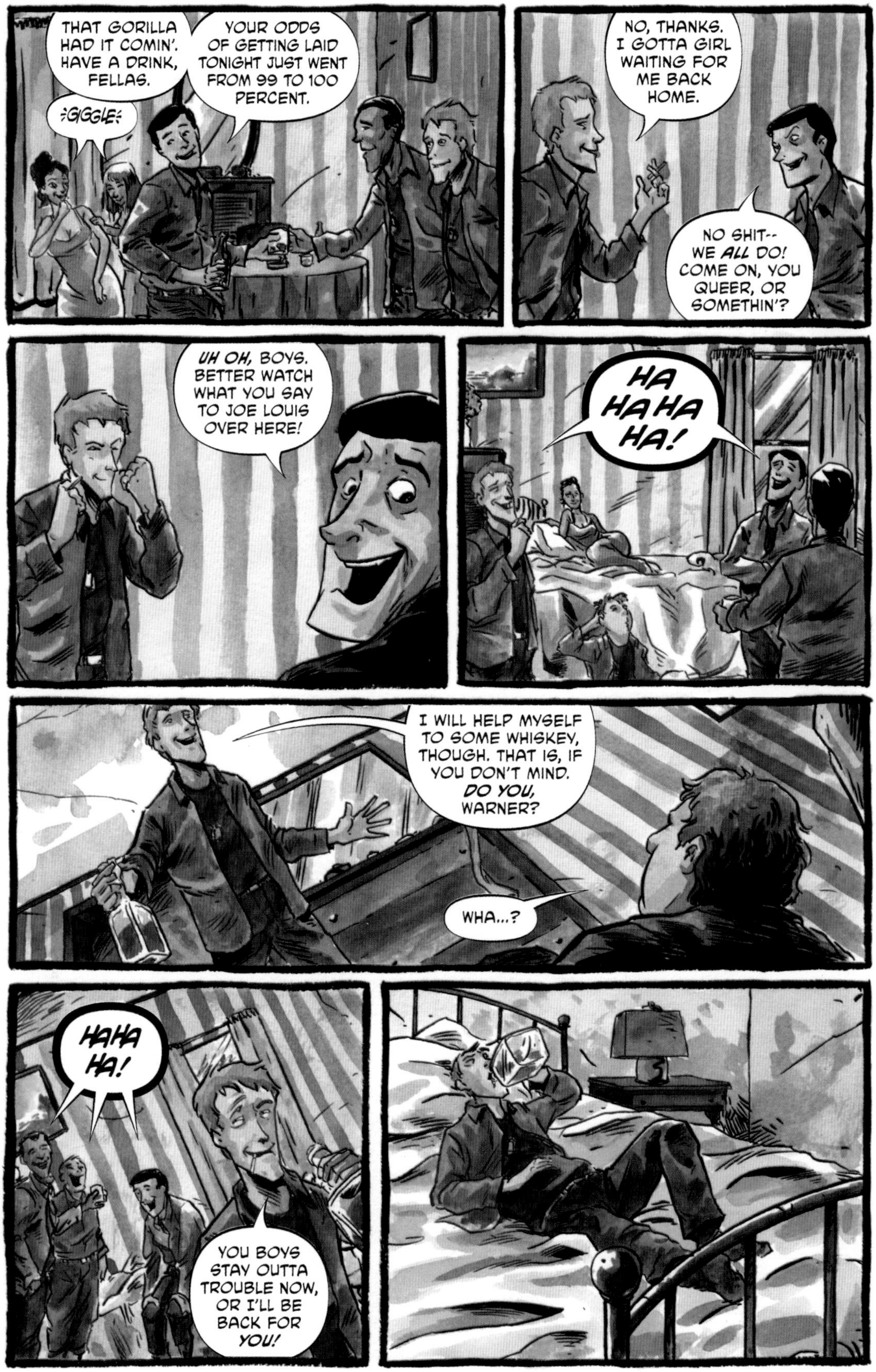
THAT GORILLA HAD IT COMIN'. HAVE A DRINK, FELLAS.
YOUR ODDS OF GETTING LAID TONIGHT JUST WENT FROM 99 TO 100 PERCENT.
GIGGLE
NO, THANKS. I GOTTA GIRL WAITING FOR ME BACK HOME.
NO SHIT-- WE ALL DO! COME ON, YOU QUEER, OR SOMETHIN'?
UH OH, BOYS. BETTER WATCH WHAT YOU SAY TO JOE LOUIS OVER HERE!
HA HA HA HA!
I WILL HELP MYSELF TO SOME WHISKEY, THOUGH. THAT IS, IF YOU DON'T MIND. DO YOU, WARNER?
WHA...?
HA HA HA!
YOU BOYS STAY OUTTA TROUBLE NOW, OR I'LL BE BACK FOR YOU!

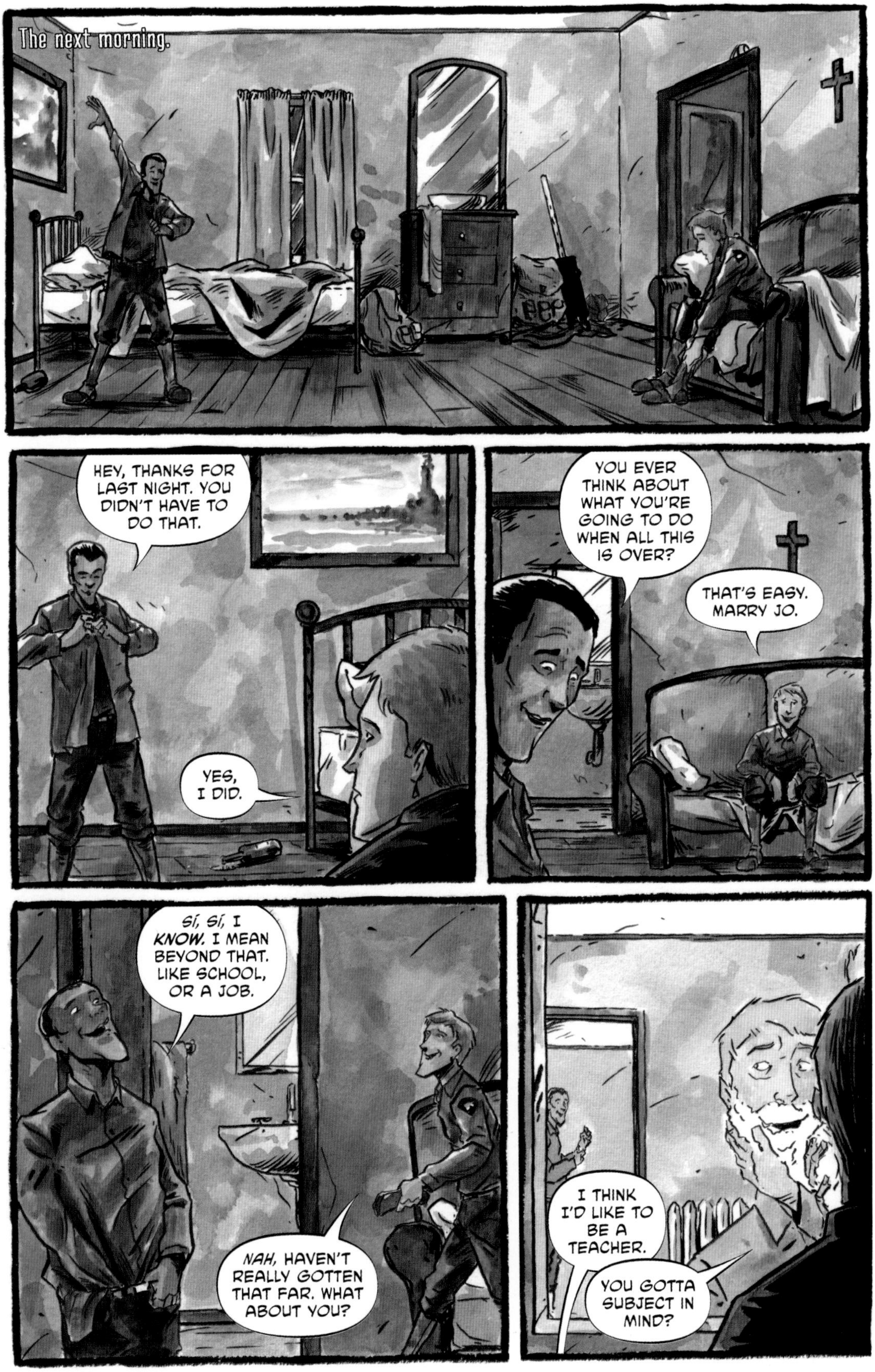

The next morning.
HEY, THANKS FOR LAST NIGHT. YOU DIDN'T HAVE TO DO THAT.
YES, I DID.
YOU EVER THINK ABOUT WHAT YOU'RE GOING TO DO WHEN ALL THIS IS OVER?
THAT'S EASY. MARRY JO.
SÍ, SÍ, I ***KNOW.*** I MEAN BEYOND THAT. LIKE SCHOOL, OR A JOB.
NAH, HAVEN'T REALLY GOTTEN THAT FAR. WHAT ABOUT YOU?
I THINK I'D LIKE TO BE A TEACHER.
YOU GOTTA SUBJECT IN MIND?

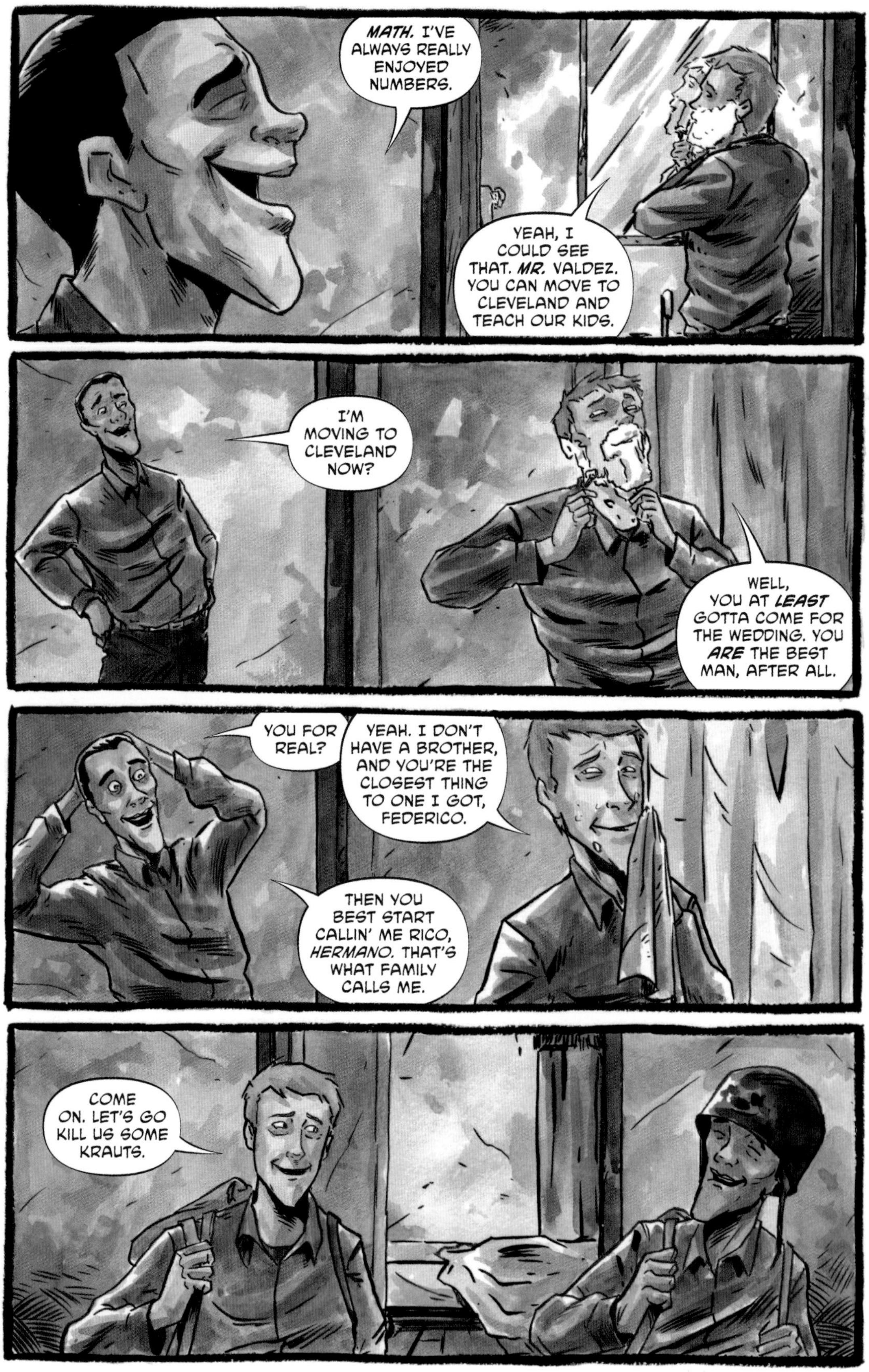
MATH. I'VE ALWAYS REALLY ENJOYED NUMBERS.
YEAH, I COULD SEE THAT. MR. VALDEZ. YOU CAN MOVE TO CLEVELAND AND TEACH OUR KIDS.
I'M MOVING TO CLEVELAND NOW?
WELL, YOU AT LEAST GOTTA COME FOR THE WEDDING. YOU ARE THE BEST MAN, AFTER ALL.
YOU FOR REAL?
YEAH. I DON'T HAVE A BROTHER, AND YOU'RE THE CLOSEST THING TO ONE I GOT, FEDERICO.
THEN YOU BEST START CALLIN' ME RICO, HERMANO. THAT'S WHAT FAMILY CALLS ME.
COME ON. LET'S GO KILL US SOME KRAUTS.

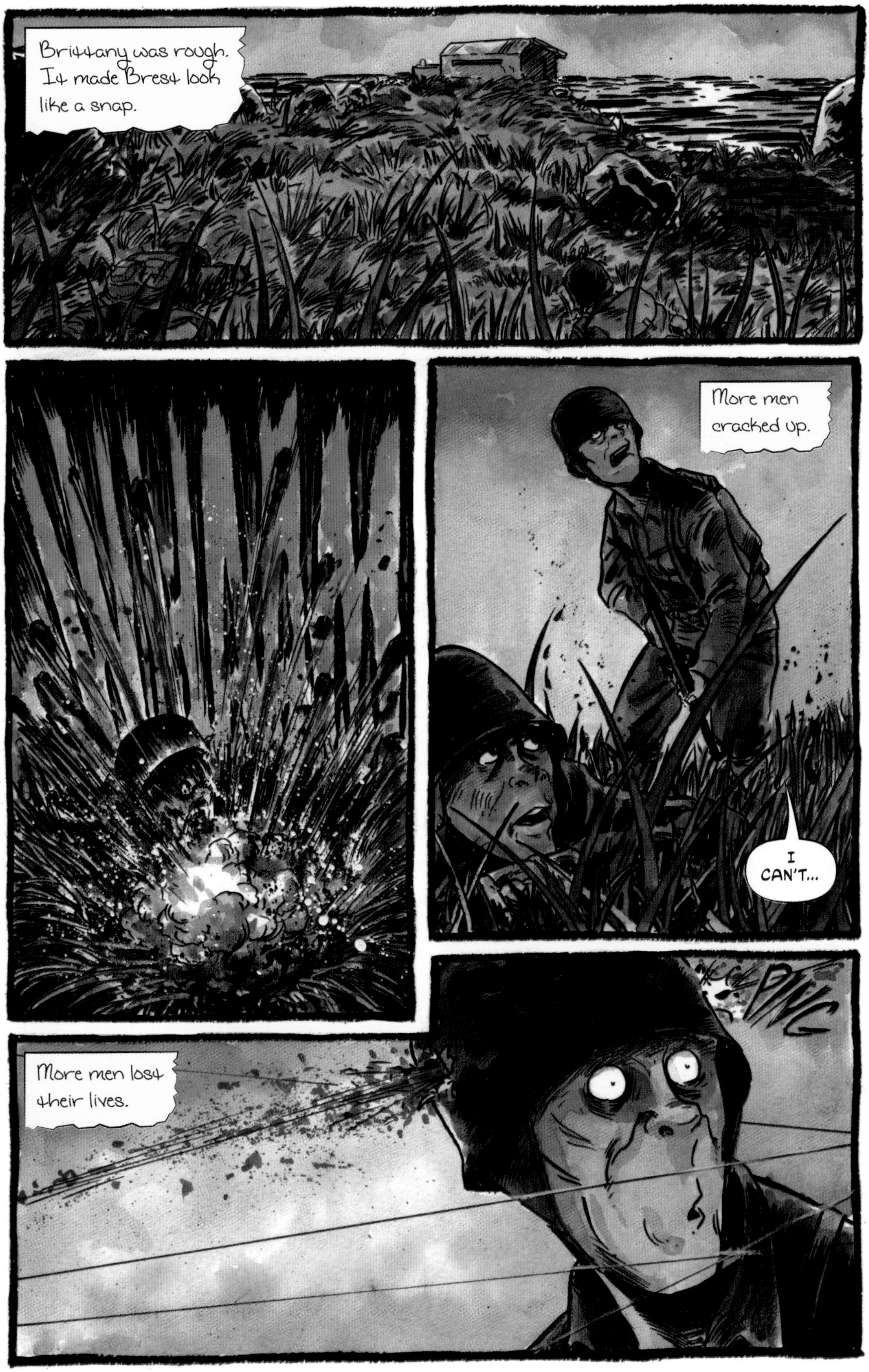
Brittany was rough. It made Brest look like a snap.
More men cracked up.
I CAN'T...
More men lost their lives.
PING

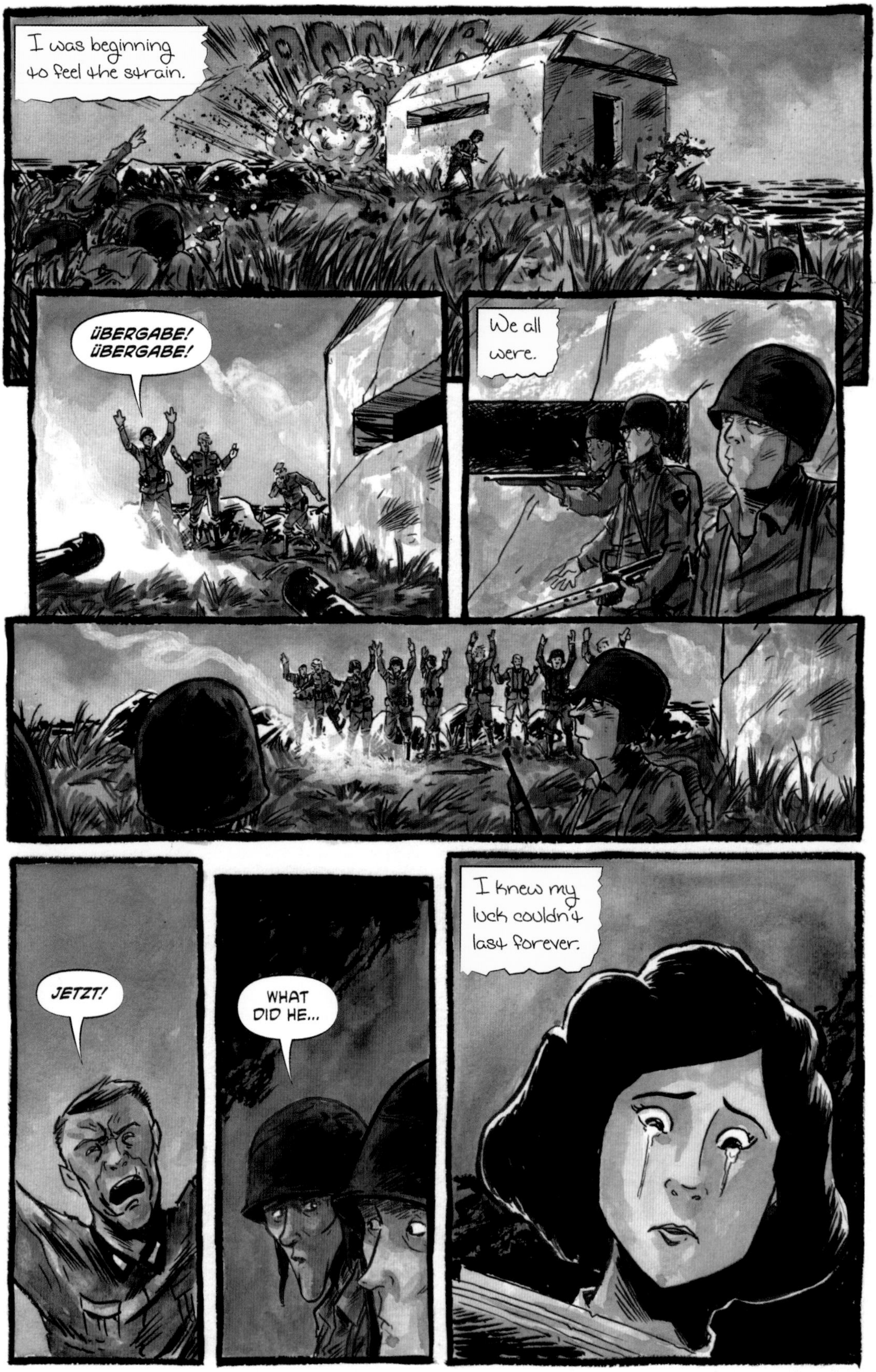
I was beginning to feel the strain.
ÜBERGABE! ÜBERGABE!
We all were.
JETZT!
WHAT DID HE...
I knew my luck couldn't last forever.

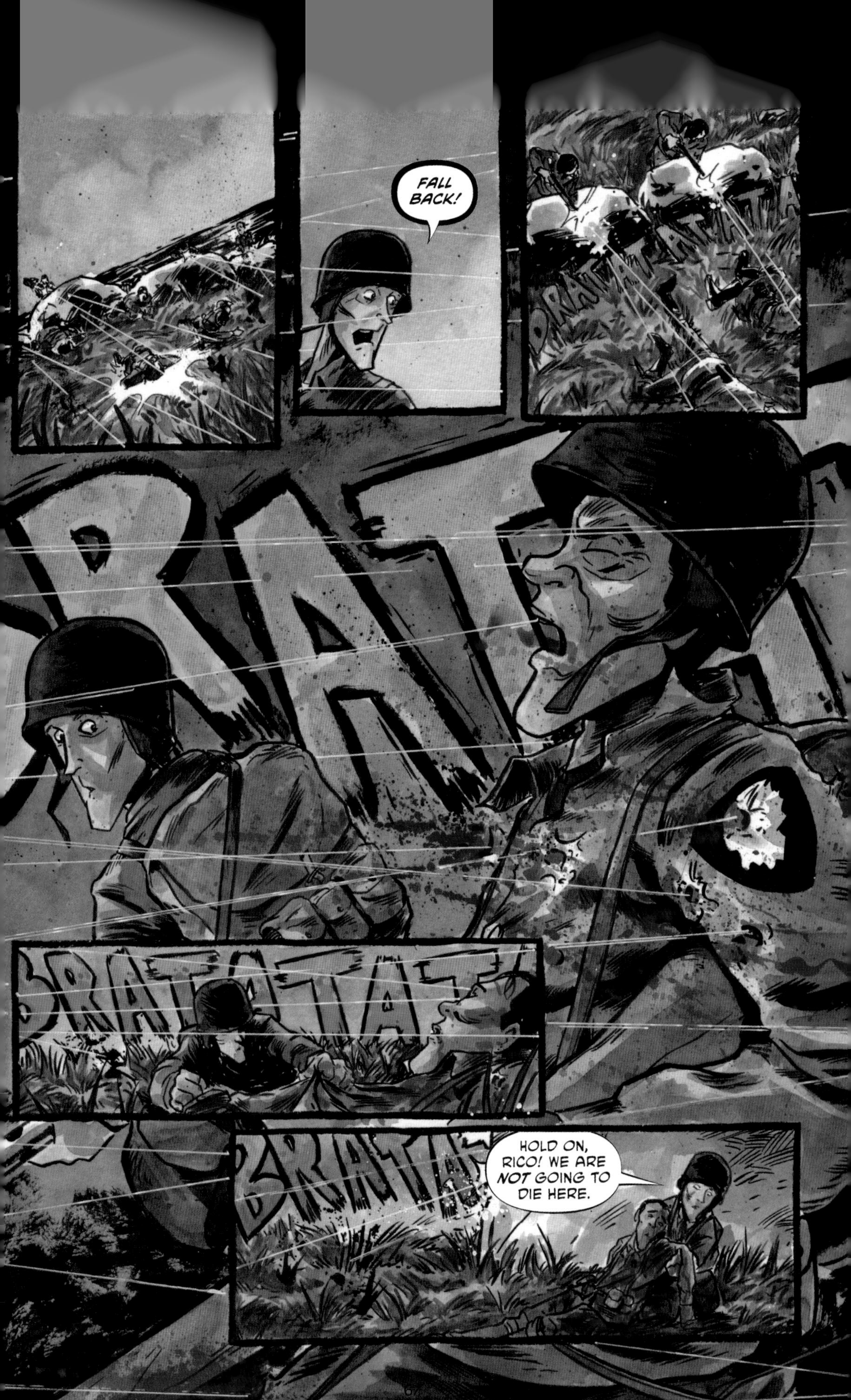
FALL BACK!
HOLD ON, RICO! WE ARE *NOT* GOING TO DIE HERE.

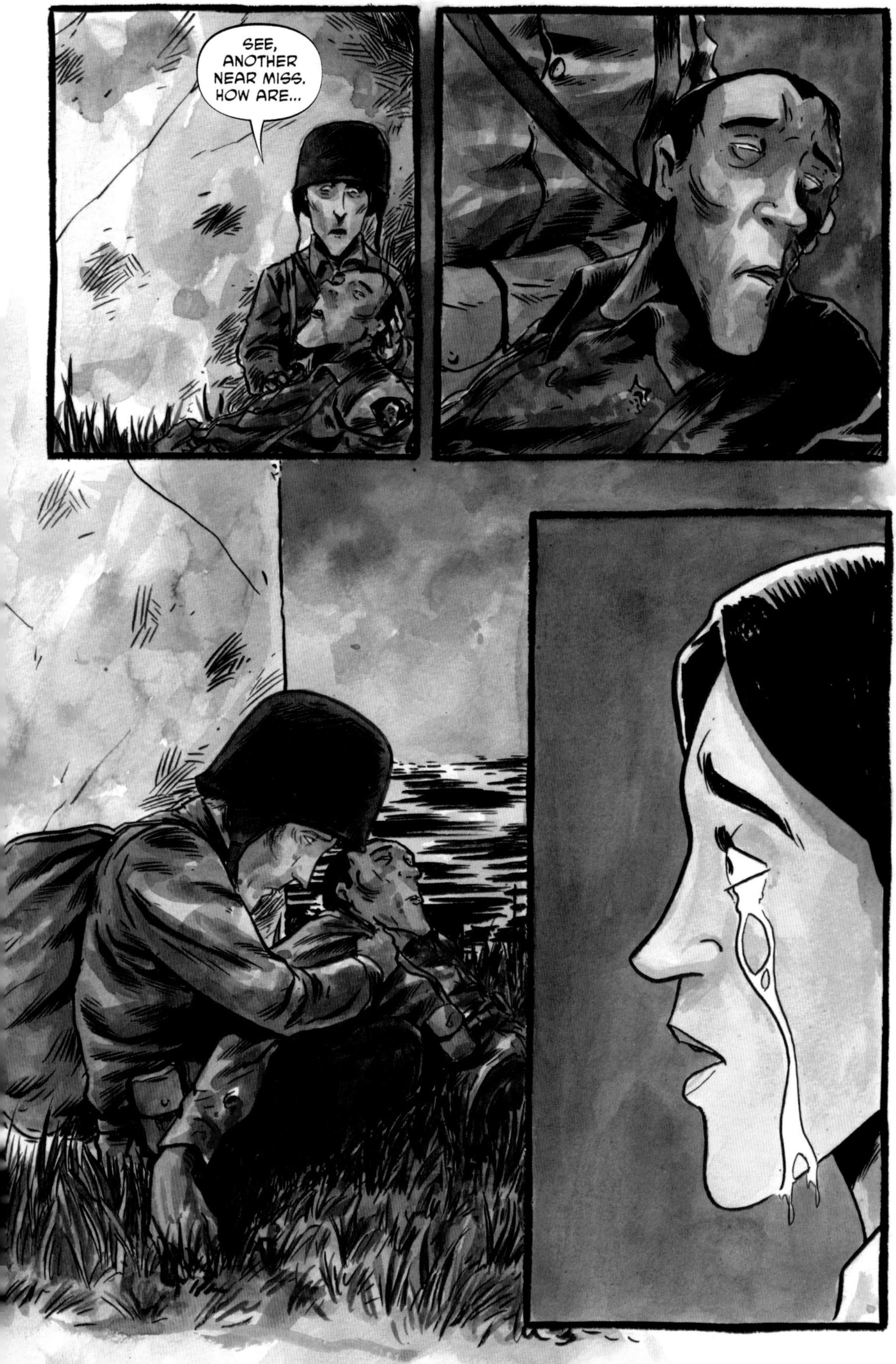
SEE, ANOTHER NEAR MISS. HOW ARE...

CHAPTER SIX
PAIN

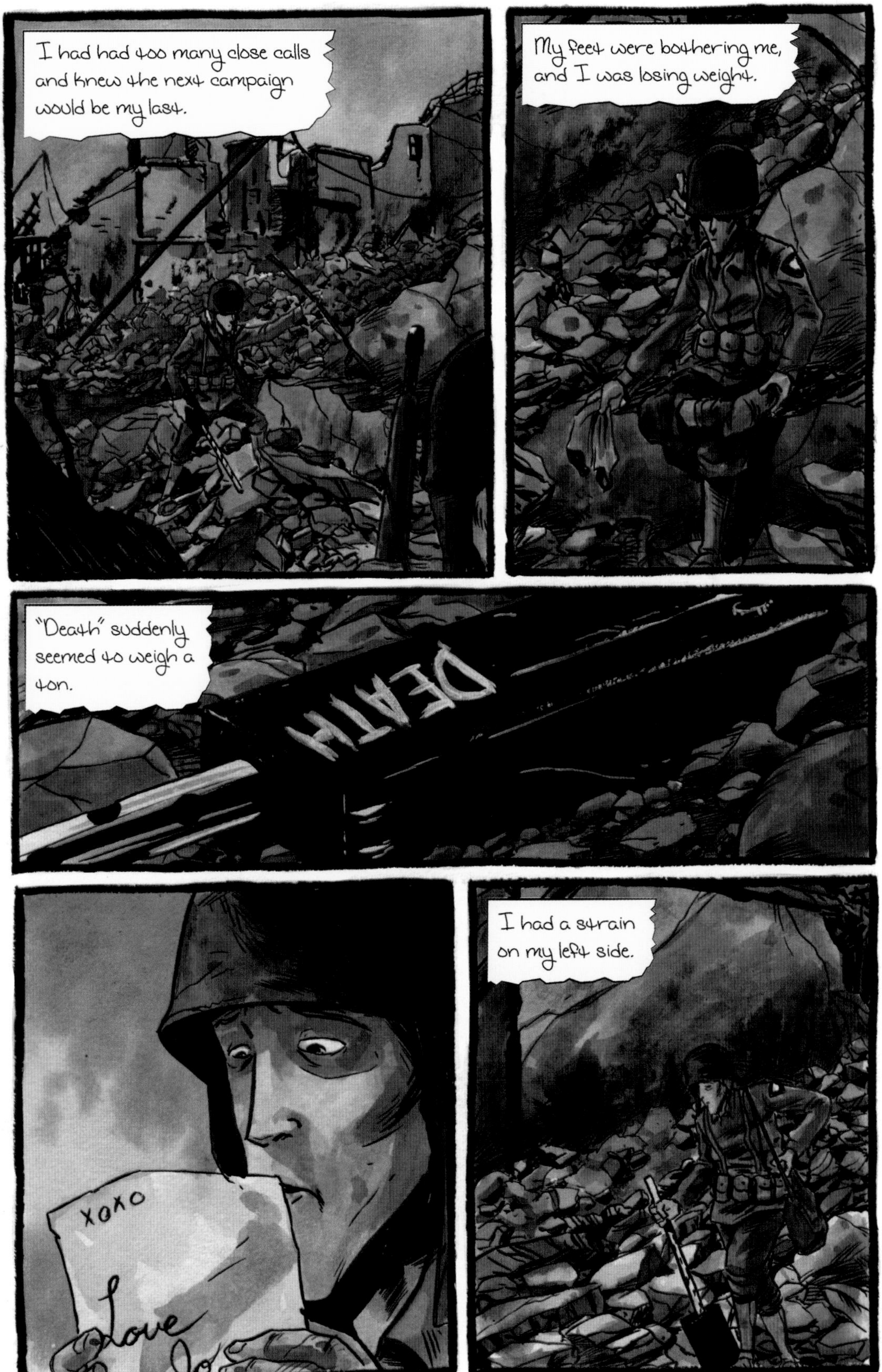
I had had too many close calls and knew the next campaign would be my last.
My feet were bothering me, and I was losing weight.
"Death" suddenly seemed to weigh a ton.
DEATH
XOXO
Love
I had a strain on my left side.

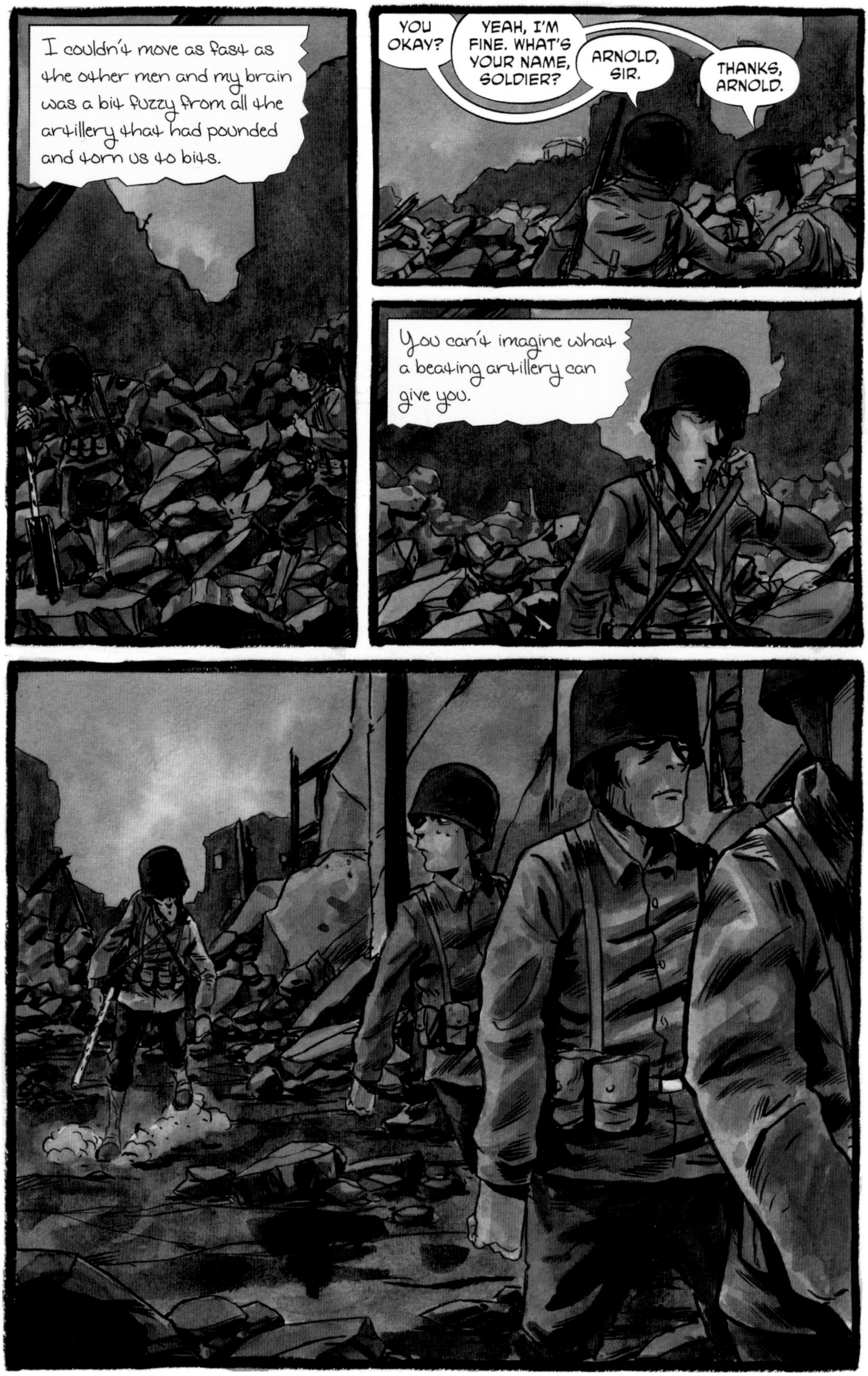

I couldn't move as fast as the other men and my brain was a bit fuzzy from all the artillery that had pounded and torn us to bits.
YOU OKAY?
YEAH, I'M FINE. WHAT'S YOUR NAME, SOLDIER?
ARNOLD, SIR.
THANKS, ARNOLD.
You can't imagine what a beating artillery can give you.

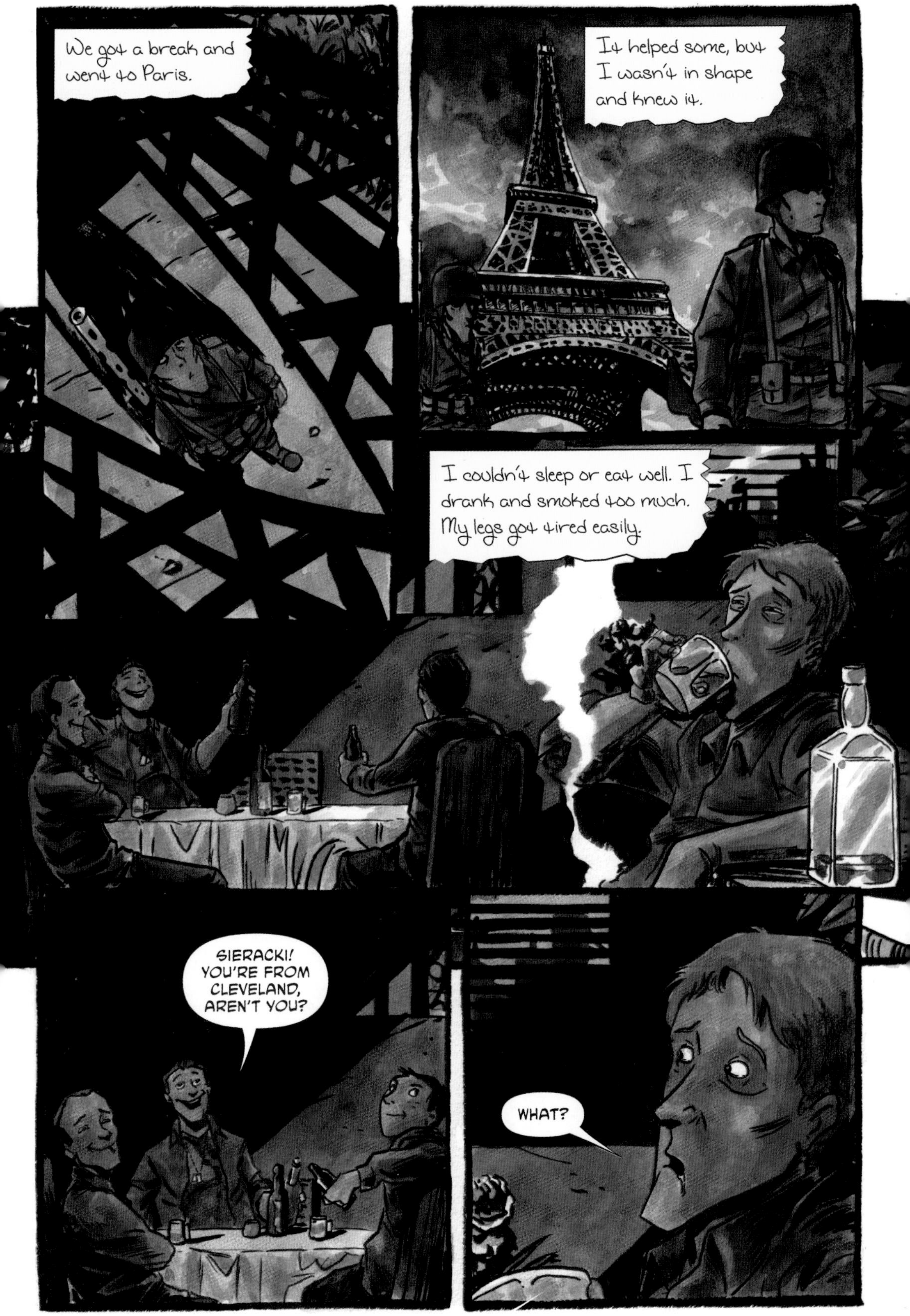
We got a break and went to Paris.
It helped some, but I wasn't in shape and knew it.
I couldn't sleep or eat well. I drank and smoked too much. My legs got tired easily.
SIERACKI! YOU'RE FROM CLEVELAND, AREN'T YOU?
WHAT?

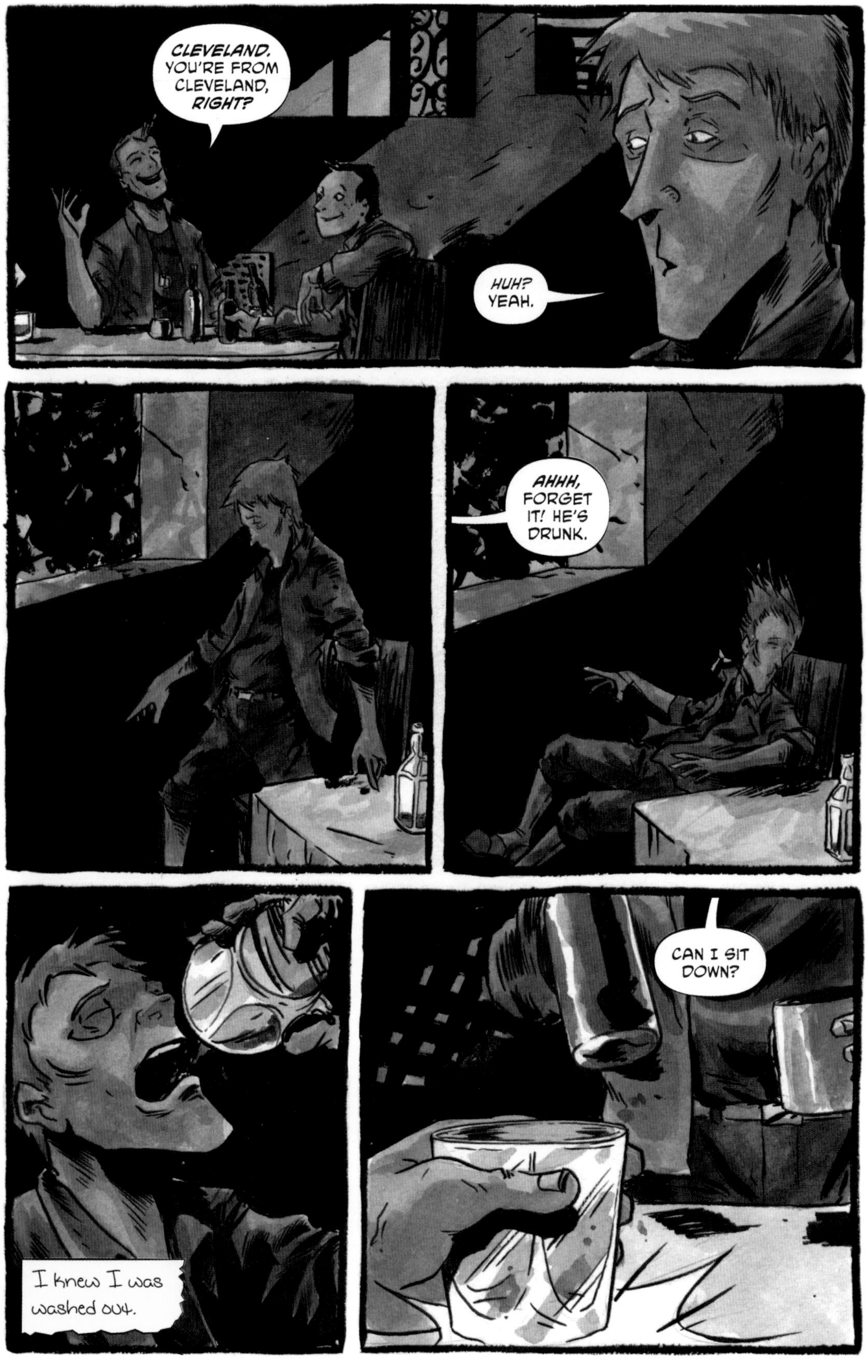

CLEVELAND. YOU'RE FROM CLEVELAND, RIGHT?
HUH? YEAH.
AHHH, FORGET IT! HE'S DRUNK.
I knew I was washed out.
CAN I SIT DOWN?

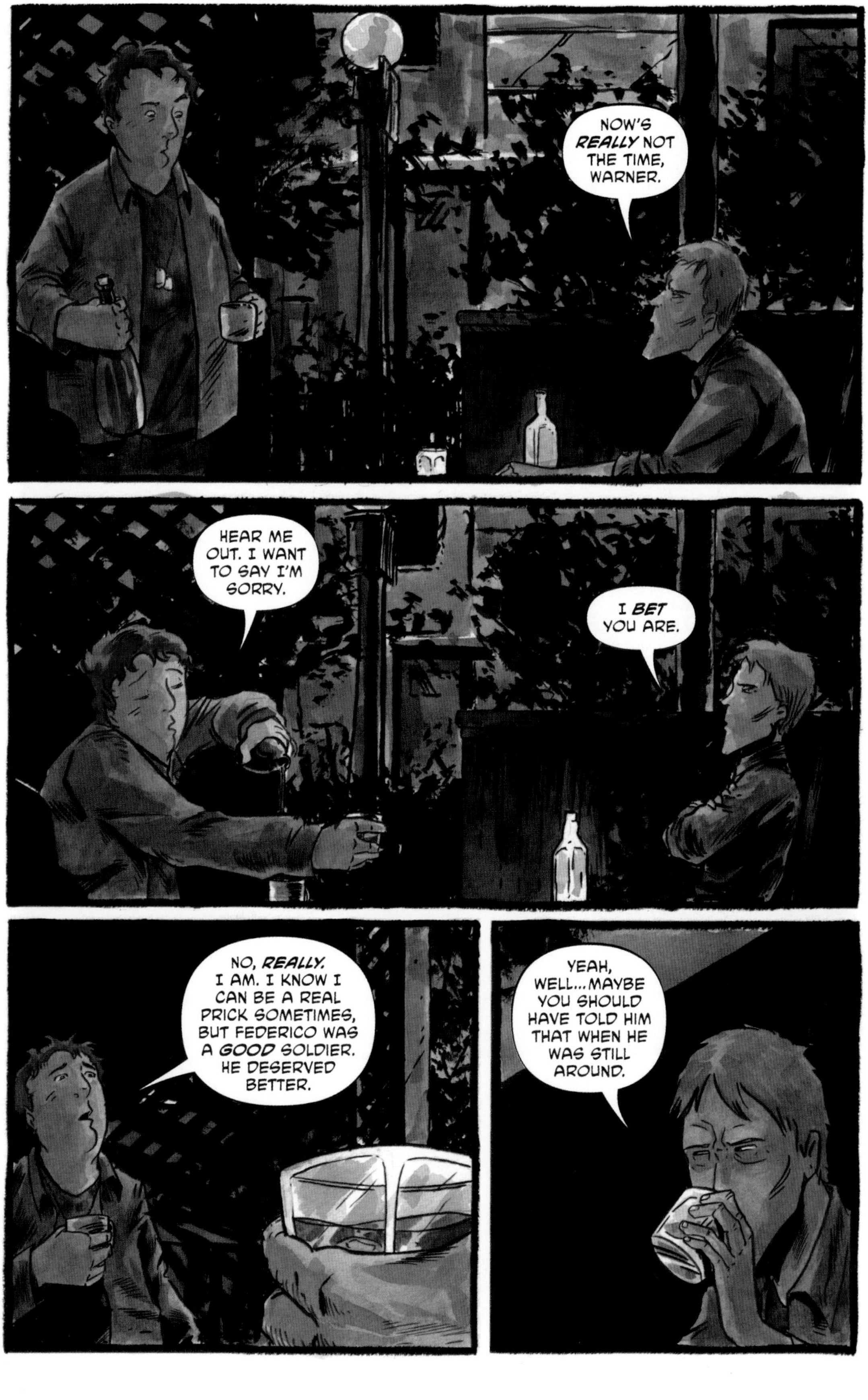
NOW'S *REALLY* NOT THE TIME, WARNER.
HEAR ME OUT. I WANT TO SAY I'M SORRY.
I *BET* YOU ARE.
NO, *REALLY.* I AM. I KNOW I CAN BE A REAL PRICK SOMETIMES, BUT FEDERICO WAS A *GOOD* SOLDIER. HE DESERVED BETTER.
YEAH, WELL...MAYBE YOU SHOULD HAVE TOLD HIM THAT WHEN HE WAS STILL AROUND.

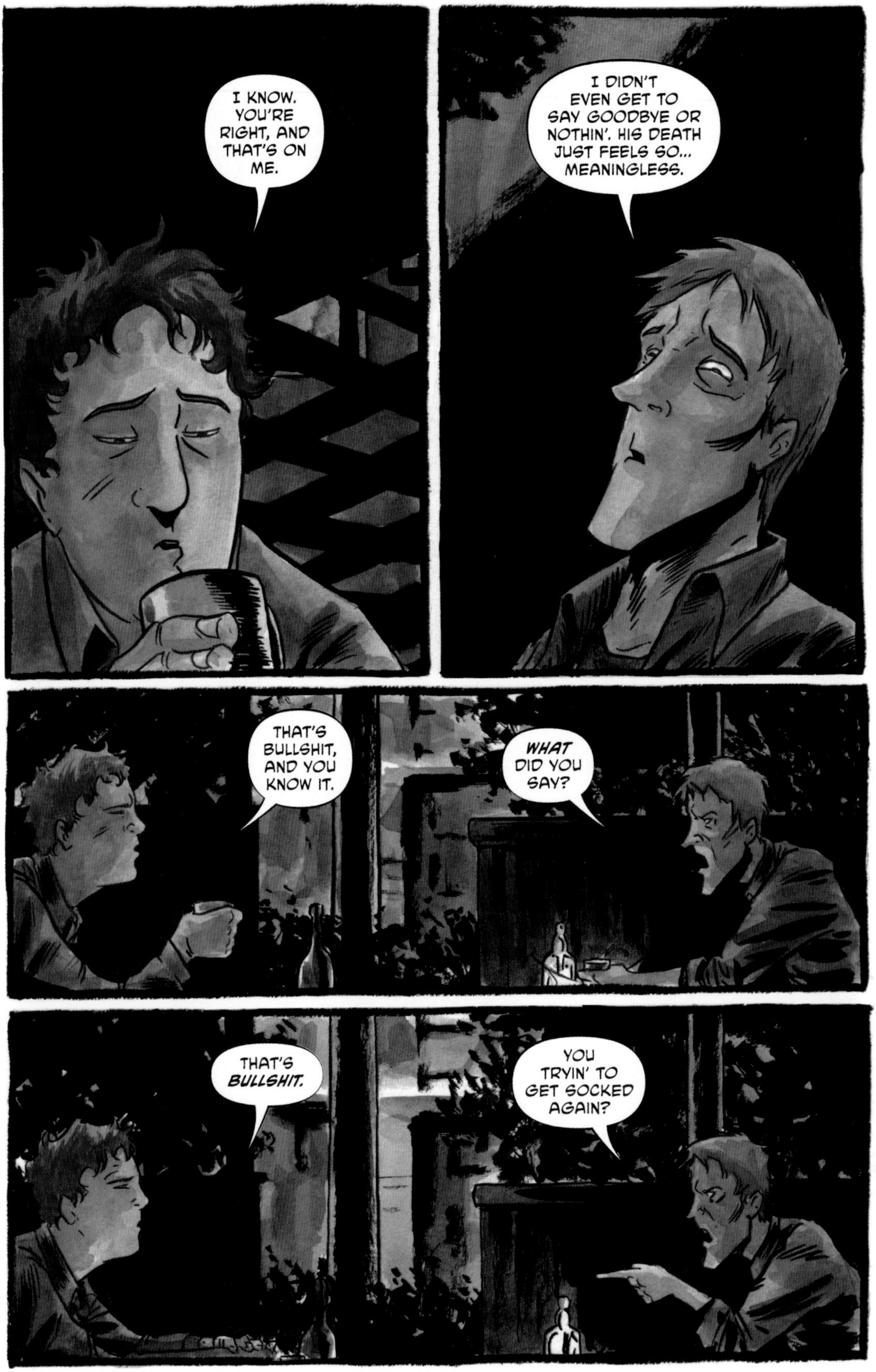
I KNOW. YOU'RE RIGHT, AND THAT'S ON ME.
I DIDN'T EVEN GET TO SAY GOODBYE OR NOTHIN'. HIS DEATH JUST FEELS SO... MEANINGLESS.
THAT'S BULLSHIT, AND YOU KNOW IT.
WHAT DID YOU SAY?
THAT'S *BULLSHIT.*
YOU TRYIN' TO GET SOCKED AGAIN?

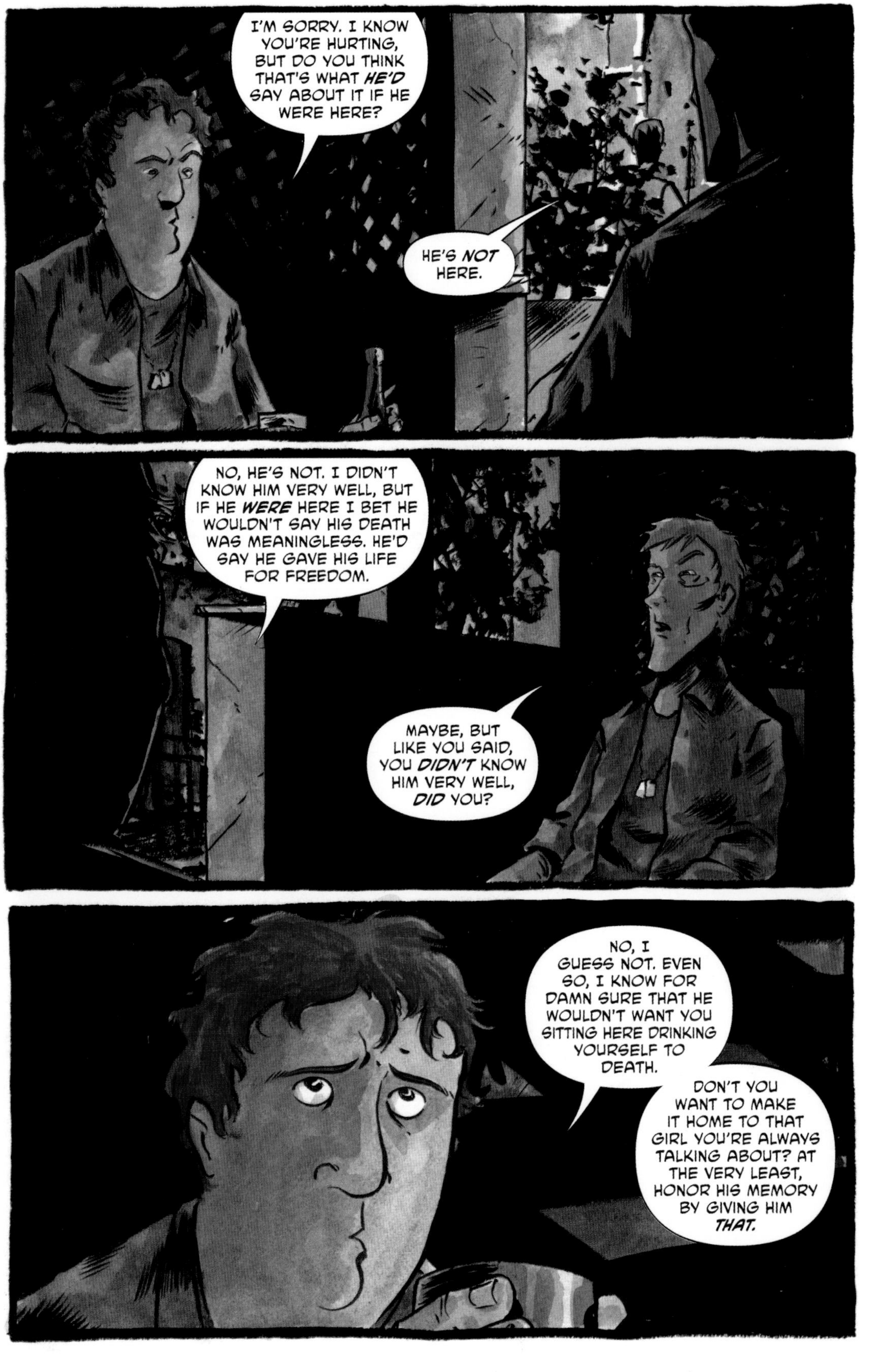
I'M SORRY. I KNOW YOU'RE HURTING, BUT DO YOU THINK THAT'S WHAT *HE'D* SAY ABOUT IT IF HE WERE HERE?
HE'S *NOT* HERE.
NO, HE'S NOT. I DIDN'T KNOW HIM VERY WELL, BUT IF HE *WERE* HERE I BET HE WOULDN'T SAY HIS DEATH WAS MEANINGLESS. HE'D SAY HE GAVE HIS LIFE FOR FREEDOM.
MAYBE, BUT LIKE YOU SAID, YOU *DIDN'T* KNOW HIM VERY WELL, *DID* YOU?
NO, I GUESS NOT. EVEN SO, I KNOW FOR DAMN SURE THAT HE WOULDN'T WANT YOU SITTING HERE DRINKING YOURSELF TO DEATH.
DON'T YOU WANT TO MAKE IT HOME TO THAT GIRL YOU'RE ALWAYS TALKING ABOUT? AT THE VERY LEAST, HONOR HIS MEMORY BY GIVING HIM *THAT.*

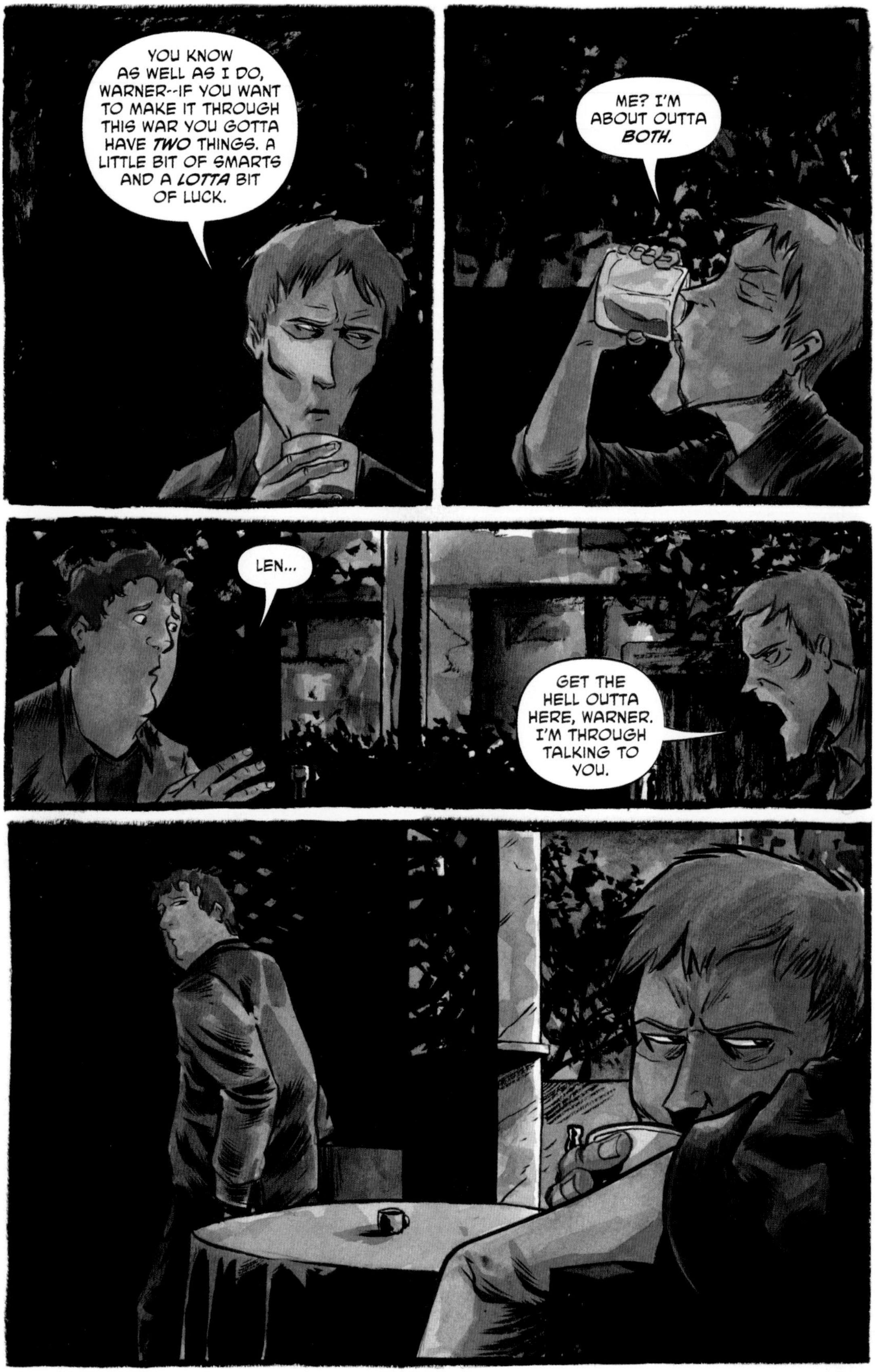
YOU KNOW AS WELL AS I DO, WARNER--IF YOU WANT TO MAKE IT THROUGH THIS WAR YOU GOTTA HAVE *TWO* THINGS. A LITTLE BIT OF SMARTS AND A *LOTTA* BIT OF LUCK.
ME? I'M ABOUT OUTTA *BOTH.*
LEN...
GET THE HELL OUTTA HERE, WARNER. I'M THROUGH TALKING TO YOU.

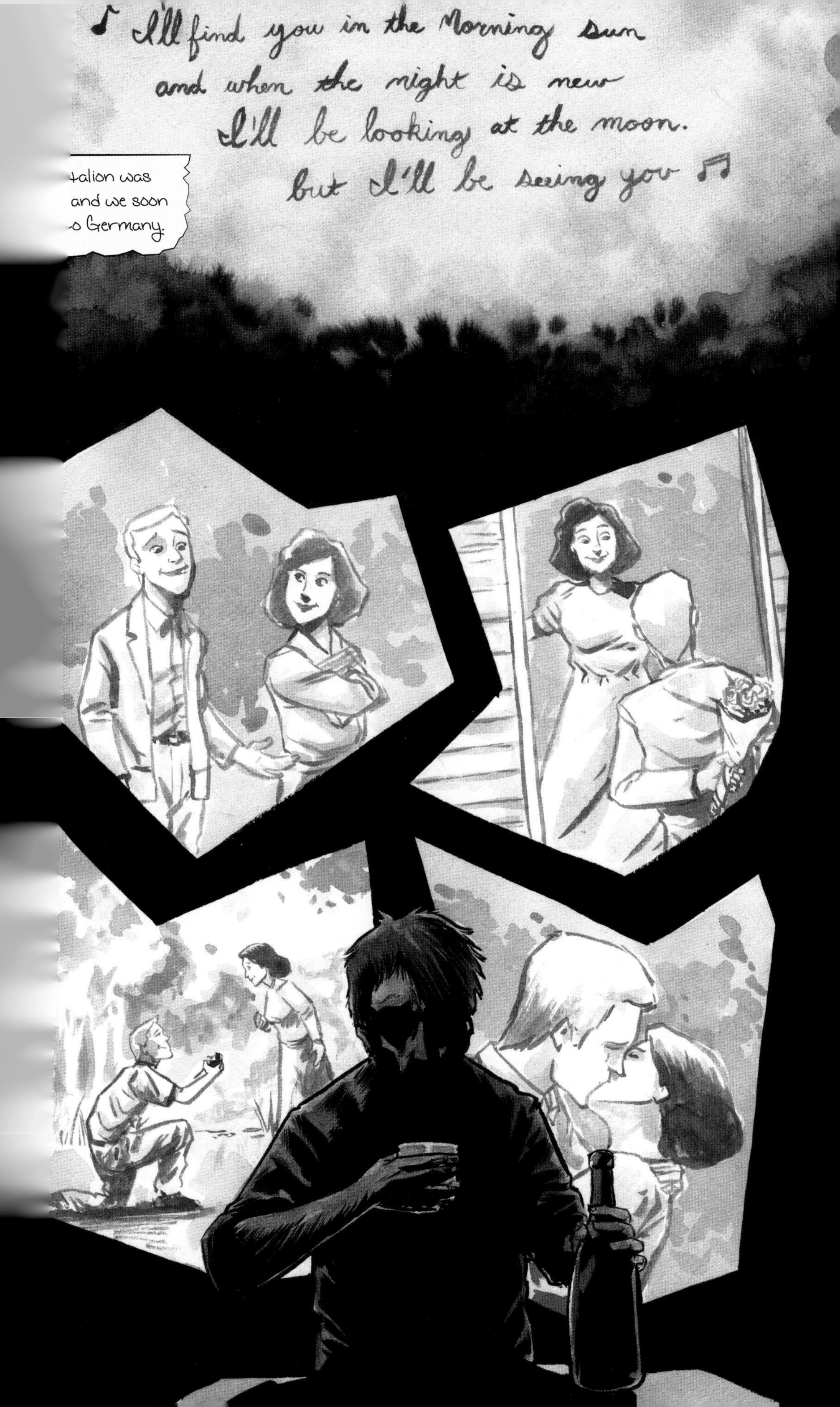
♪ I'll find you in the Morning sun
and when the night is new
I'll be looking at the moon.
but I'll be seeing you ♫
talion was
and we soon
o Germany.

CHAPTER SEVEN
DEATH

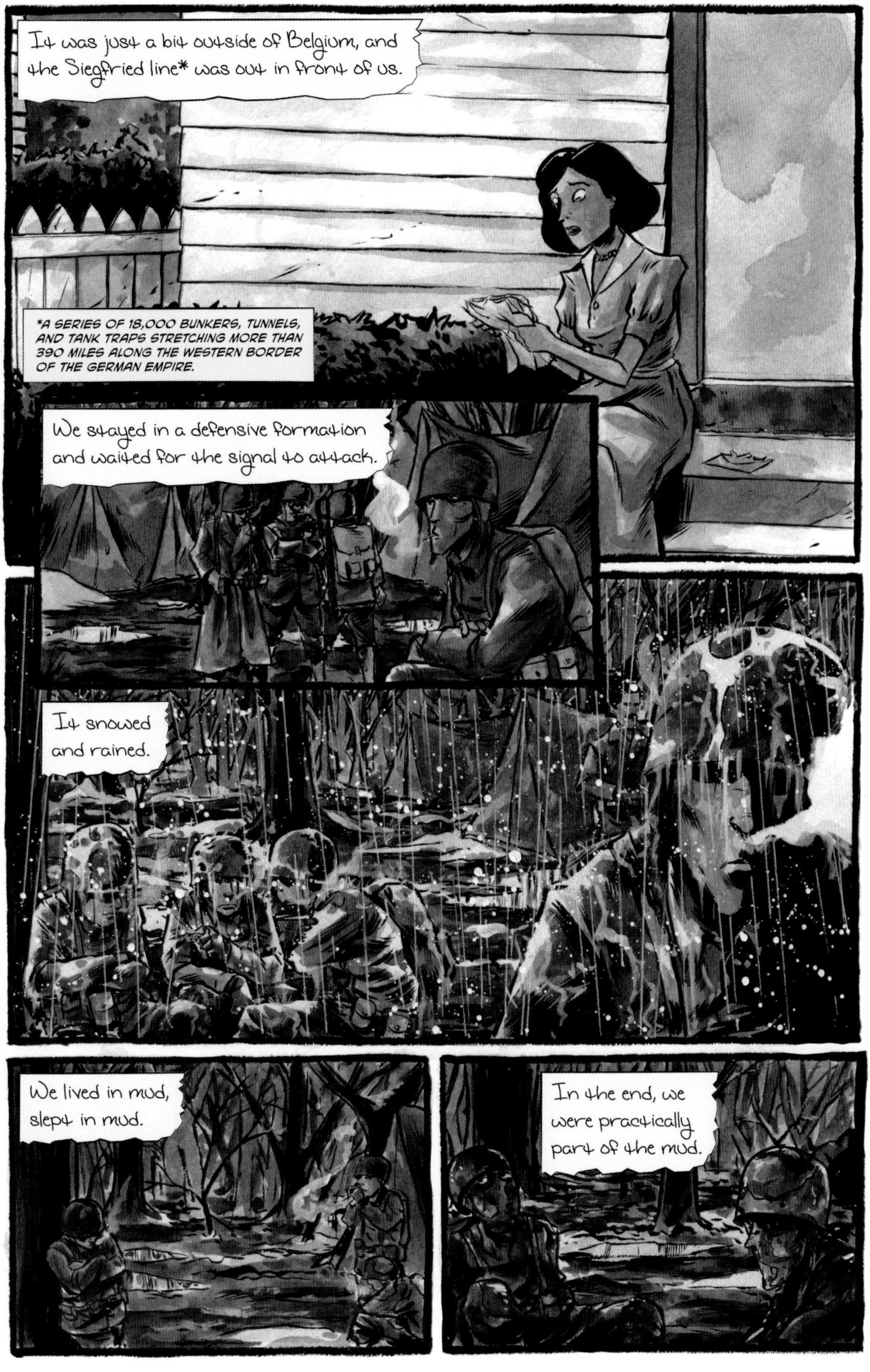
It was just a bit outside of Belgium, and the Siegfried line* was out in front of us.
*A SERIES OF 18,000 BUNKERS, TUNNELS, AND TANK TRAPS STRETCHING MORE THAN 390 MILES ALONG THE WESTERN BORDER OF THE GERMAN EMPIRE.
We stayed in a defensive formation and waited for the signal to attack.
It snowed and rained.
We lived in mud, slept in mud.
In the end, we were practically part of the mud.

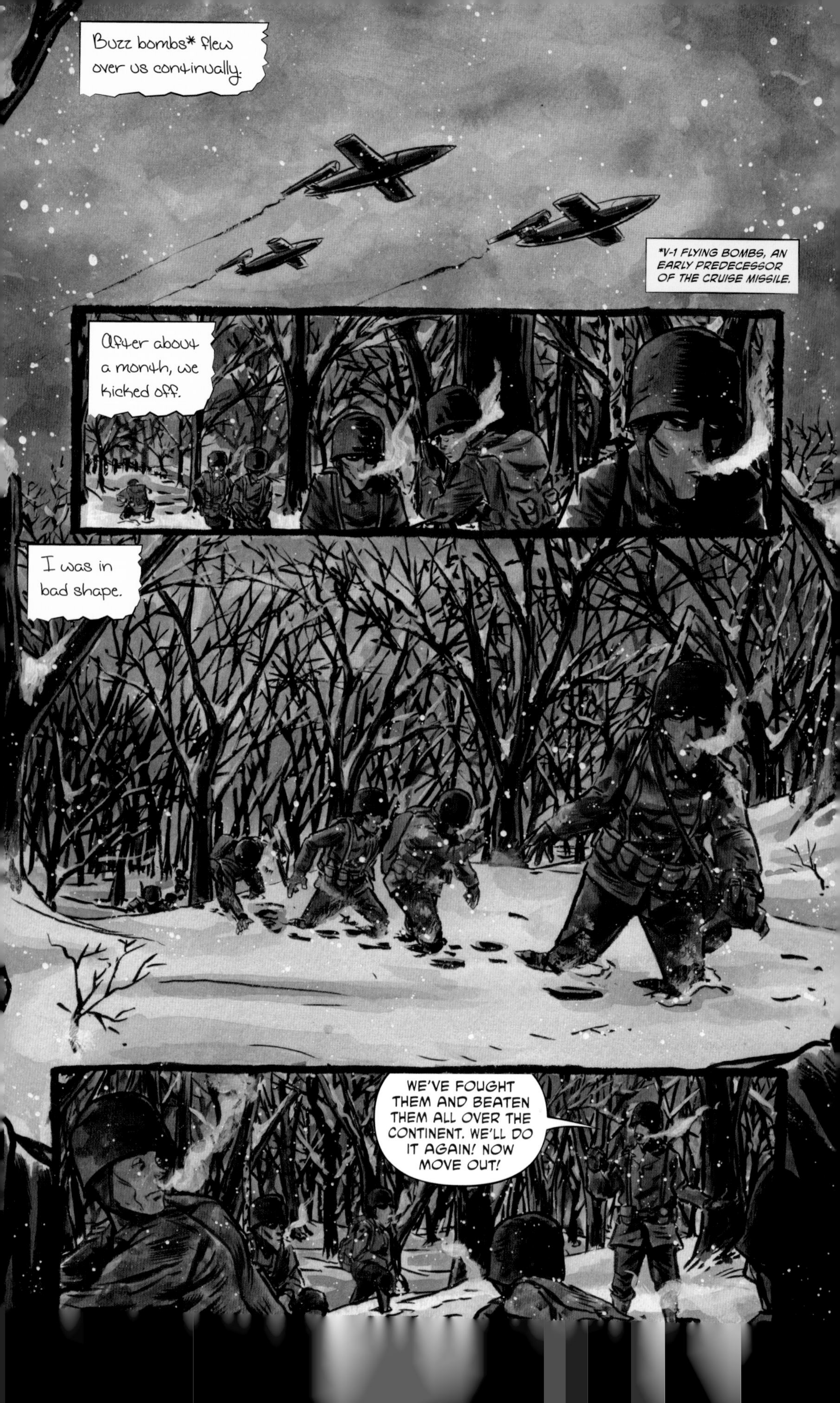
Buzz bombs* flew over us continually.
*V-1 FLYING BOMBS, AN EARLY PREDECESSOR OF THE CRUISE MISSILE.
After about a month, we kicked off.
I was in bad shape.
WE'VE FOUGHT THEM AND BEATEN THEM ALL OVER THE CONTINENT. WE'LL DO IT AGAIN! NOW MOVE OUT!

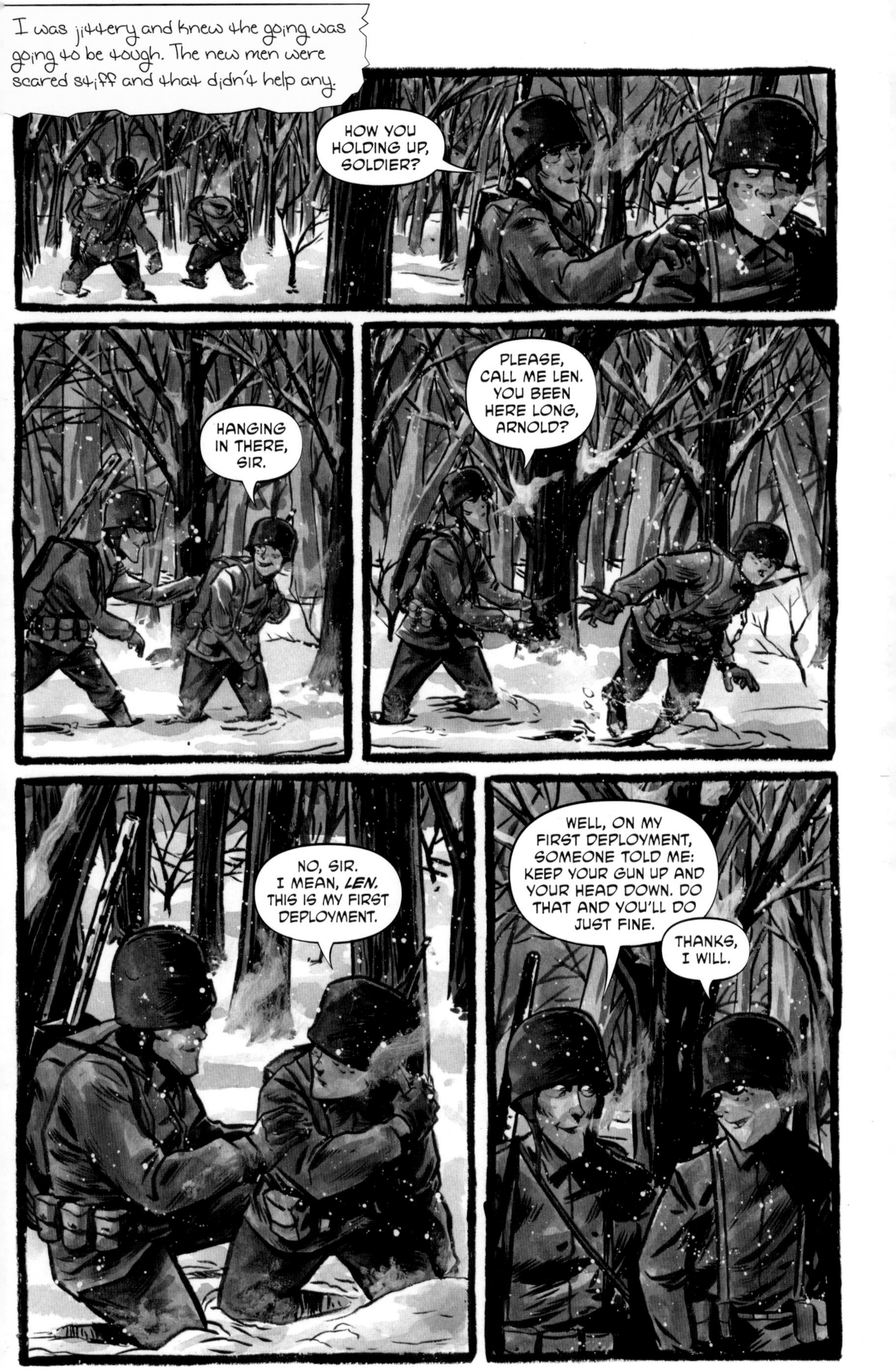
I was jittery and knew the going was going to be tough. The new men were scared stiff and that didn't help any.
HOW YOU HOLDING UP, SOLDIER?
HANGING IN THERE, SIR.
PLEASE, CALL ME LEN. YOU BEEN HERE LONG, ARNOLD?
NO, SIR. I MEAN, *LEN.* THIS IS MY FIRST DEPLOYMENT.
WELL, ON MY FIRST DEPLOYMENT, SOMEONE TOLD ME: KEEP YOUR GUN UP AND YOUR HEAD DOWN. DO THAT AND YOU'LL DO JUST FINE.
THANKS, I WILL.

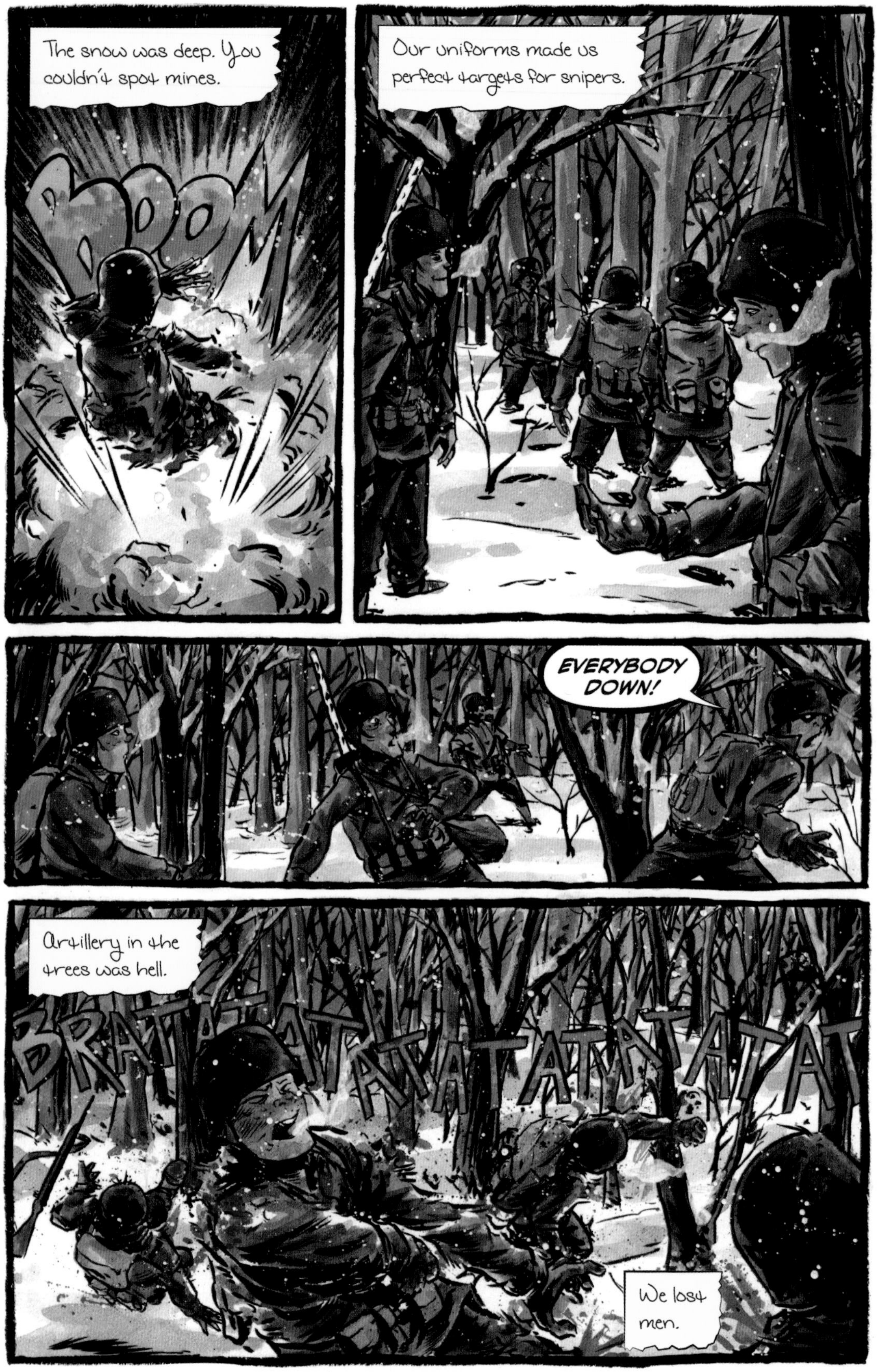

The snow was deep. You couldn't spot mines.
BOOM
Our uniforms made us perfect targets for snipers.
EVERYBODY DOWN!
Artillery in the trees was hell.
BRATATATATATATAT
We lost men.

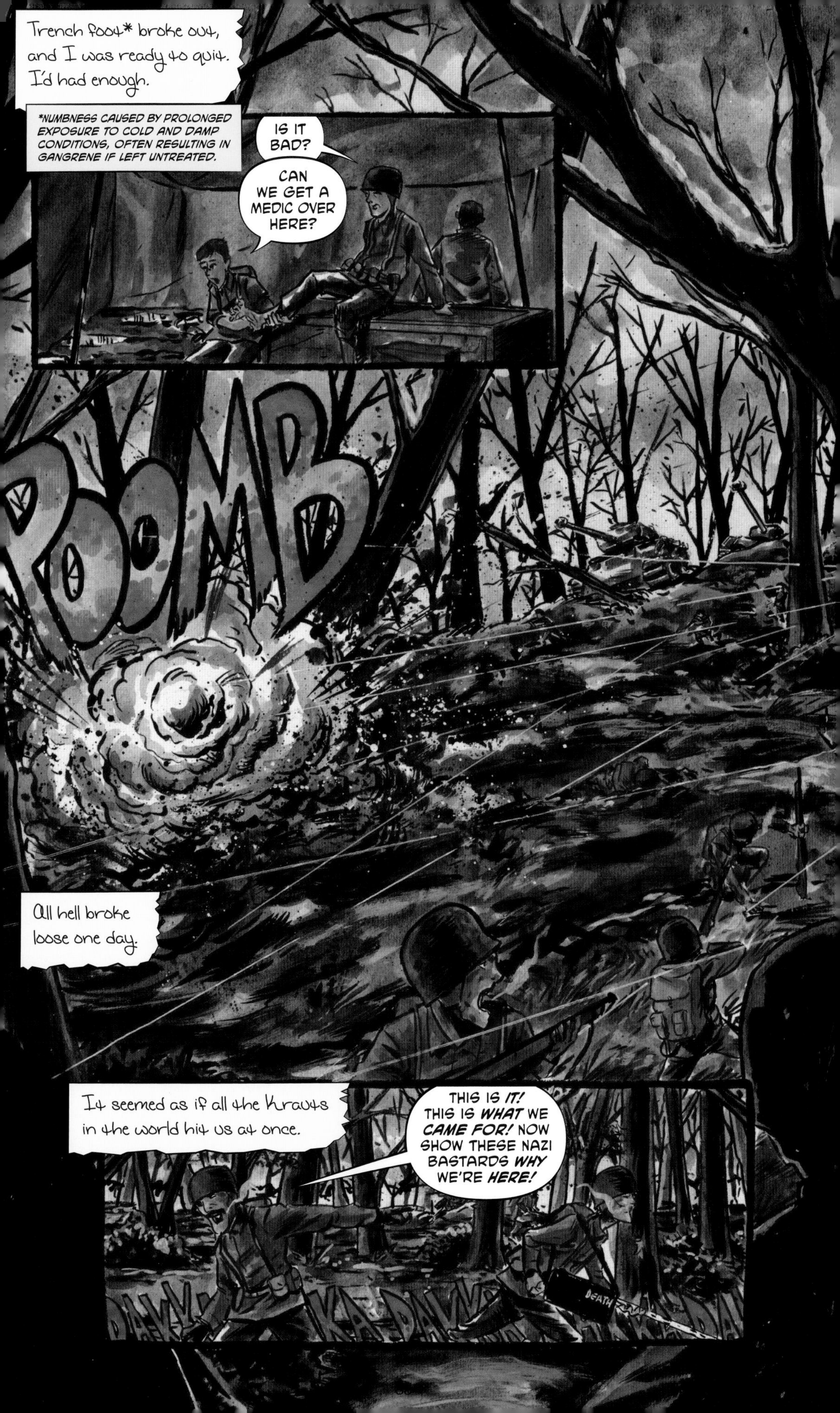

Trench foot* broke out, and I was ready to quit. I'd had enough.
*NUMBNESS CAUSED BY PROLONGED EXPOSURE TO COLD AND DAMP CONDITIONS, OFTEN RESULTING IN GANGRENE IF LEFT UNTREATED.
IS IT BAD?
CAN WE GET A MEDIC OVER HERE?
All hell broke loose one day.
It seemed as if all the Krauts in the world hit us at once.
THIS IS *IT!* THIS IS *WHAT* WE *CAME FOR!* NOW SHOW THESE NAZI BASTARDS *WHY* WE'RE *HERE!*
DEATH

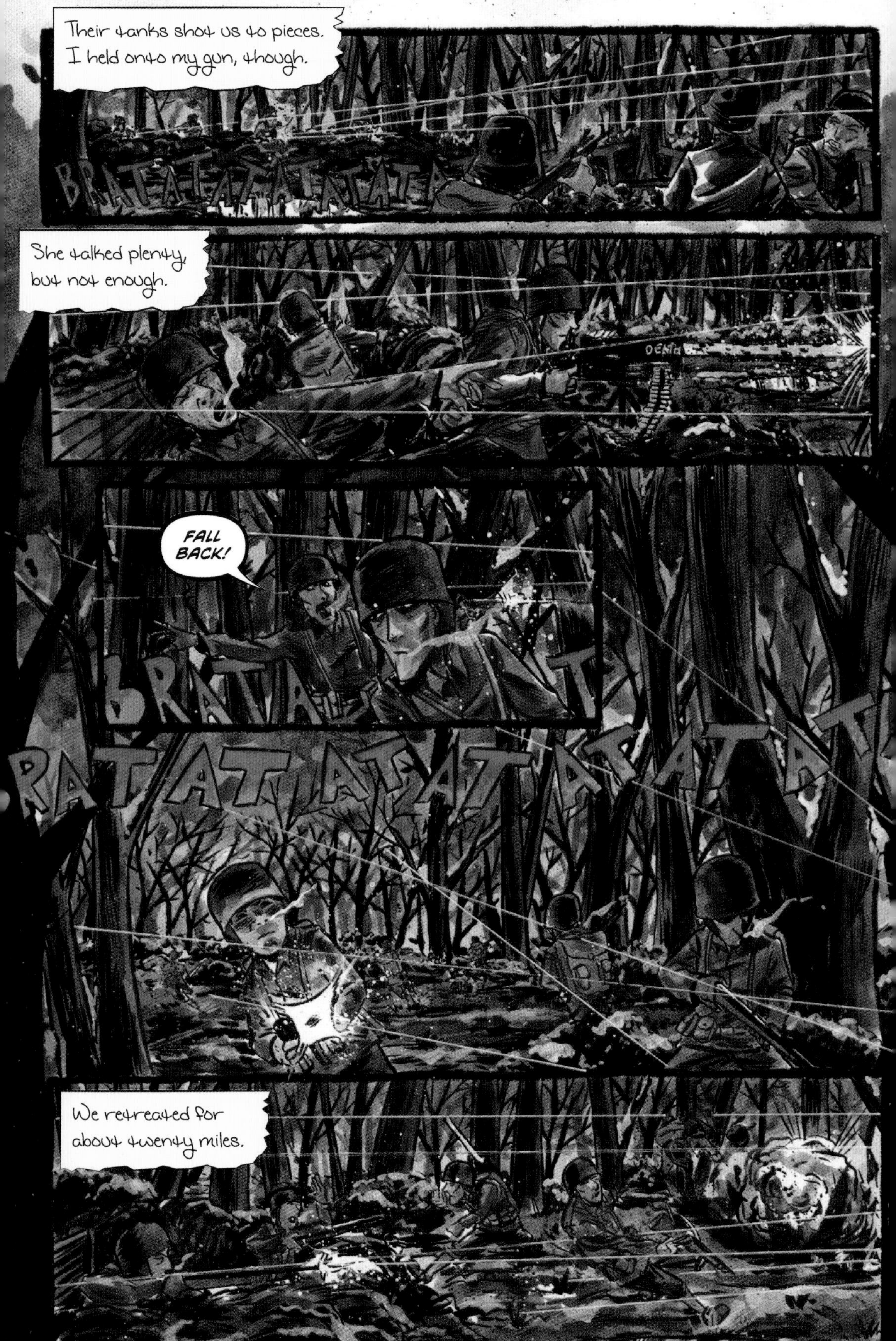
Their tanks shot us to pieces. I held onto my gun, though.
BRATATATATATATAT
She talked plenty, but not enough.
FALL BACK!
BRATATAT
RATATATATATATAT
We retreated for about twenty miles.

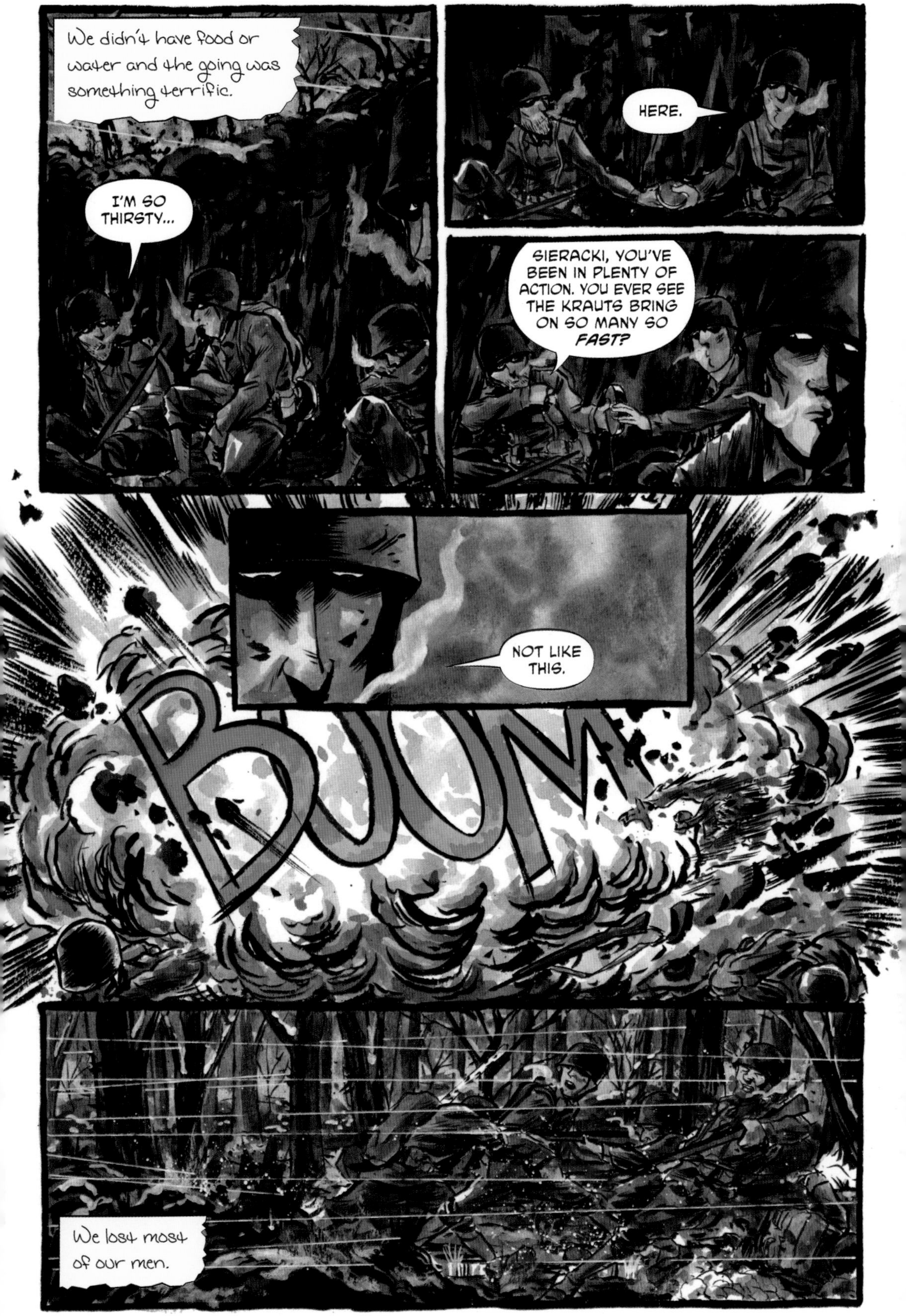

We didn't have food or water and the going was something terrific.
I'M SO THIRSTY...
HERE.
SIERACKI, YOU'VE BEEN IN PLENTY OF ACTION. YOU EVER SEE THE KRAUTS BRING ON SO MANY SO FAST?
NOT LIKE THIS.
BOOM
We lost most of our men.

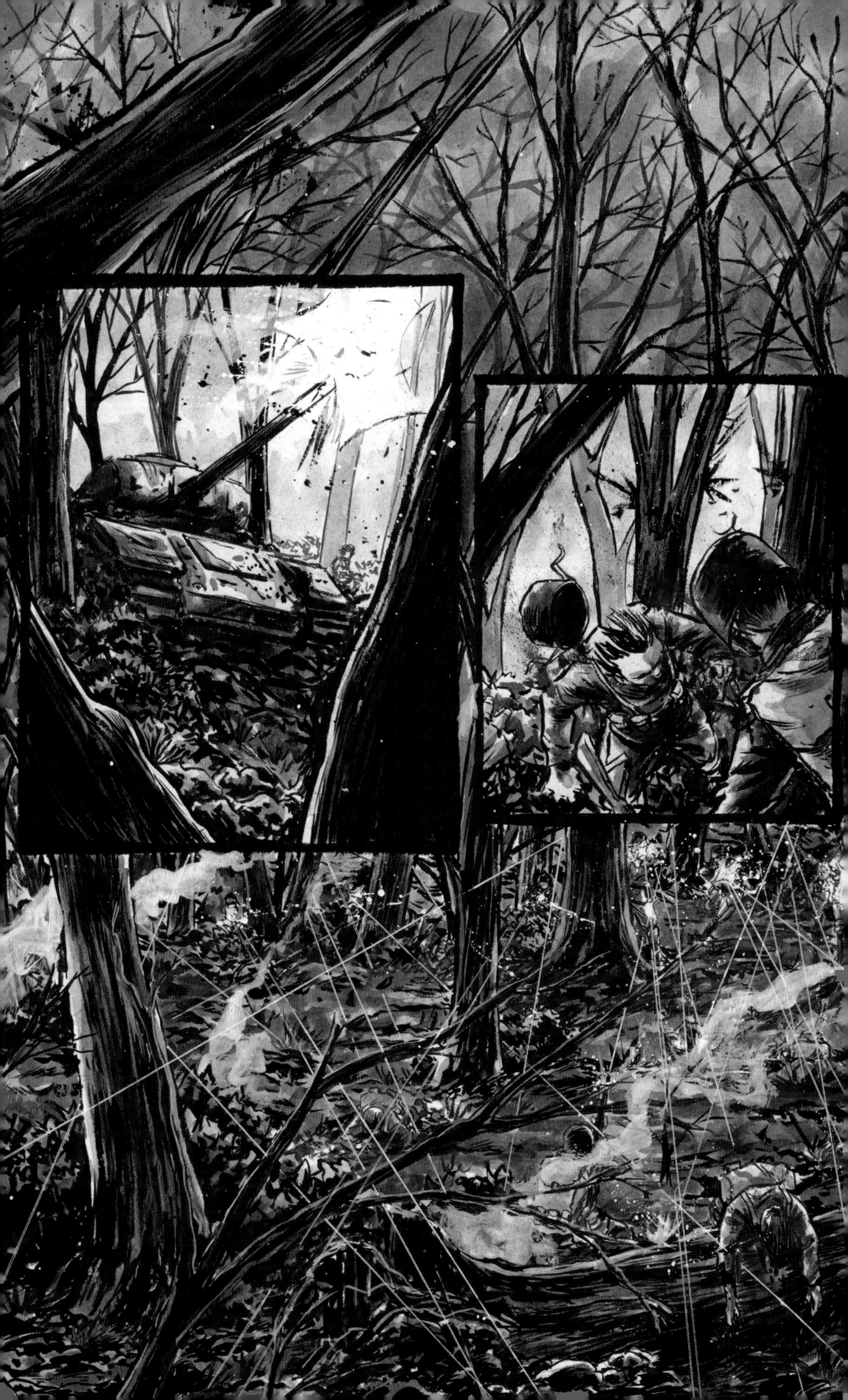

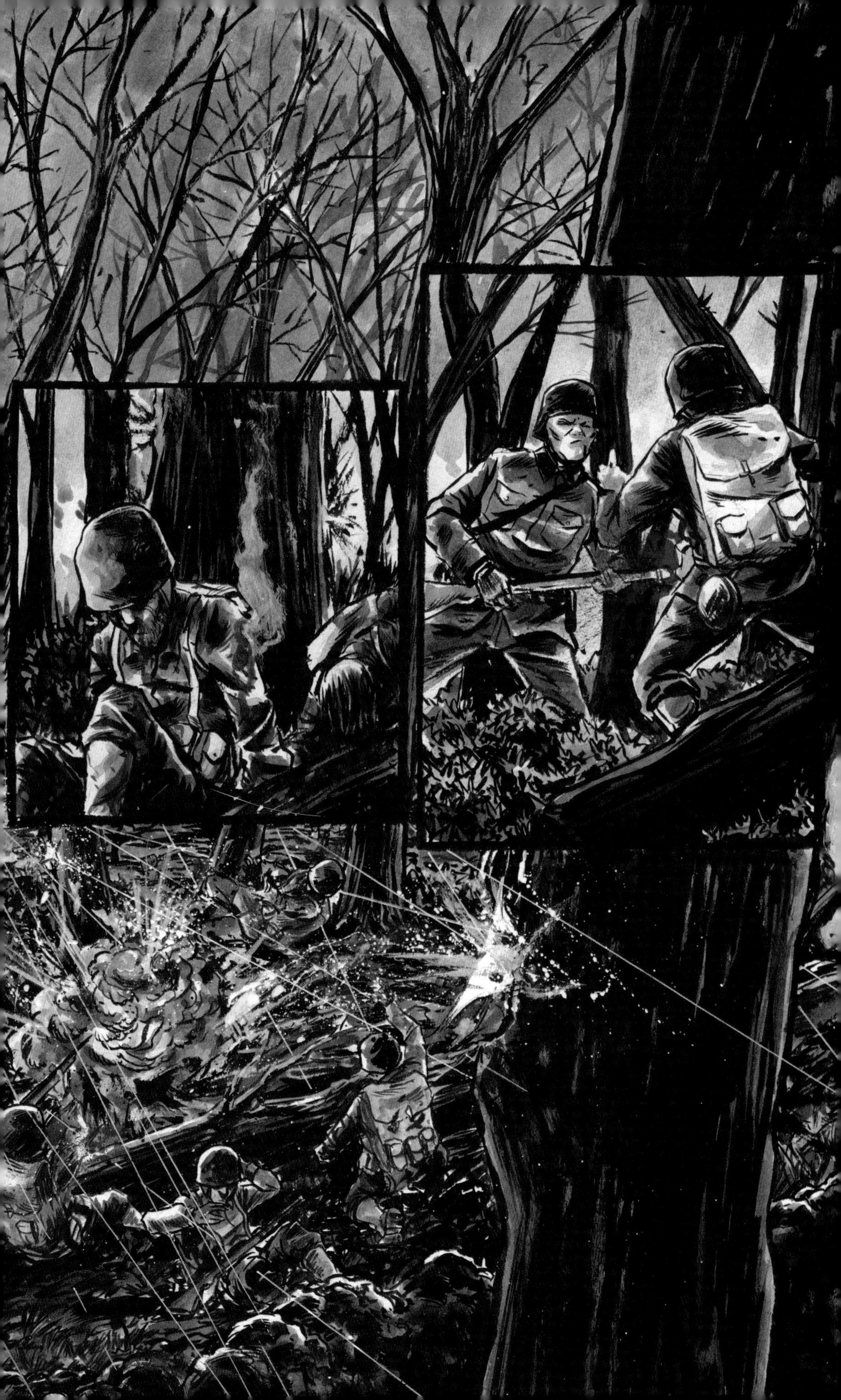

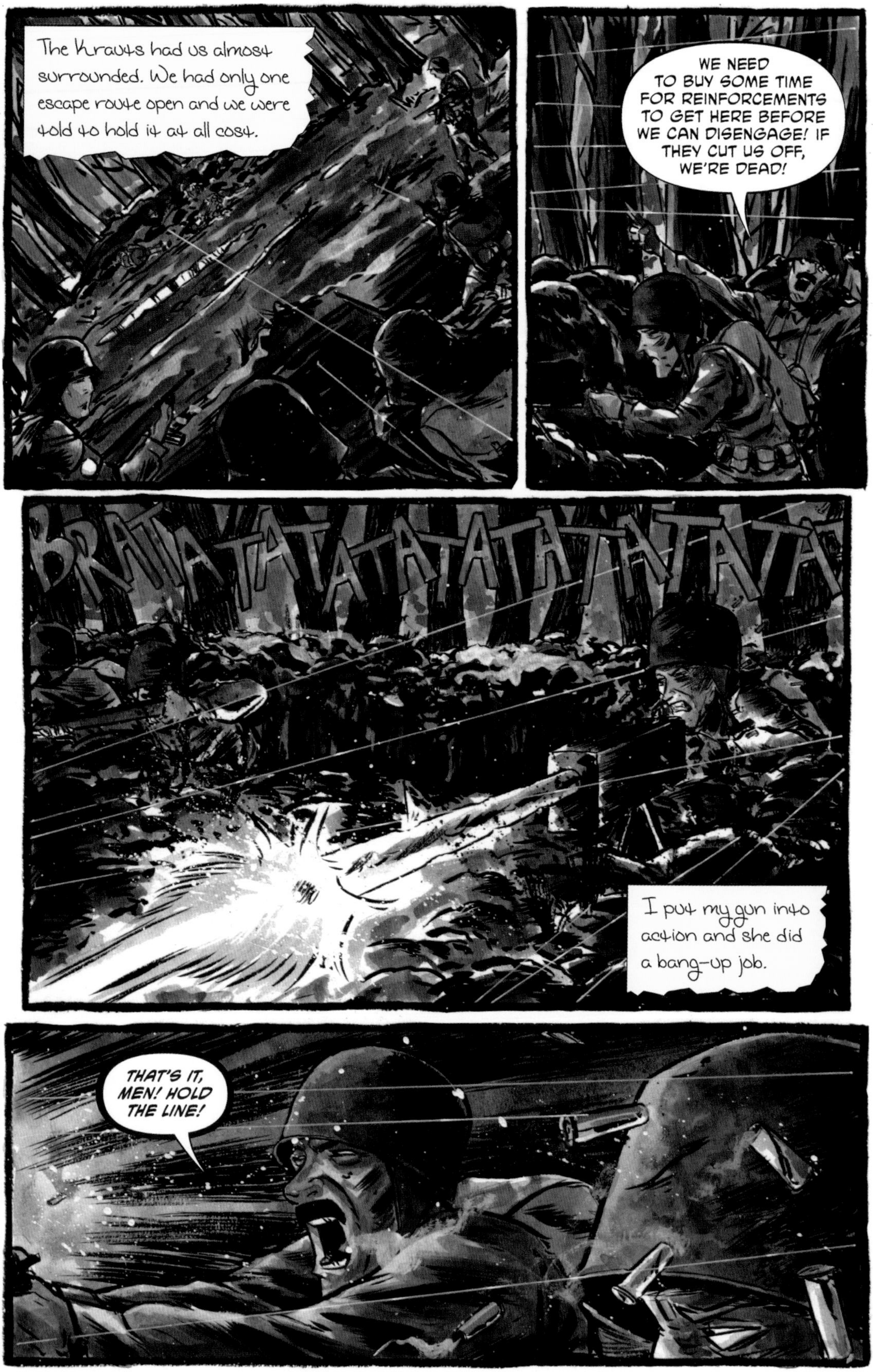
The Krauts had us almost surrounded. We had only one escape route open and we were told to hold it at all cost.
WE NEED TO BUY SOME TIME FOR REINFORCEMENTS TO GET HERE BEFORE WE CAN DISENGAGE! IF THEY CUT US OFF, WE'RE DEAD!
BRATATATATATATATATATATAT
I put my gun into action and she did a bang-up job.
THAT'S IT, MEN! HOLD THE LINE!

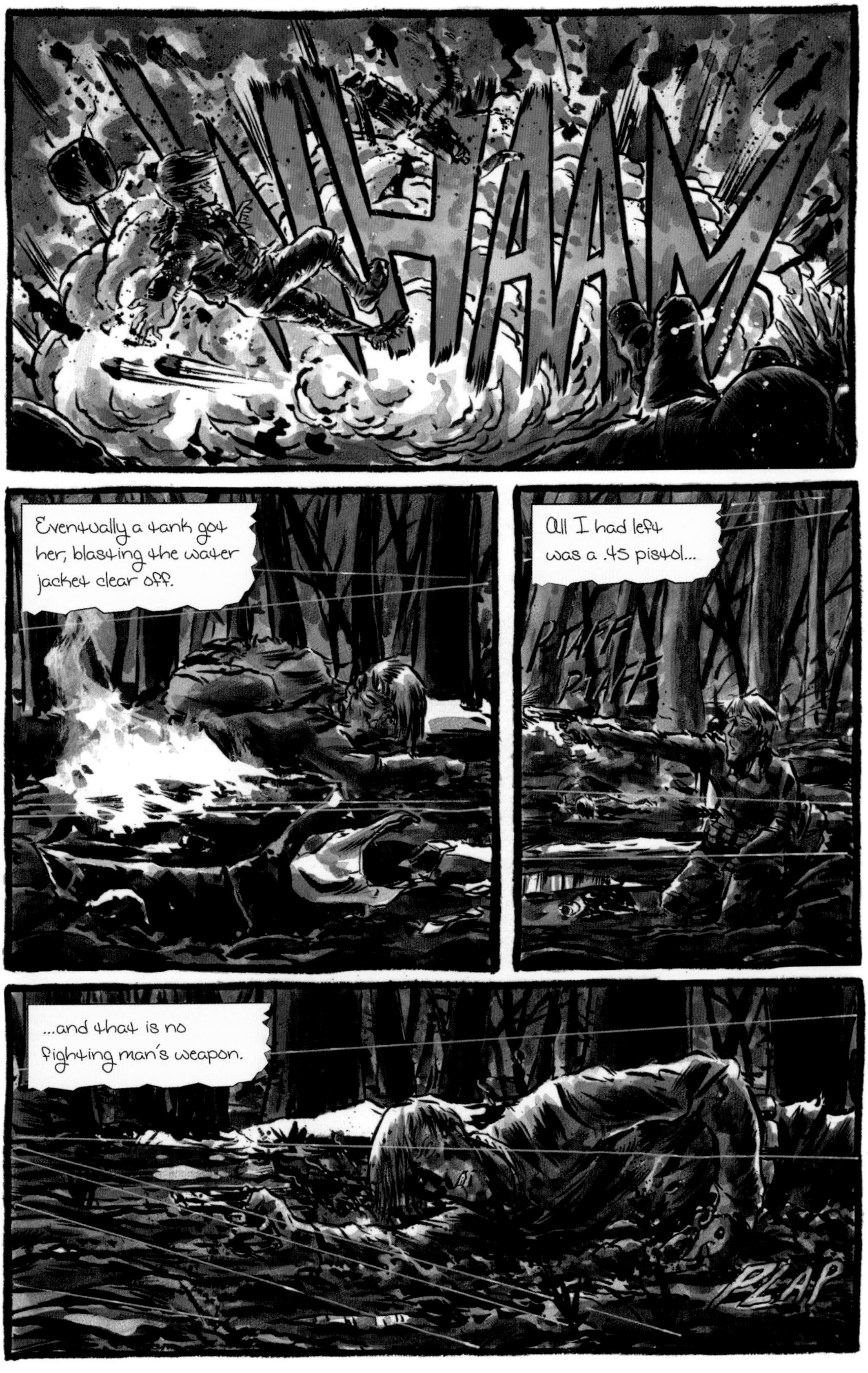
WHAAM
Eventually a tank got her, blasting the water jacket clear off.
All I had left was a .45 pistol...
PTAFF
PTAFF
...and that is no fighting man's weapon.
PLAP

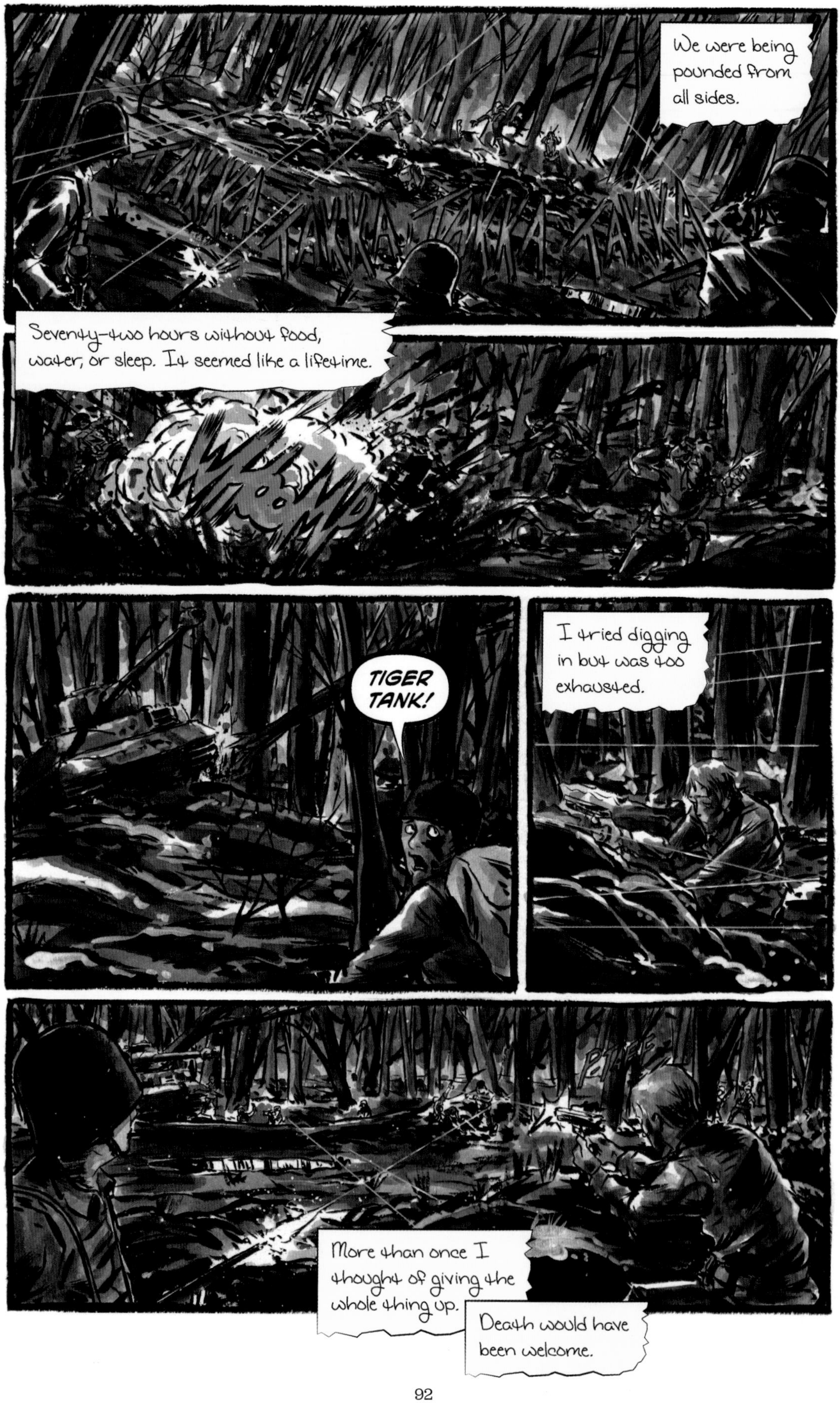
We were being pounded from all sides.
TAKKA TAKKA TAKKA TAKKA
Seventy-two hours without food, water, or sleep. It seemed like a lifetime.
TIGER TANK!
I tried digging in but was too exhausted.
More than once I thought of giving the whole thing up.
Death would have been welcome.

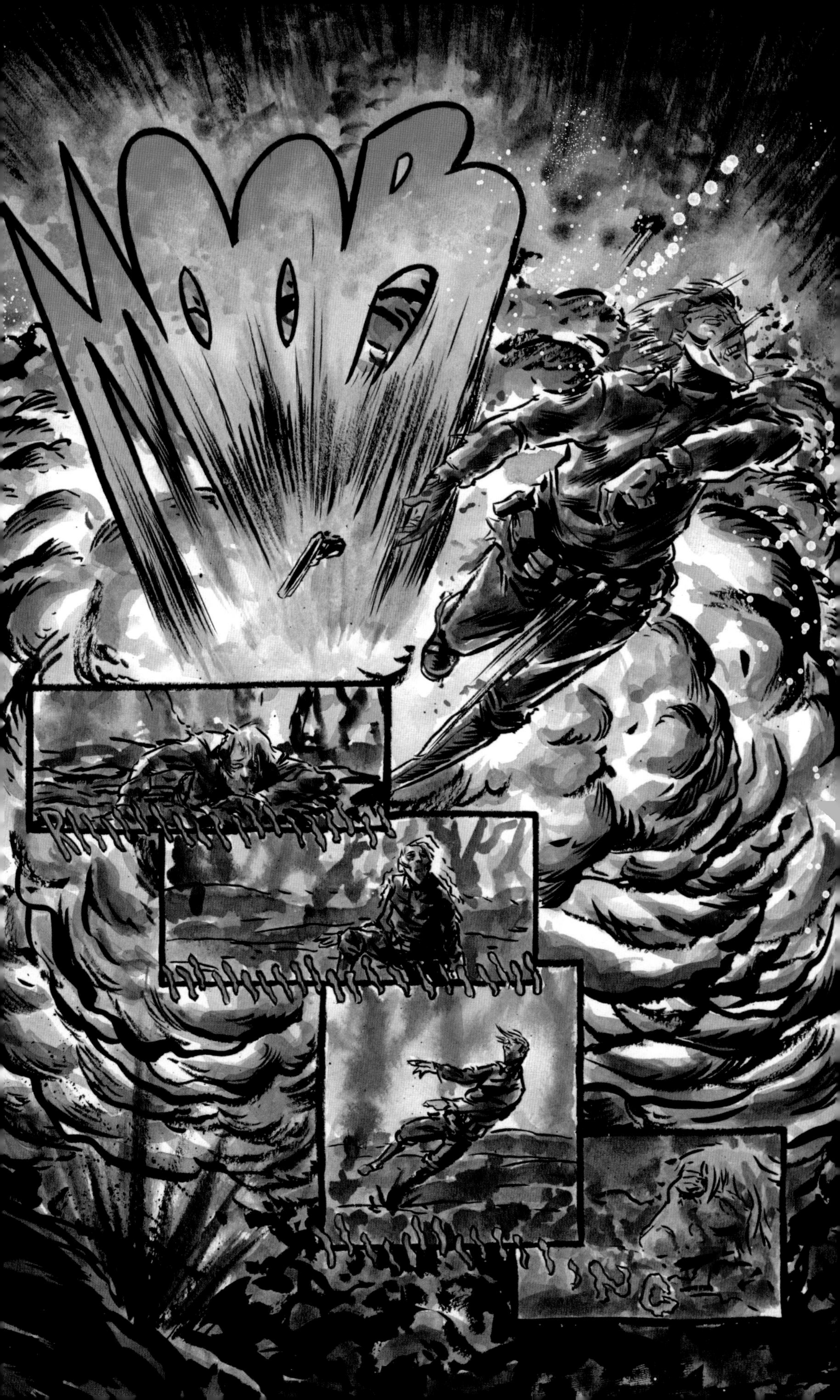

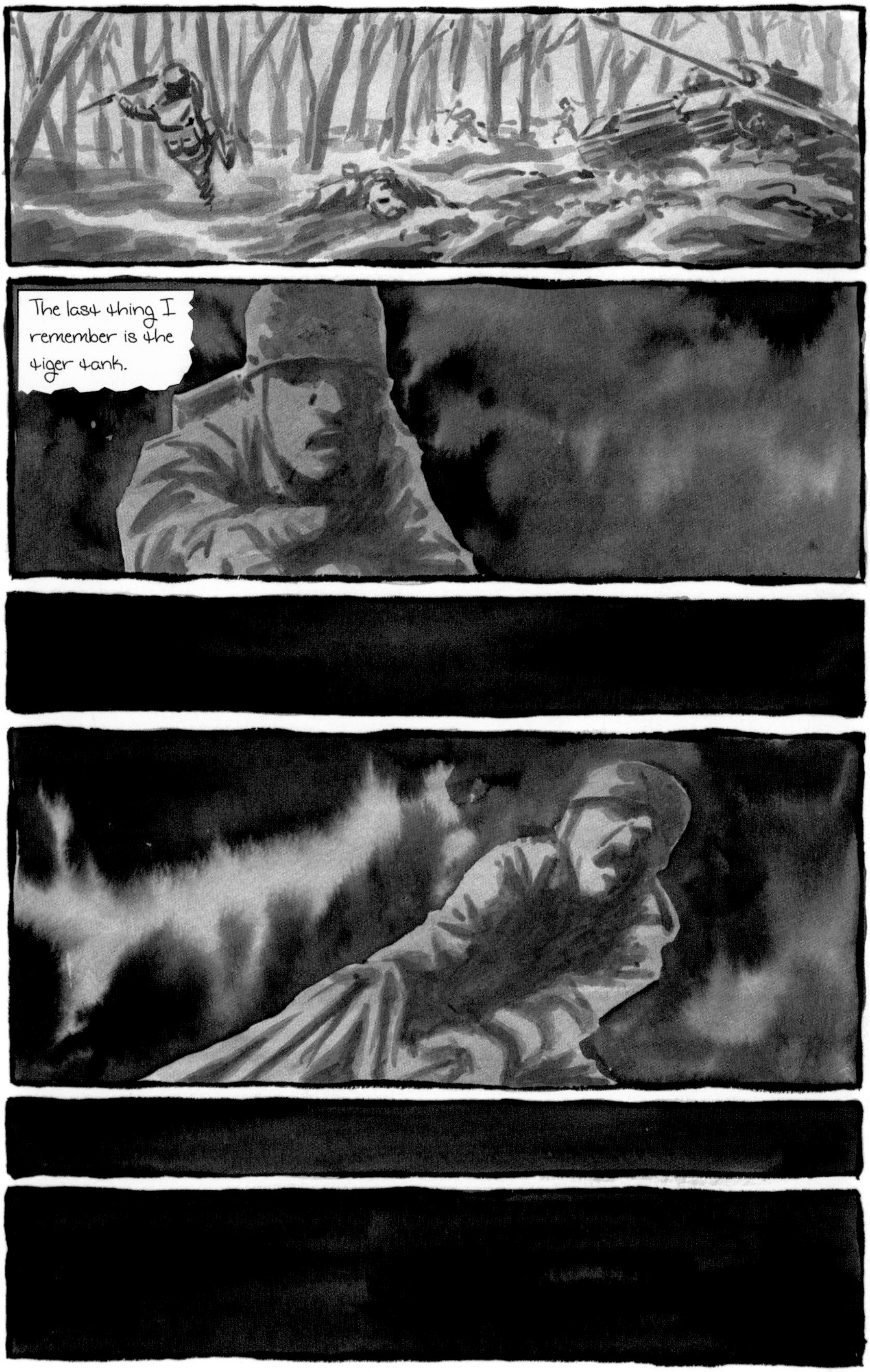
The last thing I remember is the tiger tank.

CHAPTER EIGHT
LIFE

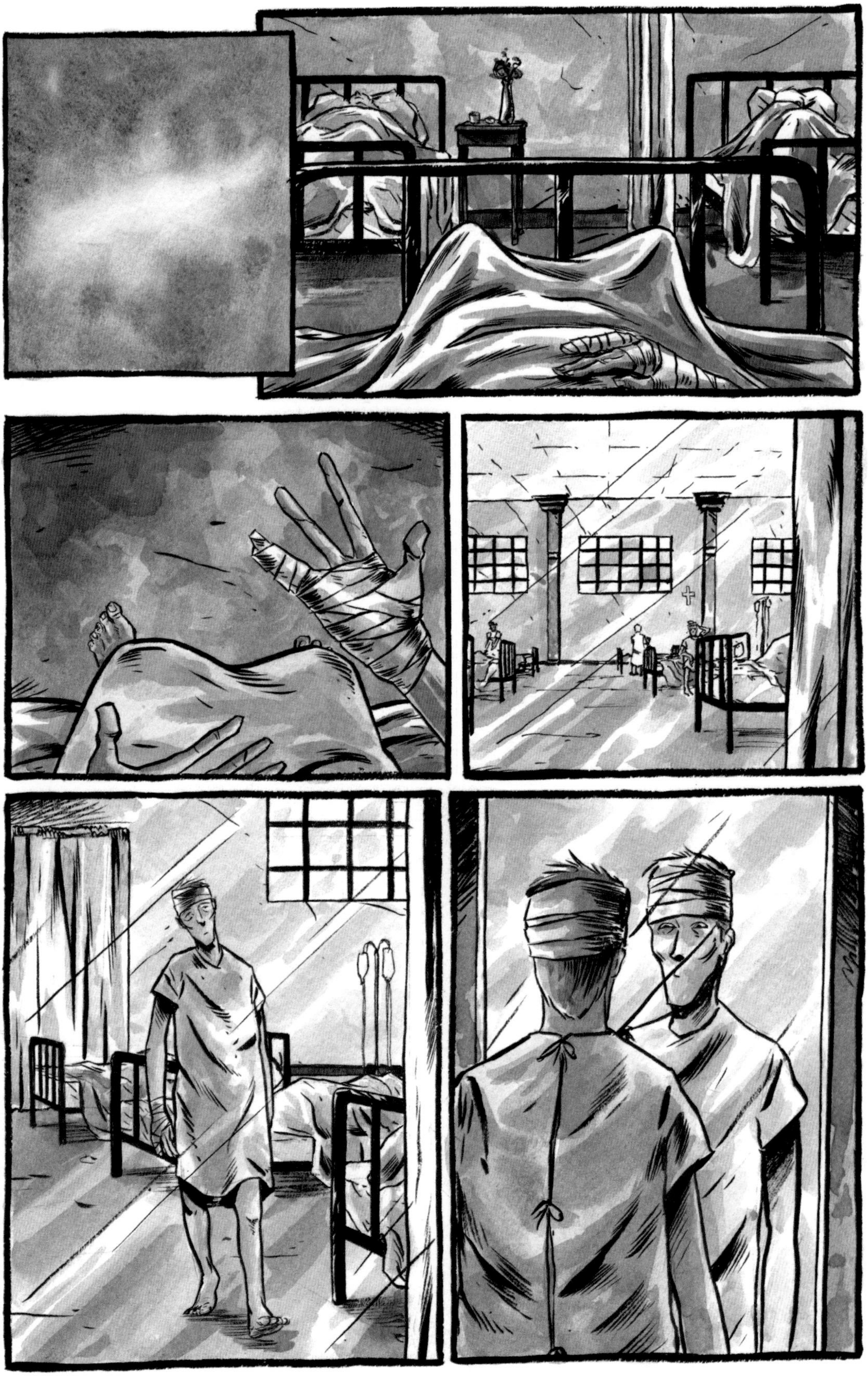

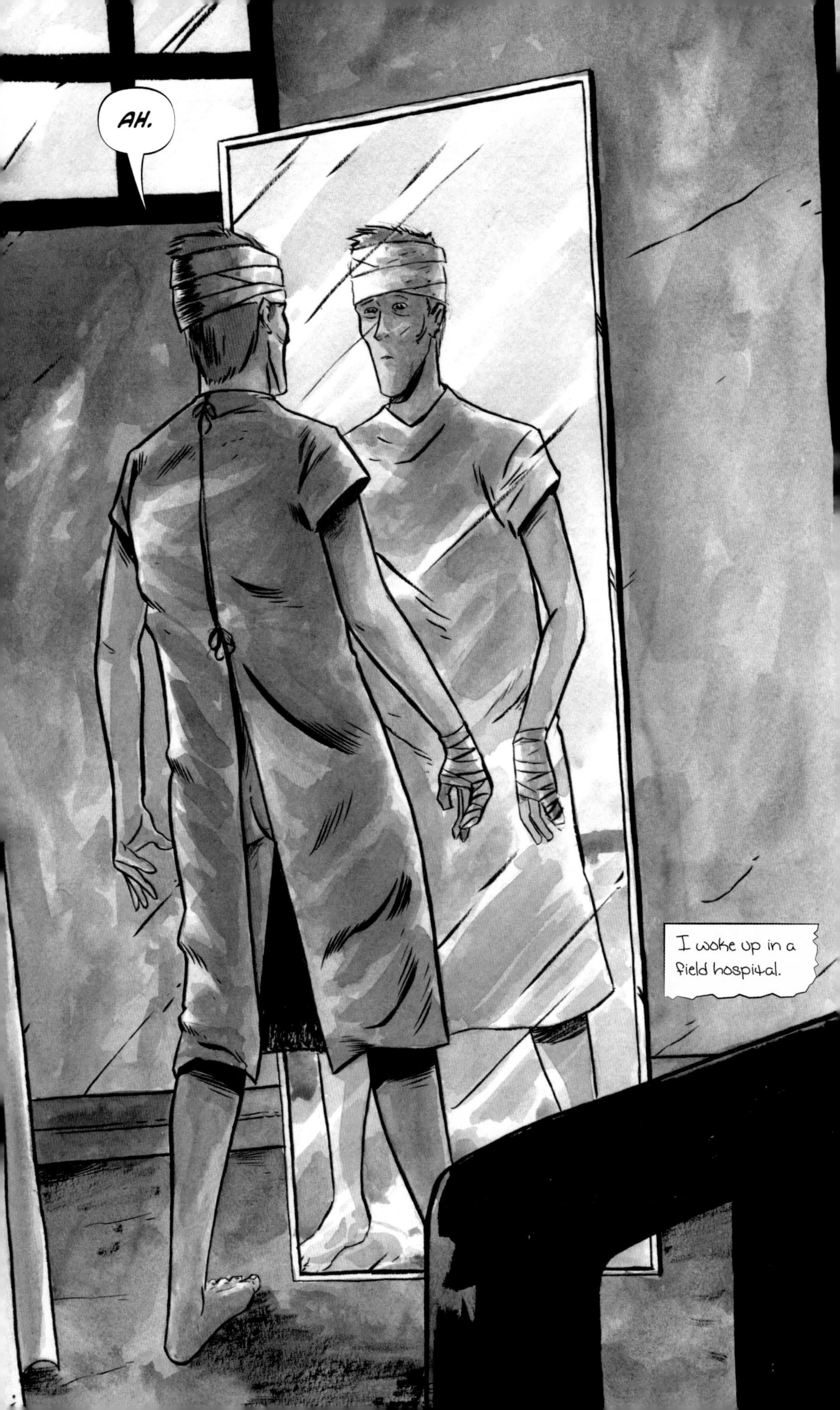
AH.
I woke up in a field hospital.

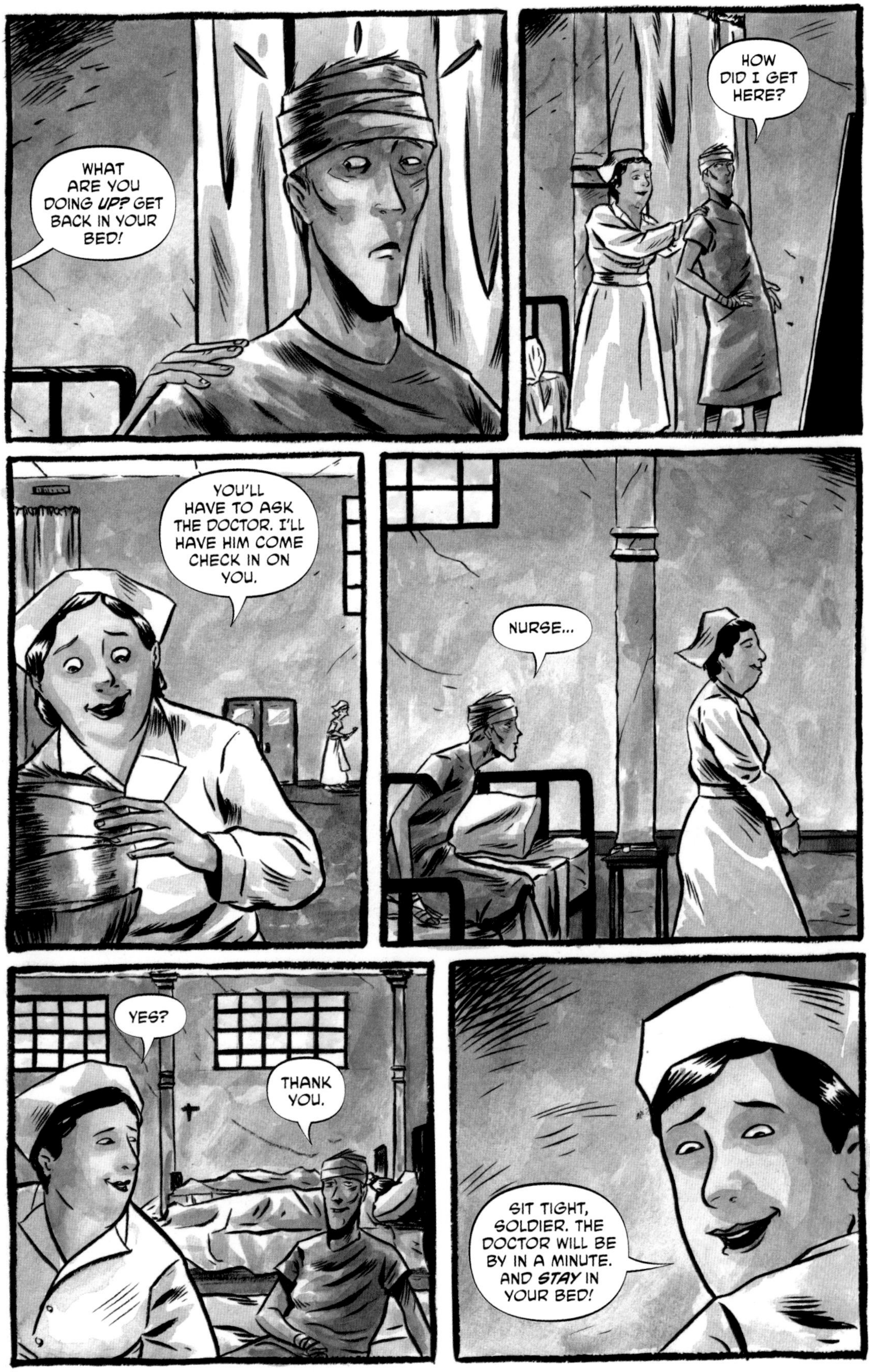
WHAT ARE YOU DOING UP? GET BACK IN YOUR BED!
HOW DID I GET HERE?
YOU'LL HAVE TO ASK THE DOCTOR. I'LL HAVE HIM COME CHECK IN ON YOU.
NURSE...
YES?
THANK YOU.
SIT TIGHT, SOLDIER. THE DOCTOR WILL BE BY IN A MINUTE. AND STAY IN YOUR BED!

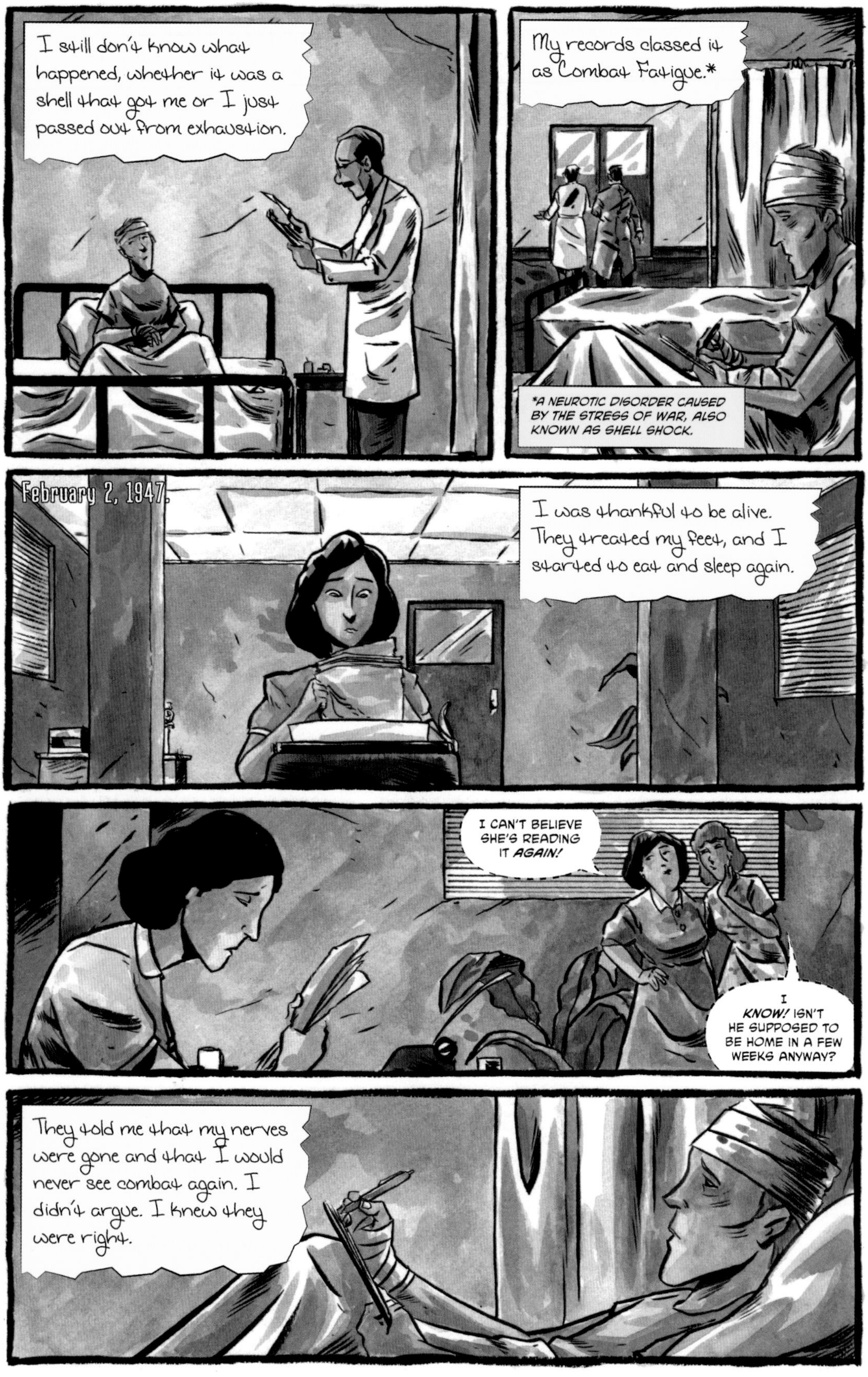
I still don't know what happened, whether it was a shell that got me or I just passed out from exhaustion.
My records classed it as Combat Fatigue.*
*A NEUROTIC DISORDER CAUSED BY THE STRESS OF WAR, ALSO KNOWN AS SHELL SHOCK.
February 2, 1947.
I was thankful to be alive. They treated my feet, and I started to eat and sleep again.
I CAN'T BELIEVE SHE'S READING IT AGAIN!
I KNOW! ISN'T HE SUPPOSED TO BE HOME IN A FEW WEEKS ANYWAY?
They told me that my nerves were gone and that I would never see combat again. I didn't argue. I knew they were right.

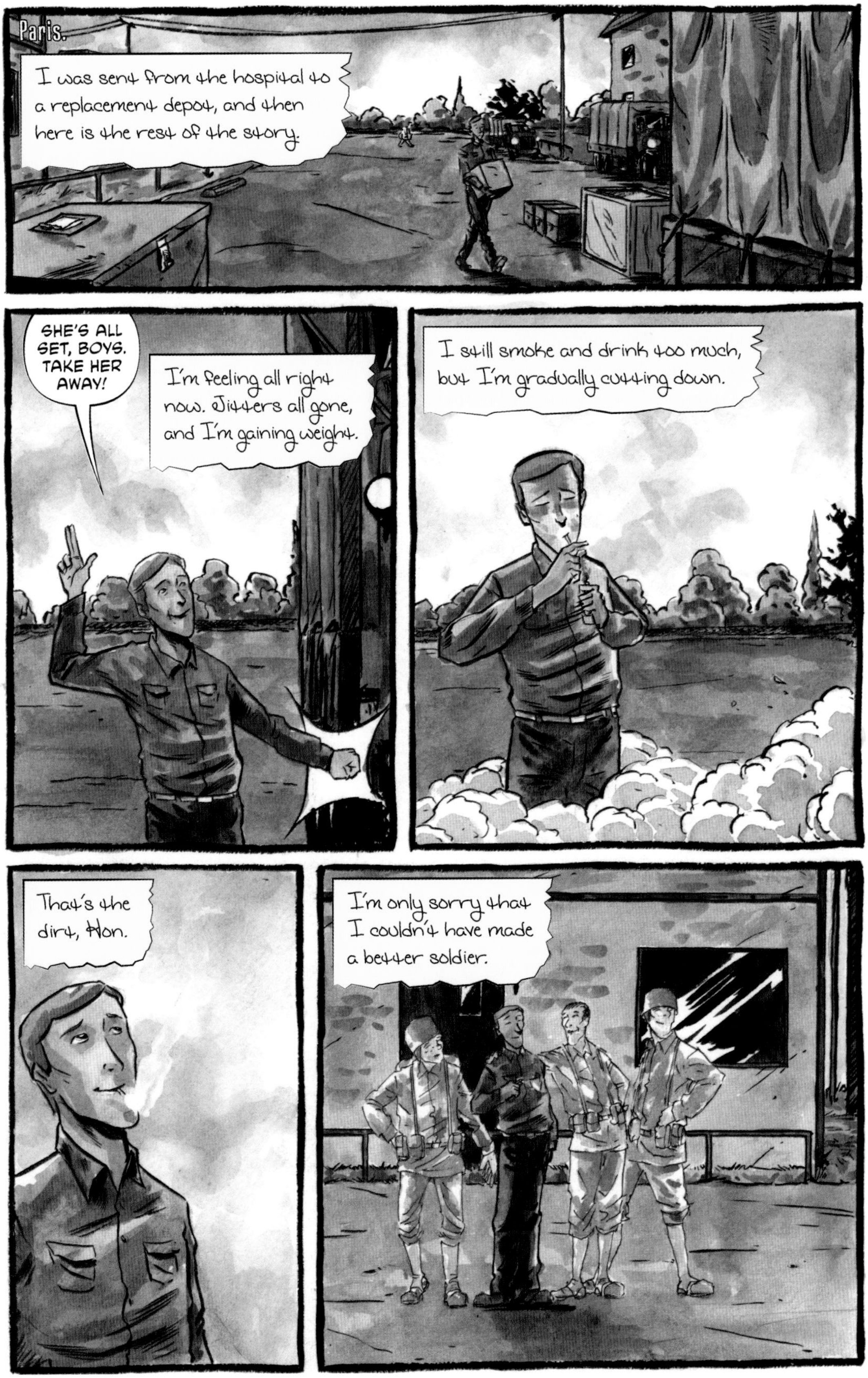
Paris.
I was sent from the hospital to a replacement depot, and then here is the rest of the story.
SHE'S ALL SET, BOYS. TAKE HER AWAY!
I'm feeling all right now. Jitters all gone, and I'm gaining weight.
I still smoke and drink too much, but I'm gradually cutting down.
That's the dirt, Hon.
I'm only sorry that I couldn't have made a better soldier.

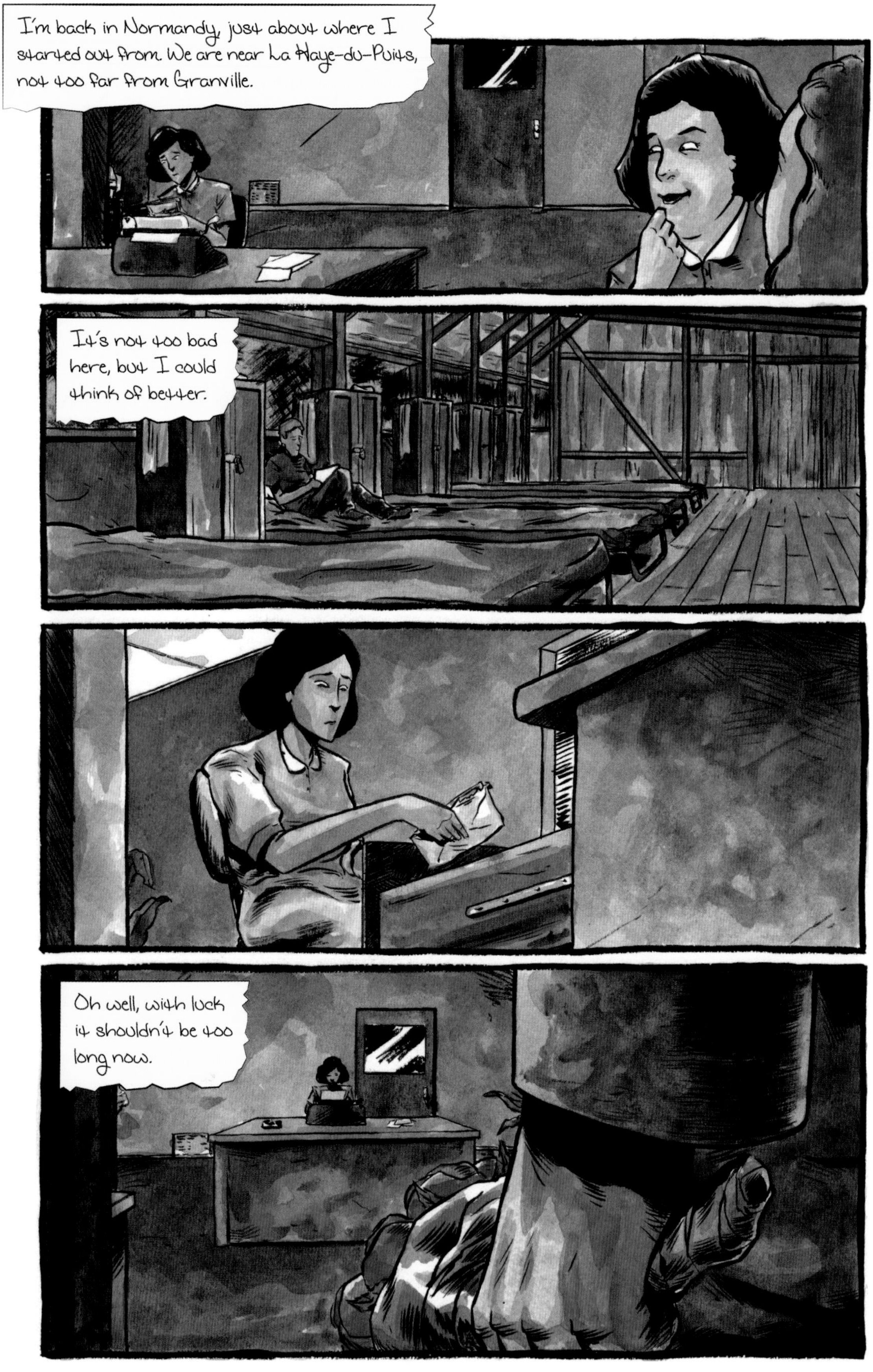
I'm back in Normandy, just about where I started out from. We are near La Haye-du-Puits, not too far from Granville.
It's not too bad here, but I could think of better.
Oh well, with luck it shouldn't be too long now.

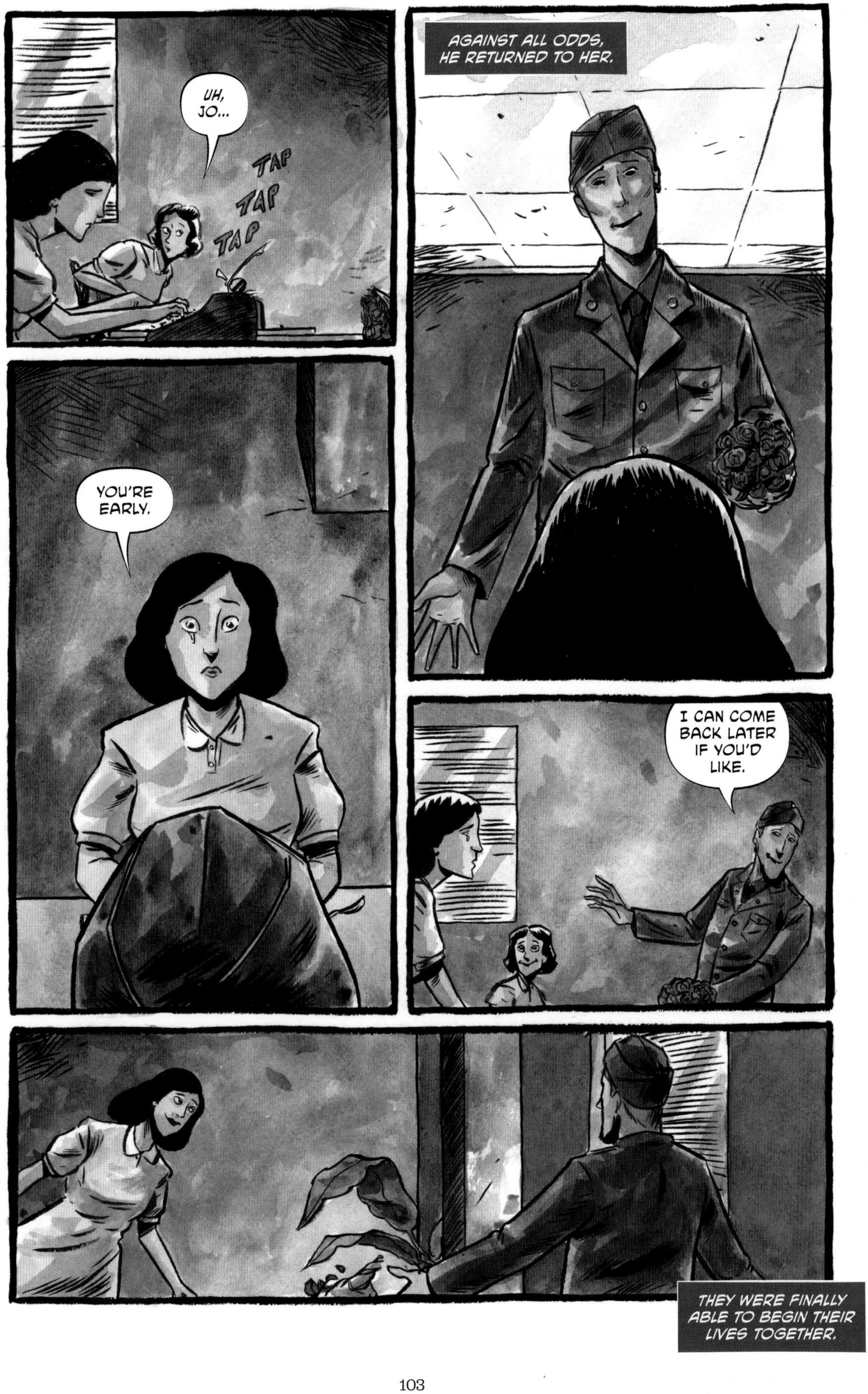
UH, JO...
TAP
TAP
TAP
AGAINST ALL ODDS, HE RETURNED TO HER.
YOU'RE EARLY.
I CAN COME BACK LATER IF YOU'D LIKE.
THEY WERE FINALLY ABLE TO BEGIN THEIR LIVES TOGETHER.

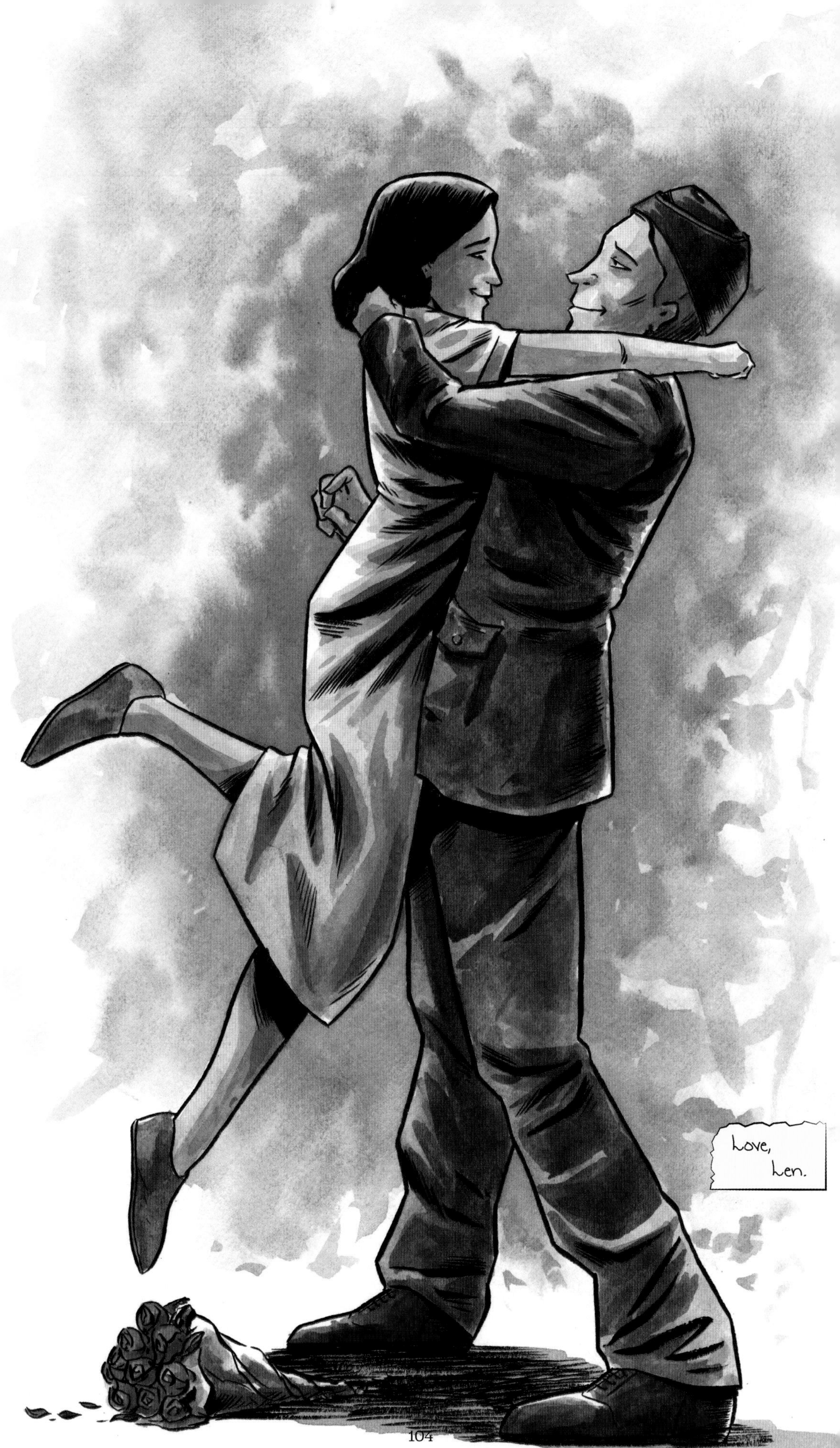
Love,
Len.

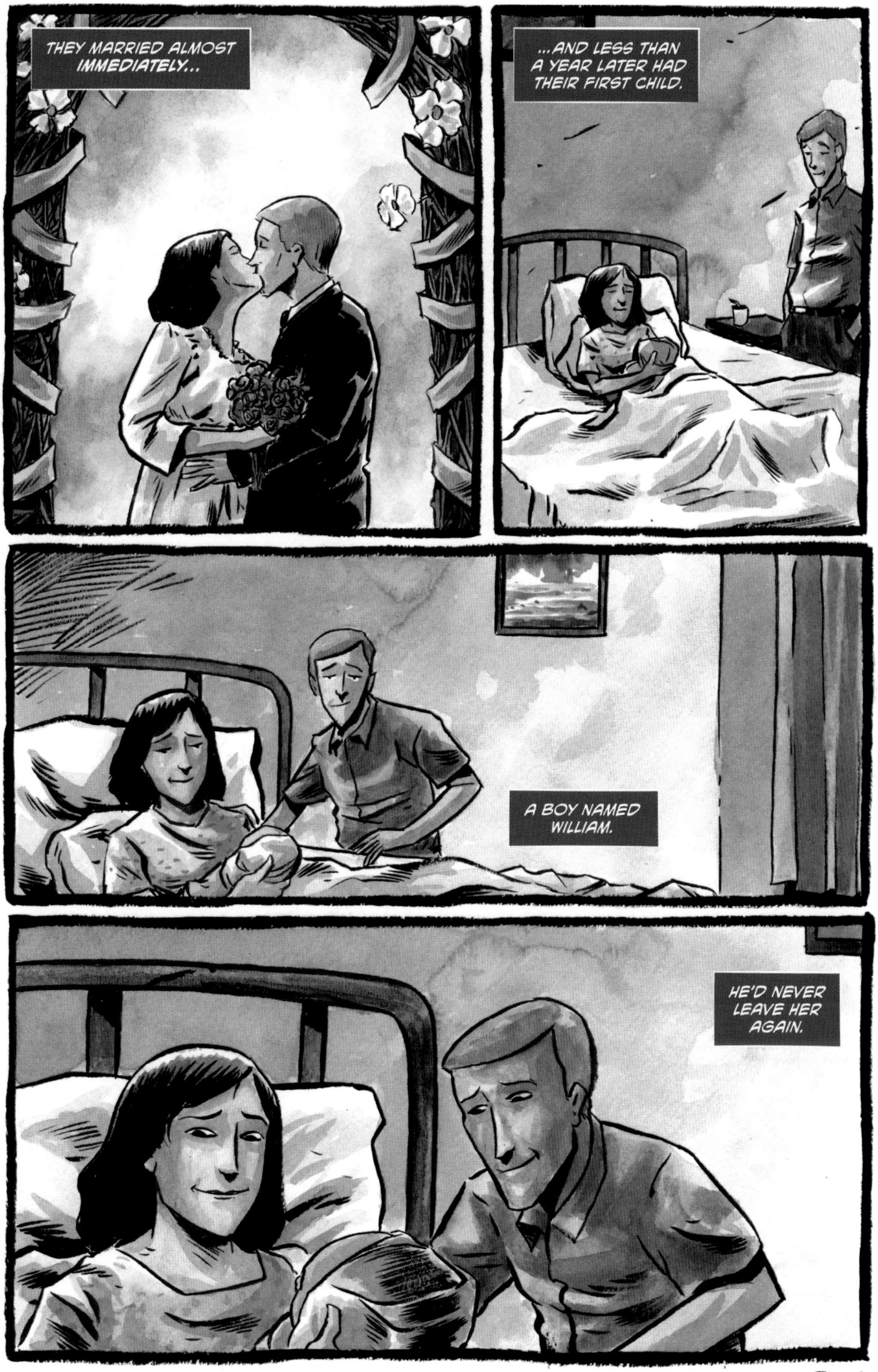
THEY MARRIED ALMOST IMMEDIATELY...
...AND LESS THAN A YEAR LATER HAD THEIR FIRST CHILD.
A BOY NAMED WILLIAM.
HE'D NEVER LEAVE HER AGAIN.

End

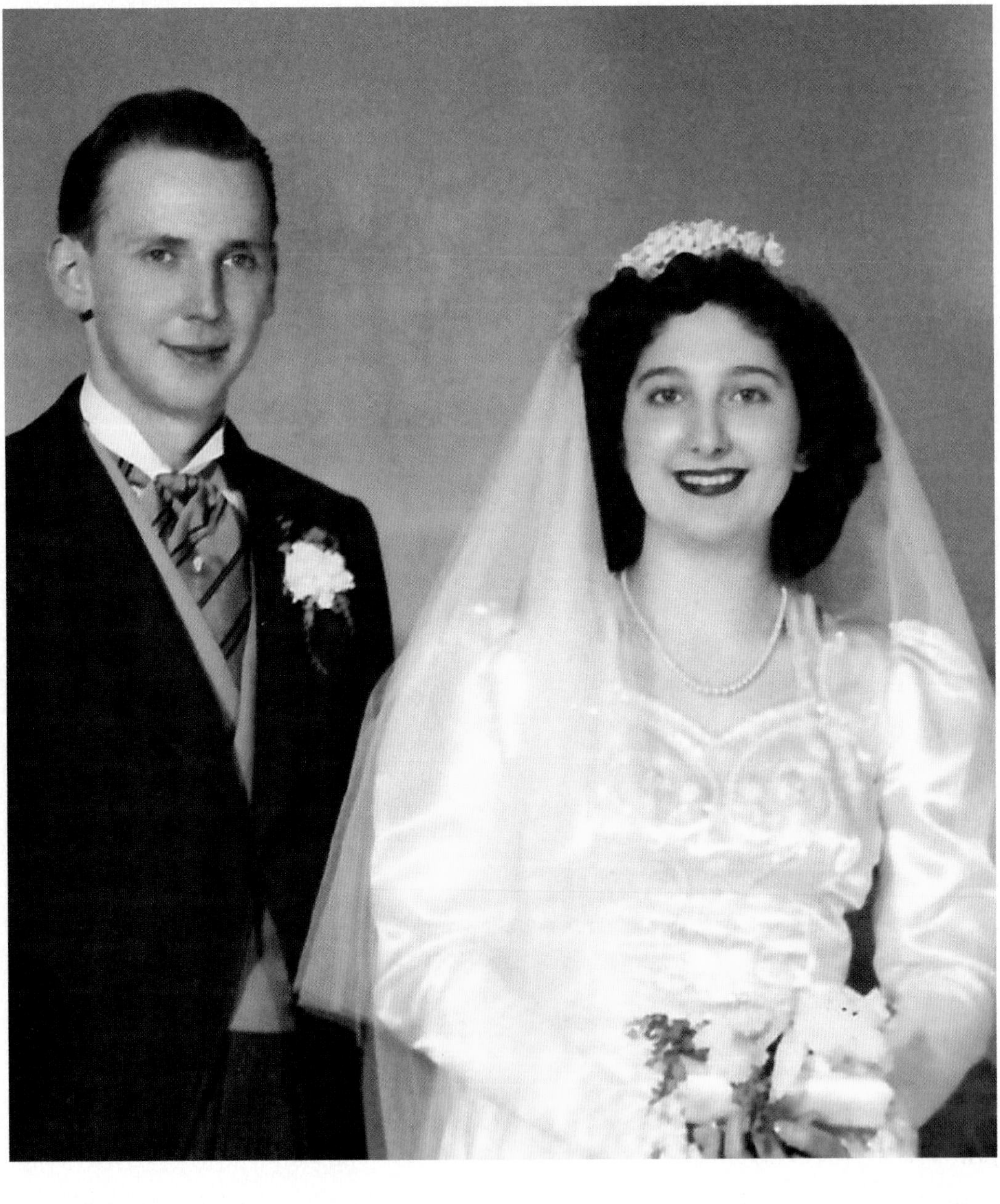

EPILOGUE

When I first began researching World War II to verify the facts of Leonard's letter, I asked my family for their memories of my grandfather talking about the war. As I suspected, he spoke very little of his time overseas, but one story did stand out.

Leonard once told my mother of a time he was riding in a truck with one of his buddies. The two were shoulder to shoulder, just chatting. Leonard had said something, but his friend didn't respond. When he turned to see why, he discovered that his friend's head had been blown clean off.

Surprisingly, it was not the subject matter of this story that shocked my mother. It was the way Leonard told it so plainly, as if it were a perfectly natural thing to happen.

When I was young, my grandfather was eager to show me his dusty old medals. He would pull them down and show them to me one by one, explaining what each was for, as I stared in awe, but for the most part he hated talking about his actual participation in the war. Especially when it came to combat. As a child, I never understood why that was, but after reading his letter to my grandmother, I finally began to get it.

Prior to reading the letter, I never thought of my grandfather as being a boy in the war. That's exactly what he was, though: an eighteen-year-old kid who desperately missed his girl back home. And, somehow, he was able to survive it all and make it out relatively unscathed.

Still, he suffered a great deal of loss overseas, and I don't think that's something that simply goes away. I believe that he carried those losses with him throughout his life, so while he was proud of his accomplishments and fully believed in the sacrifices that he and his fellow soldiers made, it was painful for him to recall the darker aspects of the war.

For the purposes of this story, I had to fictionalize certain details about Leonard's experiences in the war. While the locations of each battle are consistent with his testimony to Josephine in the original letter that can be found later in this book, he spoke little of the actual battles. I used historical texts corresponding to each battle to inform the struggles that took place there. Every action scene was based on firsthand accounts from actual participants, lending consistency to Leonard's story.

Similarly, Leonard never mentions any specific names of his fellow soldiers. He refers to "the gang," but no one individual. As such, his interactions with Graham, Federico, Warner, Arnold, etc., were all invented to assist in framing the story. Still, I believe that these relationships help to reveal deeper truths about the unique camaraderie forged only by war, and about the certain inequalities that existed within the time period.

In World War II, the United States Army was segregated, which is why you don't see African-American soldiers in any of Leonard's squadrons. Hispanic soldiers, including Puerto Ricans, however, were categorized as "white." Thus, Federico would have served right alongside Leonard. Still, despite their service to their country, it has been well documented that many Hispanic soldiers were discriminated against within their ranks, facing the same injustices that they did back home.

When he died, my grandfather willed his medals to me. I've always considered it a great honor. I keep them safely tucked away and rarely take them out, but whenever I do, I can't help but wonder why he picked me. Was it because I was one of the few family members that showed interest? Was it because of the fond memories he held of showing them to me as a child? Is it because he knew I'd take good care of them, or was it something else?

My family often say that I remind them of my grandfather. For better or worse, it's a fact that I'll always be proud of.

THE DAWN CAME

Written by
LEONARD SIERACKI

Art by
BRETT CARVILLE

The following pages reproduce a poem Leonard wrote while deployed in Europe, evoking the fear and anticipation of battle and the memory of his beloved back home. Paired with Brett Carville's vivid dramatization, created for this volume, it presents a chilling companion to Leonard's account of the war to Josephine.

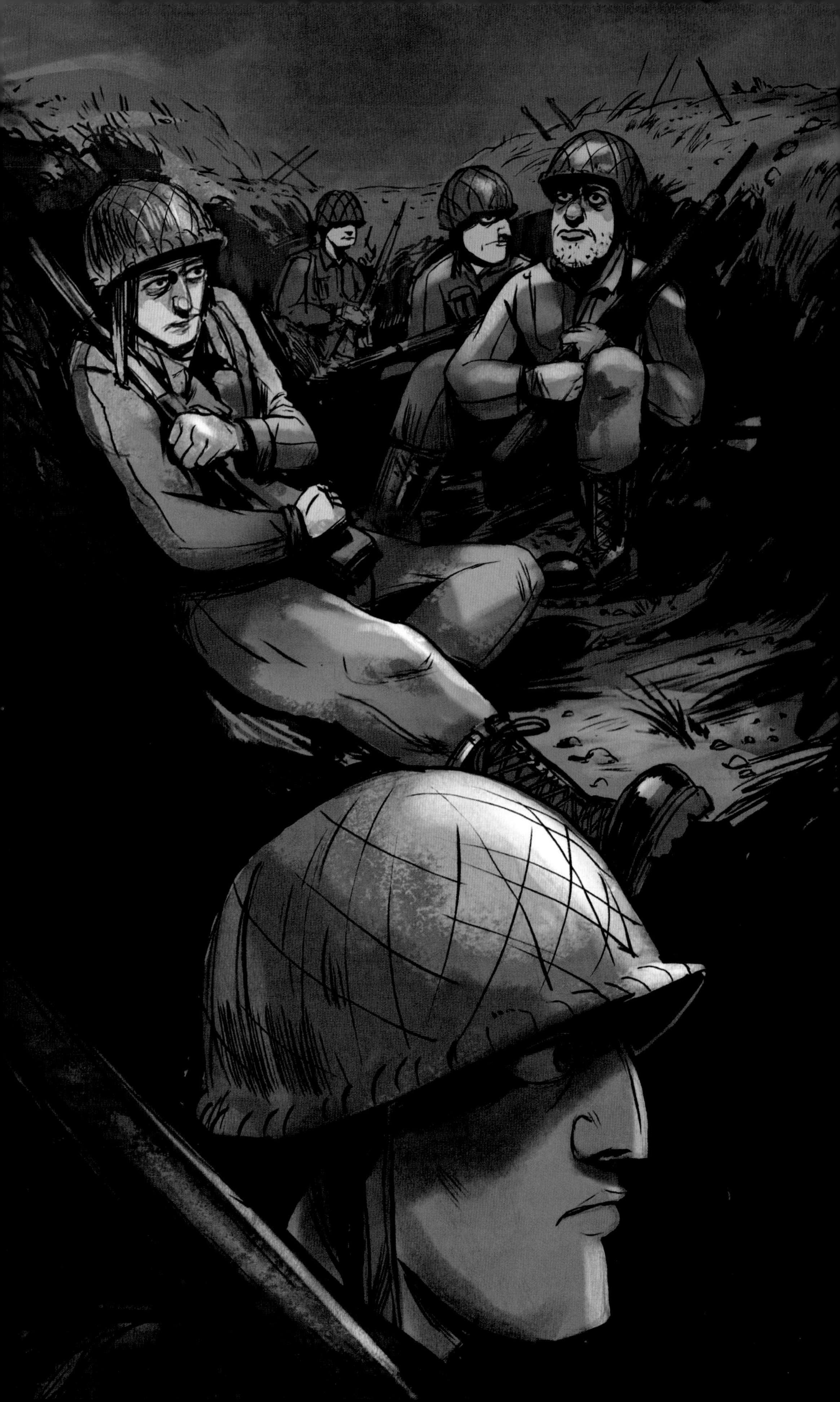

Darkness spread over us like ink,
Nothing to do but watch and think.
How long the night shall be,
Gets so dark you can hardly see.
Just sit and listen to noises of the night,
And try to control your thoughts and fright.

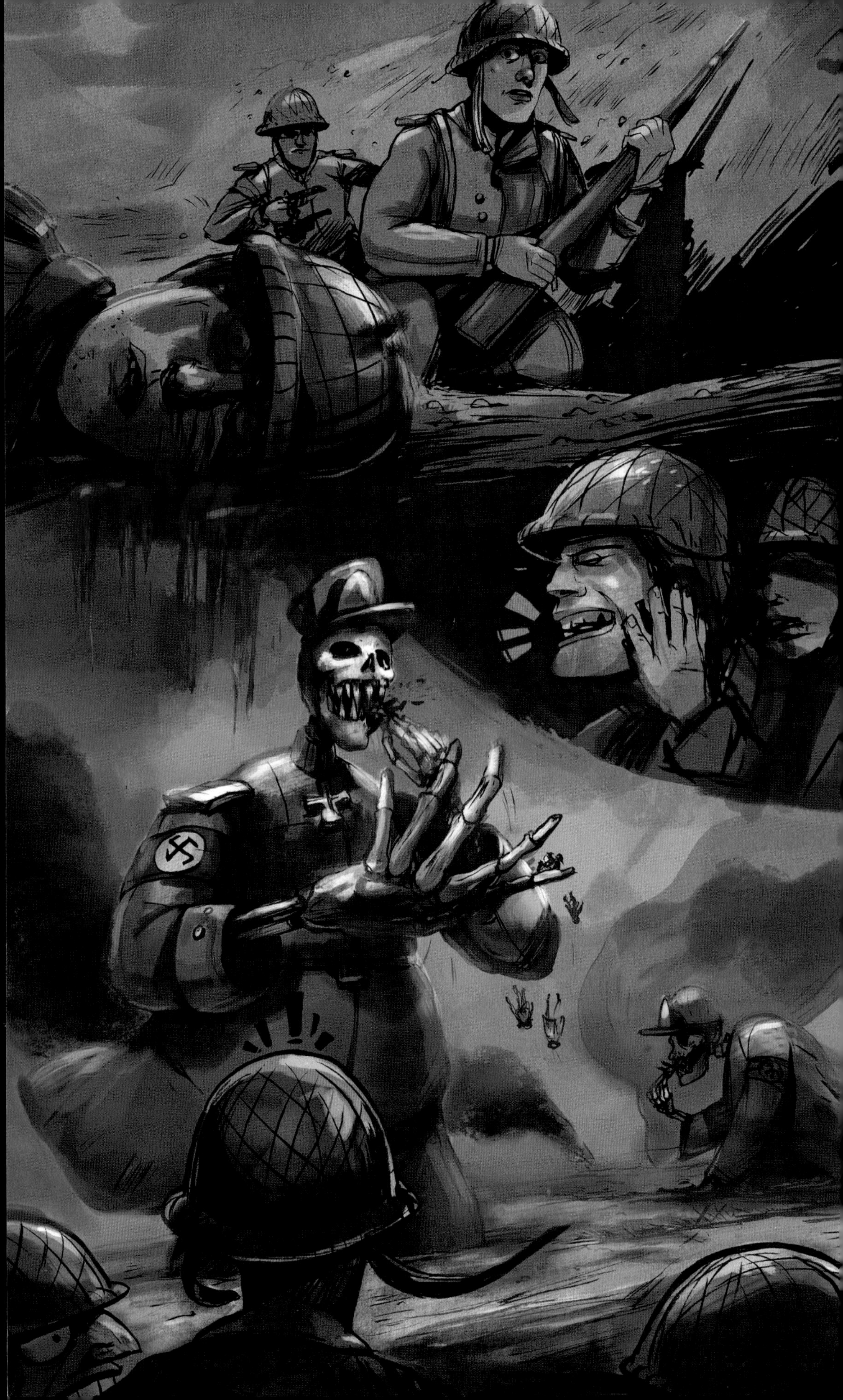

The big guns began their incessant roar,
I huddled closer to the muddy floor.
The quiet was split by the shells' crash,
A bit of light was had by their flash.

The cry of "Medic" could be plainly heard,
Out into the night they were lured.
Alas, I was wounded no doubt,
But it turned out to be a lurking Kraut.
The stillness was shattered by the rapid "burp,"
Death again was at work.

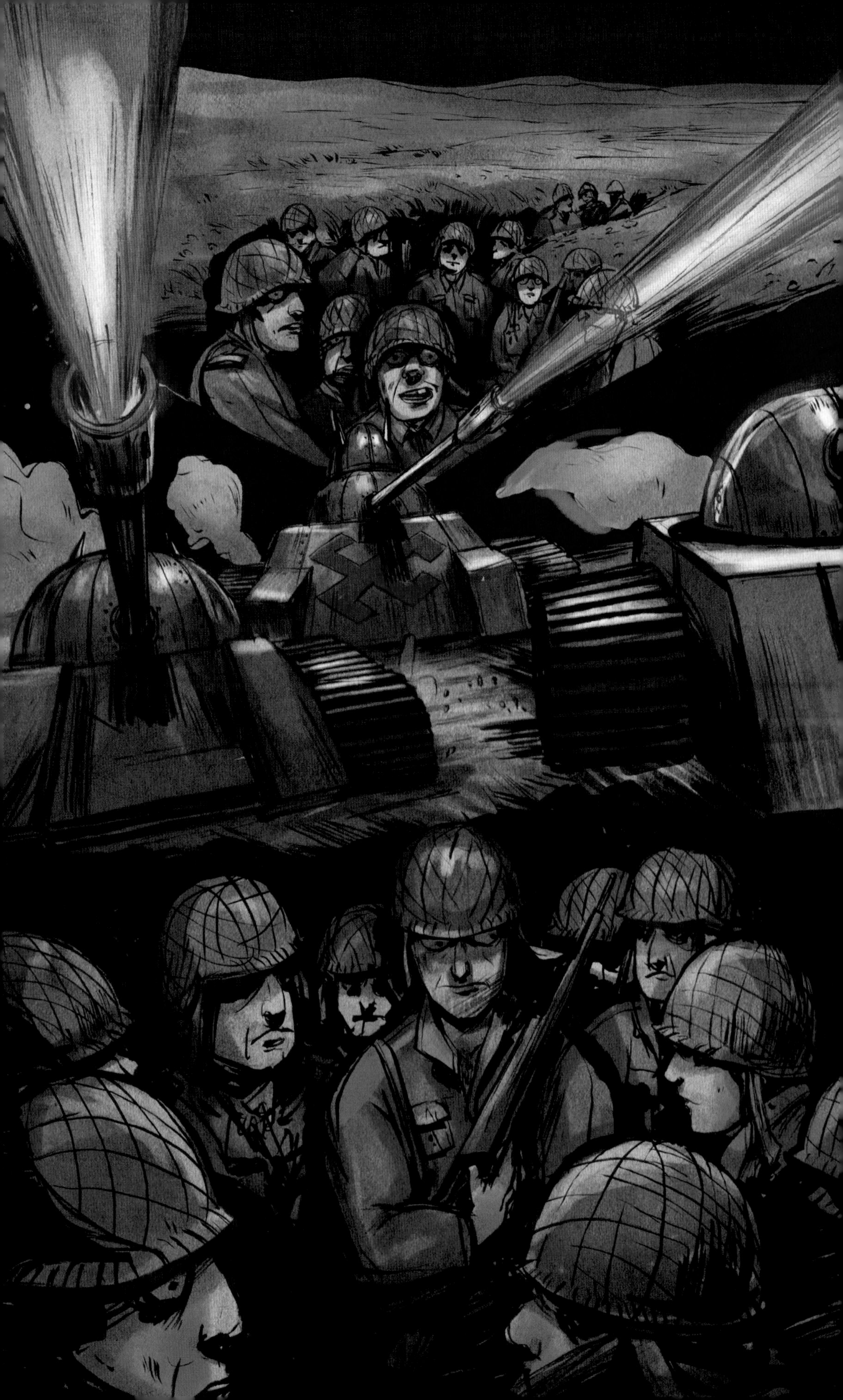

Stillness again did reign,
But that it wouldn't last, it was plain.
The night had just begun,
Oh God, will I see the next day's sun?
I laid my body close to the cold ground,
Ears alert to every sound.
The cracking of a twig,
That little noise was very big.

The cannons again did roar,
Flares in the sky did soar.
The Earth was bathed in a bluish light,
Out of the darkness these flares did bite.
Darkness once more ascended,
So quickly as if offended.

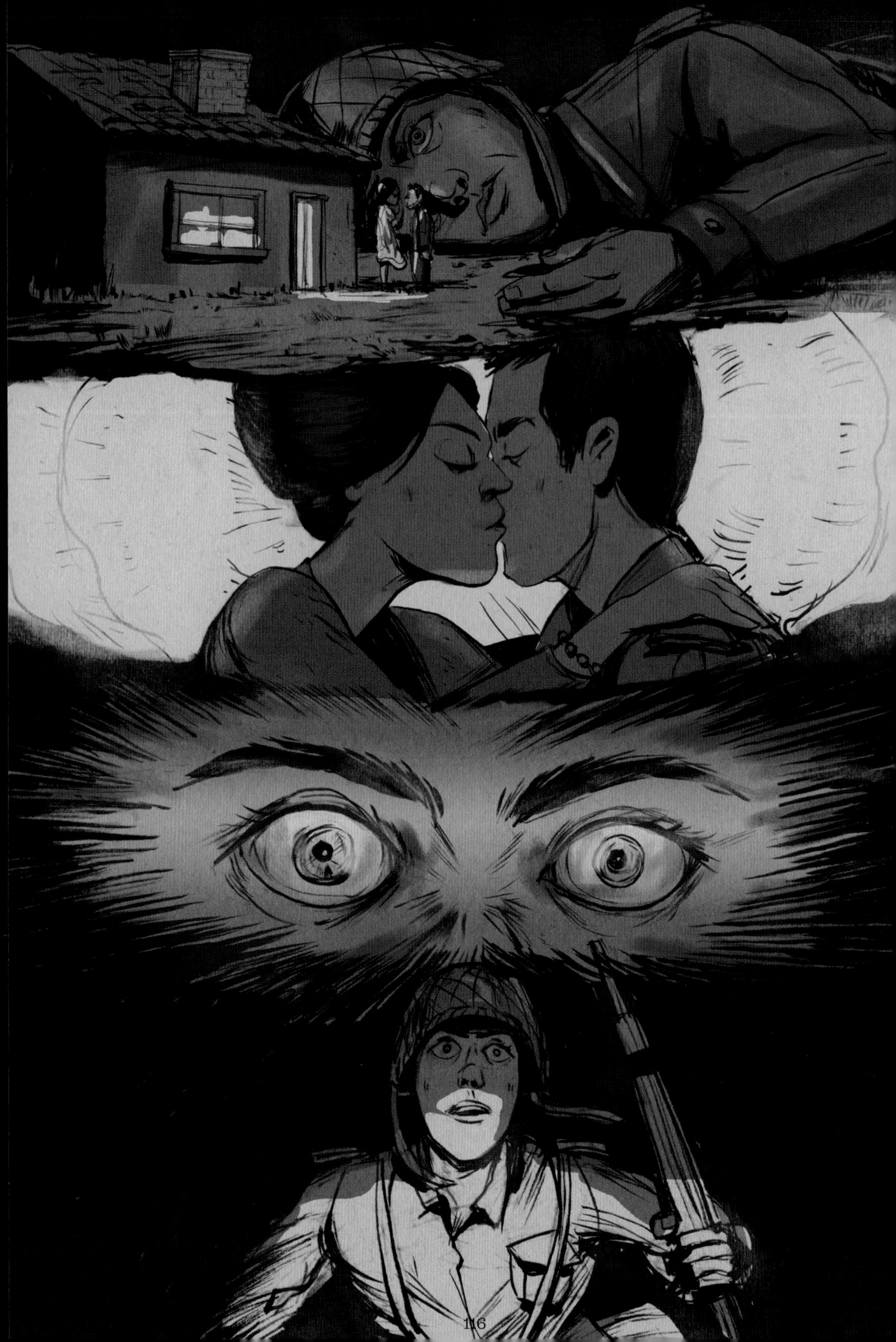

At times my thoughts were of home and you,

But those precious moments were rare and few.

There is no time to reminisce,

Or think of that last sweet kiss.

Two eyes battling the night,

If I only had a little light.

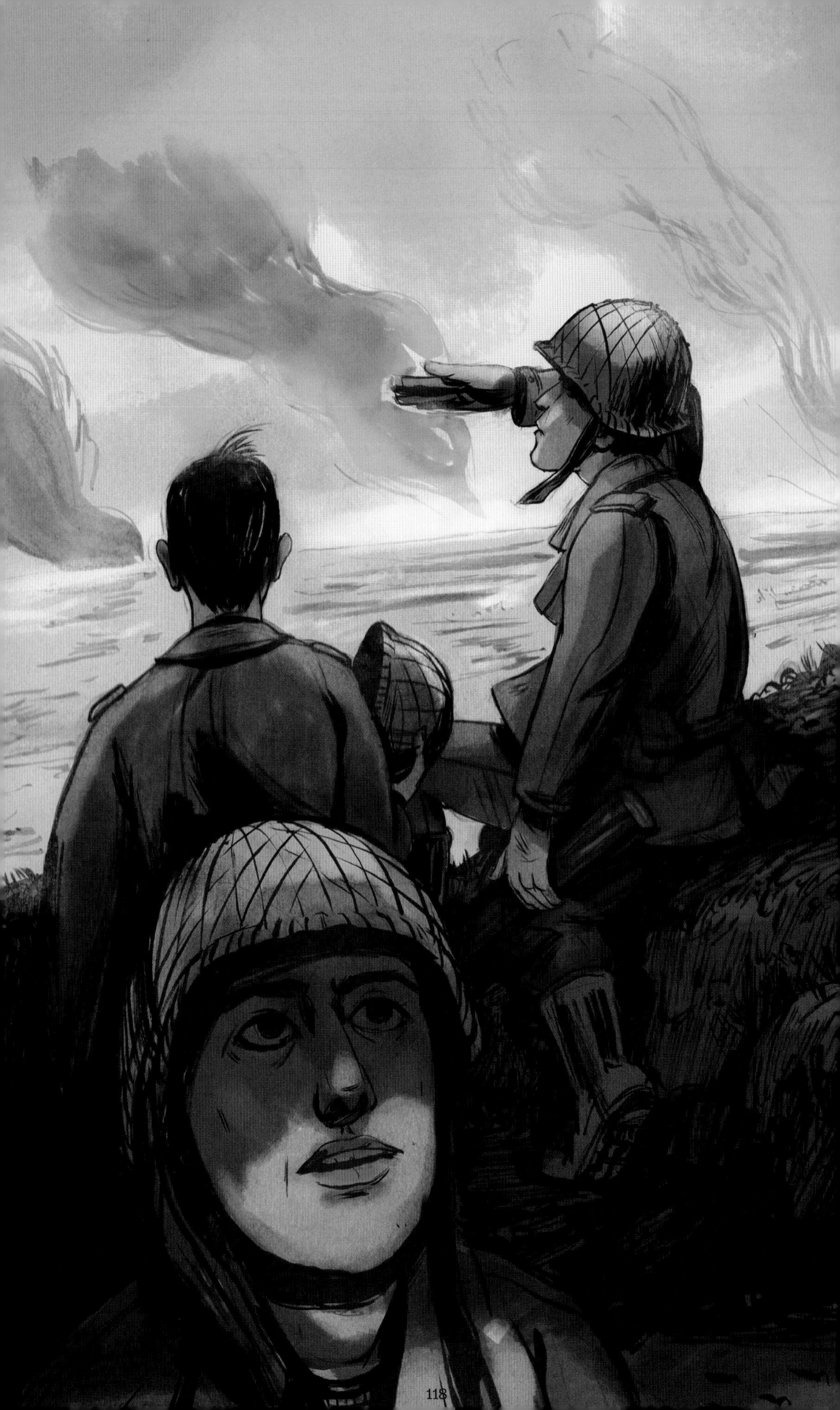

The sky grew gray in the East,

Many hungry eyes on that did feast.

There in bursting flame,

The dawn came.

THE LETTER

My Dearest Jo,

Hello hon. This is the first letter in a year and a half that wont be censored. I dont even know where to begin or what to say. I have wanted to tell you people so much and now when I can I dont know how.

I know whats uppermost in your mind hon. Lets start from the beginning and work forward to the finish. Some parts naturally will be condensed but I will try to put in all the important details.

I came across on the Queen Elizabeth and landed in Scotland about Dec. 19th, 1943. The name of the town I believe was Brenock its right off the Firth of Clyde. From there we traveled by train to Lichfield (spelled wrong) England. It was a large replacement pool and thats where all the gang was seperated. I ended up with the 28th div. a swell outfit from Pa. We were stationed in South Wales right by the town of Carmarthen. We maneuvered

This page: The first sheet of Leonard's original letter to Jo.

Following pages: A typewritten version of the letter has also been preserved, and is included here in full.

120

May 20, 1945

Hello hon, this is the first letter in a year and a half that wont be censored. I dont even know where to begin or what to say. I have wanted to tell you people so much and now when I can, I don't know how.

I know what is uppermost in your mind hon. Let's start from the beginning and work forward to the finish. Some parts naturally will be condensed but I will try to put in all the important details.

I came across on the Queen Elizabeth and landed in Scotland about Dec. 19, 1943. The name of the town, I believe, was Grenock, it is right off of the Firth of Clyde. From there, we traveled by train to Lichtfield, Enland. It was a large replacement pool and that is where all the gang was seperated. I ended up with the 28th Division, a swell outfit from Pa. We were stationed in South Wales right by the town of Carmarthen. We maneuvered all over the country, amphibious and land. We were preparing for the invasion. I had a couple of passes to Cardiff and Swansea. Life was good, we.played and worked hard also.

It was in the latter part of April that we got the invasion jitters. I was transferred to the 2nd Division. The 2nd was scheduled to make the invasion. Training slacked off and we moved to the channel city of Bournemouth. We played mostly and had little training. I was lsited to go in on the third wave which was a lucky break.

June 6th, the news broke and we were still in England. We moved that night by truck to an assembly area near Southhampton. We were jittery and touchy. Fights were commom, the mental strain terrific. I felt top notch physically and ready to go. D + 2 we loaded on boats and started to cross the channel. We reached France D + 3 and sweated out a whole day on the channel before we loaded on assault boats and came in on Omaho Beach. Things were a mess. Everything was strewn all over. Bodies of American boys and Germans were still there.

We could still hear small arms fire not far off and that renewed some of the boys. For the first time in my life, I saw violent death and real fear. We started to move and made contact with the Krauts. We pushed them back..... Treviers fell, Cerresy La Fores fell, we fought and pushed on. We dug in about 20 miles from St. Lo; we were tired men, we fought hard and had lost a lot of men. Some boys couldn't take anymore and cracked up. Death was always around us. We got replacements and tried to push for the high ground surrounding St. Lo. We got stopped. We dug in again and got more replacements. I lost a lot of my buddies, a lot of boys who will never enjoy the freedom that they died for!

Guard was tough, two hours on, two hours off. The Krauts tried several counterattacks at night but we stopped them. My machine gun sure could spit death and that is what we named her. I was offered a squad and seargent's stripes but I refused. I turned it down because I wanted to stay with my gun. I guess you can't understand that. I liked that gun, I liked to fire it.

We got tank and air support and started our long awaited push. It was the toughest fighting we ever encountered. Only two of us in our platoon came through alive. We were lucky! WE joined another platoon and I dug in with my gun. We stood guard all night and pushed again in the day. That started the St. Lo break through. We pushed for seven days, finally the Krauts outran us. That ended our tour of Normandy.

We rested a week and reorganized. I was offered a section with staff seargents stripes but refused again. I wanted to be a gunner, I liked it. We moved to Brittany and took Polgustal Penninsula just above Brest. That was rough, it made Brest look like a snap. More men cracked up, more men lost their lives. I was beginning to feel the strain. I knew my luck couldn't last forever. I had had too many close calls, my feet were bothering me and I was losing weight. The gun seemed to weigh a ton! I had a strain on my left side and I knew that the next campaign would be my last. I couldn't move as fast as the other men and my brain was a bit fuzzy from all the artillery that had pounded and torn us to bits. You can't imagine what a beating artillery can give you!

We got a break and went to Paris. It helped some but I wasn't in shape and knew it. I couldn't sleep or eat well, I drank and smoked too much. My legs got tired easily and I knew I was washed out.

The outfit (my battalion) was alerted and we soon moved to Germany. It was just a bit outside of Belgium and the Siegfried was out in front of us. We stayed in a defensive and waited for the signal to attack. It was cold and wet. It snowed and rained, we lived in mud, slept in mud and were in the end almost a part of the mud. The buzz bombs flew over us continually. After about a month, we kicked off. I was in bad shape. I was jittery and knew the going was going to be tough. The new men were scared stiff and that didn't help any. It was cold and the snow was deep. You couldn't spot mines and our uniforms made us perfect targets.

Artillery in trees was hell. We lost men. Frozen hands and feet were common. Trench foot broke out and I was ready to quit, I'd had enough. All hell broke loose one day. It seemed as if all the Krauts in the world hit us at once. We fell back and back some more. Their tanks shot us to pieces. I held on to my gun though. She talked plenty but not enough. We retreated for about twenty miles; we didn't have food or water and the going was something terrific. We lost most of our men. The Krauts had us almost surrounded. We had only one escape route open and we were told to hold it at all cost. I put my gun into action and she did a bang up job. A tank got her, blasted the water jacket right off. All I had left was a .45 pistol and that is no fighting man's weapon. We were being pounded from all sides. The last thing I remember is a tiger tank about 100 yards to my front, I was trying to dig in but was too exhausted. Seventy-two hours without food, water or sleep. It seemd like a lifetime. More then once I thought of giving the whole thing up. Death would have been welcome. I woke up in a field hospital, I still don't

know what happened, whether it was a shell or I just passed out from exhaustion.
My records classed it as Combat Fatigue. I was thankful to be alive. They
treated my feet and I started to eat and sleep again. They told me that my
nerves were gone and that I would never see combat again. I didn't argue, I knew
they were right. From a hospital to a replacement depot and then here is the
rest of the story. I'm feeling alright now, jitters all gone and gaining weight.
I still smoke and drink too much but I am gradually cutting down. That's the
dirt hon. I'm only sorry that I couldn't have made a better soldier.

I'm back in Normandy just about where I started out from. We are
near La Haye De Puits not to far from Grainville. It's not too bad here but
I could think of better. Oh well, with luck it shouldn't be too long now.

Love,

Len

PHOTO REFERENCE

The following pages display photos used in the creation of the story's visuals.

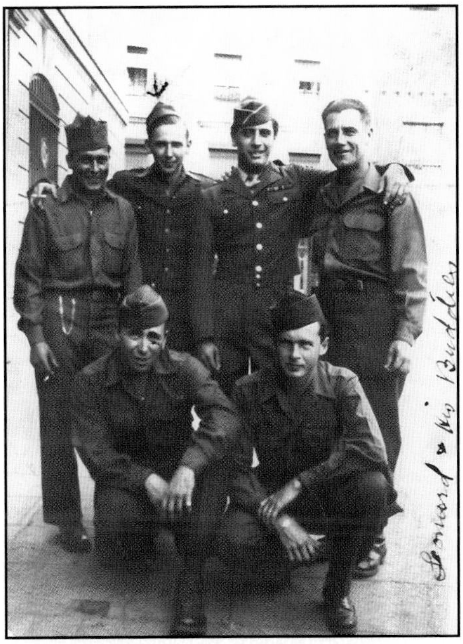

Leonard & My Buddies

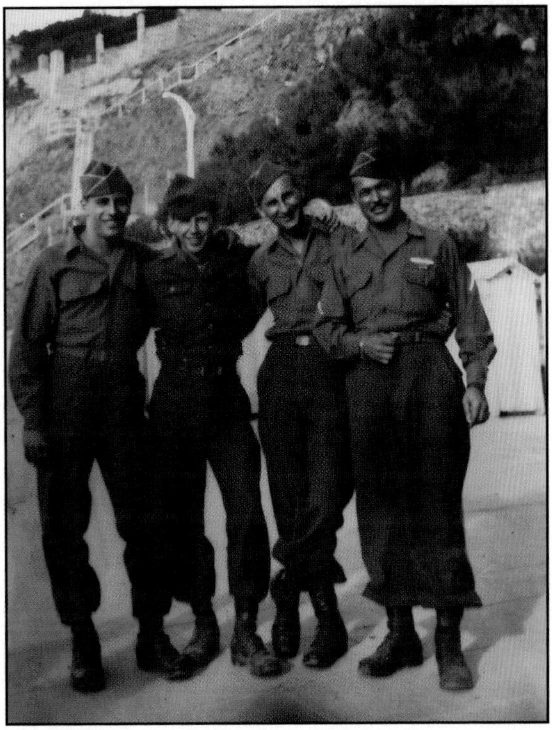

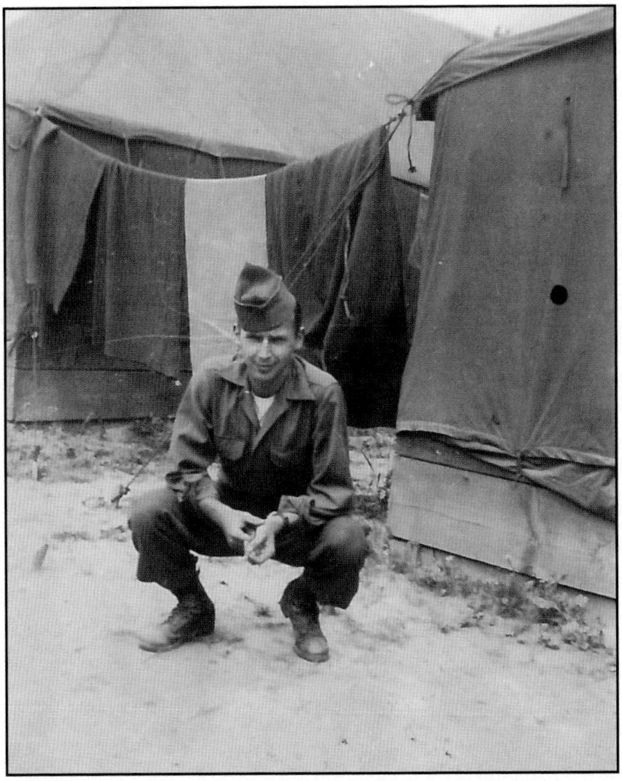

Top left: Leonard and his gang (June 15).

Top right: Leonard and his buddies.

Bottom: Len in France.

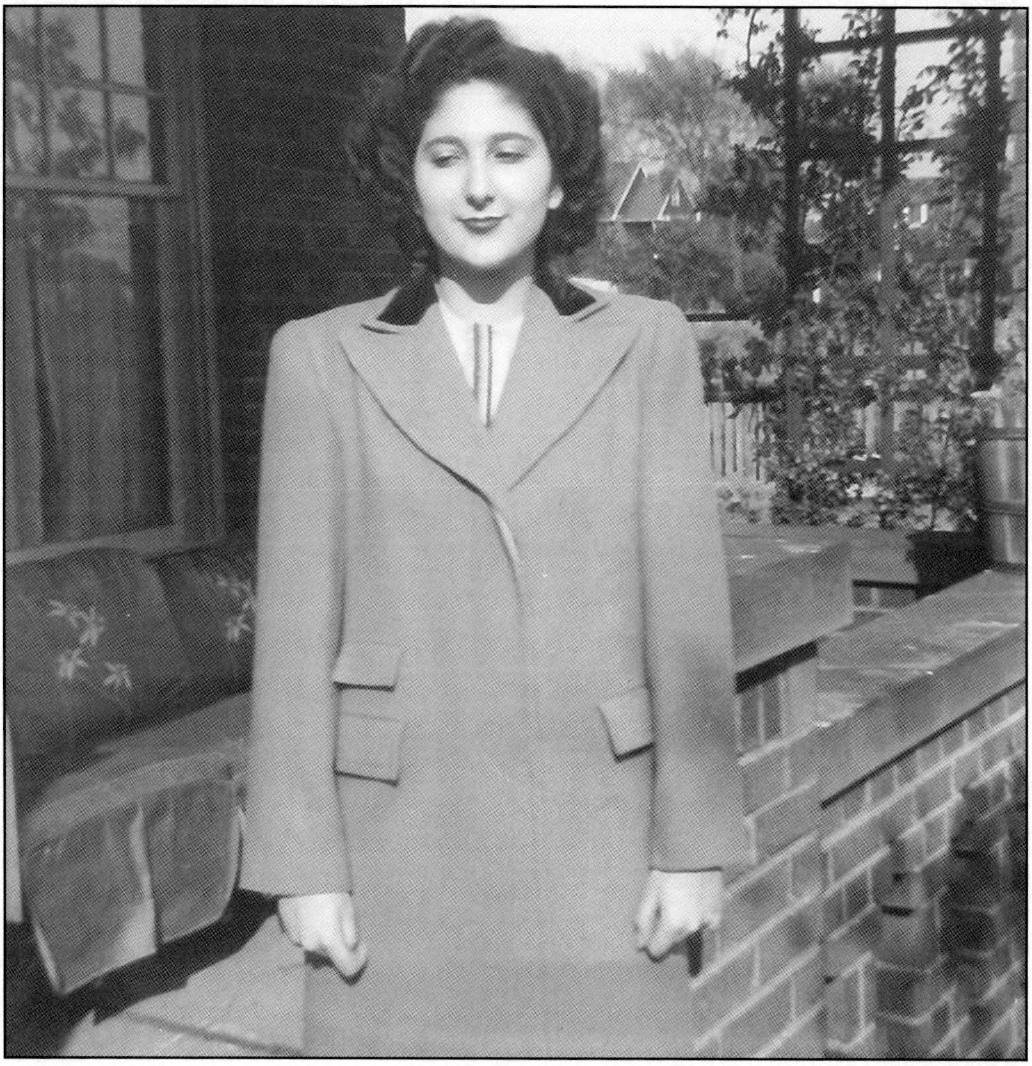

Above: Jo in high school.

Right: Army photograph of Leonard.

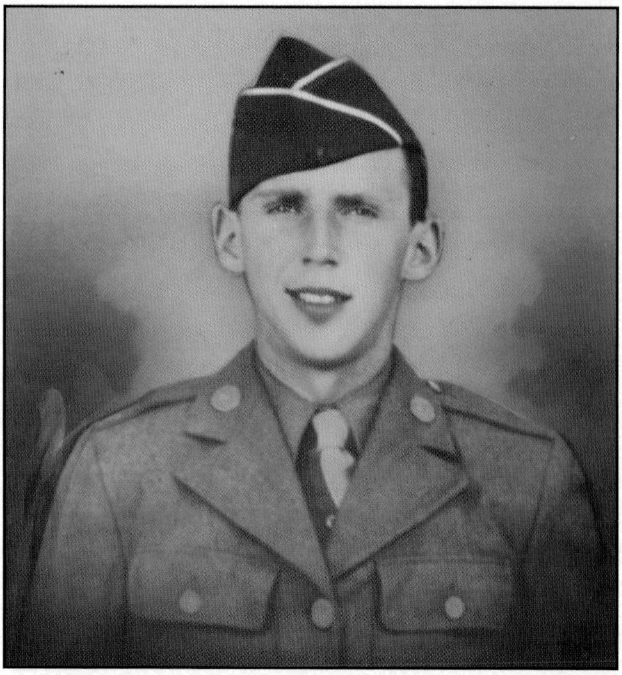

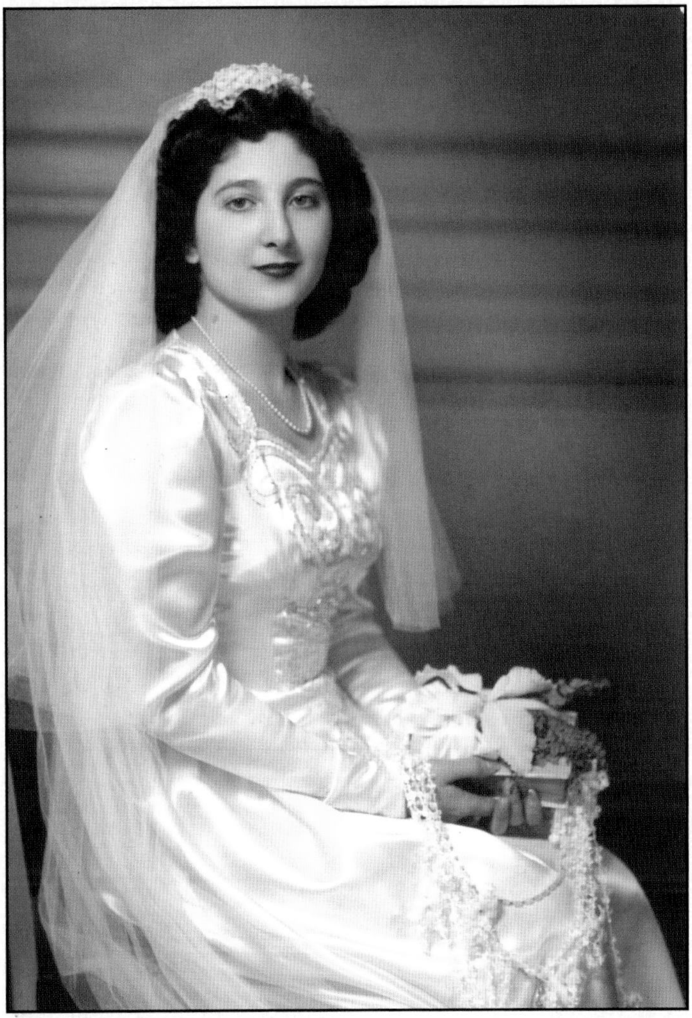

Left: Jo's wedding day photograph.

Below: Chin's Golden Dragon Restaurant, Cleveland, OH. This photo appears on page 51.

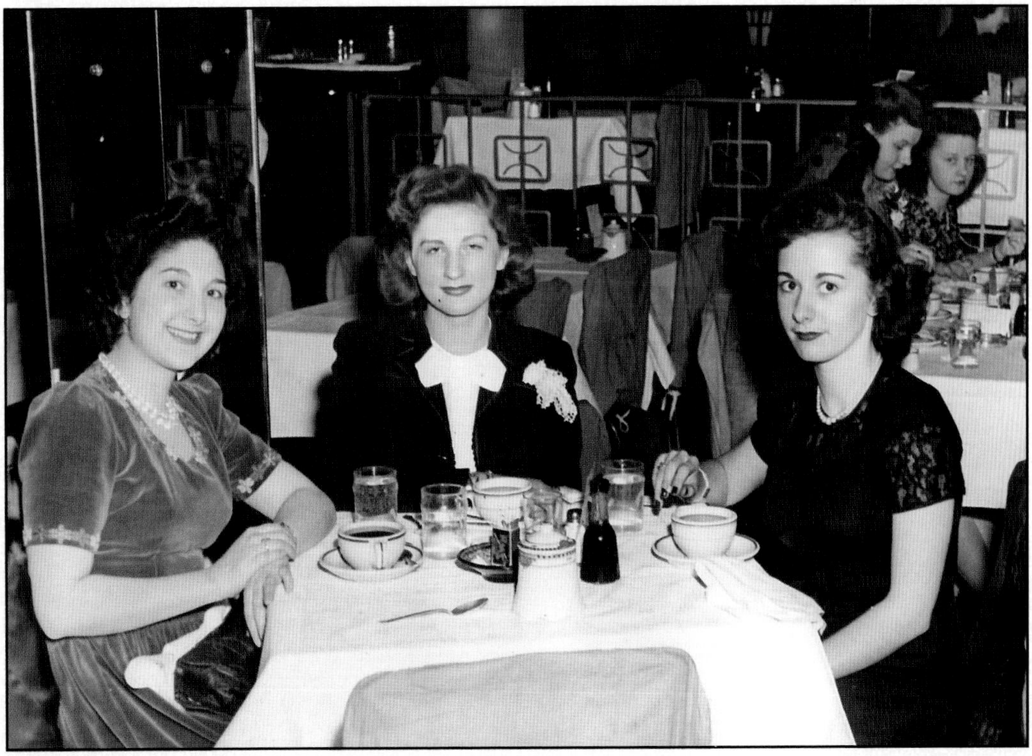

SKETCHBOOK

Notes on developing Leonard and Josephine's likenesses and creating the supporting characters, by artist Kelly Williams.

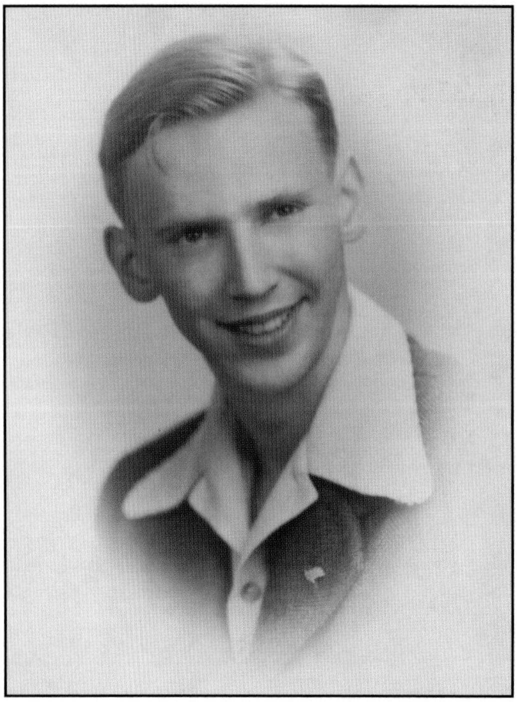

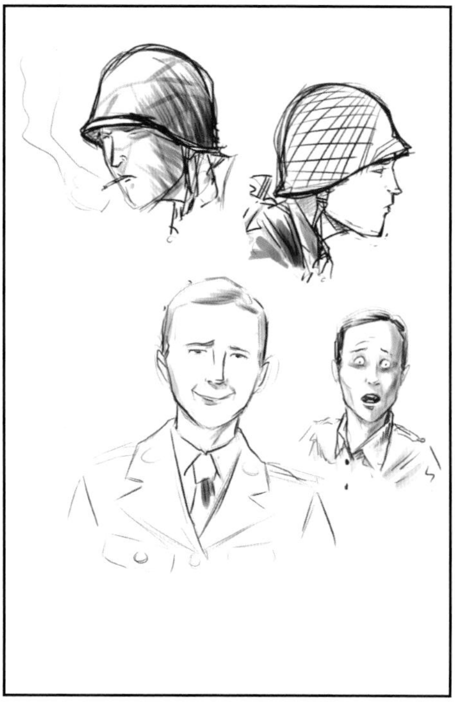

This page: In early sketches of Leonard, I focused on getting a close likeness. Later in the book, his face becomes much more gaunt and angular to show how the war has worn and aged him.

Opposite page: An early sketch getting a feel for the wardrobe of the day.

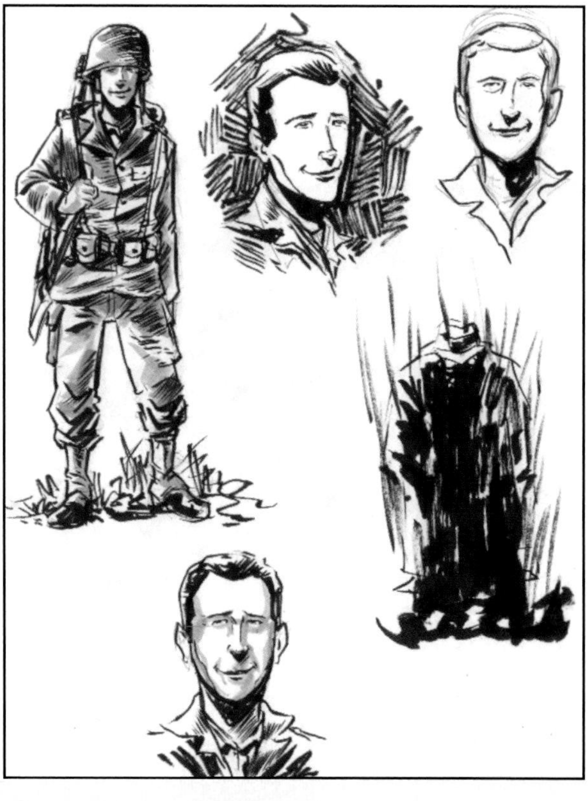

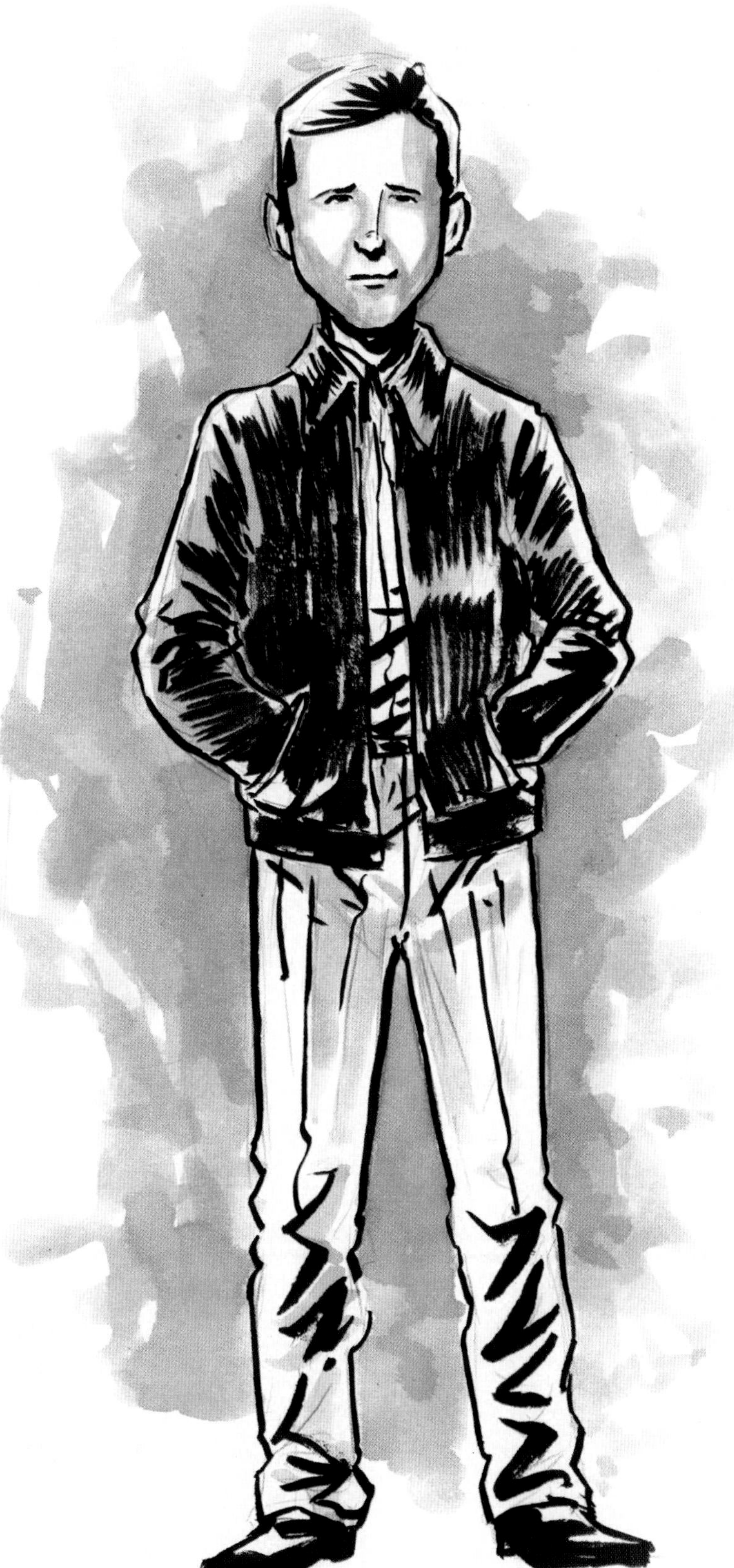

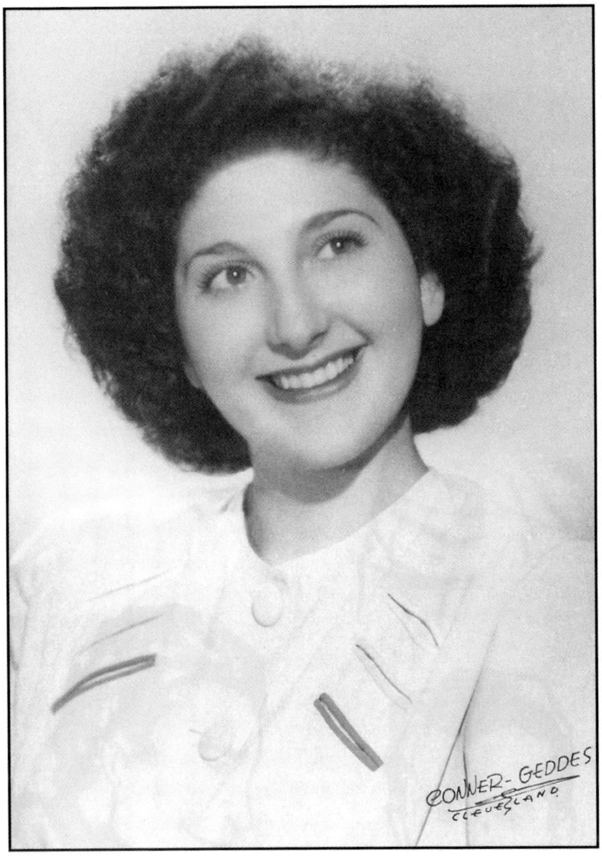
CONNER-GEDDES
CLEVELAND

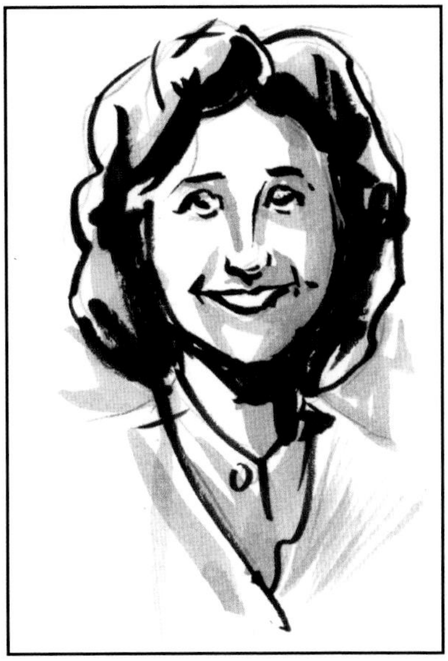

Opposite page: While Len is in uniform most of the time, I focused more on developing Josephine's wardrobe, since she is going about her normal life. A lot of my early sketches of Jo focused on clothing.

This page: Getting a good likeness for Jo was important since her appearance changes less over the course of the story. Over time I made her face a little thinner and let her hair change slightly to show the passage of time and her stress.

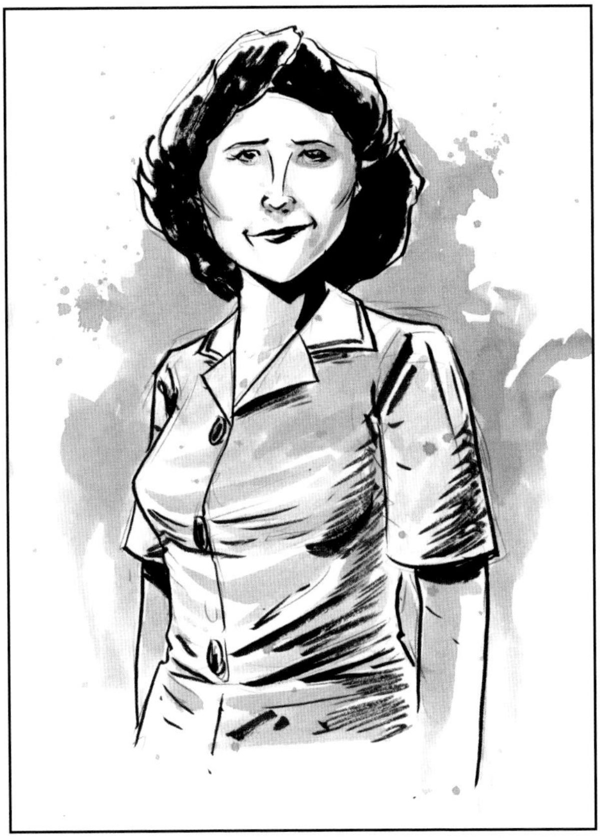

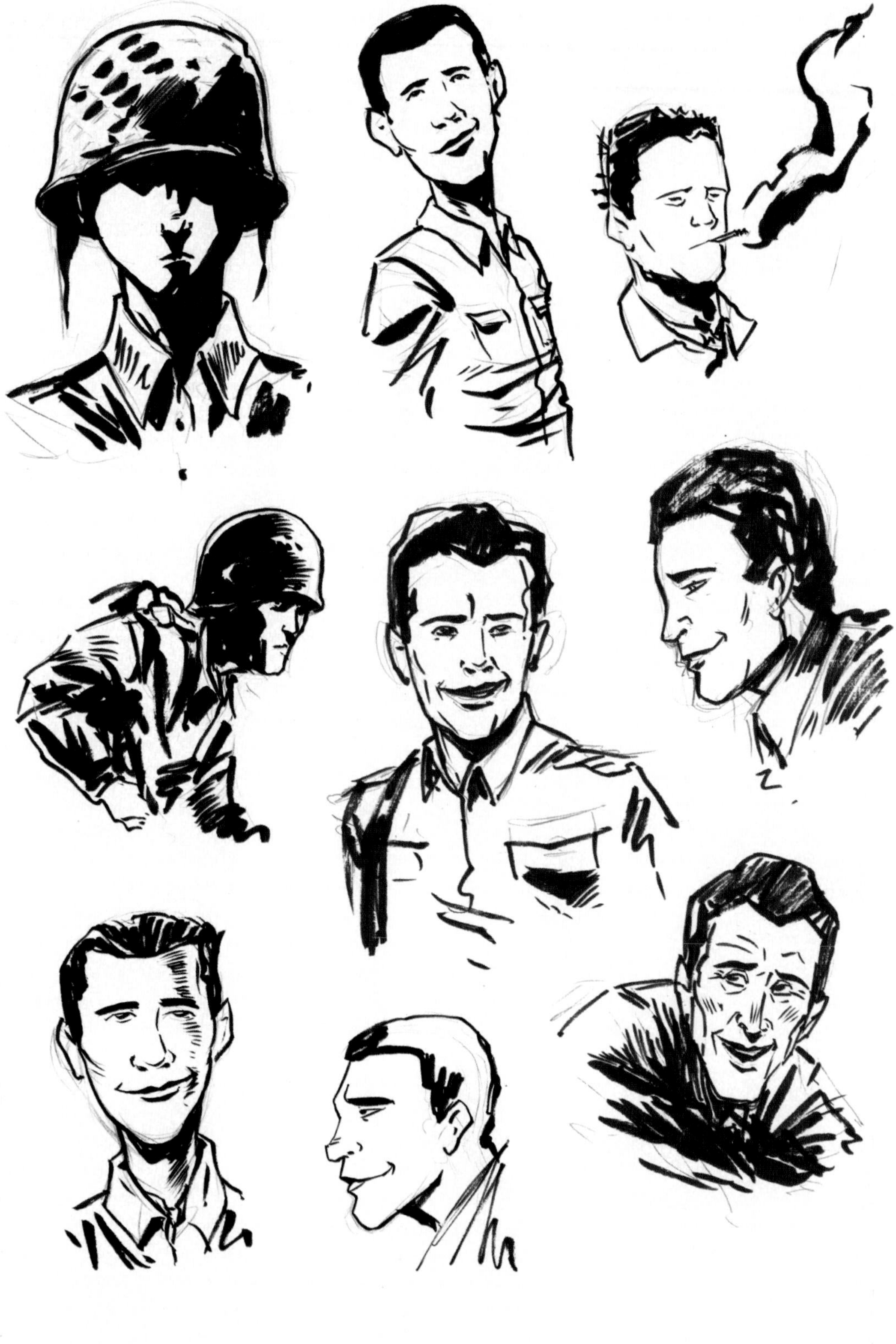

Above: I do a lot of face sketching anyway, so I had lots of loose paper and scrap pieces with different soldier characters all over the place.

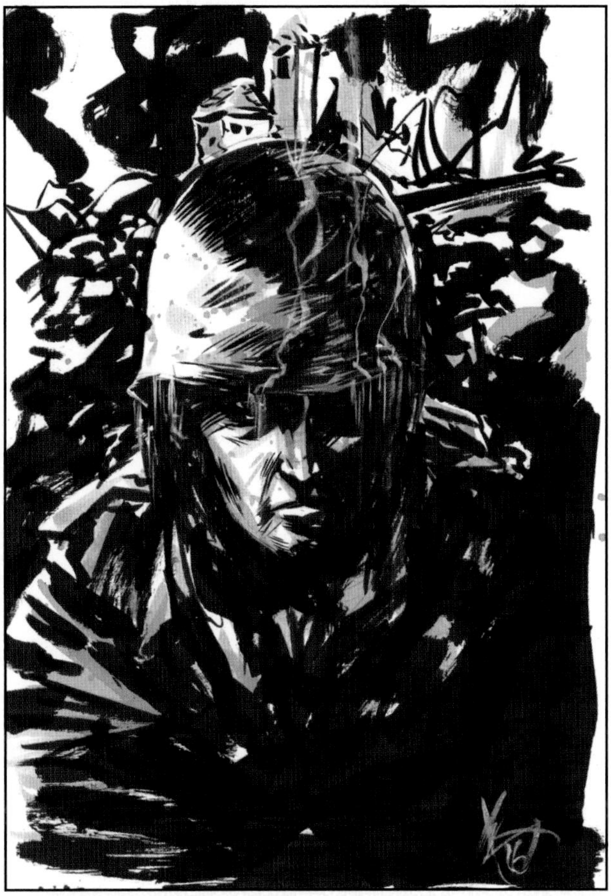

Top: As a fan of heavy shadows, my initial thinking for the war scenes was to go full-on dark. I ended up backing off a bit, as so much of the book happens during horrible war moments. We reserved this tone for the darkest parts.

Bottom: My first idea for the front and back covers. From early on, I wanted them to mirror each other emotionally, while having a strong sense of two different places, to convey the idea that these two kids are dealing with the same desire and pain.

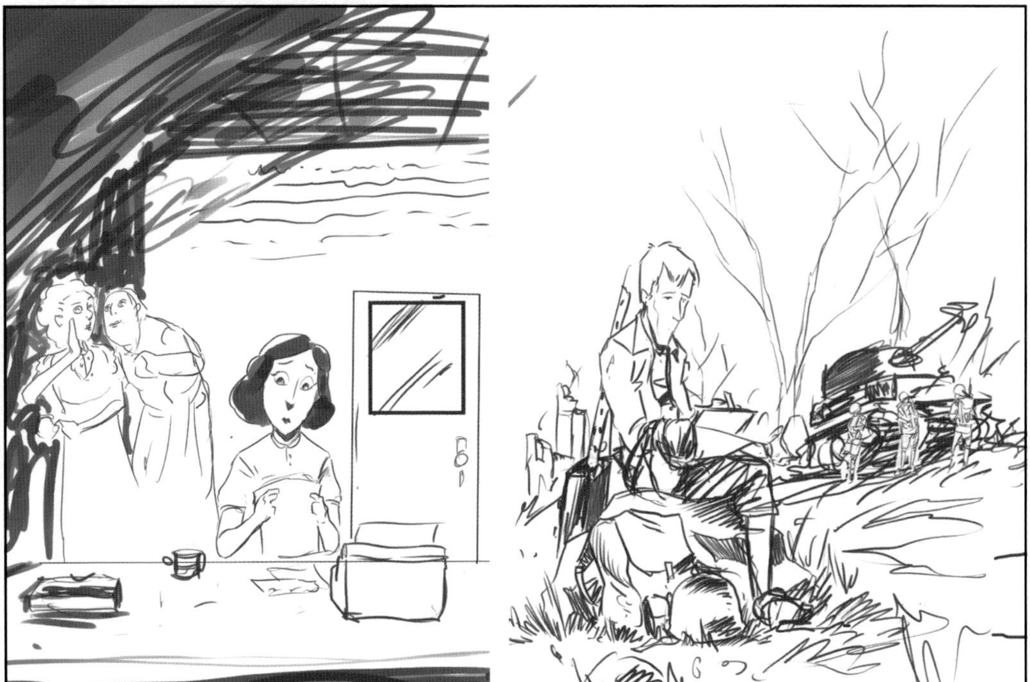

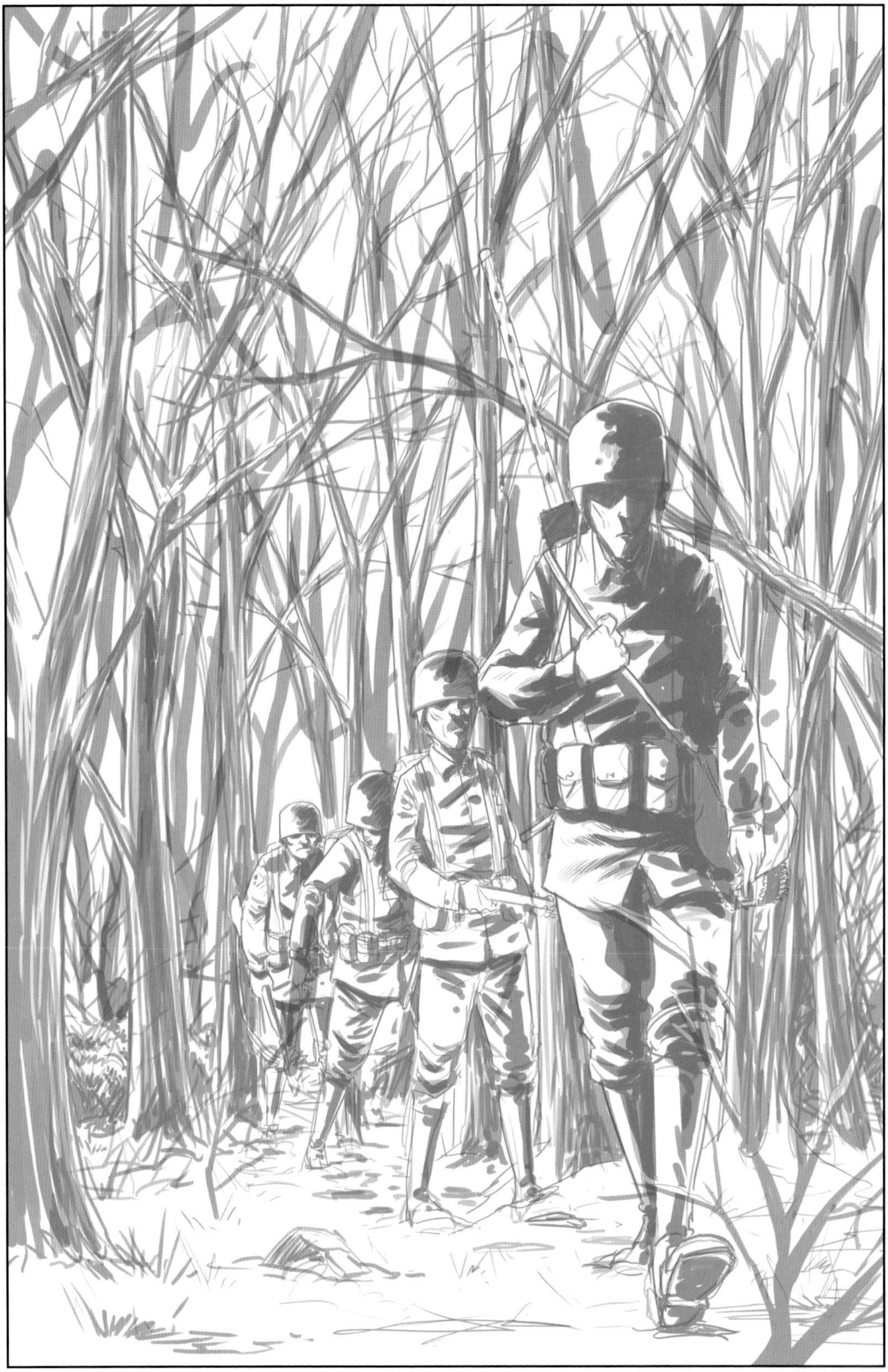

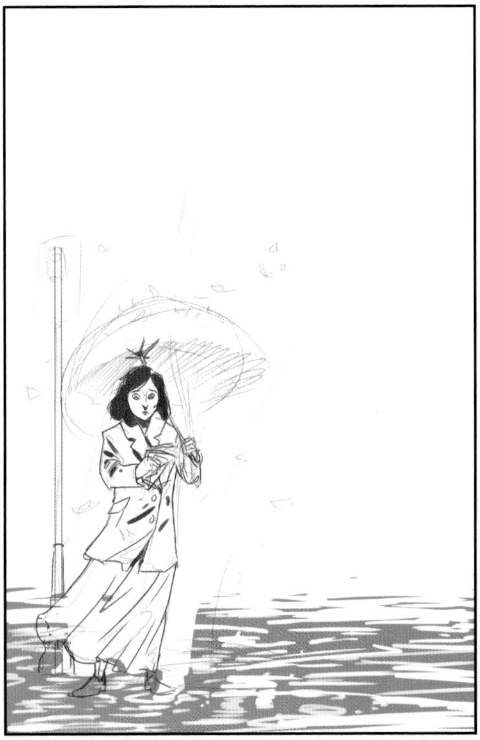

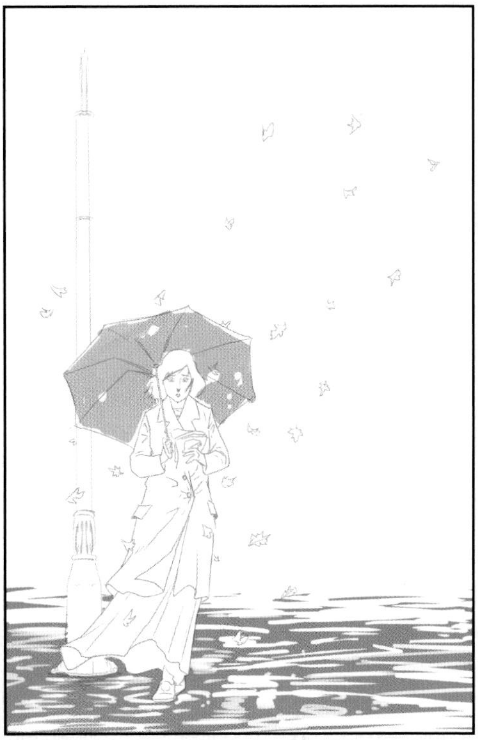

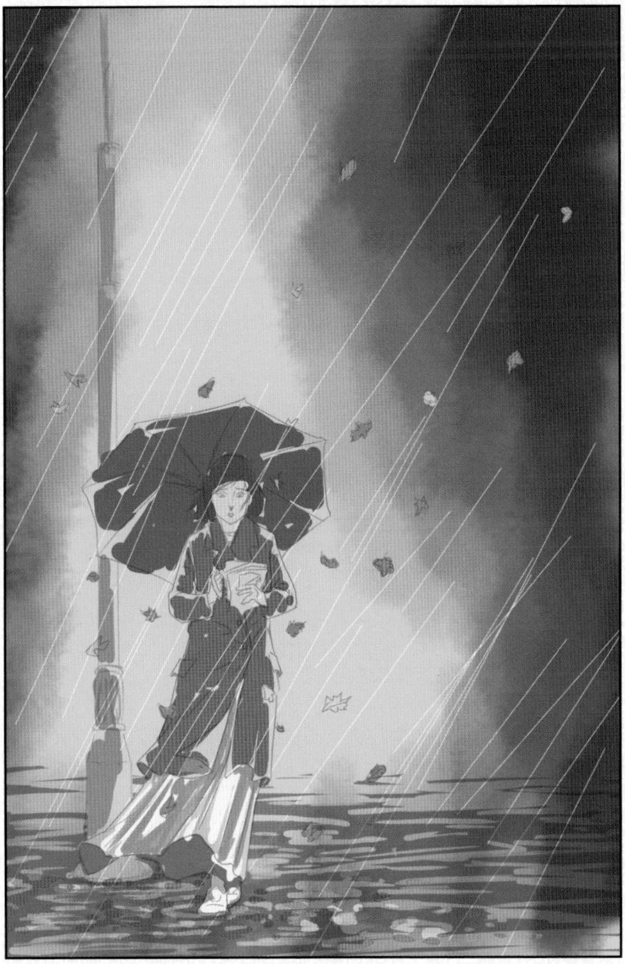

This spread: Williams's process art for the front and back covers.

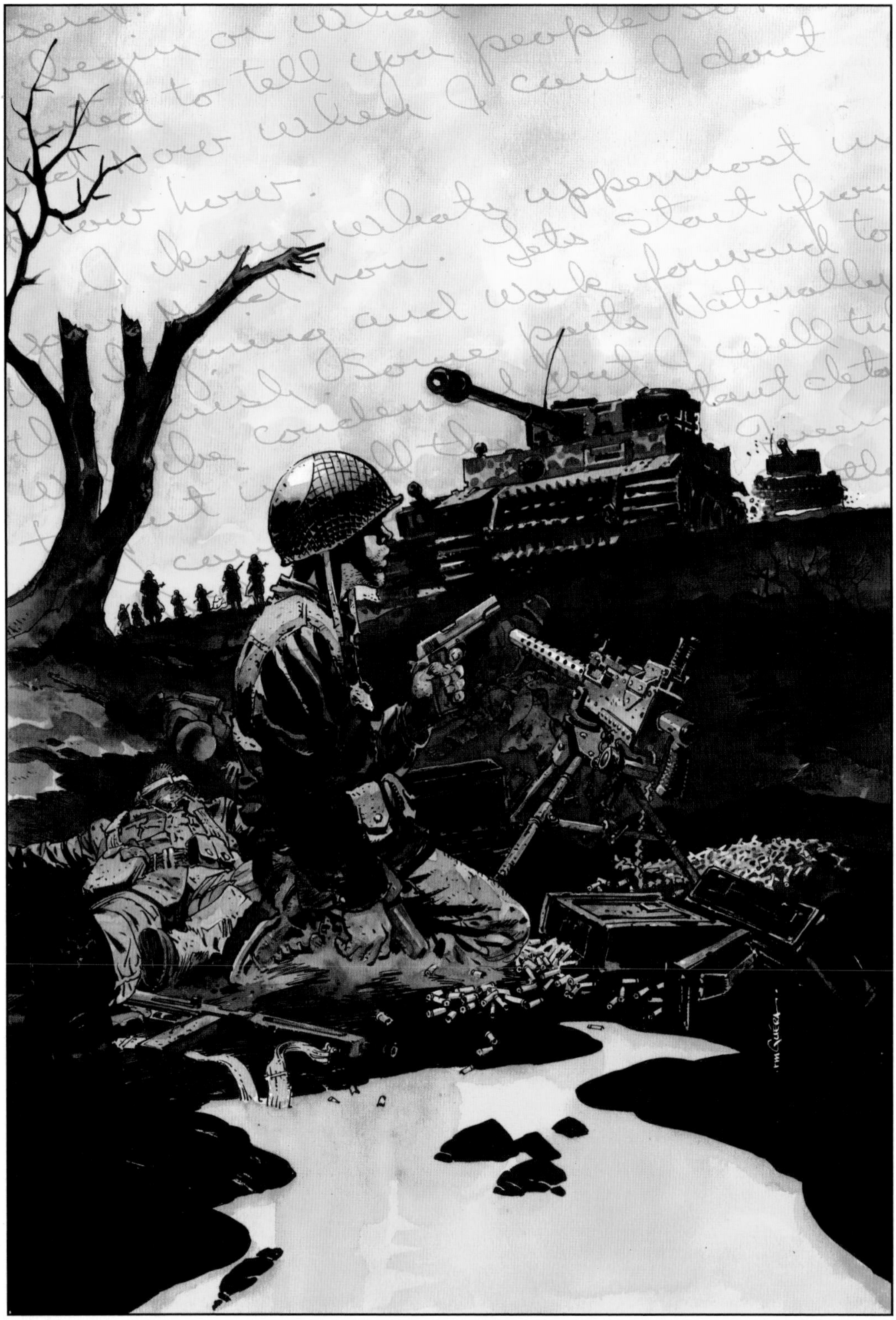

Pinup by R. M. Guéra.